Alex Gray

KEEP THE MIDNIGHT OUT

sphere

SPHERE

First published in Great Britain in 2015 by Sphere
This paperback edition published in 2015 by Sphere

5 7 9 10 8 6

Norman MacCaig epigraph on pvii reprinted by kind permission of
Polygon, an imprint of Birlinn Limited

A CIP catalogue record for this book
is available from the British Library.

ISBN 978-0-7515-5487-8

Typeset in Caslon by M Rules
Printed and bound in Great Britain by
Clays Ltd, Elcograf S.p.A.

Papers used by Sphere are from well-managed forests
and other responsible sources.

Sphere
An imprint of
Little, Brown Book Group
Carmelite House
50 Victoria Embankment
London EC4Y 0DZ

An Hachette UK Company
www.hachette.co.uk

www.littlebrown.co.uk

Alex Gray was born and educated in Glasgow. She has been awarded the Scottish Association of Writers' Constable and Pitlochry trophies for her crime writing and is the co-founder of the Bloody Scotland international crime writing festival. Married with a son and daughter, she lives in Scotland and is currently writing the next book in the Detective Lorimer series.

ALSO BY ALEX GRAY

This novel is dedicated to Val and Lawrie with love
and the memory of another special wedding

The frontier is never
somewhere else. And no stockades
can keep the midnight out.
  Hotel Room 12th Floor, Norman MacCaig

The mind is its own place
And in itself can make a heaven of hell,
A hell of heaven.
                    Paradise Lost, John Milton

CHAPTER ONE

They called it 'the splash'; though the boat that crept silently, oars dipping lightly in and out of the water creating myriad bubbles of phosphorescence, made little sound at all. It was vital to keep quiet; the time for frightening the fish would not come until the net was properly laid across the mouth of the burn. After that the oars would be raised high and brought down with force, driving the sea trout from their shadowy lairs straight into the trap. It was illegal, of course, had been for decades, but that did not stop more intrepid poachers sneaking in at dead of night and lying in wait for the fish. Unfair, unsporting, the fishery bodies claimed, though most folk here, on the island of Mull, recognised the thrill of rowing under the stars and risking some wrath from the law enforcers.

Ewan Angus Munro glanced back over his shoulder to see his son playing out the last of the splash net; the ancient cork floats now in a perfect arc across this narrow neck of water. Young Ewan looked towards his father and nodded; the first part of the deed was done and now all that remained was to ensure that the fish would be scared out from their hiding places by the sudden noise of oars thrashing on the surface so that they would rush towards the net.

The old man turned the boat with an expertise that came from many years of practice, then headed back towards the shallow channel. He raised the oars, resting them in the rowlocks, water dripping like molten rain from their blades. The small craft was allowed to drift a little before Ewan Angus turned to his son again, the eye contact and nod a definite signal to begin the second stage of their night's work.

Young Ewan Angus stood, legs apart, perfectly balanced in the centre of the boat, one oar raised high above his shoulder as the older man watched him, eyes full of approval. The boy had been given more than just his father's names: his flair for the splash, too, had been passed down from father to son.

Across the marshy strand full of bog cotton and sweet-smelling myrtle sat a small white cottage. A swift glance showed him that there was no light on anywhere; the holiday folk were doubtless sound asleep, oblivious to the small drama being played out yards from their front door.

The sound of the splash seemed magnified as it disrupted the stillness, echoing over the bay. The young man heaved the oar again and again, each whack making his body stiffen with fear and a sort of bravado. If they were caught they'd lose both the net and the boat, a heavy price to pay for a night of fun and a good catch of sea trout, fish that fetched a decent price at the back doors of the best hotel kitchens.

Several times the boat was rowed up and down, followed by a series of splashes until the old man raised his callused hand to call a halt. Now it was time to wait and see if the fish had indeed been scared witless enough to swim towards their doom.

Once more the old man rowed along the line of corks, his son lifting the net to see if anything lingered below.

'A beauty,' the boy whispered, raising the net to reveal a good-sized sea trout struggling in the brown mesh.

'Ten pounder at least!' he went on, freeing the huge fish where its gills had caught and hurling it into a wooden box below his feet.

'Be-wheesht and get the net up,' his father hissed, though the grin on his face showed how pleased he was with their first catch of the night. The old man bent towards the struggling fish, his fist around the priest, a wooden club that had been in the family for generations. One swift blow and the fish lay lifeless in the box, its silvery scales gleaming in the night.

One by one, others joined the fated sea trout as the two men made their laborious way along the edge of the net.

'My, a grand haul, the night, Faither,' Young Ewan Angus exclaimed, his voice still hushed for fear of any sound carrying over the water.

'Aye, no' bad,' his father agreed, a contented smile on his face. One of the middling fish would be wrapped in layers of bracken and left in the porch of Calum Mhor, the police sergeant. A wee thank you for turning his continual blind eye to the nocturnal activities taking place down the road from Craignure. Mrs Calum had guests staying and she'd be fair pleased to serve them a fresh sea trout for their dinner. It was universally acknowledged here on the island that the pink fish was far superior in flavour to the coarser salmon, particularly those that had been farmed.

'My, here's a big one!'

The young man staggered as he tried to haul in the final part of the splash net. 'I can hardly lift it!' he exclaimed.

'Must be caught on a rock,' the old man grumbled, his mouth twisting in a moue of disgust. If they had to tear the net to release it then it would take hours of work to mend, but the operation depended on being in and out of these waters as quickly as they could manage. Hanging about was not an option in case the Men from the Revenue had decided on a little night-time excursion of their own.

Suddenly the young man bent down in the boat, hands gripping the gunwales as he peered into the depths below.

His brow furrowed at the rounded mass swaying beneath the surface, rags of bladderwrack shifting back and forwards with the motion of the waves. Then, as his eyes focused on the ascending shape, Ewan Angus Munro saw pale tendrils that had once been fingers of flesh and one thin arm floating upwards.

He screamed, and covered his mouth as the sickness rose in his throat, then stumbled backwards. The boy flung out his arms, desperate to grasp hold of something solid to break his fall but all he felt under his hands were the wet bodies of slithering fish.

'What the ...?' Ewan Angus turned, an oath dying on his lips as the boat rocked violently, small waves dashing over the bow.

Wordlessly, his son pointed to the waters below.

Then, as the old man peered over the side of the boat, he saw the body rising to the surface, its passage out to sea impeded by their net.

Later, Ewan Angus was to feel shame, but then, under the eyes of twinkling stars, all he felt was a blind panic and a need to get away as fast as they could.

His son had blubbered a little, protesting as they'd man-handled the corpse over the side of the boat, his groans silenced by a wrathful look from the old fisherman. They had laid the boy on the grass, far enough from the water's edge so that the incoming tide could not draw it back beneath its cold waves.

'It's him, isn't it?' Young Ewan Angus had whispered, looking up at his father who had simply nodded, the sigh of regret stifled on his closed lips.

Then, as he'd pulled hard on the oars, putting distance between the land and their boat, he tried to assure himself that they had done the right thing after all. Someone would find him in the brightness of the morning light, he'd told the boy.

And what good would it do them to call the polis? They'd lose everything: fish, net, boat, the lot.

Yet, as Ewan Angus Munro made for the safety of his mooring several miles along the shoreline, his son still looking stubbornly astern, refusing to meet his father's eye, he knew he had lost something far more precious.

CHAPTER TWO

Maryka made a face as she entered the hotel kitchen. They still hadn't found anyone to replace Rory Dalgleish and she wasn't sure if she resented the red-haired boy more now that he'd gone. His constant talking had made her crash around the kitchen banging pots and pans, feverishly trying to blot out the sound of his annoyingly loud public school voice. He had been worse in the mornings after yet another night at the bottle, going on about how he was saving up to go to Thailand with his mates; a gap year before uni, he claimed. Though why a rich boy from Glasgow needed to have a summer job at all mystified her. Perhaps, Maryka thought cynically, his folks couldn't stand his loutish behaviour either and had packed him off to this country house hotel on the island of Mull.

Anyway, he had disappeared two nights ago, to the consternation of the Dalgleish parents, if not to the Dutch girl who was now lifting plates out of the big dishwasher and stacking them on the kitchen table. Breakfasts didn't begin for over an hour but she had plenty to do first. Laying the tables would have been easier the evening before but the dining room had been requisitioned by the local drama group for their weekly rehearsal, their laughter and singing continuing well into the night as Hamish Forsyth topped up their glasses, glad no doubt to have their custom. The hotel had not been full all summer and Maryka wasn't surprised. The place needed a complete facelift, in her opinion.

Kilbeg Country House Hotel had been bought by the Forsyths twenty years back, Fiona, one of the local girls who worked as a chambermaid, had informed her, but necessary refurbishment had never taken place and the same old tartan curtains, faded by years of sunlight, still hung limply against the flyblown windows. It was the drink, of course. Everybody knew that Hamish had a problem but, in the way of country folk, it was rarely mentioned; there would be just a hint or a nod towards the big florid-faced man as he knocked back a large whisky, eyebrows raised in disapproval. Maryka felt secretly sorry for Freda Forsyth. She was a small woman, straggles of grey hair tucked untidily behind her ears, who sometimes drifted into the kitchen, a vacant expression on her face as though she had forgotten why she was there in the first place. *Not all there*, Fiona had said with a smirk, tapping the side of her head when she thought that Mrs Forsyth was out of earshot. Once or twice Maryka had caught a glimpse of Hamish's wife standing on the terrace gazing out to sea as though in expectation of someone special arriving at their little jetty where the chef's ancient boat lay at anchor, the man probably snoring in there still, last night's session fogging his brain. But not a single other soul had ever landed there since the Dutch girl had begun working back in the springtime. Not even the fishermen who brought the fine sea trout in their wooden boats.

Maryka wiped her hands on the cotton apron that covered her uniform. Ewan Angus, the tall young fisherman she'd danced with at last Saturday's ceilidh, had promised them some nice fish for dinner, she suddenly remembered. *I'll just leave it in the pantry*, he'd told her, meaning the wooden hut out the back that was a cold storage facility for various bits of game and fish that came mysteriously early in the mornings. Maryka knew better than to ask questions, the grin on Ewan Angus's face telling her better than words that the sea trout was likely obtained in somebody else's private waters. She was good at keeping secrets, Maryka thought to herself, as she glanced across at the chef's old boat rocking gently on the jetty.

It had been a grand night, that ceilidh in Tobermory, the music and dancing fuelled by occasional nips from Ewan Angus's whisky flask outside on Main Street. He'd whirled her around at the dancing until she was flushed and breathless then led her away from the upstairs hall, a wee twinkle in his eye as he patted the unmistakable shape in his hip pocket. 'Time for refreshments,' he had laughed. She'd had things of her own to offer after that, Maryka remembered, smiling her secret little smile.

Maryka had brushed her long hair smooth this morning and put on a bit of make-up before coming out of the caravan that she shared with Elena, the Romanian girl, creeping quietly out to see the lad once again, her lips curling in anticipation of enjoying some mild flirtation.

The girl strolled out of the kitchen onto a strip of sheep-nibbled grass that was still wet with dew, her eyes drawn to the flower-strewn machair that swept down towards the shoreline. Above, a mere speck against the pale blue, a skylark filled the air with his song. The Dutch girl stood for a moment, breathing in the mingled scents of clover and meadowsweet, glad to be here on this Hebridean island, happy to savour a few moments of peace before the day properly began.

Then, with a sigh, she walked the few paces towards the wooden pantry. Its old grey door creaked open as she slid the latch upwards, expecting to see the promised parcel of fish under its covering of bracken. Ewan Angus had left several such packages already this summer. Maryka made a face. She hated handling the wet scaly things, their tails bent stiff, cold eyes staring at her.

As she peered into the gloomy shed, one hand was already on the skirt of her apron, ready to lift the slimy fish onto the white cotton and carry it back to the kitchen. Mrs Forsyth would settle up later, Maryka knew. She might seem a bit vacant at times but Hamish's wife wasn't stupid when it came to matters of dealing with her suppliers.

Maryka blinked. The shelf was bare. She looked around,

eyes roving up and down the wooden slats piled high with boxes containing non-perishable foodstuffs. But there was nothing, not even a sign of freshly plucked green bracken hiding Ewan Angus's spoils. The girl's brow creased in a frown. Mrs Forsyth wouldn't be best pleased: she had already printed out the menus for tonight's dinner and Archie, the chef, had annoyed them all yesterday by rummaging through every cupboard in the kitchen, seeking out the ingredients for some special sauce. It was a wonder he managed to cook anything at all, the girl thought; the number of times she had seen him stoned late on in the evenings.

She started at a noise, making her turn and gasp and, for an instant, she expected to see the young fisherman striding across the grass, a grin on his handsome face.

But there was no one to be seen, just the pantry door swinging open, taken by a sudden breeze, its chill making the girl shiver.

Detective Superintendent William Lorimer stood at the open door of the cottage, a smile of contentment on his face and a mug of freshly brewed coffee in his hand. It was just gone six o'clock, but habitual early rises in the course of his working life had set Lorimer's mental clock to this quiet time of the day. Summer was never the same without a couple of weeks here at Leiter Cottage, Mary Grant's little white house that nestled close to the curve of Fishnish Bay. They had been coming here for several years now, courtesy of

11

Lorimer's colleague, DI Jo Grant, Mary's niece. It had become their favourite place to find some peace from the hustle of Glasgow, the quiet pace of island life perfect to restore their spirits.

Framed by oaks and willows lay the curving bay, where yachts occasionally anchored, the sweeping arm of pine forest on the furthest shore providing good shelter from sudden storms. Beyond was the stretch of water known as the Sound of Mull and the gently sloping hills on the mainland. It was a view that Lorimer never tired of seeing: the changing colours of the sky reflected in the waters, the activity of car ferries or smaller boats providing interest at different times of the day, sunlight shifting over the fields and hillside by Lochaline. It was a vista waiting to be captured by an artist's skill, he often thought, but they had yet to find it in paint in any of the island's galleries.

Lorimer drained the last of his coffee, tossing the dregs into the flower bed, and wandered across the extensive lawn to a narrow path that was hidden by reeds and long grasses.

His eye was caught suddenly by the activity of birds down by the shore; herring gulls and hooded crows. Their raucous squawks made Lorimer raise the high definition binoculars that hung around his neck, but all that he could make out were the thrashing wings as they swooped and pecked at some unseen thing. A dead sheep, perhaps? Or a seal, washed up on the shore? Curious, he allowed his feet to take him along the old path, across the main road and down onto the rocky beach. Beside a crumbling sea wall lay the remnants of an ancient boathouse, its timbers silvered by years of neglect. Once it had housed good clinker-built boats, Mary Grant had told them, her sing-song voice weaving stories of times past when her late husband and his brothers had fished the bay and hunted for deer and rabbits over the hill. But the men who had worked these waters were long gone, leaving only traces of a crofter's life.

Lorimer wrinkled his nose in anticipation. If it were some dead creature the smell would certainly attract these sharp-beaked gulls and scavenging crows. The actual subject of their frenzy was hidden from view by a square black rock but the birds rose as one at his approach, with shrill calls of annoyance at this human intruding on their feast.

His feet slithered on the heaps of wet ochre-coloured seaweed as he came closer to the edge of the water. It was a high tide, he remembered. Had something been washed up from the depths and cast onto the shoreline? Here and there patches of spongy green turf made his progress easier, clumps of pink sea thrift waving in the morning breeze.

Lorimer stopped abruptly, his eyes refusing at first to believe what he saw. A sour taste rose in his throat but he swallowed it down, blinking hard as he looked at the naked body on the ground. The red hair was still wet, he noticed, trying not to stare at the place where the man's eyes should have been. The birds had made short work of them, he thought disgustedly. One hooded crow, braver than the rest, hopped closer as if to test this tall man's resolve. Without a moment's thought, Lorimer waved his arm at the bird, flinging a curse as it took off.

Hunkering down, Lorimer examined the corpse, the professional policeman taking over now. There were other marks of course, predations by sea creatures, but the body was still intact enough for identification. No tattoos, though it was obviously a young man, the white skin smooth where the birds had failed to peck and claw at it. He paused for a moment, frowning. His legs were twisted under him, giving him a stunted look, the rounded knees scarred. One pale arm lay stiffly by his side, the fingers of his hand splayed as though he had been grasping at something at the moment of death, yet the other arm was folded behind his back. Lorimer frowned, trying to make sense of the body's shape, his imagination seeing the young man struggling against the currents as he fell deep into the water. Had he landed on the sea floor, against a rock, perhaps? Was that why the body had taken on such an odd shape as rigor had set in?

There was something about it, something vaguely familiar ... he closed his eyes and tried to remember but the shriek of a nearby herring gull disturbed the moment and he raised his hand to ward off the predator.

There was no doubt in his mind about who this might be, however. The island's rumour mill had reached even the remote little cottage here at Fishnish Bay with tales of the missing student from Kilbeg House.

Giving a sigh, Lorimer rose to his feet, fumbling in his pocket, hoping against hope that the mobile would find a signal down here on the shoreline.

Then, as he dialled the number, he glanced across the bay, noting the little squall that had sprung up; dark clouds slanting shadows over the once quiet waters.

CHAPTER THREE

Glasgow

Twenty Years Earlier

The body had been laid out on the grass at the side of the river, several figures already at the scene to ascertain who it was and what might have happened. The young detective constable hovered uncertainly behind his boss, listening to what was being said, concentrating on the officer's instructions about preserving the scene. Detective Inspector Phillips turned and nodded in Lorimer's direction.

'Ever seen anything like this?' he said, his eyes flicking across the DC's face as though to examine it for any sign of weakness.

'No, sir,' Lorimer replied, drawing closer to look for himself.

The man was naked, the skin on his bloated body pale against the flattened turf and weeds. Flies had gathered already, drawn by the stink of rotting flesh, and Phillips was sweeping them away with the back of his hand as the young DC hunkered down beside him.

'What d'you make of him?' Phillips asked.

Swallowing hard, Lorimer looked at the remains of the man's face then let his gaze travel down the rest of the body. There were dark marks around each of the wrists and ankles, the legs bent back, making the corpse seem much smaller.

'He's been hog-tied?' Lorimer said, a question in his voice.

'Course he has!' the detective inspector exclaimed, his nod and fleeting smile absurdly pleasing to the newest member of A Division's CID team as his boss stood up to speak to the on-duty pathologist.

William Lorimer continued to gaze at the man on the ground: *the victim*, he reminded himself. Yet somehow using the term did not depersonalise the dead man as it was meant to do. Once, not so very long ago, this was a human being who walked and talked, swore, got drunk, maybe even did bad enough things to come to this terrible end. The hair was full of mud and weeds but under the morning light Lorimer could see the auburn glints and the reddish fuzz around his throat and chin. The beginnings of an identity, he reminded himself. Then, as his gaze lingered on the hairless torso, he wondered if the unblemished skin was that of an adult male at all. Had the river washed all coarseness away? Or, he asked himself, was this just a teenager, a mere lad?

They'd be trawling missing persons for data relating to someone fitting the description, he thought, taking out his notebook and making a few hasty observations, plus a quick sketch.

The flash made him spin round, almost losing his balance. One hand felt the wet ground as Lorimer tried to steady himself then he rose to his feet and stepped back, allowing the scene of crime photographer to shoot the necessary pictures.

He was there to watch and listen, Lorimer reminded himself, though he might well be asked again for his observations. DI George Phillips had a reputation as someone who didn't suffer fools gladly but Lorimer had found himself warming to the older man when he had been posted to CID at Stewart Street and now, seeing him in action, DC William Lorimer knew instinctively that he would learn a lot from the detective inspector.

Uniforms had called it in – something he might have done himself only a few weeks ago, before his transfer to CID – and now DI Phillips would head up an investigation into what appeared to be a suspicious death as the Senior Investigating Officer; that was the official title given to the person who took on a case like this. Lorimer took a few steps towards the DI and the pathologist, wondering if the day would come when he might be given such a designation.

'Aye, something's been cutting into his ankles and wrists. You can see the marks easy enough,' the DI was saying. 'What happened to the rope, though? If it was rope?'

The white-suited pathologist turned and smiled. 'Depends on how tightly it was tied. Immersion in the water would have made it harder to loosen off.'

'He could've been cut free post-mortem and thrown into the river? Is that what you're saying?'

The pathologist shrugged. 'We won't be able to tell much more until we get him along to the mortuary, George. Then we'll see whether he was alive or not when he hit the water.'

Lorimer gave an involuntary shudder, his imagination creating a scene where a man was trussed up and then tossed alive into the swift flowing waters of the Clyde. The victim would have known what was happening, seen the skies tumbling overhead, then struggled in vain as he sank deep, deep under the currents. If that was the true scenario, what had happened to loosen him from his bonds? Lorimer exhaled, suddenly aware that he'd been holding his breath. Much better to think that he'd been given a hammering and tossed into the river after he'd been killed. He could see in his mind's eye the figures of men crouching around the trussed-up body, cutting off the bindings on his ankles and wrists, taking away any evidence that might link them to the crime. Was that how it had happened? Were there intelligent minds behind this murder?

As he watched the body being raised from the ground and placed carefully onto a stretcher, the young detective constable realised that he wanted to know what had happened. Not simply to satisfy his own desire to succeed as a cop, but to bring the perpetrators of this crime to justice. Someone out there was missing this fellow – a mother, a girlfriend, perhaps – and it was his duty to give them the answers they sought.

CHAPTER FOUR

'What's happened?'

Maggie stood at the side of the road, her dark curls blowing in the rising wind, as Lorimer strode across the last few yards towards her. The police cars were parked on a strip of turf and she could see two uniformed officers making their way back along the shoreline, their yellow rain jackets harsh statements against the sage greens and mossy browns of the marshy ground that lay between them.

'I heard the birds making a racket,' he replied at last, turning to look down towards the water's edge. 'Thought it was a dead animal that they'd found.'

Her husband stopped abruptly, shaking his head as though unable to put his feelings into words.

'Oh, no!' Maggie put a hand to her mouth as she caught sight of his expression. There was a tightness around his mouth that she had seen many times before, usually when something dreadful had happened.

'Not ... not that boy ... ?'

'I think so. Fits his description. Red hair.'

He caught her hand as Maggie moved forward.

'Don't go down, Mags. You mustn't see that ...'

She stood still, letting him enfold her in his arms.

'Come on,' he said gently, turning her to head back towards the cottage.

The road was deserted apart from the two police vehicles stranded by the roadside, no early ferry traffic yet making its way between the port at Craignure and the towns further north. It was, Maggie thought, as if the world was holding its breath, the silence around them broken only by the cries of oystercatchers as they swept over the stony beach. She let herself be guided along the grass-covered path, feeling the dampness soak through her canvas shoes, her mind already wondering what had happened to the boy from the hotel.

Had it been the result of a boating accident, perhaps? The currents way out in the Sound could be unpredictable and if he had gone by boat from the little slipway at Kilbeg who knows what might have happened? Bodies could be lost at sea for weeks on end, washing up miles from where they had fallen into the waters.

Nobody had known what had become of the missing student from Glasgow, Mary Grant had told them just yesterday evening when she had called into the cottage. His folks were frantic with worry, it was said.

Maggie felt a sickness rise in her throat as she thought about these people who were strangers to her, whose lives would now be tenuously linked to her own. It was sometimes said that not knowing was the worst, fearing and hoping in equal measure. But was that really true? If so then these parents could be given a final answer and begin to grieve in earnest.

What was it like to lose a grown child? Maggie looked at the cottage where generations of children had played on the grass and guddled happily along the shore. Her own little ones had never taken a first breath, born too soon. The memory of these griefs had faded now, the possibility of children gone for ever. Yet somehow, Maggie could feel the pain deep within her, a knife low in her guts, at the thought of these other parents being told about their boy.

The willow gate creaked as her husband pushed it open and held it wide.

'Come on, can you make some tea? And fill the pot. I guess we'll be having visitors soon enough,' he said, squeezing her hand.

She saw him hesitate, his head turned back towards the shore.

'It's okay. I'm fine,' she said, forcing her mouth into a tight smile. 'You go on back down.'

Maggie paused for a moment, watching as her husband strode away through the reeds and bog cotton. She had come out earlier, intent on suggesting a morning walk up the hill, her eyes drawn immediately to the police cars on the roadside and the uniformed figures by the shore. A sudden trembling seized her, making her wrap her arms around her chest. Tea, she needed hot tea, Maggie told herself. Tea was good for shock . . .

Yet it wasn't the shock of having a body washed up on the shore here that troubled her, she realised, walking across the lawn towards the door of Leiter Cottage, but the thought that horror could visit this special place, their sanctuary from the outside world.

The two policemen were standing on either side of the body when Lorimer returned. As they looked up, the tall man from Glasgow thought he saw a flicker of resentment in the eyes of the older man, Sergeant McManus from Craignure. Calum Mhor. *Big Calum*. He was a broad-shouldered fellow, right enough, though he merited the name on girth rather than on height, his waterproof jacket straining across his stomach.

'Need to get something to protect that from the rain. Preserve the scene,' he muttered.

'You don't think he died here?' Lorimer blurted out.

'Well, nothing is certain, is it?' The police sergeant turned and nodded at the wet stones lying against the grassy banks. 'Tide's going out now. You found him at high tide. So . . .' He shrugged and pursed his lips as though he were a small boy trying to calculate a particularly difficult sum.

'Wasn't he washed ashore?' Lorimer ventured.

'Ach, must have been, eh?' McManus shrugged again as though his brain could wrestle no further with the problem.

23

'We'll check the tide charts when we get back up the road, though.'

'And now?' Lorimer asked, nodding towards the body lying near their feet.

McManus looked at the detective superintendent through narrowed eyes. 'You'll be on holiday here . . . ' he began.

'Yes.' Lorimer frowned. Calum Mhor knew fine they were taking their annual break.

'So you'll have a camera with you?'

Lorimer's face relaxed as he understood the question. 'You need to take some photos of the body in situ,' he said.

'Aye. If it's no trouble, sir,' McManus replied, his eyes flicking back to the little house sheltered in the lee of the hill. 'It's not every day we find something like this on the island,' he continued with a grimace. 'And this wee mobile does not take a good picture. Jamie, away you go up and get the camera from Mrs Lorimer,' he said, turning to the young police constable who was standing by their side, a bleak expression on his face.

The two men watched as the young man strode swiftly away, glad no doubt for an interlude away from the sight of the corpse, its damaged flesh exposed to the elements.

'He's no' seen any sights like that,' McManus said quietly as they watched the young constable cross the road and head towards Leiter Cottage. 'No' even in Inverness,' he added wryly.

Lorimer did not reply. Part of him was remembering himself

24

as a younger detective, standing beside the bloated body of an unidentified man. He felt a sudden sympathy for Police Constable Jamie Kennedy. Being a police officer in Tobermory was a far cry from the sorts of cases that he might have had to deal with in Scotland's largest city had he been sent south to Glasgow.

The opening notes of 'The Hen's March to the Midden' interrupted Lorimer's thoughts and he smiled as the big police sergeant snapped open his mobile phone, cutting off the Scottish tune. Calum Mhor turned away as though not wishing to be overheard and Lorimer walked back along the shoreline, keeping a discreet distance between the officer and himself.

The waters were lapping against the coloured stones where tiny red fronds of sea anemones waved back and forth as the current took them. A whole miniature world continued down below the surface, oblivious to whatever was happening to the human race. Watching the pebbles roll beneath the tide's swell, seeing a pale crab scuttle sideways under a dark rock was somehow comforting to Lorimer, hunkering at the sea's edge. Life would go on in the world despite the vagaries of mankind.

The crunch of stones under the big sergeant's boots made Lorimer stand up again.

'We'll be expecting a team from the mainland,' Calum Mhor said, waving the mobile phone in his fist. 'Probably on the afternoon boat,' he added.

'Anyone I might know?'

Calum McManus gave him a shrewd look. 'Detective Inspector Stevie Crozier?'

Lorimer shook his head. It was not a name he had heard of before and McManus did not seem to want to enlighten him further. Whoever this guy was, he would be SIO as soon as he set foot on the island. And, despite Lorimer being the one to have found the body, Crozier would probably not want the senior officer from Glasgow interfering in his case.

'Here's Jamie with your camera,' McManus said, nodding towards the approaching figure.

Lorimer bit his lip. There was something in the way McManus was standing, arms folded, as though he were barring the way back to the corpse on the grass. *You can go now*, his body language seemed to say. *We can take over from here.*

'Will you come up for a cup of tea once the ambulance has been?' Lorimer suggested.

McManus nodded. 'Aye, and we'll need a written statement from you. And permission to hold on to your camera.'

'It's digital,' Lorimer told him as they watched the constable picking his way across the marshy ground, the camera slung over his shoulder. 'There's a printer at the cottage. We can run off copies for you.'

'Right,' McManus said shortly. 'We'll see you in a bit, then.'

The view of the Morvern shore was almost blotted out now by low rainclouds sweeping across the Sound of Mull, and the two figures heading back across the shore were bent against the sudden wind. It was the sort of rain that could soak a person in moments, soft and sweet-scented as it fell off the hillside, but persistent as a nagging wife.

Jamie Kennedy heaved a sigh, wishing he were anywhere else but on the island right now. Bad enough to have to be involved in a sudden death, but to have to talk to the senior policeman from Glasgow who was staying at Fishnish made him feel the weight of his years of inexperience on the Force. Coming back to Mull had been great after his training in Inverness. *No more violent clashes with neds in the wee small hours*, his mum had remarked with a note of triumph in her voice. *Better to be at home and see to things here*, she'd added. And it had been better, hadn't it? Boring sometimes, but good fun, too, and on the island the uniform was given plenty of respect, not like the sneers and filthy looks that had sometimes come Jamie's way in the city. Here they were *officers*, not just *your lot*, as the mainland neds were wont to say.

'D'you think he'll have spoken to anyone in Glasgow?' he asked the man toiling at his side.

'Not if he wants to act like a professional,' the police sergeant retorted. 'He's on holiday. And I hope he's not getting any ideas about sticking his nose in,' he grumbled, as though he was already suspicious that the detective superintendent might wish to pull rank and leave the island officers adrift.

'What d'you know about him?' Jamie asked as they walked

27

along the single track road that led to the whitewashed cottage.

'He comes here a fair bit,' McManus admitted. 'Birdwatcher. Helps out the RSPB boys now and again. Mary Grant speaks highly of the pair of them,' he added grudgingly. 'Told DI Crozier as much when we called it in.'

'No, I know all that,' Kennedy said. 'I mean, d'you know anything about what he's done? Cases, I mean ...'

'Och, he's aye on the telly, that one. *Crimewatch* and stuff. He's been SIO in lots of big murder cases. DI Crozier'll make sure he keeps his paws off this one though,' McManus said, smiling grimly, holding his collar tighter in a vain effort to stop the trickles of water soaking his shirt.

'What d'you mean?' Kennedy stopped in astonishment. 'The DI coming here? But ...' He stopped and stared at the older man. 'The wee lad ... you don't think he was murdered?'

McManus gave the young cop a sharp look. 'Did ye no' see his hands and feet?'

Kennedy shook his head, ashamed. He'd not wanted to look long and hard at the dead body once he'd seen what the gulls had done to its face and genitals. And he was relieved that the paramedics were down there right now taking over, putting the lad on a stretcher, taking his corpse to the cottage hospital in Craignure.

'He's been tied up,' McManus said quietly. 'Someone did that to the boy, Jamie. It was no accident.'

They stepped along the road in silence, their boots making wet imprints and vanishing again on the narrow tarmac, each man wondering what the officer from Glasgow would say when they reached the little house that overlooked Fishnish Bay.

CHAPTER FIVE

Glasgow

Twenty Years Earlier

'No missing persons fitting his description, sir,' Detective Constable Lorimer said, looking up from the masses of lever arch files that were stacked on his desk. It had taken him days to trawl through the missing persons data, reading each and every description of men who had been reported missing over the last couple of weeks. The waterlogged body had been taken to Glasgow City Mortuary where the pathologist had confirmed what George Phillips had suspected: death had occurred prior to the man being put into the Clyde's flowing waters. Asphyxiation was a possible cause of death, there being no signs of knife wounds or bullet holes, the more common method of dispatch used by some of Glasgow's gangland fraternity.

'How d'you think he died, sir?'

Phillips shook his head. 'He'd been trussed up, possibly

gagged as well,' he shrugged. 'Why, we don't know. Did something to upset someone, obviously. Maybe it was a warning that went wrong? Maybe they didn't mean to kill him, just give him a fright.' He sighed heavily. 'We'll probably never know unless we find out who he was.'

'Maybe if we ran it past the press office . . . ?'

'Aye, well, I'll leave that with you to sort out. Let me see your written description of him first, okay?'

'Yes, sir,' Lorimer nodded, already imagining how he could phrase a short paragraph for the newspapers.

He glanced up at the DI as Phillips turned to leave. There was a gloomy cast to the older man's countenance as though he had already given up hope of finding any clues that might help solve the case.

'Hm.' DI Phillips gave another sigh. 'Don't like it, young Lorimer, don't like it at all.' He paused as though he were about to say more, then, shaking his head, turned and left the CID room, leaving William Lorimer to stare after him.

Turning over a fresh page in his spiral-bound notebook, the detective constable began to write. *Missing person found*, he began, then scored it out. *Body of man found in River Clyde*. He stopped and frowned, twirling the pencil between his fingers. Maggie would know what to write, he thought. His wife was great at putting stuff into words; she spent her working life teaching kids how to do just that at the secondary school where she worked.

A smile crossed his face as he thought of his wife. Her once

31

slim body was filling out now as she entered the third trimester of her pregnancy. Just another few weeks and she would be on maternity leave. Pity that didn't extend to husbands, he thought, imagining the time when the baby arrived and they could begin life as a complete family. It would never happen, though, he told himself. And certainly not for serving police officers: they were perennially short on manpower in Strathclyde Region, as everywhere else in the country. Just as well Maggie's mum would be round to help when the baby was born.

Funny how life worked out, he mused, looking at the lined notebook, the effort of juggling words and phrases temporarily forgotten. Had it not been for that identity parade, then William Lorimer might still be at the university and studying for his doctorate. While he was working during the holidays, a chance likeness between a bank robber and the student who was innocently counting notes in the bank's own vault had brought Lorimer to be part of a line-up in one of the city's police stations. Discouraging frowns from his manager and the alarming thought that he might be mistaken for a real criminal had given him quite a shake at the time. But then talking with the officers over a cup of tea – after he had been eliminated from that particular part of their inquiry – had intrigued the young man. Folk who committed criminal acts might be people who looked just like him. How did you tell the difference? He wanted to know and it was a question that was to begin the journey away from his studies in History of Art and take him into the role of a serving police officer.

At least his time at university had served some purpose, he thought, the smile lingering around his mouth as he brought an image of his wife to mind. Maggie and he had met at the University of Glasgow, after all. Maybe their kids would grow up to be students there one day.

He flicked the pencil back and forward in his fingers, remembering the lad that had lain on the grass beside the river. He'd looked in his late teens. What was his story? Had he ever had the chance to go to university? Or was he one of the unfortunates in the city who had slipped in with the wrong crowd? Whoever he was, his life had been cut short and he deserved the same amount of time and attention as any other murder victim to bring his killers to justice.

CHAPTER SIX

'That'll be the boys in blue.' Lorimer attempted a grin as he heard the door being knocked; three determined raps of meaty knuckles against the pebbled glass.

Maggie nodded and walked briskly from the cosy sitting room through to the kitchen.

A brief glance showed the outline of two dark figures standing at the door, one of them the thick-set police sergeant from Craignure, Calum Mhor.

'Good day, Mrs Lorimer, sir ...' Calum was brushing his boots on the coir mat inside the porch, a few paces away from where Lorimer's wife was standing, busying herself with cups and plates.

'Terrible business, just,' he added with a shake of his head, then followed Lorimer and the younger officer into the main room of the cottage.

Lorimer had put a match to the kindling on the hearth and already the birch logs had caught, giving warmth and light to the room, but he still knelt down, leaning across the red stone fireplace to loosen the wood a little with the poker – a proprietorial gesture, perhaps. *This is our place for now*, that small action might have said, *but come in and be welcome*.

'Tea or coffee?' Maggie's dark head came around the door.

'Oh, tea for us both, thank you,' Calum replied, giving no opportunity for the younger officer who simply nodded his agreement.

'Well, now, what can I say?' Calum Mhor heaved a sigh as he watched Maggie approach with the tray.

'You can say anything in front of my wife. If you want to stay, that is …?' he asked Maggie, looking up at her from his place down by the fireside.

'No, I'd rather not,' Maggie said stiffly. 'There's milk and sugar and a selection of biscuits. Mary Grant's own shortbread,' she added with the ghost of a smile.

Lorimer watched as she left the room, closing the door behind her. The swishing sound of her waterproof jacket being removed from its peg and the soft thuds as she put on the necessary rubber boots made him realise that she had decided to set off up the hill, just as she had planned to do before the discovery that had shattered their day.

'Mrs Lorimer won't be going near the shore …?'

'No, Calum, she won't,' Lorimer replied, standing up and reaching for the milk jug and sugar bowl.

'Ah, just so, just so.' The big police sergeant nodded, his eyes flicking towards the large window that looked out to the bay, alerted by the sound of her feet crunching on the pebbled path as Maggie passed them by, the hood of her jacket pulled forward against the incessant drizzle.

'It's a bad business, Mr Lorimer, sir,' Calum began again, his hand stretched out to take one of the pieces of sugary shortbread.

'You're sure it's the boy from Kilbeg? Dalgleish?'

Calum gave a sigh. 'Who else could it be, man? The lad goes missing more than forty-eight hours ago and you find the body washed ashore here. Stands to reason it's him. Same hair colouring an' all,' he said with a grunt. 'We have the description though I never set eyes on the boy myself,' he added, a note of sadness in his gruff voice.

'What's been happening on the island to find him up till now?' Lorimer asked, deliberately looking at the younger officer from Tobermory. 'It would come under your jurisdiction, I suppose?'

PC Jamie Kennedy looked up, startled at being asked such a direct question.

'Well, we checked with MacBraynes to see if he'd bought a ticket to Oban. The staff at the hotel thought he might have just pushed off.'

'But you didn't think so?'

'No, sir. All his belongings were left behind in the wee attic room he had.'

'Everything? Nothing missing there that you noticed?'

The young man's cheeks bloomed with sudden colour.

'Well, just what you'd expect a kid to take with him. So, no mobile phone, no wallet or credit cards, that sort of stuff ...'

'And no trace of him using a card since he was last seen?'

'Still waiting for an answer to that, sir,' Kennedy replied, lowering his eyes guiltily.

Lorimer bit off a reply. It was obvious that nothing much had been done to trace any activity on the lad's credit cards or mobile phone, something that his own officers would have been smart enough to do. He'd done it often enough as a uniformed officer and as a young detective constable; though the technical support that they had nowadays was a whole world away from the days when they'd depended on British Telecom and the credit card companies for help.

Besides, it was none of his business to criticise how these island officers went about their business. Life here went on at a slower pace altogether and crime, never mind murder, was not something most folk thought about.

'What do you know about him?' Lorimer asked. 'The missing lad.'

PC Kennedy sat up a little straighter before replying. He was on safer ground here, Lorimer thought.

'He is ... or he *was* a student. Up here to work at Kilbeg Country House Hotel for his holidays, seemingly.'

'Anything else?' Lorimer was surprised. Surely they knew more about the missing student than that?

'Well,' Jamie Kennedy began, glancing at the big police sergeant nervously. 'Some of the staff at the hotel didn't seem to like him very much,' he said. 'Not good to speak ill of the dead . . .'

'He hasn't been officially identified yet, constable, so I think your conscience is clear,' Lorimer said kindly.

Jamie Kennedy nodded, taking a quick slurp from his tea before continuing.

'He seems to have been a loud type of bloke; bit of a Hooray Henry, if you know what I mean. Came from a well-off background and wasn't shy about letting them all know it, too,' he went on, nodding his head all the time as if he were embarrassed for the lad. 'His first name was Rory but the girls in the hotel made fun of him. Talked about him as Roary, as in to roar, see?'

'So he wasn't a popular lad?'

'The owners seemed to like him, sir. Said he was an asset to the place. He had the sort of manner that guests like, Mr Forsyth told me. Suppose he meant that he was well spoken, and all that.'

'What sort of work did he do in the hotel?'

'Oh, waiting on tables. He knew his silver service all right. Must have worked somewhere else, I suppose, to learn that. And lately he'd been given the job of wine waiter. That was something else that riled the younger members of the staff. He was always showing off his knowledge of the wines of the world, seemingly.'

PC Kennedy sat back, his face flushed from the heat of the fire. 'That's all I've found out about him so far,' he mumbled.

'Well, it's a start, isn't it?' Lorimer said. 'Your SIO will be glad to have something to go on.'

Jamie Kennedy drew in a deep breath and nodded silently.

Just then Lorimer caught the glimpse of a smile playing around Calum Mhor's mouth. Maybe this DI Crozier was a stickler for detail and that was why the younger officer seemed so tense.

'I looked this out for you.' Lorimer handed over a small red booklet to the detective sergeant. 'Tide tables,' he said. 'I wasn't sure about today's tide,' he added, a question in his voice.

Calum Mhor flicked through the booklet till he came to the page where the date and times for July tides were given.

'Aye, a spring tide right enough.' He nodded, handing the booklet back. 'Just what I thought.'

Lorimer took the booklet and slipped it into his pocket. The tide had been particularly high this morning. Unnaturally high, he knew, given the conjunction of the sun and moon. And yet ... the boy's body had been on a bank of soft grass about a foot higher than the damp line showing where the tide had turned. Almost as if it had been placed there by other hands ...

His thoughts were interrupted by the big policeman.

'Perhaps we could take that statement from you now, sir?' Calum Mhor asked, setting down his mug by the fireplace and reaching into his jacket for a black-bound notebook.

'Of course.' Lorimer attempted a wry smile. 'I'll be as

detailed as I can,' he said with a nod, his eyes flicking over to PC Kennedy and back to McManus. Whatever he said now would be integral to the beginning of this case, an investigation that the DI from the mainland would soon be taking over. His own suspicions and memories of that other unsolved case from so long ago would have to remain unspoken, at least for now.

CHAPTER SEVEN

Dr Rosie Fergusson clicked on the send button, her reply to the police officer winging its way to the DI's BlackBerry. The team was already on their way to Mull and she hoped to join them within twenty-four hours. It would be Rosie's job as senior consultant pathologist to carry out the post-mortem. But, before that could happen, the victim's parents were also heading to the Western Isles. The discovery of a red-haired young man washed up on the beach two days after he had gone missing told its own sorry tale. Rosie shook her head. Something bad had happened up there to allow a senior officer to investigate. Not just an accident, she told herself, not a simple case of drowning, then; not if DI Crozier was involved.

Her husband had raised his dark, bushy eyebrows when Rosie had described the death. Solly was not one to make puerile statements, but one look could say such a lot. His background in behavioural psychology had involved Solly in several cases of multiple murder in the past, many of them with cases headed up by Lorimer.

How bizarre that it should have been Lorimer who had found the body! The Lorimers spent at least two weeks every summer up in their hideaway. It was a release for them both: Maggie from the stresses and strains of teaching and Lorimer from the urban jungle that was Glasgow. Rosie sighed and blinked at the screen. She ought to send Maggie an email. After all, the Lorimers were close friends, godparents to her daughter, Abby, and the four of them had hoped to meet up during Maggie's summer break. But the pathologist hadn't reckoned on it happening quite like this.

A holiday in Balamory, Rosie had suggested, seeing three-year-old Abby's eyes light up at the idea. The children's TV programme that was based on the colourful houses around Tobermory had taken the little girl's fancy and plans had already been made for the Brightmans to head north. Solly had found a place in Tobermory for them to stay and she would have time to fulfil her duties on this new case before taking a short break, Rosie realised. And maybe taking Bill and Maggie away from the scene of a crime would do them both a favour. Abby's incessant chatter about her favourite characters in *Balamory* could be the perfect antidote to the horrors of finding a body practically on their doorstep.

She would also be able to catch up with her old friend and one-time mentor, she thought, images of a tall, grey-haired lady who now resided in Mull coming to mind. That would be good.

The pathologist's eyes sought out the pencil icon and she

began to type in Maggie's email address. They had broadband up there, didn't they? She shook her head, wondering if this email would reach them, letting them know that she, too, was involved in the fate of the boy.

Pamela Dalgleish stood on the deck of the *Isle of Mull*, the big car ferry that ploughed through the seas between Oban and Tobermory, looking out at grey skies and choppy waters. Minke whales had been sighted here, Rory had told them, but somehow she doubted whether she and Douglas would see more than the occasional herring gull on their trip to the island. A long spit of land, dominated by a stark, white lighthouse, loomed out of the mist, the current heaving harder beneath the ship. Lismore. That was the place. Pamela had read about it somewhere, hadn't she?

If she could only stay here for ever, mesmerised by the waves foaming past the bow . . . it was a fate she desired more than anything. *Stop all the clocks*, Auden had written, and now she knew how he had felt. If she could make time stand still, keep sailing out to the west, away from landfall, away from the necessity of speaking to people, away from whatever horror lay ahead, then Pamela Dalgleish would choose that here and now.

He found her at the top of the hill under one of the ancient oak trees. Maggie was turned away from him, sitting on a long, low branch that generations of children must have used to

43

bounce up and down. Did she miss them? These phantom children? And had the death of this boy brought back thoughts of what might have been? So many pregnancies, so much hope invested in a family life, all come to naught.

Lorimer came to sit beside her, his weight making the old branch creak.

Maggie was staring out to sea through a gap in the trees, the shore beneath them and the ribbon of road blanked off by the curving hillside from this point. The hill mist was a fine, gentle rain but larger drops fell from the trees, plopping onto their waterproof hoods.

Lorimer took her hand, twining her fingers in his own. 'You're frozen,' he remarked, but she did not answer, simply kept looking at the grey seas and the dark green outline of pine forest across the bay. He reached across and took both her hands in his, gently massaging them to bring some warmth back into the cold flesh. Maggie placed her head against his shoulder then he felt a huge sigh as she nestled into his body.

'I feel so selfish,' she said at last, her voice small under the dark hood.

'Why? You've done nothing to feel selfish about.'

Another sigh, then, 'I was angry,' she said quietly. '*Am* angry. That it happened here. Spoiled this place for ever.'

He put an arm around her shoulder, drawing her closer. 'That's not selfish,' he replied.

'Isn't it?' Her tone was scathing so he said no more, for

hadn't he felt that spurt of betrayal too? That moment on the shore, the feeling that their special place had become tainted with something evil?

'There's no getting away from it, is there?' she continued, a note of bitterness in her voice.

'What d'you mean? The job?'

'No,' Maggie answered, 'not that. I'm not blaming you for being a policeman.' She looked at him seriously. 'I meant, there's no getting away from the *world*.'

It was Lorimer's turn to sigh. 'I suppose not,' he agreed.

Then, as something caught the corner of his eye, he placed a finger over his lips, nudging Maggie to follow his glance.

A large brown hare had come out of the mist, lolloping across the wet grass and onto the narrow road. They sat still on the branch, watching as it came closer and stopped. For a moment the animal seemed to stare at them, nose twitching, long dark ears erect, then it turned and began to make its way downhill, stopping again, sitting up on its haunches, turning to look back at them.

'Time to go?' Lorimer asked, and Maggie nodded.

The branch swung upward as they climbed off, a faint swish and groan as though the oak was tired of bearing its burden.

'He's waiting for us,' Maggie whispered as they stepped onto the tarmac and followed the hare back down towards Leiter Cottage. Sure enough, the hare appeared to be looking at them with its steady, glassy eyes, as if certain the two humans were following his lead, then it turned and began to lollop its way down the road. They walked on, hand in hand, their eyes fixed on the creature. When the white house came into view it stopped once more and turned to watch them, ears twitching. Then, as though satisfied that they were safely home, the hare leapt across the burn and vanished into the bracken.

Lorimer and Maggie walked towards the edge of the road but there was nothing to be seen, not even a green frond disturbed by the animal's passing.

There was no need for words when they crossed to the gate, hand in hand, the sound of boots crunching on pebbles as they made their way back to the front door. It was a moment that would be hugged to themselves and taken out some other time to be remembered, a moment a poet might have mined for symbolism or meaning. For now all that mattered was that the bold hare had lifted their spirits and restored their delight in this special place.

CHAPTER EIGHT

Glasgow

Twenty Years Earlier

The baby would be born in September, around the time of the equinox when summer finally gave way to darker nights and autumn tints. They hadn't decided on names but Maggie favoured Susan for a girl and David if it was a boy. She wrinkled her nose as she recalled Bill's choices. She didn't fancy Brian for her son's name; it reminded her of the naughtiest child in her first-year class at school, a snot-nosed kid who always forgot to bring a handkerchief. Helen was okay for a girl, but it would always be a reminder of the mother-in-law she'd never had, Bill's mother having died some years before they had met.

She smiled as the baby moved, instinctively placing her hand to feel some tiny limb stretching beneath her rounded belly. 'Susan Lorimer,' she murmured into the dark. It felt at that moment as if there was a little girl in there, listening.

There would be books to read to this little one, stories to tell, songs to sing at bedtime. Maggie sighed, the prospect of motherhood stretching ahead in a haze of pastel-coloured baby clothes and nursery wallpaper. Such plans they had! The new house was far more expensive than they'd intended to buy, but Bill had managed to secure a mortgage for them and now she lay by his side, letting her dreams take her into a future where children played in the big back garden, maybe in a tree house like the one next door.

Her husband stirred, murmuring something indistinct, a dream escaping into the darkness. It was no wonder, Maggie thought. He'd been tasked with trying to identify a dead man pulled from the Clyde. She wrinkled her nose, the idea of death at odds with the new life growing inside her. It wasn't something Maggie wanted to think about and she looked across at her husband's sleeping form with pity. His was not a job she could ever have done. Being a policeman took a certain sort of strength, the sort that William Lorimer seemed to have in abundance. He'd told her briefly about the case, not dwelling on the details; it was the sort of things that working couples did, share the elements of their respective days over an evening meal. Perhaps she ought to tell him that she didn't like to think about dead people right now, Maggie told herself, one hand on her belly as the baby moved again. He'd understand. He always understood things . . . She yawned and closed her eyes, sleep taking her back to her own dreams.

*

48

It was still early when he woke but sunlight filtered through a gap in the thin summer curtains, harbinger of another beautiful day. Maggie, slumbering on her side of the bed, was on holiday now from her school, Lorimer reminded himself, so he would try not to waken her. He had saved his own leave for the arrival of their child, so this fine July day meant a return to the city and a final attempt to crack the case of that unidentified man.

There was so much about this case that troubled the detective constable. *He probably had it coming to him*, one of his colleagues had remarked gloomily, hinting that such deaths always involved the dark side of this city, its drug barons ruthless in dispatching any troublesome elements. The words had been spoken when DI Phillips was well out of earshot. The SIO had already told them more than once that justice should be even-handed. Lorimer had mentioned this to his wife who had quoted lines from Shakespeare's *Macbeth*: *This even-handed justice commends the ingredients of this poisoned chalice to our own lips*. He'd nodded, remembering the quotation from his own schooldays. But he didn't think that was quite what Phillips had meant. It was more the point that all human life was worth something and that the dregs of society deserved the same quality of police time as anyone else. It was not a sentiment that all of his fellow officers shared. And now the case was being wound down, fewer man-hours spent on trying to find out who the red-haired man had been and why his young life had ended in such a brutal manner.

*

Detective Constable Lorimer could have taken one of the pool cars, a Ford Escort or an Astra, but parking spaces behind the mortuary were limited and the walk through the city appealed to the young man. It was always hard to equate the brightness of a clear July day like this with the sorts of things that had happened overnight. The duty sergeant had left notes about the knifing: a drunken brawl that had left one man in hospital and fighting for his life; the other incarcerated, howling with remorse.

Yet there was no trace of that anguish in those city streets as DC Lorimer walked down Buchanan Street past the old model lodging house, the crumbling tenements giving way to a vista that stretched all the way to the river and his destination. Already much of the place was derelict, properties having been purchased to make way for a new shopping complex. Lorimer smiled to himself, remembering Maggie's mother's words on seeing the architectural images in the newspaper. *As if the good folk of Glasgow needed more shops. We've already got that new St Enoch Centre!* she'd exclaimed, tutting loudly and going on to extol the virtues of older emporiums up in Sauchiehall Street like Pettigrew & Stephens or Copland & Lye where she'd shopped as a girl. But things were changing in the heart of Glasgow and soon these old Victorian buildings in Buchanan Street would give way to something that his mother-in-law would no doubt consider as brash and modern as the glass-topped edifice of the shopping centre that had been built beside St Enoch's Square.

He crossed Argyle Street, skirted the new mall and headed towards Paddy's Market, smiling to himself: the old way of buying and selling clothes was still rubbing shoulders with the newcomers here in Glasgow. Paddy's was a frequent haunt of ne'er-do-wells, more for the resetting of stolen goods than anything else, though word had it that drugs were also being channelled through some of the street vendors.

A small man in a flat cloth cap looked up from behind a table strewn with old clothes, one swift glance that did not meet Lorimer's blue gaze. As the detective walked on, he could hear the sound of hawking followed by a spit onto the pavement; it was a mark of the man's bad feelings towards the polis. Even now, in plain clothes, Lorimer was finding it hard to hide his identity from those in the Glasgow underworld; it was as if they could smell a copper the way an animal smelled its enemy.

Saltmarket was an old part of the city, the river not far away, the tenement buildings towering overhead, closing in on these narrower streets. It was hard to imagine the expanse of Glasgow Green so nearby. He turned a corner and there was the High Court of Justiciary, its Greek portico dominating the other buildings, pale sandstone columns like raised fingers of admonition to those in fear of their lives. In contrast, the city mortuary was a squat, grey place, its back doors facing the grand courts, ready to admit the dead.

He was to meet the procurator fiscal at the mortuary – some-one new in his limited experience of CID. There had not been much contact with the Crown Office so far, such liaisons not considered vital during the start of an investigation. A quick glance at his wristwatch told him that he was still on time; Donald Anderson was not someone he would want to keep waiting, Lorimer had been advised.

The man whose body had been dragged up from the river was the sort of anonymous person that Americans referred to as a John Doe. Here, in the west of Scotland, the authorities had no such terms of reference for these unidentified souls whose corpses were kept in the refrigerated cabinets awaiting the time when a friend or relative might come to claim them.

The mortuary superintendent gave him a nod as he entered.

'Just over there, son,' he said with a grin above his closely clipped white moustache. 'They've not begun yet so you'll be able to see the entire process.'

The man smiled at Lorimer with a knowing look in his bright eyes. Here was a rookie detective constable, the expression seemed to say; we'll be able to have some fun with this one.

Lorimer stepped up to the viewing platform and looked at the room through the huge window that would separate him from the pathologist's activities. Several figures appeared from another door; the pathologists gowned and masked, wellington boots on their feet as though to protect themselves from some awful deluge of blood and guts, with several gowned students trailing in their wake. Lorimer shuddered in spite of his earlier resolve to be as objective as he could be. Then his eyes were drawn to a slim shape emerging from the wall as if by magic. A couple of mortuary attendants arrived, lifting the body from its refrigerated cabinet onto the stainless steel table where the two pathologists waited, one pulling at her silicon gloves as though keen to begin. Beside them, on a cloth-covered table, lay an array of surgical instruments, the scalpel blades glittering in the shaft of sunlight that filtered from the windows above.

It was the same boy that he had seen lying on the grass by the River Clyde but somehow here in this mortuary room his body appeared diminished, smaller and waxen, like a model for a corpse, not the real thing at all. The idea comforted him a little as the pathologist took her instrument and began the first incision.

It had been an interesting experience, he told himself, nothing that would bother his dreams. The detective constable had been pleased by his own sense of objectivity, able to look at each and every stage of the post-mortem examination, not even flinching when the sound of the saw had whined through the intercom. DC Lorimer had even been able to ask a few questions during the process, mainly to the fiscal by his side who was far less threatening than he'd been told.

'What would happen to his body, sir? In the event that he remains unidentified?' he asked Donald Anderson as they stepped back into the corridor.

'We keep him,' the fiscal said bluntly. 'He's ours in law,' he added, glancing back at the door they had just left.

'But surely you can't keep unidentified corpses here indefinitely?' Lorimer protested.

The fiscal shrugged. 'We'll see,' he remarked blandly. 'I believe you've been tasked with finding out who he is? George Phillips seems to think you may have the necessary skills to complete that particular action.' He raised doubtful eyebrows at the younger man.

'I hope so, sir.' Lorimer swallowed hard. 'Someone's bound to be missing him.'

'Any progress with that?' the fiscal asked as they left the mortuary.

'No, sir. Everything we have looked at so far has been a dead end.' Lorimer blushed as the fiscal gave a yelp of laughter.

'Sorry, didn't mean that . . .'

'No, Detective Constable, I'm sure you didn't,' the fiscal replied, patting the younger man's arm. 'Well, keep on doing what you can. If this chap has nobody out looking for him we may well have to conclude that there simply are no relatives around. And nobody else who wants to be involved,' he added darkly.

'You think it might be gangland related, sir?'

'George Phillips hinted as much,' the fiscal agreed. He sighed. 'What's happening to this old city of ours, eh? Once upon a time, long before you decided to become a copper, m'boy, we had a sort of honour among thieves.' He shook his head sadly. 'Now with these drugs flooding into every corner of the country, there's nothing like that. Dog eat dog. Nobody in that racket cares a fig what happens to one of their henchmen.'

'There isn't anything to show that the death was drug related,' Lorimer said.

The fiscal shrugged. 'Just because he didn't have needle marks all over his arms doesn't mean he wasn't part of the scene. They aren't all users.

'Anyway. Time I was off,' he said, sketching a brief wave. 'Good day to you, young Lorimer. Good hunting.'

Then, without a backward glance at the police officer he stepped out into the sunlight and headed towards the sleek grey car that was parked at an angle in the small parking space behind the building.

Lorimer watched as the fiscal drove off. It was just another routine morning for the man from the Crown Office, but for the young detective constable it had been so much more. For a moment he looked up at the sky, seeing twin white streaks of vapour, the distant aircraft a mere speck of silver against the blue: up there hundreds of people were jetting off, placing their mortal lives in the hands of the man at the controls. What were they all, when it came down to it? Were human beings simply a mass of flesh, bones and fluids? The stuff that he had seen displayed on that steel table? He blinked suddenly, realising his fingernails were digging into the soft skin on his palms as though to remind himself that he was still alive. Then, stepping between sunlight and shadow once more, Lorimer headed back across the city, resolved to do his duty, not to the bits of human corpse that he'd seen exposed on that table, but to the living young man, whoever he had once been.

CHAPTER NINE

This hospital looked like a nice place to be if one were recovering from an illness, Pamela Dalgleish thought as the car came to a halt on the gravel drive. The view alone would raise one's spirits, the mist lifting off those green hills and the water sparkling under a welcome beam of sunlight. There were large tubs of flowers either side of the front door; the delicate blooms of red and yellow begonias fringed by dark blue trailing lobelia. Someone cared enough to tend these plants and make the place attractive to visitors to the hospital. Somehow it made facing what lay inside a little easier for Rory's mother, though she could not have explained why. Their journey was at an end now, a uniformed policeman ushering her and her husband Douglas inside, his voice lowered out of respect for the bereaved. That was still to be proved so, she thought, clinging to a last fragment of hope. Perhaps the dead person lying inside this building would have nothing to do with them.

A white-coated woman that she took to be a doctor came forward; she saw Douglas shaking her by the hand, followed them meekly along a well lit corridor with doors on either side then around a corner where another policeman stood as if to guard the place against intruders.

'Before you go in to look at him, I do need to ask you not to touch the body,' the doctor said, an apologetic smile appearing for an instant. 'There will have to be a post-mortem examination carried out and a full forensic examination will take place before that so we cannot allow any risk of contamination.' She hesitated, then placed a hand on the sleeve of Pamela's coat. 'I hope that doesn't sound harsh,' she said.

Pamela saw her husband shake his head, murmuring something that she failed to catch. Her ears seemed to be full of a buzzing sound that grew louder as the door opened and they were permitted to step inside.

It was a small room, unadorned in any way, a simple bed in the middle of the room, the sheet spread out across the form beneath. She felt Douglas's fingers grasp her own as the doctor stepped to the top of the bed then slowly and carefully lifted the sheet away from the body.

Rory might have been sleeping, his mouth opened slightly the way it always was after a night out with his pals. Lying there, his hair combed to one side (the way it never had been in living memory), he seemed more like a waxwork than a real flesh and blood human being. And why had they placed that thin strip of bandage across his eyes?

She heard Douglas's cry, felt her husband's fingers slip from her own as he moved towards the bed.

Then the buzzing sound grew louder and louder until it completely filled her senses, blurring her vision, weakening every muscle as everything tilted sideways and the floor came up to hit her.

'It's him all right, then,' the big police sergeant said shortly. 'Parents have identified the body.'

Lorimer nodded quietly. It had been good of Calum Mhor to come by the cottage with this news.

'What now? Can they transport the boy back to the mainland for the PM?'

Sergeant McManus tipped his cap to one side to scratch his forehead. 'Well, now, that won't be done just yet. Our SIO arrives on the next boat. Might have to wait till then before we know any more.'

'Where will he be taken? Inverness?'

The big man shook his head. 'No. Some top-notch pathologist down in Glasgow's coming to do the PM here with our own Dr MacMillan and then there's a forensics team arriving to take a look at things. Think your place may well be of interest to them,' he continued, turning to nod towards the shore where Lorimer had discovered the body.

The silver Mercedes slid off the edge of the green ramp with a double clunk, momentarily jolting the two people in the front of the car. Craignure village appeared even smaller than it had from the boat, a few shops and cottages lining the road, not a place that would seem to boast a four-star hotel complete with leisure centre. The need to dive into a cold pool, swim a few lengths and clear her head made her sigh for a moment. But taking any time off duty was out of the question. The woman at the wheel waited impatiently for the traffic to clear before swinging the big car to the right and heading out of the village. Besides, she hadn't brought a swimming costume and she hoped that a couple of nights on this island would be as much as they would need.

'Check in first, boss?' the man by her side asked.

The woman nodded, raking fingers through her short, blonde hair. She had risked a few minutes up on deck, letting the salty air blow across her face, pondering the fate of the boy from Newton Mearns in Glasgow. He may well have stood on that selfsame spot, watching as Duart Castle came into view, excited by the prospect of a summer job on the island of Mull. And now he was dead. Killed by person or persons unknown, something that concerned this DI from the mainland.

The wheels of the big car crunched to a halt on the gravel driveway and Stevie Crozier alighted, swinging a pair of shapely legs that had elicited many an admiring wolf whistle from city workers as she'd walked along their streets.

Leaving her detective sergeant to carry in their overnight bags, Stevie strode towards reception, staring fixedly to catch the eye of the young woman dressed in a tartan pinafore behind the desk.

'May I help you?' The smile seemed genuine and the

lilting voice held a note of warmth that made the senior police officer suddenly glad that she had chosen to stay in the Isle of Mull hotel.

'Detective Inspector Crozier and Detective Sergeant Langley,' she said briskly, sensing Langley's arrival.

'Ah, yes, two single rooms. Will you be having dinner here this evening, Ms Langley?'

Stevie frowned. '*I'm* Detective Inspector Crozier,' she said between gritted teeth, glancing behind her in time to catch the tiniest trace of a grin on Langley's face. He was enjoying her discomfiture, Stevie knew. She was not unaware that the older detective sergeant was the type that chafed against having a female as his immediate superior.

'Oh, beg pardon, I thought . . .' The girl bit her lip, cheeks reddening, her confusion made worse by the admission of her assumption.

'Our keys, please, and no, I don't think we will be eating here tonight,' Stevie snapped. She stooped to pick up her bags, glaring at Langley, daring him to smirk.

Two plastic keys were slid across the counter with a form requiring the senior detective's signature. She heard Langley murmur 'thanks' in an apologetic tone but Stevie Crozier was already heading for her room, overnight bag slung across one shoulder and handbag and laptop case on the other.

A shower would have been nice, a poor substitute for a dip in the pool, but even that luxury was to be denied as her mobile began to ring almost as soon as she entered the room.

'Crozier.'

'This is Sergeant McManus, ma'am. I heard that you had arrived.'

'News travels fast,' Stevie answered crisply.

'Thing is, ma'am, we wondered if you should be seeing Detective Superintendent Lorimer in the first instance.'

'Lorimer?'

'Aye, ma'am. 'Twas Lorimer found the laddie's body,' McManus explained. 'Did no one tell ye?'

There was a pause while the DI digested this piece of information, then, 'I think my first call should be to see the Dalgleish parents, don't you?'

'Of course.' Calum Mhor's cough could be heard clearly over the telephone. 'They're still at the hospital. With the doctor.' He hesitated. 'Shall I come by and bring you there myself? It's not far from the hotel.'

'Right. See you in reception. Ten minutes.' Stevie snapped the mobile shut. It gave her precious little time to freshen up before facing the bereaved parents. They might be in shock, she thought. Maybe the medics had doled out something to deaden the mental anguish. Else why would a mother and father want to keep a vigil beside the bed of their dead son – if that was what had actually happened to make them stay there for so long?

The man wearing the tweed jacket and worn corduroy trousers sat nursing a cut-glass tumbler of whisky, his eyes darting towards the stairs from time to time. His was a face that elicited trust; a kindly smile often broke open the floodgates of confidences and he had learned over the years to become a sympathetic listener. It was a pity, he often thought, that these same faces bent close to his own would harden once they read their own words in next day's newspapers. For his sympathy was usually genuine, despite his motivation in garnering their stories.

When the blonde woman stepped into the reception area and shook hands with the big police officer, neither of them noticed him rise from the winged chair and walk slowly after them, a copy of the *Oban Times* tucked under one arm.

Jim McGarrity knew fine where they were heading, just as he knew the identity of both Crozier and McManus. It was his business to know such things and McGarrity was well aware that he needed to search out the Dalgleish parents and offer his condolences before he filed his copy for tomorrow's edition of the *Gazette*.

Most of it was already written, of course, the subs no doubt waiting with a headline such as BODY ON BEACH IDENTIFIED AS MISSING STUDENT.

So far McGarrity had managed to type up a preliminary draft.

The body discovered on the shores of Fishnish Bay in Mull has been identified as that of missing student, Rory Dalgleish. The young man was last seen following a ceilidh dance in Tobermory on Saturday evening. Police were alerted when he failed to return to Kilbeg Country House Hotel and fears were raised for his safety.

A Police Scotland spokesman said, 'Inquiries are continuing into the circumstances of Rory's death and a report has been submitted to the procurator fiscal.'

It wasn't enough, though. Not nearly enough. It lacked the human interest that readers craved. And the gentle-faced reporter in the tweed jacket had decided that only a first-hand account from the grieving parents could satisfy that sort of demand.

Stevie Crozier cursed herself for her hasty departure from the hotel as her high heels tip-tapped along the corridor, the sound bouncing off the hospital walls. It would have been far better to have worn the pair of comfortable flat shoes that she'd packed for this island visit, but years of needing to be that bit taller to challenge her male counterparts had made the wearing of high heels second nature, and McManus's call had driven the thought of footwear from her mind.

She was glad, though, when they rounded a corner and her eyes fell on the tall, dark-haired man standing outside a room. His face was vaguely familiar; had they ever met? Stevie asked herself as McManus walked ahead, ready to introduce her to the man who had found the body. That was what he was, she reminded herself as his figure loomed over her. Not her superior officer, but a witness in this case where *she* was SIO.

'Detective Superintendent Lorimer, DI Crozier.' McManus grinned as he made the introductions, seeing the surprise in Lorimer's face. It was evident that Stevie Crozier's name – and reputation – had eluded the officer from Glasgow and that he had been expecting a man; a small fact that the police sergeant had deliberately kept to himself, just for a little bit of fun.

Stevie tried not to blush as the detective superintendent took her hand and gave a gracious nod. He had the brightest blue eyes she'd ever seen, eyes that seemed to look right into her mind, and for a moment Stevie Crozier felt a sense of acute discomfort that this man might be able to read her thoughts.

'I didn't know you'd be here,' Stevie said bluntly.

'Dr MacMillan called me,' Lorimer replied. 'Rory's parents asked if I would come. I do hope that you don't mind my being here.'

Was that a note of apology in his tone? That smile crinkling the corners of those maddening eyes in any way contrite? Stevie Crozier could not be sure, her usual skill at summing people up deserting her momentarily. She had arrived expecting to be the senior ranking officer here, a feeling she had lately begun to relish.

'Why would they do that?' Stevie looked at both men in turn.

'I think Mr and Mrs Dalgleish may want to see where Rory was found,' McManus explained. 'With your permission, of course,' he added, touching the edge of his cap in a gesture of deference.

Stevie's jaw hardened. She'd see about that, but, as the door opened, all thoughts of who was in command of the situation vanished at the sight of Pamela and Douglas Dalgleish.

She may have been just in her early fifties but it was an old woman who emerged from the shadowed room, bent and stumbling between the man clutching her arm and the tall grey-haired doctor who appeared to be leading them both away from that shrouded figure on the bed.

'Mrs Dalgleish?'

Rory's mother looked up at the sound of the DI's voice and Stevie saw her puffy eyes, half closed with weeping. The policewoman took a deep breath, steeling herself against what had to be done.

Afterwards, Pamela Dalgleish could not have said with any certainty what the female detective inspector looked like but she did remember the tall, dark man who had waited while all these awful questions had been asked. There was something about him, a certain stillness from which she felt they could draw strength.

Douglas had withdrawn into himself, his replies to the probing voice of the woman detective making him shrink further and further into a place that even his wife could not reach. The man who had been captain of their local golf club, who had won so many boardroom battles in his career, had finally retreated, beaten by the loss of his youngest child.

What was fatherhood? Pamela wondered as they walked

closely side by side along this hospital corridor. Douglas had never been the sort to attend school sports days or even parents' nights, leaving all that sort of thing to his wife. Not that he had ever been bad to his children; his had been the role of provider for his family, something that was expected of him. Sure, there had been times when he'd bowled balls on the lawn for Rory at weekends and summer holidays, taken him through to Murrayfield to watch the rugby. Yet there had rarely been displays of affection between the two of them. And now there never would be. Pamela felt inside her coat pocket but the handkerchief was sodden and she pushed it back, a hiccup escaping from her, threatening a fresh storm of weeping.

'Here.'

She turned to feel the touch of the policeman's hand on hers, the folded cotton handkerchief slipped gently into her grasp.

Pamela nodded her thanks, too full for speech, the kindness of that small gesture more than she could bear. Still, it was comforting to have this tall man hovering near their side, a shadow guarding them against the outside world.

The daylight made her blink as they walked towards the waiting car. She was aware of other voices now, the tall man speaking to another chap who was looking their way.

'I will see you later, Mrs Dalgleish.' The woman detective put her hand on Pamela's sleeve as she opened the back door of the silver Lexus and ushered her in. Douglas had already drifted to the front passenger seat and was slumped there, staring into space.

The short journey was made easier by being able to look out of the window at the view, much of the road running parallel with the sea. It did not fill her with any horror to think of Rory's body washed by the tides. The horror lay in what had happened before he had died; it was a route into darkness where the woman wanted her to go and Pamela Dalgleish was not yet ready to take that particular journey.

Neither of the men spoke as the car sped smoothly over the ribbon of road leading them to Fishnish Bay; the man at the wheel might have been a taxi driver, the silence was so natural but, Pamela realised, this man, Lorimer, understood their need for an interlude of quietness. She had seen the other man, the one in the tweed jacket, nodding in acquiescence at something he'd said before they had left the hospital grounds: Lorimer was someone to whom people deferred, Pamela had noticed that. She heaved a sigh of relief, the tremble through her chest lessening as they drove on.

When the car turned off the main road onto a tiny single track, Pamela realised that they were almost at their destination and she turned to look towards the shore. Was this where her boy had finally come to rest? This pretty bay with a forest of trees to one side, the little white cottage nestled under the gently sloping hills? As the car turned into a pebbled driveway she saw a slim woman approaching, her dark curls blowing in the breeze. Taking a deep breath, Pamela

Dalgleish prepared herself for the niceties of social encounter once again.

The world still turned on its axis, she thought, as Lorimer helped her out of the car and she stood on firm ground once more. Life would go on, though their particular world could never be the same.

CHAPTER TEN

'I need an incident room set up right away in Tobermory,' DI Crozier told the chubby sergeant who was driving them through the village of Salen where a proliferation of flowers spilled from tubs and window boxes. 'That's where he was last sighted, right?'

'Yes, ma'am,' Calum Mhor agreed. 'What exactly have you in mind?' he added. Such things had never once featured in the man's professional career and he was unsure what this feisty woman expected him to do.

'We need a visible presence,' she told him frostily. 'Somewhere the public can come to us with information. I've requested a police mobile unit but we've been told it will take another three days till one is available. Hoped to have this done and dusted by then,' she added sourly. 'How difficult can it be to find a killer on a place this size?'

'So,' Calum Mhor began ponderously, ignoring her last remark, 'you'll be wanting something like a *caravan*?' He said the word as though it were something foreign, the stress on the last syllable.

'Possibly. Can you arrange that?' She twisted in her seat to give him a cool appraising look.

'I think so. My son's pal works in the campsite. There are always caravans empty, even in high summer. They don't do as well as they might up there,' he told her, shaking his head. 'Even when the bed and breakfasts have no vacancies and turn folk away they don't think to toddle over the hill to the campsite.'

'So you can get me a caravan?' Crozier asked impatiently.

'Aye, ma'am.' He swung the police Land Rover around a corner and slowed down, the road out of the village narrowing to a single track.

Calum Mhor sighed inwardly. He was used to extolling the beauties of his island home to new visitors, slowing down just here to point out the grey seals lolling on the rocks, waiting for the gasps of delight as the crumbling ruins of Aros Castle came into sight, the bay below like a millpond, a swan or a lonesome heron completing the picture. But, as he drove up the steep slope that took them past forests and the breathtaking vistas of the Sound of Mull, he knew he would be wasting his time with this one. She was staring straight ahead, her mind on the murder case. And who could blame her? Since the discovery of the boy's body Calum had been wakening a lot during the night, the picture of that ruined face haunting what was normally a dreamless sleep.

71

'You've secured the crime scene, I take it?' Her words snapped Calum out of his reverie.

'Well, we don't know if the edge of the bay is the actual scene of the crime, ma'am . . . ' he began.

'It was where his body was found, wasn't it?'

'It was where he was washed ashore,' Calum told her patiently. 'Tides might have carried him for miles.'

He could hear her sigh from where she sat beside him. 'Could be he went into the water much further up the coast,' he mused. 'Has been known for these tides to take someone a long way down the Sound. And it was a very high tide that particular morning – a spring tide.'

'Oh?'

'Sometimes spring tides can wash right up to the edges of people's gardens, given the right conditions.'

'And how does that affect this case?'

'Well the lad's body was washed up high on the shore, much higher than anybody would have expected. 'Twas laid out on the grassy banks way above the normal tideline. Lorimer said he found it because of the gulls.'

'The what . . . ?'

'The seagulls, ma'am. They'd been attacking the poor boy lying out in the cold. Och, it doesnae bear thinking about,' he added in disgust, slowing the Land Rover down and turning into a passing place as a couple of cars approached. Calum gave a wave as the driver of each car drew level.

'You seem to know everyone here,' Crozier remarked as they moved off again.

'Oh, no, ma'am, these are visitors. It's just a common courtesy to acknowledge one another,' he explained. 'Something that doesn't happen on the mainland much,' he added, allowing himself a smile.

Stevie Crozier did not reply. Life on this island was very different from anything in her experience, it seemed, and she was irked by the thought that this bumbling sergeant was teaching her things that most of the inhabitants took for granted. Sure, she was becoming used to life in Oban after years spent in the Borders towns, but the people on these islands seemed to behave as though they were a law unto themselves, something Stevie found hard to take.

She stared out of the window as the vehicle climbed higher: the Sound of Mull seemed so far below now, a few yachts under sail mere specks of white against the blue. Somewhere down there the boy's body had been swept along, these strange tides taking it from ... where? Had he been cast into the waters near Tobermory? Or had someone transported the corpse further south? Craning her eyes, the detective could see the steep hills that tumbled down and down into the rocky coastline. Who had taken that boy? Had it been the task of more than one man to heave the dead weight from a car into the depths? The DI had decided to begin answering these questions in the town where Rory had been last seen. Perhaps someone would share a nugget of information about

73

who had been with him, then the team could begin to piece together the boy's last movements in an attempt to discover what his terrible fate had been.

'That's Tobermory,' Calum told her, though he used the Gaelic words, *Tobar Mhoire*, a sound that was suddenly alien to the blonde woman who gazed at the curve of little houses ranged against a sloping hillside. Then the sight was lost as they descended once more, the road straight and smooth taking them to the place where she would set up her incident room.

'It's peaceful here,' Pamela Dalgleish said at last. The sun was still masked by a few stray clouds but there was a brightness in the sky, patches of earlier rain already dry on the ground.

'That's why we like it,' Maggie said simply.

'It's where I would have liked to come for a holiday,' the older woman admitted. Then she fell silent, sipping tea from the nicest porcelain mug that Maggie Lorimer could find in their kitchen cupboard. Maggie nodded. She could understand that this woman was unwilling to talk about holidays or times past that may have been reminders of her dead son, superficial things now that this dreadful event had stolen him from her.

They continued to gaze shorewards, the two figures of their husbands clearly defined against the background of Fishnish Bay; one standing tall and straight, the other seated on a rock, back bowed as he looked out to sea.

'You don't want to go down . . . ?'

Pamela Dalgleish shook her head. 'I thought I would but, no.' Her voice faded as she swallowed hard. 'It was bad enough having to see him back there,' she admitted, stealing a glance at the dark-haired woman sitting beside her on the garden bench. 'I couldn't bear the thought of him . . .'

Maggie reached out and took the other woman's cold hand in hers, feeling the fingers clasp her own. They sat there in silence once again, two women pondering the vagaries of life, watching while their menfolk dealt with this tragedy in a different way. She had known so many cases where her husband showed compassion to the victims of crime; often it was the impetus that drove him on to discovering what had happened and whose hand had committed that most terrible of deeds. But here he was simply a witness, not the person in charge, and Maggie Lorimer wondered just how that must feel right now as he tried to find words of consolation for that broken father down on the shore.

'He was our youngest, you know. The baby of the family,' Pamela Dalgleish said suddenly. 'A bit of an unexpected addition, actually.' She smiled vaguely. 'Thought we had finished. A gentleman's family,' she went on. 'Phillip and Jennifer. That was all we really wanted.' She drew her hand away, searching for her handkerchief. 'I was appalled when I found out I was pregnant again. Didn't want a third. Felt far too old to begin all over again. Nappies and sleepless nights, you know?'

The woman turned her head as if she expected a child to

come wandering out of the cottage then turned back again. 'He was a funny little thing when he was born,' she continued. 'All that red hair. God knows what side of the family that came from.' She sighed. 'Douglas suggested we name him Ruaraidh because of his colouring but I thought it was too hard for a little boy to be given such a difficult name so we agreed on Rory instead.' She shook her head. 'Never realised just how appropriate that would turn out to be.'

'Why?' Maggie asked, puzzled.

'Oh, dear.' Pamela Dalgleish heaved another huge sigh. 'They say it's wrong to speak ill of the dead but Rory was a loud sort of boy. *Very* talkative. Could be quite annoying at times. His friends nicknamed him *Roary*. You know, with an A in the middle.'

She paused then bowed her head, crumpling the handkerchief in her hands. 'Funny how much I would give to hear his voice again.'

Maggie said nothing, letting the woman wipe away the tears that were coursing down her pale cheeks. Her heart felt sore inside her chest as though she too had been weeping, an aching sympathy for this bereaved mother.

'You have children?' The inevitable question that Maggie had expected.

'No. We couldn't,' she said shortly.

'Well, you're lucky. You'll never know what this sort of loss feels like,' the older woman replied, a note of bitterness in her tone.

Maggie sat very still, remembering the way she had stroked her rounded belly, feeling the life within. Then, afterwards, the agony of seeing the tiny form, lifeless in her arms. It would do this woman no good to share such pain, let her know that yes, she had suffered *that sort of loss*; and had her grief been so very different? A sigh shuddered from her before she could stop it.

'I'm sorry ...?' Pamela Dalgleish had turned towards Maggie, a look of concern on her face.

'It's all right,' Maggie tried to reassure her. 'It was a long time ago.'

CHAPTER ELEVEN

Glasgow

Twenty Years Earlier

'I'd like a boy,' she said, laying down her book beside the chair.

'So long as it's like the world,' her mother replied, looking up from her knitting. Already there were several tiny little garments folded between sheets of tissue paper awaiting the day when Maggie would bring home her first child from hospital. And, well wrapped up in a plastic carrier bag, was the complete pram set that Mum had made, blankets all edged in satin, a crocheted cover meticulously crafted.

Maggie nodded and smiled at the old-fashioned phrase. Mum had also promised to buy a pram. It was ordered but would not be paid for or delivered until baby Lorimer made his or her appearance for fear of bringing ill luck on the expected infant, a superstition that had lingered in the west of Scotland over countless generations.

'Still working in white?' Maggie cocked her head to one side as her mother smoothed out the piece of knitting, its intricate pattern of diamond-shaped leaves almost invisible under the lamplight.

'I can buy pink or blue when the time comes,' Mrs Finlay told her daughter. 'And if it's anything like you were, you'll need plenty of changes of clothes, let me tell you.'

'Why? What was I like?'

'Oh, a sickly baby. I was forever running out of gripe water.'

'Everyone uses muslins now,' Maggie murmured. 'I've seen girls with them draped over their shoulders. Seems to keep mother and baby clean.'

'And you would fill your nappy just when I was all ready to take you out in the pram. Wee frilly pants, lacy tights, under-skirts. Och, sometimes I had to change the lot!'

Maggie laughed at her mother's wrinkled nose. 'See what I'm in for!'

'Well, it's not all rock-a-bye-baby,' the older woman told her tartly. 'I can remember pacing the floor for hours when you were cutting your teeth. Poor wee lamb,' she added with a sigh, looking into the distance as though she could see baby Maggie all over again. 'But you were a bonny wee thing, I'll say that. Good-natured, too.'

'Well, if I have a girl maybe she'll take after me,' Maggie said. 'But I'd love to have a son as my first-born.'

The sound of a car turning into the drive made both women look up. The light was fading from the summer sky and Detective Constable Lorimer was only now arriving back home, hours after Maggie and her mother had finished dinner.

'Late again,' Mrs Finlay remarked.

'It's a murder case,' Maggie said quietly. 'They don't know who the victim is. That's what Bill's trying to find out,' she explained.

'Well, he'll be glad to get away from all of that and come home to a decent meal, I dare say.'

Maggie smiled. Her mother had brought one of her home-made steak and kidney pies, enough for two meals at least, and it would be the work of just a few minutes to warm it up again.

'Hello, Alice, hi, gorgeous.' Lorimer bent to kiss his wife before she could heave herself out of her armchair. 'Sorry I'm late.'

'Well. You need to keep better time once Maggie's due date comes closer,' Alice Finlay told him. 'I might not always be here to keep your wife company.'

'Ah.' Lorimer's eyes twinkled. 'Planning that trip to Australia, then, are you?'

'Don't be silly,' his mother-in-law scolded, but her smile had joined his already. 'Come on, go and get yourself washed. I'll see to your dinner.' She rose from her chair and nodded at her daughter. 'You stay where you are and keep your feet up,' she ordered in a tone that brooked no refusal.

Lorimer winked at his wife behind the retreating back of her mother. He loved Alice Finlay dearly but there were times, like now, when she made him feel like a little boy again, not a grown man whose job entailed dealing with life and death.

The afternoon had been hot, the air-conditioning units in the mortuary scarcely able to diminish that feeling of oppression in the viewing room. There had been several students there too, wilting in their green scrubs, watching as the lady pathologist, Dr MacMillan, performed the post-mortem examination. He'd noticed that one of them was a girl, her blonde curls escaping from the cap on her head. She'd looked far too young even to be at university, Lorimer had thought, yet hers was the face that expressed most interest in all of the surgery, hers the hand that was raised first to answer any of the consultant pathologist's questions. The young woman's cheeks had turned pink when she'd praised her. *Well done, Miss Fergusson*, she'd said.

Lorimer had watched and listened, fascinated by the entire procedure, not at all squeamish as Donald Anderson, the fiscal, had hinted he might be. The marks on the young man's neck were discussed at length by the pathologist, her explanations about neck injuries giving Lorimer as well as the students gathered around a great deal to think about. The pathologist had drawn back the victim's eyelids, pointing out the petechial haemorrhages; signs, she told them, of an asphyxial death.

'Seen typically in the eyes, face and neck,' she had continued, her voice strong and enthusiastic, making the students look more closely; even Lorimer found himself peering right up against the glass of the viewing window, fascinated by the woman's discourse.

Of course, the main things to look at were the marks around the fellow's neck, clear signs that something had been applied to cut off his last breath. And he'd been dead before he'd hit the water, the pathologist explained, showing the internal signs after exposing the thoracic area.

A case of manual strangulation, she had concluded, well satisfied that her audience had seen such evidence that she might well have to bring to court should an arrest for the man's murder ever be found.

Dr MacMillan had given them time to suggest what sort of materials had secured the wrists and ankles, the body twisted and misshapen in rigor mortis.

Only the young blonde girl had asked, *Why would they do that?* Her question showing a keen appreciation of motive as well as interest in the surgical details.

The pathologist had shaken her head and smiled. *Something for our colleagues over there to find out*, she'd answered, making them all look up at the window where Lorimer and the fiscal stood observing the post-mortem. It was right that she had prevaricated, Lorimer thought. Putting ideas of bondage and sexual fetishes into students' heads was not a good idea, even though that was one line of thought that had cropped up at a briefing meeting back at police HQ. Some of the police officers had looked distinctly uncomfortable as DI

Phillips had spelled out the possibility that the victim might have been indulging in some sort of sex game as he sought to find an explanation for the state of the dead man's body. *And it might also explain why these bonds had been cut before the victim had been cast into the river*, Lorimer had suggested. But shakes of the head and disgusted looks from his more senior colleagues had stopped him pursuing that idea.

'Any luck with finding out who the victim is?' Maggie asked.

They were in bed at last, Mrs Finlay had gone home after insisting on washing up the rest of the dinner dishes, and the summer twilight had deepened to a burnished blue. Lorimer had watched the sky as they lay side by side, Maggie turning this way and that, trying to find a position that would be comfortable enough to let her drift off to sleep.

'No. Maybe we won't ever find out,' he said quietly. 'Fiscal seems to think he might not be missed by anyone.'

'That's awful,' Maggie sighed. 'How terrible to be of so little importance that nobody would miss you.'

'Go to sleep, darling.' Lorimer stroked her bare arm gently. 'Don't think about my job, all right?'

Her smile in the fading light was all he ever wanted, Lorimer thought as she closed her eyes. Yet, even as his wife's breathing became the measured tones of slumber, Lorimer lay awake, staring at the ceiling, wondering about the man whose body had undergone such extensive examination and whether they would ever be able to dignify him with a name.

CHAPTER TWELVE

They had passed the entrance many times but had never actually been to the hotel itself, preferring the smaller bistros and cafés in Salen or Tobermory. So it was with a sense of curiosity that Lorimer turned off the road and drove along the tree-lined route past the sign that proclaimed *Kilbeg Country House Hotel*, the narrow slip of painted wood attached with *Vacancies* turned towards any passing trade. Had they been full up till the death of one of their staff? Lorimer wondered. Or was there a problem attracting sufficient custom in high season? It was unusual for any of the big hotels on this island to have vacancies during the summer months. Anyhow, he would not have thought to bring Maggie here; the restaurant wasn't said to be particularly good and the only reason for his visit was the Dalgleish parents' request: would he pick up Rory's things for them? He'd called DI Crozier, of course, and obtained a curt assent. She would see it as interference, of course she would. But Lorimer had succumbed to the couple's entreaties, realising that already they had begun to warm towards Maggie and her policeman husband.

The thick pines and rhododendrons either side of the narrow road blotted out what sunshine there was and more than once the Lexus bucked into a pothole before Lorimer had time to see it. Then, round a sharp bend, the trees fell away to reveal a huge expanse of grass and a large grey stone mansion beyond, its turrets and balustrades testament to the style favoured by Victorian architects.

Lorimer parked beside the other three cars that were neatly lined up to one side of the hotel and got out, gazing over the smooth land and the sea opening out before him. It was easy to see why this place had been built all those years ago, the view of the sea and hills must be wonderful from the rooms that faced the Morvern shore. A well-trodden path beside the hotel led down to the water's edge where an old cabin cruiser lay at anchor, bobbing gently against the tide. Then his eye was caught by the flutter of an orange windsock to one side and it came as a surprise to see that there was a landing strip for planes. That explained the long flat fields, he told himself. Had this place once been popular enough for tourists to fly in, perhaps? It certainly didn't seem busy now, if the few cars here were anything to go by, he thought as he ascended the stone steps to the entrance of Kilbeg House. And that old boat didn't look like a pleasure craft for the guests.

There was no need to knock on the door or ring a bell for the double doors were wide open as though someone had wandered out just for a moment. Hesitating, Lorimer retraced his steps and wandered around the back of the building where he found, to his astonishment, a vast kitchen garden, half of which was overgrown and unkempt, swathes of rosebay willowherb towering above rows of shot lettuce and several wigwams of garden canes, dry wisps of old peas or beans clinging to the bamboo. There were signs that someone had tried to weed several of the rows but the small heaps of dried foliage on the path suggested they had given up the task in disgust. His eyes roamed over this sad, neglected place but there was no one to be seen so he walked back to the front, surprised to see that the doors were now closed. Had his arrival been noted, then? Lorimer looked up; the hairs on the back of his neck seemed to shiver, giving him a strong sensation that he was being watched.

The reception desk was a curve of polished rosewood and, as he approached, a young woman with long, silver-blonde hair came out of a door at the back marked *Private*.

'Oh,' she gasped, taking a step back as she saw Lorimer standing there. 'You gave me a fright!' she exclaimed in an accent that he found difficult to place. Polish, perhaps? There were so many Polish youngsters in the hotel trade here in Scotland now; they made a good living with pleasant efficiency, something they could teach some of the locals, he'd heard several folk grumble.

'Sorry.' Lorimer smiled and placed his hands upon the edge of the desk. 'I was looking for Mr or Mrs Forsyth. I've come to collect Rory Dalgleish's things. The name's Lorimer.'

'Oh, yes, you rang earlier,' the girl said. 'I think they were packing them all up.' She vaguely waved a hand to one side. 'Mr Forsyth's gone into Salen but he won't be long. Would you mind waiting in the lounge till I can find Mrs Forsyth? It's this way.' She came around from the desk and ushered him through to a large airy room filled with light from enormous bay windows that looked straight onto the sea.

'Can I fetch you anything? Tea? Coffee?'

Lorimer shook his head, noticing for the first time the small name badge attached to the girl's waistcoat. 'No thanks, Maryka,' he replied. 'I'm fine.' Then, curiosity overcoming him he asked, 'Where is it you're from? Poland?'

The girl laughed, showing perfect teeth. 'No, not me. I'm from Holland. I was lazy at school. Never did get the English accent right.' She smiled again. 'Sure I can't get something nice for you?' Her eyelids batted in what might have been a coquettish overture.

Lorimer shook his head again, amused at her flirtatiousness. She couldn't be more than twenty and here he was, old enough to be her father!

'Well, maybe a coffee, then,' he conceded. 'Black, please.'

He didn't want anything to drink but perhaps it might give him the opportunity to ask the girl about Rory Dalgleish.

Lorimer looked around. There was a sense of faded grandeur about the place: the long floor-to-ceiling curtains flanking the windows were dusty with age, their tartan bleached by decades of sun, and he could see traces of wear on the red carpet. It was little wonder, he thought, that the place had a vacancies sign dangling at the road end. There were far nicer hotels in other parts of the island, though few commanded such impressive vistas. The Forsyths were finding it hard to pay their bills, local gossip had told him; money was tight and they were thinking of selling up, though rumour had it that Freda Forsyth wanted to stay. Well, there was no excuse for dirty windows, Lorimer thought, gazing up and down at the dust-streaked glass, even if there was no cash to refurbish the place. He frowned. Something wasn't right. And he didn't think it had anything to do with the dead student who had been working here for the summer.

'Thanks,' he said, looking up at the girl as she laid a cup of black coffee on the table in front of him. 'Maryka ...' He watched as she turned back, surprised to hear her name. 'Did you know Rory Dalgleish?'

There was something in her face, he saw, something like a shutter closing as she shook her head. 'Not very well,' the girl shrugged. 'Why do you ask?'

'Come and sit down,' he said, patting the chair beside him.

For a moment she hesitated, glancing back towards the reception desk in the hall as though to see if she were needed.

'You're police?'

'Detective Superintendent Lorimer,' he nodded. 'Though I'm not officially in charge of this investigation.'

She frowned, clearly puzzled. 'Then why are you here?'

'I'm on holiday.' He smiled. 'And the body was washed up near where my wife and I are staying.'

'*You* found his body? A policeman?'

'Policemen and women have to take holidays too, you know,' Lorimer laughed. 'It's not exactly like the television where they always appear to be on duty.'

He saw the smile come to her lips then, the way her shoulders relaxed. That last bit had been true to a point; there had been many times when he had denied himself sufficient sleep during particularly difficult murder cases.

'I told the policeman from Tobermory everything I knew about him.' Maryka shrugged, folding her hands on the lap of her short black skirt.

'Hm, yes, I'm sure you did, but, see, his parents are wondering what happened to Rory and anything you know might be helpful in finding that out.'

'He wasn't a friend, or anything,' Maryka said suspiciously. 'If that's what you're thinking. I didn't actually like him very much,' she admitted, pursing her lips.

'He was quite a loud chap, as far as I've been told.' Lorimer smiled encouragingly.

'You can say that again,' Maryka agreed. 'Loud and a show-off. Why he was even here to work was a mystery to us all.'

'I think his parents wanted him to earn his passage for that big holiday he had planned,' Lorimer told her.

'But they are so rich!' the Dutch girl protested. 'Why didn't they just give him the money?'

'Not every well-to-do parent wants their kids to exist on handouts,' Lorimer said. 'Learning a work ethic is quite important, you know.'

'Well, he wasn't a bad worker, I suppose,' she said grudgingly.

'Did you all travel up to that ceilidh together?' Lorimer asked, changing the subject.

She raised an insouciant shoulder then nodded. 'Yes, we did. There were four of us in Lachie's van.'

'Lachie?'

'Oh, he's supposed to be the gardener and handyman.' Maryka raised her eyebrows significantly. 'Have you seen the state of the place? Can't say he's done very much to make any improvements,' she added, dropping her voice and leaning forwards. 'They don't have enough money, Lachie told me.'

'Who else was with you apart from Rory?'

'Elena. She's one of the other summer workers. We share a caravan out there.' Maryka waved a hand towards the back of the hotel. 'And Fiona.'

'And were you expecting to return with Lachie?'

'The other policeman asked that,' Maryka sighed, as though the whole conversation bored her.

'So how were you going to get home?'

'Lachie was staying over at his sister's in Tobermory. That's where he lives. Fiona usually stays with a friend or her aunt. Elena and I hoped to find a lift back.' She gave him a roguish smile.

'And, did you?'

She nodded, cheeks blushing.

'What about Rory? How did he intend to come back to the hotel?'

'I don't know. It was his day off on the Sunday so I think he wasn't too bothered about that.'

'Did he have friends in Tobermory?'

Maryka hesitated. 'He *said* he knew folk who were on a boat. There are lots of big yachts in the bay just now.'

'And did he intend to stay over with them?'

She made a face. 'How should I know? I was just glad to get there and be rid of his big mouth.' She bit her lip. 'I didn't mean that to sound horrible,' she said swiftly.

'It's usually better to tell the truth. A remark like that can't hurt him now, can it?'

'Suppose not.' She hung her head.

'Who else works here, Maryka?'

The girl made a face. 'The chef,' she said. 'Archie, his name is. Archie Gillespie. He lives on that smelly old boat out there.' She wrinkled her nose. 'He's not such a brilliant cook, you know,' she added, holding a hand over her mouth as though to shield her words from anyone who might overhear them.

'So, no gourmet nights in the restaurant?'

'The food is okay,' she conceded grudgingly. 'A lot of fish. But my mother is a better cook than *this* man. Too many flavours in his sauces,' she said, tilting her nose in the air. 'Better to keep it simple with good food.'

Lorimer smiled. This girl from Holland knew a thing or

two and perhaps she had been frustrated at being kept in jobs less suited to her talents.

'I better get back,' Maryka murmured. 'Mrs Forsyth should be here any minute and I need to be behind the desk.'

She left Lorimer sipping the now lukewarm coffee.

The police had this information. Kennedy and his colleagues must surely have investigated every yacht that had been moored that night in the harbour. It would be the harbour master's duty to keep a careful log of what crafts entered Tobermory bay and when. If Rory Dalgleish had slept over in a friend's boat then that might explain a few things, not least why his body had been found miles down the coast at Leiter.

His thoughts were interrupted by the arrival in the lounge of a grey-haired woman who was lugging a silver ridged suitcase. He glanced up then away, supposing for a moment that this was one of the guests about to depart. Then he looked again, curious. The suitcase was one fitted with wheels, so why was this grey-haired female carrying it by the handle, its weight pulling her to one side?

Suddenly the woman was right beside him and letting the case fall with a thump.

'That's it,' she said. 'All of his things are in there. At least, all that I could find. The police officers already took away his laptop.'

Lorimer sprang to his feet.

'Mrs Forsyth?'

'I don't know why his parents won't come themselves,' she

said, avoiding his glance. 'I could have told them nice things about their son. He was a good worker, you know. Kept the bar spotless,' she added. Then, raising a pair of pale blue eyes to his, she frowned. 'Who are you, anyway?'

'I'm Bill Lorimer,' he replied.

She nodded, scrutinising his face as though it were important to remember him again.

'You're a policeman, aren't you? But not with that other lot.'

'My wife and I are on holiday. Down at Leiter Cottage,' Lorimer explained.

'That's where he was washed up.' She spoke in a flat monotone as though reciting facts from a newspaper.

'Yes,' Lorimer agreed. 'Mr and Mrs Dalgleish came to see us today. They asked if I could fetch his things for them.'

'Why?' She glared at him, her mouth half open as though she would say more, but the question lingered between them.

'Why did they want me to come instead of them?' Lorimer asked, surprised at the vehemence of her tone, hoping that the hotelier might clarify what she meant. 'I suppose it's very hard for them to speak to strangers right now. They only just identified his body, after all,' he protested. Why was this strange woman making so much of it?

'Well, here it is. Better take it away, hadn't you?'

Then, without another word, Mrs Forsyth drifted back towards the hallway and walked out of sight.

Lorimer looked at the suitcase. The exterior zip was not even fastened all the way around, the end of a black tie

93

hanging out at one side. He laid the case onto its side, unzipped it and opened it up. She had evidently made no effort whatsoever to pack Rory's things properly, Lorimer saw with disgust. Clothes had just been jammed in any old way, dirty laundry rolled up in balls, a few books sliding to one end. He frowned, gazing at the mess. Couldn't she have packed it better than that? It was, he thought, as though she had hurled his stuff into the case in a temper.

Rising to his feet, Lorimer searched in his jacket pocket for his mobile phone. It was the matter of a moment to photograph the opened case, a small thing perhaps, but something to discuss with the unsmiling DI.

Kneeling down, he rearranged the dead boy's clothes and toiletries, stuffing socks into hiking boots and making the case far neater so that his parents would not be shocked at the way his belongings had been packed by his employer. Had she felt that the search of the boy's room and his belongings by the local police had tainted them somehow? The idea caught hold as he thought about the woman, trying to find a reason for the way she had packed Rory's bag. Something had certainly sparked off that strange behaviour.

Mrs Forsyth had wanted to see Rory's parents, he thought, zipping the case back up again. She'd even spoken quite kindly of the boy.

So, why fling his possessions into the suitcase as though she had been in a rage? Like some impassioned wife ridding herself of an errant husband?

CHAPTER THIRTEEN

The irony of using the Aros Hall where the victim had been enjoying a ceilidh the evening before his death was not lost on her. Several times the DI had glanced over her shoulder, imagining a band playing on that raised platform, the sound of whoops and hands clapping in time to the music a distant echo. Since taking over at the Oban station, Stevie Crozier had been invited to one of the dances there, her feet tapping to the rhythm whenever she was a mere spectator. Yet, despite her posting to the 'Gateway to the Isles', as Oban was known, she knew herself to be an outsider, born and bred in the Lowlands, no family connections up here to make her more interesting to the natives. That was why she had insisted that the local cops should be included in her team: she was wise enough now to understand that local knowledge counted for so much. The DI had fully intended to visit each and every one of the islands under her command but had not yet had the time to do so, hampered by the swathe of paperwork left by her predecessor, a taciturn, disappointed man, by all accounts, who had drunk himself into a fatal coronary.

The caravan had been brought into town and sited on the old pier next to a mobile fish and chip van. *Everyone will see it there*, the big police sergeant had assured her. It was in as central a spot as it could possibly be, right enough, the notice taped to the door asking for any information the public could give.

'We need to examine his laptop as a matter of priority,' Crozier told the small team of men assembled in the upstairs room of the Aros Hall overlooking Tobermory Bay.

'I did an IT course, ma'am,' PC Kennedy offered. 'Would you like me to have a look at it?'

Crozier frowned. She was accustomed to having experts delegated to her cases and the absence of the usual technical staff was making her feel exposed in this small holiday town. At least they would have a professional from Glasgow before the day was out, she reminded herself. Another woman, too, sparing Stevie Crozier from the sudden feeling of isolation that washed over her as she looked at the faces of the men seated in front of her.

'Can you download all the files from the hard drive? We need some memory sticks. Do you have any spare?'

'I can get them from Browns,' Kennedy murmured.

Crozier nodded her agreement. A quick walk along the main street had shown her the limited possibilities of the town and Browns the ironmongers had been pointed out to her as a place where almost anything useful could be obtained including, strangely, some fine vintage wines.

She studied the faces waiting for her instructions. DS Langley was sitting next to Kennedy and McManus, then, sitting slightly apart as if they were still uncertain of their role, the two community officers from Salen and Bunessan, one ruddy-cheeked like a farmer, the other a thin dark-haired man with a neatly clipped moustache who reminded the DI of a card-sharp from an old black and white movie. Stevie Crozier glanced at the paper in her hand, reminding herself of their names: Police Constable Roddy Buchanan was the farmer lookalike, PC Finlay Simpson the skinny one darting nervous glances towards the other officers along the row. She stifled a sigh. They were more used to hunting down poachers and the sort of vandals who attempted to steal eagles' eggs than the killer of a young man. They were all out of their comfort zone, she realised, seeing Buchanan take a large handkerchief from his pocket to mop a sweating brow.

'I need someone to man the caravan all hours of the day,' she began.

Buchanan looked up hopefully, his hand paused in wiping his face.

'Someone who knows the locals well enough for them to talk freely,' she added, ignoring the expression on the burly man's face. 'Kennedy, you're a local man, aren't you?'

Jamie Kennedy grinned back at her. 'Yes, ma'am, though I was in Inverness for a few years,' he said, tilting his chin upwards as though to assure her that he had seen the tough side of policing in a way his fellow officers might never have done.

Crozier tried hard not to return the smile. There would be no favourites here while she was in charge of the case.

'Very well, you take charge of the caravan. See to the laptop while you're there. Buchanan, I want you there too,' she said, turning to the sweating man. 'And no sloping off together,' she warned. 'Make sure there's always one of you in that caravan during the day.'

She looked hard at each of them in turn. 'DS Langley and I will be doing the bulk of the groundwork, talking to the staff at Kilbeg House, attending the post-mortem once the pathologist arrives.'

She had been surprised that there was a mortuary at all on the island; one of her colleagues in Oban had told her that it was in the hospital at Craignure, a necessary feature for any unexpected deaths although murder had never been one of them till now. Dr MacMillan was in charge until the fiscal could make his way across from the mainland later today; Dr Rosie Fergusson, the consultant pathologist, was meeting him on Oban pier. Tomorrow she would be performing the post-mortem. Then, and only then, would they have a definitive cause of death; had he been alive when he entered the cold Atlantic waters? Or had the hands that had bound him taken his life then tossed him into the depths like so much rubbish?

'Will Lorimer be at the PM?' McManus asked, his face

turned to the DI with an expression of innocence that didn't fool Crozier for a moment.

'Why should he be there?' Crozier snapped. 'He's a witness, not SIO, for goodness sake!'

'Just wondered,' McManus replied meekly. 'Word has it that he and the pathologist are close friends.'

Stevie Crozier gritted her teeth. That was all she needed, a senior detective sticking his nose in where it wasn't wanted. She had a good mind to stop off at the holiday cottage and tell the man just that.

'Right, everyone know what actions they're responsible for? McManus and Simpson, you're doing house-to-house here in Tobermory, Langley, you'll come back to Craignure with me after we've been to Kilbeg House.'

She looked at the team as they shuffled to their feet, wondering for the first time if she had been right to put such a big matter as a murder case into the hands of these island men. At least she had Langley, an experienced detective who had walked the mean streets of Glasgow in his younger days.

'Seagull!' Abby bounced up and down, her chubby hand pointing in the air as Solly and Rosie led her along the rows of cars that were parked on Oban pier awaiting the ferry to Mull. They had driven up through Inveraray and the winding roads of Argyll, arriving much earlier than the mandatory half-hour needed to stake their claim in the queue.

'That one's a herring gull,' Solly remarked, hunkering

down and watching the bird alight on a stone bollard. 'See the red on its beak?'

'Aye, it'll give you a nasty bite if you put a finger anywhere near it,' Rosie warned drily. 'Big brutes, so they are,' she whispered under her breath, seeing the three-year-old laugh as the seagull took off and landed again on another bollard, its great wings spread out, a guttural noise coming from that fearsome beak.

The seabirds had done a lot of peripheral damage to the boy's body, Lorimer had warned her. And the sight of them now was a harsh reminder of what lay ahead.

Somehow the prospect of performing a post-mortem on the island was faintly nauseating, not something that had ever happened to the pathologist. The presence of her husband and daughter had given her a different outlook today: Abby's excitement at the thought of travelling to Balamory and the sight of Solly in his windproof jacket and sturdy shoes were at odds with what they were really doing here.

'What's that, Daddy?' Abby had turned away from the herring gull now, her eyes lifted towards a strange structure like a stone crown outlined against the pale skies.

'That's called McCaig's Folly,' Rosie answered, seeing the look of bewilderment on Solly's face. Her husband adored Scotland but a London upbringing had not prepared him for every feature in his adopted country.

'Once upon a time,' she began, earning Abby's immediate attention, 'there was a man who wanted to build a big, big tower. Bigger than anything in the land,' she exaggerated, spreading out her hands and making Abby's eyes widen. 'But he ran out of money and it was never finished,' she ended lamely.

'No big tower?' Abby asked, shaking her head at the strange ways of grown-ups and seeing the stone structure with different eyes.

'No big tower,' Rosie agreed. 'Folk said he was foolish to have begun it when he didn't have the money to finish it. Folly is a word meaning something that comes from foolishness, see?'

'Mr Folly's tower,' Abby declared, sticking a thumb into her mouth and nodding sagely.

Above her head Rosie and Solly exchanged amused glances. No doubt McCaig's Folly was destined to be called 'Mr Folly's Tower' in the Brightman household from now on. It was something she must remember to share with Maggie, Rosie thought.

They had reached the end of the pier now and were turning back when Rosie felt a hand on her shoulder.

'Dr Fergusson?'

The man who stood beside them was looking at them with an enquiring smile.

'Yes?'

Rosie looked at him closely. Derek McClure had changed dramatically since the last time she had met him. It had been in the high court in Edinburgh, a case involving the victim of multiple stab wounds, she recalled. The defence had tried to tie them in legalistic knots but had failed.

Rosie smiled back, trying to hide her astonishment. The fiscal appeared so much older than she remembered him: the thinning white hair and the shining bald patch on top had taken her quite by surprise. She'd held a mental image of a dark-haired man of middle years, cheery and slightly over-weight, not this ageing man before her. But the hazel eyes were the same, the shrewd smile crinkling his haggard face the smile she remembered.

'Derek! Hello, good to see you,' she said, clasping the fiscal's outstretched hand. 'This is my husband, Solly,' she added, stepping aside a little to allow the two men to shake hands.

'Ah, the celebrated Professor Brightman!' McClure exclaimed. 'I've read all of your books, you know. Should be mandatory reading for every law undergraduate, never mind the psychologists,' he laughed.

Then, bending down, he stretched out a kindly hand. 'And who is this pretty young lady?'

Abby slid behind her daddy then peeked out, giving the stranger a shy smile.

'This is Abigail Margaret Brightman,' Solly announced grandly. 'And we are on an expedition to discover the amazing Balamory!'

'Balamory!' McClure gave a mock gasp, joining in on the fun of the moment. 'Well, well. If you see PC Plum, give him my regards, young lady.'

He rose to his feet again and drew Rosie aside out of the child's earshot.

'It's a bad business, Dr Fergusson. There has never been anything like this on the island in living memory. Or,' he paused, 'in any records that we know of.'

'Do you think someone from the mainland came to target the lad?' Rosie asked, walking in step with the fiscal towards the queues of parked cars.

'I hope so,' he said slowly. 'It isn't something we would think any of the islanders capable of, you know. We have the odd rumpus after drinking hours, doesn't everybody? And a few domestics, but nothing, *never* anything like this.' He drew a hand across his scant white hair as a breeze from the sea threatened to blow the wispy strands upwards.

'I retire soon, you know,' he went on, lowering his voice. 'Health grounds,' he added, seeing Rosie's raised eyebrows. 'And I didn't want my final months spent searching for a killer on one of my favourite places on earth.'

'You're from Mull?'

He shook his head. 'No, but my grandparents lived there and my mother was born in Tobermory before the family moved to Glasgow. I still feel the connection, though.' He sighed, looking over the waters to the distant grey-green hills.

'DI Crozier is a fine detective,' he said suddenly. 'But I hope she has the sense to ask Lorimer for advice if she needs it. You know what *he's* like.' There was a grin on the man's face as he spoke the detective superintendent's name.

'Oh, aye, I know fine what Lorimer's like,' Rosie agreed. 'Won't rest until he can give some peace of mind to the family, is my guess. But he won't interfere, either,' she added, looking squarely at McClure. 'He's far too professional for that.'

'But why won't you take the case on yourself?' Douglas Dalgleish paced up and down the hospital corridor where he and his wife were waiting to see Dr MacMillan.

'It's out of my jurisdiction,' Lorimer replied.

'But it's all Police Scotland nowadays,' Dalgleish protested. 'Doesn't that make a difference?'

Lorimer shook his head. 'The Oban officers would have to put in a request for a more senior officer to take charge . . .' he began.

'So . . . ?' A gleam of hope appeared in the man's eyes.

'The fiscal has to determine whether the gravity of a case necessitates that,' Lorimer explained. 'If it is reckoned that there is a danger to the public then perhaps a more senior officer than a detective inspector would be appointed as SIO.'

'SIO?'

'Senior Investigating Officer,' Lorimer said. 'Sorry, it's a habit we have in the police force, speaking in acronyms.'

'But there's a murderer running around loose somewhere!' Dalgleish exploded, thumping one fist against his open hand. 'Doesn't that constitute a danger to the public?'

'We don't know that, sir,' Lorimer began. 'Yes, the signs are that Rory's life was taken, but until we know more then I am afraid the fiscal's position is clear. DI Crozier leads the investigation.'

'Well, I'll have something to say to this fiscal whenever he arrives,' Dalgleish said, his lip trembling with emotion.

'He will probably tell you just the same as I have, Mr Dalgleish,' Lorimer said, laying a placatory hand on the bereaved father's arm.

He could feel the shuddering sigh in the other man's body and knew from experience that tears were not very far away.

'I'll be at Leiter if you need me,' he said, patting the arm before turning to walk back along the corridor.

Why did he feel as though he were betraying this poor man and his wife? he thought as he emerged from the hospital into an afternoon of sunshine and shadows. Was it because, deep down, he wanted to take over from the DI? Was it his policeman's curiosity making him want to find out what had happened to the boy? Or had there been a moment on that morning shore when something had stirred, the memory of a different red-haired lad to whom he still owed a satisfactory outcome?

CHAPTER FOURTEEN

Glasgow

Twenty Years Earlier

'No identifying marks at all,' George Phillips concluded. 'Not even a wee mole or a birthmark. Some of these red-haired types have such fine skins,' he mused.

'What happens now, sir?' DC Lorimer asked.

'We keep the case open for a while,' Phillips shrugged. 'But if the body is never identified then the fiscal may well decide it should be donated to the Royal College of Surgeons. God knows what sort of life the victim led when he was alive, but he may as well do some good now he's dead.'

The comment raised a laugh from the assembled officers in the room, all except the tall detective constable who was biting his lower lip and frowning.

It wasn't right, he had told Maggie the previous evening. *They should make a more concerted effort to find out who the victim was.*

Couldn't they make a splash in the newspapers, put his image on television? his wife had asked, but he had shaken his head. *It doesn't work like that, besides, the state of the poor man's face wasn't what the broadsheets would want on their front page.* She had grimaced at that and he had changed the subject. Gruesomeness was not the order of the day for this heavily pregnant woman.

George Phillips looked over the team of men and women, his glance stopping at his newest detective constable.

'Now that this case is winding down we must turn our attention to other matters in the city,' he said. 'Lorimer, I want you to look into a spate of burglaries on the south side. Not too far from your own neck of the woods,' he grinned.

Lorimer listened as other actions were given out, then they were dismissed.

He was surprised as he left, the DI's hand tapping his shoulder.

'A wee minute, son,' Phillips grinned, beckoning him into his office. 'I know you're keen to find out who that lad is. And if time allows you can still look into that. But remember it's important to serve the public in whatever capacity. An old lady whose precious jewellery has been stolen is just as much a victim of crime as that wee lad down in the mortuary. Okay?'

Lorimer nodded, suddenly ashamed of his moment of pique. Wasn't that what he had signed up for? To protect the public from wrongdoers of whatever ilk?

The bathroom mirror was steamy from the shower he had recently turned off, the windows still shut tight against the night air. Taking an edge of the frayed bath towel he wiped away the moisture and looked at his reflection in the glass.

It didn't look like the face of a killer. There was nothing monstrous about the man looking back at him. The damp had misted up the corners of the oval looking-glass, making it seem as though his face was floating apart from his body. Sometimes it felt that way. He wasn't the same person he had been before it had happened though his body still went through the everyday motions of being alive while his head was somewhere else entirely.

It was a bad place, a place of darkness and of recurring nightmares. It was also a place of regrets but wasn't it also tinged with the memory of . . . what? A thrill? Yes, but the word barely did justice to what they had experienced together. It had been a thrill so immense that now, standing in front of the mirror, he found himself holding his breath tightly, imagining the scene all over again.

His fingers twitched as though a latent memory of those final *moments possessed them.* Harder, harder, *they seemed to say in the same mocking tones that he would never hear again.*

He grabbed the tin of shaving foam, shaking it fiercely, in command of his hands, his fingers once more, then slathered the face in white foam, a Santa Claus beard and moustache covering the dark shadows. But nothing could blot out the shadows that lingered below those grey-green eyes. They regarded him with a cynicism that he found disquieting, making his hand tremble again so that he stopped, the razor in mid-air, fearful of cutting into his cheek, a teardrop of blood sliding downwards. He could imagine the sight of his face, blood dripping down as the razor bit into soft flesh. The fingers holding the razor wanted to cut, to tear: should he give in to their insinuation?

The idea was tempting. It would be a kind of recompense for what he had done, the face in the mirror suggested. And didn't he deserve to suffer?

A long shuddering sigh escaped him as he took the razor and began to slide it through the foam. He worked slowly, carefully, not wishing to leave a single scar, nothing that would be a reminder of his other self: that hidden man looking out at him from the other side of the looking-glass.

CHAPTER FIFTEEN

'It reminds me of a case I had twenty years ago,' Lorimer told his friend.

Solly and he were walking up the single-track road behind the cottage, Maggie content to stay behind and read a story to her goddaughter who was sleepy after the long journey.

'We never found the identity of the victim,' Lorimer continued, looking at the moss-covered ground as he spoke. 'Young man, maybe the same age as Rory Dalgleish,' he mused. 'I remember some of the details. He was a redhead as well. But it was the manner of his death that made me think about this one.' He glanced across at the bearded psychologist who was walking, hands folded behind his back. Solly returned his glance, nodding the policeman to continue his narrative.

'There were marks on the wrists and ankles that showed he had been bound up. Tightly. With stiff rope or something really strong. The marks had survived immersion in water. And this lad, Rory, had something similar.'

Solly nodded sagely once more but said nothing for a few moments. Lorimer wondered if the psychologist's mind had sprung to the same sort of conclusions as his own: had the victims been involved in some sort of deviant sexual behaviour? Were these bondage marks signs of earlier sadomasochistic activity?

'Coincidence?' Solly suggested at last, then he grinned, showing perfect white teeth against his black moustache. 'Ah, but Detective Superintendent Lorimer doesn't believe in coincidences, isn't that what they all say?'

'Do they?' Lorimer stopped, a look of surprise on his face. 'Goodness. I thought it was just me ...' He gave a laugh. 'Anyway, I might just run this past DI Crozier, see if she wants to make anything of it.'

'Do you think that's a good idea? It was twenty years ago, after all, and your other case was in Glasgow, not the island of Mull.'

'It isn't always place that matters,' Lorimer said. 'It's the MO that counts, especially when it's recorded on a database as extensive as HOLMES.'

'Ah, yes.' Solly nodded. 'Of course, it's been updated since your earlier case. Lots of things have,' he murmured.

Lorimer walked on at the psychologist's side, thinking hard. The Home Office Large Major Enquiry System had been in place all right when he had joined the force, something that had been sparked off in the wake of the Yorkshire Ripper investigation. Nowadays it afforded officers all over the country a basis for comparison of cases no matter where they had occurred, something that the professor also found interesting, particularly in cases of multiple murder when it paid to look at the geographical scatter of incidents.

'She will look for another similar crime, though, won't she?'

'I would hope so,' Lorimer agreed. 'It's standard practice.'

'So, no need to risk putting her nose out of joint with a suggestion in that direction?' Solly smiled meaningfully at his friend.

'Do you think she'd mind my mentioning it?'

'I don't know,' Solly replied. 'I haven't met her yet.'

The vibration from his phone made Lorimer stop and take it out. Lifting it up to the light he read the text message and smiled.

'Looks as though you won't have long to wait. She's on her way here now.'

Stevie Crozier clenched and unclenched her fists, the anger she felt suffusing her cheeks with colour. These Forsyth people deserved to be reported for the way they'd spoken to her. The woman had hardly said a word, just nodding in agreement with everything her husband said, like some sort of puppet. *A wee bit of a want*, McManus had said, tapping his head meaningfully when she had asked him about Freda Forsyth. And she could see what he had meant. There had been a gleam of something fervent in the woman's eyes, though, when she had looked at Stevie. It was as if there was

112

a deep-seated resentment against the police and against this female officer in particular.

He'd been overtly charming, the sort of Mine Host who talked into the wee small hours with his clientele, encouraging them to spend their money at his bar. But Hamish Forsyth hadn't fooled Stevie for one minute. He had shown them the paperwork that comprised an agreement between Rory Dalgleish and themselves for his summer job at Kilbeg House, even drawing her attention to the original email that Rory had sent in response to the advertisement for seasonal staff. *Didn't know the lad well at all*, he'd told her, avoiding her eye and looking over his shoulder as if to see what the weather was doing out on the Sound. *Good worker, though*, he'd admitted. The loss of eye contact had interested her. She was well enough versed in a person's body language to tell when someone was lying, and for some reason Mr Forsyth wanted to give the impression that he hadn't known the boy when in fact there may have been something between them. Yes, very interesting indeed. But then to dismiss them so hurriedly as if there were guests clamouring for his attention was just plain annoying. And the cheek of that Forsyth woman who had simply told her to go away and stop bothering them! Stevie had been lost for words.

They would have to go back again, speak to other members of staff who might have been Rory's friends. That was how it was done, after all. Look at the victim's background, speak to family and friends then cast the net wider and wider, taking in things like his emails, his financial transactions, anything that could give a clue as to what had happened in the days leading up to his death. Pity the mobile was missing. Records of phone calls while they waited for the phone company to get back to them could be extremely useful.

Stevie found herself gazing out towards the water. A fish farm of some sort lay just offshore, then they had passed it and a line of overgrown birches obscured her vision. The DI sighed. She couldn't see too clearly in this case yet, but she was damned if she was going to ask that tall detective super-intendent for help.

Lorimer and Solly watched as the silver Mercedes turned from the main road and made its way along the single-track road below them.

'Must be her,' Lorimer said, quickening his pace towards the cottage.

There were two main gates into Leiter, one that had to be swung open for cars to park on the pebbled drive, the other a smaller gate leading to the front garden. Most of the islanders enclosed their properties against the predations of sheep and deer. Traffic could often come to a halt too for a ewe and her lambs idly trotting along the road, apparently oblivious to the fact that they were blocking the way of vehicles.

'They're parking at the lay-by,' Solly murmured, looking at the car turning into a large area just short of the cottage.

'That's all right, gives us time to get home before them.'

Lorimer grinned. 'Wonder if Maggie can woo them with her latest batch of scones?'

'If my daughter hasn't finished them,' Solly laughed, remembering the sticky raspberry jam around Abby's face as she'd demolished her Aunty Maggie's home baking.

The cottage was quiet when they arrived and Maggie lifted an admonitory finger to her lips as she saw the two men.

'She's sleeping,' she whispered. 'Poor wee lamb was tuckered out.'

'We've got visitors,' Lorimer said. 'DI Crozier.' He tilted his head towards the open door and Maggie looked up, hearing the crunch of feet on pebbles.

'Oh, I better put the kettle on, then,' Maggie exclaimed, hurrying into the kitchen and closing the door behind her.

Lorimer stepped out of the cottage to greet the two officers. A small wind had sprung up and the blonde woman had put a hand up to smooth her hair back in place as she approached the doorway. It was a small gesture, but one that made her seem suddenly vulnerable, reminding Lorimer how hard it could still be for senior female officers even in these enlightened days. Crozier stepped out in front of her colleague, her eyes shifting to the man standing behind Lorimer, her lips parted as though an unspoken question hovered there.

'DI Crozier, DS Langley.' Lorimer shook their hands in turn, beckoning them into the cottage. He turned towards the entrance where the bearded psychologist was standing just inside the porch.

115

'Allow me to introduce Professor Solomon Brightman, Dr Fergusson's husband,' he said, stepping aside to allow for more polite handshakes.

'I don't think we've met before.' Solly smiled benignly. 'This is our first time here in Mull,' he explained.

'Well I'm sorry you had to be dragged up for a murder inquiry, sir,' Crozier said, blinking hard as though she could not quite believe that she was seeing the man in front of her. Even the full black beard and horn-rimmed spectacles could not disguise this handsome and engaging man, Lorimer realised. Used as he was to Solly's exotic appearance, it came as something of an amusement to see a new female reaction to his friend.

'Please, come in and sit down, my wife will be bringing in some tea and scones. Or would you prefer coffee?'

'Oh.' Crozier seemed nonplussed for a moment. As they followed Lorimer into the lounge she said, 'We weren't going to stay long . . . '

'She makes great scones.' Solly smiled winningly. 'And the raspberry jam's home-made too.'

'I'd love a cuppa, boss,' Langley nodded, putting the woman at a sudden disadvantage.

'Well, okay, then, fine. Tea's fine, I mean,' she agreed helplessly, sitting down on the edge of one of the ancient armchairs that were angled towards the fireplace.

'Hello.'

Lorimer smiled as Maggie entered the room, DS Langley

immediately on his feet, Crozier hemmed in where she sat next to the coffee table. The DI's discomfiture was all too apparent as she sat looking up at her fellow officer and the dark-haired, smiling woman bending to put the tea things beside her.

'This is my wife, Maggie,' he said, taking the teapot and beginning to pour tea into the four mugs that were on the tray next to a mound of freshly buttered scones and an old-fashioned china pot full of jam.

'Sorry to butt in on you like this,' Crozier murmured, taking a scone from the pile that Maggie was offering.

'I'm used to it,' Maggie said simply. 'Being a policeman's wife makes for lots of interruptions.' She shrugged. 'But we didn't expect to be in the middle of a murder inquiry. Here, of all places.'

'I'm sorry to intrude,' Crozier repeated. She took a deep breath before continuing. 'There is something that I wanted to make very clear, though,' she began, ducking her head to avoid their glances.

'You don't want me sticking my Glasgow nose into your case,' Lorimer said softly, a wry smile on his face. 'Don't worry. I don't intend to interfere. Or pull rank. You are the SIO, after all, and I'm supposed to be on holiday. There is one thing you ought to know, however.'

'Oh, and what's that?' Crozier's face was pink.

'The Dalgleishes did ask me to take over.'

'And what did you tell them?

117

'That it's your case. Though I could tell *he* wasn't happy. I think coming here to see where Rory was found made them feel like that,' he explained.

There was an uncomfortable silence as they sat drinking tea, Maggie now perched on the arm of Lorimer's chair, the psychologist gazing at each of them in turn with a faint contemplative smile on his face as though he were reading their body language.

'Is this your own place?' Langley asked at last, looking around the cottage, its old-fashioned decor in keeping with a bygone era, not quite what he may have expected from the Glasgow couple.

'No,' Maggie replied. 'It belongs to the aunt of one of Bill's colleagues, Mary Grant. We rent it as often as we can.'

'Though if she were ever to sell we'd want to have first refusal,' Lorimer chipped in.

'It's such a haven of peace and quiet,' Maggie enthused.

'You must have been pretty upset then when the body was washed up,' Crozier said.

'I was.' Maggie nodded. 'We both were,' she said stiffly.

'You know what householders say whenever they've been burgled?' Lorimer asked. 'They always seem to feel that they've been violated. That was how it felt to Maggie and me.' He looked around the room with its low ceiling and deeply recessed windows. 'Leiter's special,' he said, 'even though it doesn't belong to us.'

DI Crozier nodded, a small frown on her face as though she

were slightly embarrassed at this personal disclosure. 'Well, thanks for the tea, your scones are lovely,' she said, looking at Maggie with undisguised admiration. 'I never learned how to bake.'

'*My* wife makes great scones,' Langley grinned. 'Almost as good as yours, Mrs Lorimer.'

There was an uneasy silence as DI Crozier appeared to bite back a retort. Then she rose from the armchair and laid her mug back onto the tray. 'We'd better be going,' she said. 'I think your wife may be waiting for us at Craignure,' she added, nodding to Solly. 'Nice to meet you, Professor Brightman.'

The psychologist had risen to his feet but remained where he was as Lorimer led the two detectives out.

Maggie waited until she was sure they were out of earshot before whispering, 'What do you make of her?'

'Hm.' Solly began stroking his beard and looking out of the window towards the lay-by where the officers had left their car. 'She was certainly spoiling for a fight. But I think your tea and scones completely disarmed the detective inspector, Maggie.'

Maggie laughed. 'She's quite a pretty girl. Reminds me of Laura, one of my younger colleagues at school. Husband and three kids. Not a path that DI Crozier seems to have chosen,' she added thoughtfully. 'So many female officers appear to be married to the job.'

'Maybe she just hasn't met anyone she wants to settle down with,' Solly rejoined. 'But I think you're right. I would guess DI

Crozier's had to work jolly hard to get to where she is. I'm not sure she has much support from her detective sergeant, either,' he mused. 'I would guess he isn't too happy about having a woman as his superior officer.' He looked out of the window thoughtfully. 'And this case must be a big deal to her. I'd guess she's never covered a murder case on her own before.'

'How can you tell that?' Maggie asked.

'She's desperate to hold on to it,' he replied. 'Can't be too many incidents of this nature, even in the wild town of Oban,' he chuckled.

'He seems a decent sort,' Langley remarked as they drove back onto the main road and headed around Fishnish Bay.

Stevie Crozier did not reply. She was thinking hard. Lorimer had agreed to meet them again tomorrow after the post-mortem and give them a blow-by-blow account of where and how he had found the boy's body. He was cooperating so nicely, maybe too nicely, she thought darkly. His politeness and charm hadn't quelled her suspicions that the detective superintendent might yet try to take over, pulling strings that would leave her sidelined.

The views of the forest and the distant hills of Morvern were lost to her as they sped along the road, her thoughts now turned to the people who were expecting them in Craignure; she was curious to meet the wife of the enigmatic Professor Brightman.

*

Why hadn't he told her? Were there such doubts in his mind that to relate his thoughts might prove embarrassing at the very least, professionally risible at worst? He had rehearsed the words to himself several times before the DI's arrival. *There's an old case you might be interested in ... There's something I wanted to run past you ...* But he had said nothing, seeing only too well that such a matter would be taken as blatant interference in her case.

As Lorimer gazed out at the bay and the shadows chasing each other across the Morvern hills, he was seized with a sense that there had been an opportunity missed and that now it was too late to bring up the subject of the unknown red-haired boy who had come into his life all those years ago.

It was a time he wanted to forget, of course. Wasn't it, after all, part of the human condition to stifle all memories that surrounded profound grief? The days and weeks that had followed the discovery of that unknown victim were all a blur now; and perhaps, he told himself, there was a part of him wanting it to stay that way.

CHAPTER SIXTEEN

The tall blonde woman walking towards her reminded Rosie of a former fellow pathologist, a stylish young woman who had always donned her highest heels and designer outfits after a post-mortem, insisting that wearing scrubs and plastic aprons for the day job made her all the more aware of her appearance outside the mortuary. Rosie grinned, recalling Dr Jacqui White, the woman who was now enjoying the television career she had carved out for herself.

DI Crozier's cream-coloured heels were modest in comparison and her sharp grey suit with a pale lemon blouse might have been purchased in any high street chain, but she carried herself with the same self-possession as Jacqui White. The DI's attractive face might not grace the public's TV screens but, as the senior police officer in the busy harbour town she would probably have been photographed often enough for the *Oban Times*.

'DI Crozier? I'm Dr Fergusson.' Rosie got up from the bench outside the hospital and smiled as the DI was almost past her.

'Oh.' The woman stopped in her tracks and stared at Rosie. What had she been expecting? Rosie wondered in a moment of amusement: a white-coated professional instead of a small woman dressed in jeans, open-toed sandals and a cotton top? Crozier towered over her as she took Rosie's outstretched hand, trying to overcome her surprise.

'I guess you've already met my husband and our little girl?'

Crozier nodded. 'Not your daughter, I only met Professor Brightman and the Lorimers,' she replied.

'Ah.' Rosie smiled as they walked together into the shade of the hospital porch. 'Abby would be down for a sleep, I expect. Bill and Maggie are her godparents,' she explained.

'Right.'

Rosie hid a smile, watching the way the other woman's lips tightened. It would be interesting to see what Solly had made of this woman. The very mention of Lorimer seemed to make her stiffen.

'I've seen Dr MacMillan,' Rosie began as they walked down the hospital corridor. 'She's fine for me to do the PM first thing tomorrow. Will you be there?'

'Of course.' Crozier threw her a suspicious glance. 'I'm not the squeamish type, you know.'

Rosie laughed. 'I bet you're not! In my experience it's usually the young guys who faint at the sight of me cutting open a cadaver.'

Crozier managed a smile, making Rosie see for the first time what might lie beneath that buttoned-down exterior. She was an attractive woman, probably in her mid-thirties, but the worry lines around her eyes and creasing her forehead made her seem older.

'It isn't the first post-mortem I've attended. There were cases in Lothian and Borders,' she said.

Rosie nodded, waiting for her to elaborate, but no further information about the DI's background appeared to be forthcoming.

'Dr MacMillan is going to assist me,' Rosie told her. 'She'll be recording all the information should it be required in court later on.'

'Can she do that? I thought you needed two pathologists.'

'She trained in surgery,' Rosie explained. 'Did pathology for a while then went back to hospital work after she was married and came to live up here in Mull.'

'Oh.' Crozier seemed nonplussed that Rosie had found out so much about the doctor from Craignure in the short time since she had arrived.

'We had quite a chat, catching up on this and that,' Rosie grinned.

'And she told you all about Rory Dalgleish, I suppose?'

'No.' Rosie looked at the DI seriously, suddenly concerned at the bitterness in the woman's tone. 'I was waiting for you to tell me that, DI Crozier. All I know so far is what you told me on the telephone and by email.'

'Well, that's a surprise. Thought your friend Lorimer would have given you all the details.'

124

'I know he found the body,' Rosie said slowly, staring at the woman, disturbed by her sarcastic tone. 'And I expect he will tell me how he feels about that, but I was expecting the SIO to be the one to give me all the necessary information about where the body was washed up, how it appeared. I take it you have photographs of the body in situ before it was moved?'

Crozier nodded, her expression almost miserable. 'The local police took them. With Lorimer's camera,' she added.

Rosie hid a smile. Her friend's helpfulness had not gone down well with the detective inspector from Oban and she guessed that Crozier would be more than relieved when the Lorimers' holiday came to an end, taking them back to Glasgow.

Just then a door opened and Dr MacMillan emerged from her office.

'Ah, good to see you again, Detective Inspector Crozier.' She beamed at them both. 'And you've met Rosie now?'

'Rosie?' Crozier looked at the pathologist, a puzzled expression on her face. 'You know one another?'

'Dr MacMillan was my tutor when I was at Glasgow Uni,' Rosie explained. 'Taught me all I know.'

The older woman threw back her head and laughed, a long whooping sound that echoed down the corridor.

'Hardly that, my dear!' she exclaimed. 'Just glad I didn't put you off forensic pathology. The drop-out rate was quite alarming,' she added, turning to the DI. 'Only hardened wee souls like our Rosie stuck it out.'

There was a look of relief on the DI's face as she glanced from one doctor to the other.

'Aye, well, look where it's got me,' Rosie laughed.

'Only to the top of the tree, my dear,' Dr MacMillan said. 'A fine achievement to be director of the department at your age.' She beamed at her protégée. 'And I am so glad it's you here, Rosie. I know we will all be in safe hands.' She put an affectionate arm around Rosie's shoulders. 'Okay, shall we say a nine o' clock start?'

'Fine for me,' Rosie replied. 'DI Crozier?'

'Yes, I'll be here.'

'Good, that's settled then. Shall we see you tonight, Rosie? Martin and I were hoping to take you out in the boat after dinner. It's been anchored most of the summer in Tobermory but he brought it back today.' She smiled at Crozier.

'My husband's been photographing minke whales in the Sound for the last few weeks,' she explained. 'Sometimes I don't see him for days if he sleeps over on the boat,' she laughed, 'but he'll be with us tonight.'

'That would be lovely. See you at six.'

'Right.' The tall woman consulted her wristwatch. 'Time for me to do my rounds, then. See you later.'

Dr MacMillan shook hands with them both then DI Crozier and Rosie turned to walk back along the corridor.

'She's nice, isn't she?' Rosie began. 'Was everybody's favourite tutor at uni.'

Stevie Crozier cleared her throat. 'I wasn't aware that she was a pathologist as well.'

'No? Well, I suppose it's been a long time since she practised, right enough. And she married a bit later in life. Martin and she met at Earls Court at the Boat Show when they were both there to suss out buying a yacht. Ended up buying one together and coming up here.'

'Mr MacMillan's retired, then?'

Rosie shook her head. 'No. Martin must be well into his seventies now but I doubt he'll ever retire. And he's not Mr MacMillan. The doc still uses her maiden name for work. So do I, as it happens,' she added. 'Her husband is Martin Goodfellow. You've maybe heard of him? He's a freelance writer and photographer. Does loads of wildlife stuff. You've probably seen some of it on television.'

'Don't get a lot of time to watch TV in my job,' Crozier replied stiffly.

They were out in the sunshine once more and Rosie saw the woman shading her eyes as she looked towards the waiting Mercedes.

'Well, I'd better be getting back to Leiter to pick up my family. Solly's stranded there,' she laughed. 'He doesn't drive.' She grinned as the detective's eyebrows shot up in surprise. 'Says he has too much on his mind to concentrate on mundane things like roads and traffic.'

'I'd better be off, too,' Crozier replied, nodding her farewell but not enlightening the pathologist as to where she was heading or what the next stage of her investigation entailed.

High above the small car park, hidden amongst swathes of bright green bracken, a glint of sunlight bounced off twin orbs of glass that were trained upon the two women.

Nobody noticed the watcher, halfway up that hillside, nor the way those powerful binoculars turned to see the silver car leave the village and head back towards the north of the island. The man behind the field glasses nodded to himself then leaned back, an invisible figure, his camouflage jacket blending in with the sunlight playing across grasses and heather.

CHAPTER SEVENTEEN

'Of course I'd been drinking!' the man in the battered panama hat scoffed. 'It was a Saturday night and we were in the Aros Hall. What did you expect, young Jamie Kennedy?'

The police constable's face reddened as he looked back down at the lines he had written on the screen of his laptop, his eyes shifting momentarily to the unopened Toshiba lying to one side. People had been coming to the caravan all day and he hadn't yet had time to look at the dead boy's laptop.

'Would you say the drink might have affected any of your ability to recall details, though, Jock?'

Jamie Kennedy stifled a sigh. Jock Maloney was a man well known for his ability to drink all evening and still be blethering on in the wee small hours. The man's mild boast at being able to drink any of the other locals under the table had been put to the test countless times in the police constable's experience but he was also prone to embroider his stories. Not to lie, exactly, just to embellish truths about people.

'You want to know if I'd seen that boy, eh?'

'And did you?'

''Twould have been hard to avoid him,' Jock Maloney grinned. 'With his kilt swirling on the dance floor and these ridiculous boxer shorts showing underneath!'

'Boxer shorts?' Jamie murmured.

'Aye. Emblazoned with a Union Jack, would you believe!'

The man's face twisted in disgust. Jock Maloney might be half Irish but he was one hundred per cent Scottish Nationalist and could often be heard to declaim loudly on the incomers from south of the border who had made their first or second homes on the island. *White settlers*, he'd say to anyone who was willing to listen to his rant. *From Englandshire*, he'd add, as though that part of the UK was somehow tainted. It wouldn't be the first time that PC Kennedy had had to warn him about his racist tendencies, something that Maloney brushed off with a joke and a disarming shrug of his shoulders as though he hadn't really meant any offence.

'So, did you see the lad leaving the Aros Hall, Jock?'

'Aye, well, maybe,' the man admitted, his grin fading a little. 'He was there at the interval, downstairs with a crowd from the Mishnish Hotel, yachties by the look of them.'

'Half-time drink?'

The man in the panama hat nodded. 'That would be right.'

'And did you see him afterwards? Was he upstairs dancing later on?'

A shadow of doubt crossed the man's drink-reddened

130

features, bristly dark brows drawn down as he considered the question.

'I believe so,' he said at last. 'There was a Strip the Willow and I'm sure he was in the set next to ours. Dancing with the local lassie from the hotel.'

'And which lassie would that be?'

'Och, Fiona, *your* wee pal.' He winked. 'They'd all cadged a lift up with Lachie Turner in his van.'

Jamie added this to the paragraph he had already written down, making a mental note to tell the DI that his old school-friend, Fiona Taig, had been seen with Rory Dalgleish but had not yet come forward to tell them so.

'And later on? When you were leaving yourselves?'

Maloney tipped back his hat and rubbed his weather-beaten forehead. 'Naw, nae sign of the laddie out on the street when we were going home. And I'd have remembered.'

'Oh? How's that, then?'

Maloney grinned. 'Only man wearing a kilt, wasn't he? Typical bloody Lowlander!'

Jamie straightened up and gave the man the benefit of his harshest stare. 'May I remind you, Jock, that we're dealing with the laddie's death. It's a serious matter.'

'Sorry.' The grin on the man's face turned to a twisted smile but there was nothing of contrition in his eyes. 'Anyway,' he blustered, 'I would have expected you to have Detective Superintendent Lorimer up here working the case.'

'You know him?' Jamie's face registered surprise.

Maloney tapped the side of his nose. 'Old pals, aren't we?'

'Oh? How come?'

'Fixed his old Lexus plenty of times before he bought that silver job.' Maloney grinned. 'Had some good craic with the man, too.'

Jamie shook his head wearily. This was getting them nowhere fast.

'Look, I need to know about Rory Dalgleish. Did you happen to see who he was talking to during the evening?'

'Not really.' Maloney shrugged. 'Just knew he was there; I mean who could help avoiding him? That thatch of red hair and yon loud voice? Well, you could hardly miss him.'

Jamie Kennedy swallowed his annoyance. Maloney just didn't seem to understand the gravity of this situation at all.

'And there was no trouble at the dance?'

Maloney frowned. 'Trouble? What kind of trouble could there be? Everyone was having a right good time.' He paused, staring at the policeman. 'D'ye mean like a fight breaking out?'

Jamie nodded.

'Naw, nothing like that. 'Twas a quiet enough night on that account, I'd say. No trouble.' He paused for a long moment, staring over the policeman's head as if something had indeed come into his mind.

Jamie waited, hoping that the man might have something, anything that would give a clue to what had happened to the boy. But Maloney simply shrugged.

'That's as much as I remember, young 'un. All done, are we?'

Maloney sketched a mock salute against the bent rim of his hat and opened the door of the caravan, letting in some of the sweet salty air and the sound of raucous seagulls.

'*Arrivederci, commissario*,' he said, slipping down the two steps to the ground.

Jamie Kennedy shook his head and sighed. Maloney was one of the leading lights in the Mull drama club and his Italian accent was nigh on perfect, reminding Jamie of *Inspector Montalbano*, his favourite Saturday night viewing.

'Aye, *arrivederci* to you too,' he muttered under his breath.

The cheery expression on Maloney's face vanished as soon as he had closed the caravan door again, his usual jaunty stride slower and more measured as he walked back along the street towards the Mishnish Hotel. A dram or two was in order, he told himself, a shudder passing through his body. Just to clarify his thoughts, not banish them altogether.

Though the image that came into his mind's eye was one that Jock Maloney would prefer not to see ever again in this life.

CHAPTER EIGHTEEN

Lorimer was sitting beside the man and woman on a bench outside their hotel, saddened that the view of the gardens sweeping down to the shore and the hills beyond was lost to these grief-stricken parents. Would they always associate this island with death and despair? They had urged him to sit with them during this interview with the reporter from Glasgow: *He's known to you*, Rory's mother had said. *And we don't know what to expect.*

'He's late,' Douglas Dalgleish grumbled, looking at his watch.

'No, dear, we're early,' Pamela chided. 'Look, here he is now.'

The three people turned as one at the reporter's approach. McGarrity gave a slight bow in the direction of Mrs Dalgleish; it was not an ostentatious gesture, just a brief courtesy and Lorimer knew that the man was prepared to be as sympathetic to these bereaved folk as he could be. Today he had discarded his tweeds and was wearing a light linen jacket over an immaculately pressed shirt that was open at the neck, a concession to the sunshine that was blazing down from an azure sky.

'Thanks for agreeing to see me,' McGarrity said, offering a hand to each of them in turn. 'I understand how hard it must be.'

'Do you?' Pamela Dalgleish blurted out then gazed at her lap.

'It's part of my job to talk to people who have experienced some terrible things,' McGarrity said gently. 'Part of being a crime reporter.'

'Suppose someone's got to do it,' Douglas Dalgleish grumbled, making it sound as though the reporter was little better than the lowliest street sweeper. 'Well, let's get it over with,' he added testily.

Lorimer watched as McGarrity picked up a metal chair that was nearby, angling it so that he was near enough to the trio but not invading their space. He was being sensitive towards these poor people, but Lorimer knew that he was also a consummate professional who would not leave until he had all the information he wanted.

'Let's start with Rory,' the reporter began. 'Tell me about him. What he did at school, his friends, his hobbies, the things he excelled in.' He smiled at them encouragingly. 'Readers always like to think of the life that a young person has enjoyed. It helps to make them more real in their eyes,' he explained.

Pamela Dalgleish stared at him then nodded. 'Hard to know where to begin,' she whispered.

'Just take your time,' McGarrity told her.

A shuddering sigh went through her body then she straightened her shoulders as though preparing for a hard physical task.

'Rory was our youngest,' she began. 'He was at Hutchie like the rest of the children, but he didn't particularly shine at school. Not like his siblings.'

'Too many things had changed since they'd been there,' Dalgleish put in. 'Too much choice. All that extra-curricular nonsense.'

'Rory did like to go to the after-school clubs,' Pamela agreed. 'Computer club was his favourite.'

'Never away from the blasted thing!' her husband retorted.

'Well, he was good at it, dear. He could always show me what to do if anything went wrong with mine.'

'What was he going to study at university?' McGarrity asked, as though sensing that this line of questioning was not particularly fruitful.

Dalgleish cleared his throat noisily. 'Ah,' he said, then stopped.

The two parents looked at one another then Pamela nodded as though there had been an unspoken agreement.

'He hadn't exactly been accepted for a course,' she said. 'He was going to travel first then apply later on.'

'And had he any course of study in mind?'

136

'Media studies,' Dalgleish said, shaking his head. 'Fat lot of good that would have done him in the job market. Oh well, not a problem now—' He broke off, his hand across his mouth, sudden tears filling his eyes. He rummaged in a pocket and took out a handkerchief then blew his nose as the reporter looked on, an expression of utter contrition in his eyes.

'Is this too hard for you?' McGarrity asked.

'Sorry, sorry, no, please go on. It's just . . . ' He stopped and swallowed hard.

'Phillip and Jennifer chose such traditional professions,' Pamela explained. She's a doctor in Edinburgh Royal Infirmary and Phillip's a lawyer.'

'And Rory had his own ideas about what he wanted to do?'

'Something like that.' She attempted a tremulous smile. 'He was good at designing things.' She looked up as though she had suddenly remembered. 'Games for the computer, I mean. He could have made a career out of that, couldn't he?' She turned towards her husband, a mother protesting her son's worth.

'Plenty of youngsters have made a fortune from the internet,' Lorimer agreed.

McGarrity nodded. 'Shall I say then that Rory had advanced IT design skills? That he hoped might lead to greater things?'

As the two parents nodded as one, Lorimer hid a sardonic smile. McGarrity would have the dead boy as some sort of technical genius who was a loss to the modern world. His piece would be exaggerated, as they all were, but hopefully harmless. Still, it was an interesting bit of information and he wondered just what the police had turned up on the dead boy's laptop.

'Any girlfriends?'

Lorimer saw the dark look that passed between the Dalgleishes. It was a small enough thing but in that momentary exchange the senior detective suddenly understood.

'No,' Douglas said, a shade too firmly.

McGarrity smiled. 'Lots of pals, though, I suppose.'

A momentary look of relief swept across Pamela Dalgleish's face.

'Oh, yes, lots,' she agreed swiftly. 'The house will be so quiet now without them all there,' she added, biting her lip.

Lorimer sat back, watching and listening, forming his own opinions and wondering if the reporter had also picked up on the parents' body language. Probably. McGarrity was no fool.

If he was not mistaken, here was a secret that the Dalgleishes wanted to die with their boy. Had it been a secret kept from others, though? Had Rory, the loud lad, shared the fact of his sexuality with his schoolfriends? Or had the shame that emanated from his own parents made him more reticent about the fact that he was gay? It didn't explain the boy's death but perhaps it would make things more complicated.

And, for the first time since he had discovered the body, Lorimer allowed himself to speculate about the marks around the wrists and ankles.

*

'What do you reckon?'

'I would have said wire.' Rosie peered more closely at the ankles where some form of binding had cut into the boy's flesh. 'But it hasn't left the sort of impression you would expect. Maybe some sort of binding twine.' She paused, examining the surface wounds with a magnifying glass. 'There's a definite pattern. Won't be any traces after being so long in the water, but I want some photos sent to our friends down in Glasgow. Chap I know there is a whizz with this sort of thing.'

Grace MacMillan angled the camera carefully, zooming in on the spot that Rosie was indicating with a scalpel blade, the ruler next to the boy's ankle to give an idea of scale. Despite the tragic circumstances of Rory Dalgleish's death, the older woman found that she was enjoying this. Having her former protégée undertake the post-mortem was hugely gratifying; it was something that she and Martin would talk about over an evening whisky for years to come.

Stevie Crozier stood as far away from the two doctors as she could manage, DS Langley by her side. It was not out of any sense of nausea at watching a PM, rather a desire to give the medics as much space as possible. There was no viewing platform here, as in a city morgue, and so the police officers had donned scrubs and slunk against a wall, angling themselves to see what was happening as Rosie moved around the stainless steel table. The harsh lights beamed down to illuminate the pathologist's work, a necessity in this windowless room. She felt a strange sensation, as though they were all cut off from the real world, adrift in some timeless place where death ruled supreme. She watched as Rosie opened the boy's body, revealing the internal organs.

Was that all a person amounted to in the end? A load of dark red pieces being weighed on the scales, facts and figures about them written down in a notebook? Where was the loud boy she had heard so much about? Where was his laughter, the exuberance of a young life?

Stevie sensed Langley shifting uncomfortably by her side and she glanced at him, hoping that the detective sergeant wasn't going to disgrace her and throw up. *He'd* have told her that Rory's spirit was elsewhere. In heaven, whatever that meant, she thought sourly. Langley was a churchgoer of the traditional sort but he had surprised her when she had remarked on the waste of a young life being cut short.

We can't know why it's their time, Langley had said, looking obliquely at his boss, *we can only trust that their spirit is safe in the arms of God.*

Somehow, watching the small blonde woman at work, Stevie found it hard to imagine a spirit of any sort. It was all flesh and bones, nothing more. Wasn't it?

Rosie turned and looked at the two police officers. 'You've been very patient,' she smiled. 'And I know you want as much information as possible, so here's what we have.' She turned back to indicate the neck area. 'Broken hyoid bone suggests

140

that some person has inflicted this injury. It cannot have happened during his passage at sea and the cause of death was most certainly not drowning. The lungs and air passages confirm that,' she continued. 'He was dead before he hit the water.'

'So they tried to dispose of the body by chucking it into the ocean?' Crozier said, not masking the bitterness in her tone.

'That is a likely scenario,' Rosie agreed, 'but not my part of the ship. All I can tell you is how he died as far as the injuries on his body will show. Whether it's a they or a he or even a she that put him into the water is not my call, Detective Inspector.'

'Can you tell if he was tied up before or after he died?'

Rosie shook her head. 'That's a bit harder. But he was still warm when he was trussed up. Rigor setting in established the shape of his limbs like that,' she said, nodding at the bent knees where the bonds had pulled his lower limbs back.

'But he might have been restrained while he was still alive?'

Rosie nodded. 'Might have been, but I would never categorically state that he *was*, not here nor in a court of law. We deal in possibilities.' She smiled, exchanging a knowing look at her former tutor who smiled back as though the phrase was something that had been learned and passed on from Dr Grace MacMillan years before.

'We'll have to send all the photographic material to Pitt Street but I can do the toxicology here. See what his bloods and the stomach contents reveal.'

'D'you mind if I go out for a bit?' DS Langley said suddenly. 'Bit stuffy in here.'

'No, that's fine, we're almost done so no need to come back in if you don't want to,' Rosie said.

Langley slipped out of the room, closing the door almost reverently as he left, as though to disturb the dead was some sort of sacrilege.

'Sorry about that,' Crozier apologised. 'Didn't know he was the squeamish sort.'

'Can't be too many post-mortems for a police officer to see in this part of the world,' Rosie said sympathetically. She glanced back at the cadaver, the flaps of skin that lay open, exposing the workings of the human body. It was a sight she was used to seeing in her job, but for a moment she saw Rory's body through the eyes of the policeman and shuddered. It was fascinating to her, as a pathologist, but pretty grim, perhaps, if you weren't used to it.

Jim McGarrity was waiting for her as Rosie emerged into the sunshine.

'Oh, it's you,' she said. 'Lorimer didn't mention that they'd sent you this far north.'

'Big story.' McGarrity shrugged. 'Bad thing to happen on a place as nice as this,' he said, spreading his arms wide to encompass the hills, sky and sea around them.

Rosie followed his gesture. It was a lovely place, too lovely for such a death to have been committed here and she could see why the chief crime reporter at the *Gazette* had wanted to come to see it all for himself.

'I've spoken to his parents,' McGarrity continued. 'And now I wonder, Dr Fergusson, if you could give me any indication of the cause of the poor boy's death?'

'Och, you know I can't do that yet,' Rosie protested. 'It'll have to be done through the proper channels.'

'Did he drown?' McGarrity persisted. 'Was it an accident?'

Rosie shook her head. 'You'll know soon enough,' she said. 'The police press office will let you know by the end of today, I would think.'

McGarrity grinned. 'Thanks, Doc,' he said.

'What for? I haven't told you a thing!' Rosie protested, but McGarrity was already walking away, one finger tapping against his nose as though he had read what he wanted to know in her unspoken words.

Martin Goodfellow's hand pushed the tiller to starboard, feeling the tension on the sheet as the yacht cut through the waves. He bent low as the boom came around, feeling the boat swing beneath him like a living creature. Then, as he steered his course across the Sound of Mull, the photographer lifted his face to the afternoon sun, feeling the sharpness of the wind against his stubbled cheeks. It was a perfect day for sighting the minkes, a perfect day to leave the little village behind with all its talk of death and despair.

His eyes caught sight of the fish box tucked neatly to one

side, wrapped in several strands of plastic twine. There was a fishing line in there, the one with nine hooks that was called a 'murderer'. Maybe he would head later to the buoy for a spot of fishing. The ling were supposed to be plentiful at this time of year and Grace might like to invite her young friends back for dinner.

He smiled to himself, feeling the field glasses bump against his chest as the yacht swept up and over a wave. It was good to keep an eye on these people from the mainland. So many of them meant well; but occasionally something like the death of the red-haired boy would happen to wreak havoc in their peaceful lives. The man's smile faded as he faced the sun, his eyes half closed as he remembered his wife's words and the bleak expression on her face. He would do *anything*, Martin thought fiercely, anything at all to protect his Grace from the world she had left behind all these years ago.

CHAPTER NINETEEN

Glasgow

Twenty Years Earlier

A red-haired young man, she read, *possibly in his late teens*, the short article went on.

Mona Daly put down the newspaper with a sigh. Had that been the lad she'd seen the other night, after work? The young chap she had seen here before ...? She shuddered, remembering the two men standing in the shadows of the building where she worked. It had been the shock of seeing grown men do something so horrid that made her remember them so well. She'd looked at them for a moment, expecting one of them to be a daftie, a poor soul who didn't know any better. That would have made it kind of sad, but understandable. These sorts hadn't a clue what was right or socially acceptable, did they? And Mona had heard it said they were extra affectionate, these Mongol laddies who hadn't the brains to understand what they were doing with their own bodies.

But the one with red hair, she'd seen his face and he wasn't like that at all. He was actually an okay-looking sort of guy, shorter than the other one who had bent down towards him, their faces so close that Mona had stopped suddenly, horrified that she was about to see two men kissing one another. Then the younger one had slid his hand onto the other man's trousers, fondling his groin, and Mona had turned and fled from the window, gasping, not wanting to see any more.

Then, to see them again in the middle of the town ... disgusting types!

Could it have been him? Had he come to grief in the river afterwards? Mona twisted her lips in a moment of indecision. Was it something in her – God forgive her! – that wanted the laddie dead? A punishment for having offended her sense of decency? She re-read the notice in the *Gazette* and shook her head. There were thousands of red-haired lads in the city; Scotland was full of them. And no doubt there were queers everywhere too, only she hadn't been used to seeing the nasty sort of things they got up to: not in broad daylight.

No, it couldn't be the same person. There had been something mendacious in the red-haired young man's face, something that made Mona think he could look after himself. And if it was him? Well, it was none of her business, was it? Nobody had come forward to identify the body, the police spokesman in the article said. But someone knew that lad she'd seen. The older man; the one who hadn't even flinched when his private parts had been touched. He would have come to the city morgue, wouldn't he?

But what if that had been the lad's killer? a small voice whispered in Mona Daly's ear. She folded the newspaper and stuffed it into the wire mesh bin under her desk.

She wouldn't think of it again. It didn't concern her. There were too many other important things to take up her time, she told herself, pulling herself in to the desk and preparing to tackle another day with this new computer system that had been given to all the secretarial staff.

'Not a thing.' Lorimer shook his head as he sank back into the ancient armchair that had been a cheap saleroom purchase when they'd bought the house. 'Not one single person in the whole city has responded to it,' he said tiredly.

'That's a shame,' Maggie said. 'To think that nobody loves you enough to keep in touch.'

'Oh, there could be any number of reasons why he wasn't identified,' Lorimer mused. 'Probably wasn't even from Glasgow. Most of the missing persons who are never found again have left their old haunts and live a life amongst strangers.'

'Yes, you hear about old folk who are found behind their doors months after they've died.' Maggie sighed. 'It's such a sad part of your job, darling,' she sympathised.

'Och, it's the frustration of knowing that someone out there really does know who the boy is,' he said wearily. 'At least whoever trussed him up and threw him in the water does, but they won't be letting on anytime soon,' he grumbled.

'It couldn't have been an accident?'

Lorimer shook his head. 'No. Phillips reckons it's probably gang-related. But I'm not so sure.'

'Why?'

'Well, most of the Glasgow gangs are local, aren't they? And even a bad lot has a mother or a sister who would be worried about them when they disappeared.'

'What if they're warned not to go to the police?'

'Aye, well, that's one of the things that Phillips said.' Lorimer grinned suddenly at his wife. 'You should be a polis, pet.'

'Hard to see me in a uniform of any sort right now.' Maggie smiled back, stroking the folds of her maternity dress.

She looked down. 'Just a few more weeks and you'll be out of there, wee one,' she crooned. 'And I can begin to get my figure back and not be such a huge big elephant.'

'You're gorgeous just as you are, d'you know that?' Lorimer bent forward and patted his wife's knee. 'Pregnancy becomes you,' he mused, smiling into her eyes. 'And I don't care if you're never a skinny wee thing again.'

Maggie laughed. 'Well you'll be nothing but skin and bone if I don't get your dinner.'

'Here, sit where you are,' Lorimer protested, rising to his feet. 'I'll fix the dinner. What are we having?' He strode towards the kitchen part of the large, airy open-plan room that

148

stretched the width of the house and beyond into an extension that the previous owners had built.

'Mum made a casserole,' Maggie called back. 'A bit hot for this weather but it'll be nice. There's rice ready to be heated up in the microwave.'

'Ah, the age of modern conveniences!' Lorimer laughed, opening the microwave with a ping and slipping the covered dish inside.

Maggie Lorimer closed her eyes and sighed contentedly. They would never be rich people on a schoolteacher's and policeman's salaries, especially if she were to go part time after the baby was born; but right now she wouldn't have swapped their lives for that of the wealthiest folk on the planet. Nobody could have as much as they had, she thought, feeling the ripples of movement across her swollen belly. They were the luckiest couple in the world.

They had been good together, he thought, blinking the tears that threat-ened to blind his vision as he chucked the last of his belongings into the rucksack and pulled the draw cord tight.

We make a good pair, don't we? the boy had said, and he remem-bered smiling at that, imagining a future together where they made one another happy.

That would never happen now. The red-haired boy was dead, lying on some cold mortuary shelf, an unnamed victim.

He yanked the straps of the rucksack, gritting his teeth against the images that would not go away.

It was time to leave, time to go far away from this city of night-mares and vile memories. He would find a place where he was known and liked, he told himself. A place where he would make sure that nothing like that would ever happen again.

CHAPTER TWENTY

Stevie Crozier snapped her mobile shut and stuffed it into her pocket. Damn the man! Could he not just get on with his holiday and leave her to carry on with the job? But, no, it appeared that Detective Superintendent know-it-all Lorimer had something important to discuss and was she free any time this morning? Stevie slammed out of the hotel room in annoyance, wishing she'd had the nerve to tell him to get lost.

Yet he hadn't sounded as though he were pulling rank, she admitted, heading to the car park; his tone had been rather contrite, as though whatever he had to say might actually be a bit sensitive. And, if she were totally honest with herself, DI Stephanie Crozier was curious to know what it was that the detective superintendent wanted to share with her.

He was already at the water's edge when Stevie drove up in the Mercedes, Langley having been dispatched to interview the staff at Kilbeg Country House Hotel. As she closed the car door, Stevie looked at the tall figure standing in his wellington boots, arms folded and gazing out to sea as though deep in thought. She clicked the lock, a spasm of annoyance crossing her face as she realised there was absolutely no need to secure her vehicle in this part of the world. 'Old habits,' she muttered under her breath and began the short walk along the narrow path where countless feet over the years had trod from the roadside to the wreck of an old boat shed.

It was a windless morning, the still waters reflecting the swathe of pines from Leiter forest in a mirror image, the sun a hazy suggestion behind a grey veil of mist. Looking up, the policewoman noticed clouds of tiny flies descending from the oak trees that sheltered this part of the bay. She cursed inwardly, remembering, too late, the anti-midge repellent sitting on the bathroom shelf back at the hotel. By the day's end her fair skin would be peppered with tiny red marks, causing itching for days. Why on earth did someone who enjoyed his sort of salary come here year after year when he might have been swanning off to any part of the globe? Stevie raked slim fingers through her hair, hoping that the midges weren't already feasting on her scalp. A lone buzzard swooped past and disappeared into the trees, hunting something more substantial than flies. Of course, the Lorimers were bird lovers; she remembered McManus telling her. And Mull was a haven for all sorts of wildlife.

There was a pebbled area that might have been a slipway at one time, the different-coloured stones bright under the clear water, and this was where Lorimer stood, letting the tiny waves of the incoming tide lap over his feet.

'Good morning.'

He turned and smiled as she approached. 'Good morning. Thanks for coming. Hope I didn't take you out of your way.'

Stevie made a face and looked at her watch. 'I don't have all day, so let's get on with it, shall we?' she said brusquely. *Let him know who's in charge here*, she was thinking.

He gave her an apologetic smile then stretched a hand out as if to encompass the scene before them: quiet waters with the backdrop of the dark green trees and the sloping hills beyond, a thin line of mist draped languidly across them like a woman's silk scarf.

'Never tire of this view,' he remarked. She saw his back heave with a sigh and for an instant Stevie Crozier understood what this place really meant to him. It was the peacefulness, so at odds with the noise and bustle of the big city where he spent his working hours, she realised suddenly, following his gaze and beginning to see how the hills, sky and sea worked a certain magic on this quiet morning.

Then he turned and she saw his lips tightening as he regarded the fluttering lines of police tape that indicated where Rory had come to rest, the moment gone, the memory of a dead boy tainting this idyllic scene.

'You'll have seen the photos that were shot when we found the body,' Lorimer began, waving a hand at the spot where Rory's body had been, empty today of any ravening gulls.

'Yes?'

'It was a spring tide, really high, the highest on record for

153

quite a few years, in fact,' he continued, wading out from the water and walking towards an area several feet above the water's edge where clumps of sea pinks sprouted from the bright green turf. 'This is the exact spot where his body was lying. I knelt beside him . . .' He was bending down slowly, giving Stevie the impression that he was reliving the scene in his mind. 'I put my hand on the grass, here' – he was kneeling now, one knee on the turf – 'and do you know what?' He turned to give her a quizzical look.

Stevie shrugged, not knowing what on earth he was on about.

'It was bone dry,' Lorimer said. 'There hadn't been any rain for days and the sun had dried all the residual dew. I think the shock of finding him and chasing off these damn gulls—' He broke off, rising to his feet. 'That's one of the things I needed to tell you,' he said. 'Or, maybe to ask you?'

'Ask me?'

'How had Rory's body come to be above the tide mark on dry ground?'

'Washed up by a particularly big wave?' She shrugged, puzzled for a moment, her eyes turning towards the quiet lapping of the little waves as they caressed the stones.

'Okay,' she said at last. 'No big tides at this inlet, then?'

Lorimer nodded. 'No. So how did the body come to be lying above the water like that?'

'You think someone dumped it on the shore? But that doesn't make sense,' Stevie protested.

154

'No, it doesn't,' Lorimer agreed. 'It doesn't make much sense at all. But I think someone did move the boy's body. Maybe for it to be found,' he added thoughtfully.

'And is that it? Did you drag me all the way to Fishnish Bay just to tell me that?'

'I wanted you to see it for yourself,' Lorimer explained, a look of mild surprise on his handsome face. 'But that wasn't all I wanted to tell you.'

Stevie waited, arms folded defensively across her chest. There was something in his manner, something hesitant that had her wondering if he was about to say that he'd been appointed to take over the case. *Her* case.

'It was something that happened twenty years ago. When I was a young DC in Glasgow. Just starting out, really.' He smiled as though embarrassed by the thought of his younger self. 'We had a case where a young man was dragged out of the River Clyde. A red-headed boy, possibly around Rory's age.'

Stevie frowned. Where was he heading with this?

'There were marks on his arms and legs that showed where he'd been trussed up. Just like Rory,' he added, giving her a meaningful stare. 'He'd also been dead before he hit the water.'

'So? You want me to look at whoever killed that lad, do you?' Stevie asked, nodding. It would be okay, they'd access HOLMES, the database that was so up to the minute these days that cold cases were being reopened all the time, many of them to satisfactory conclusions.

'That's just it,' Lorimer said, catching her glance and holding it with his own blue stare. 'The perpetrator was never found. And, even worse, the boy was never identified.'

'Dear God!' The words were out of Stevie's mouth before she could stop herself. 'And you think there might be a link? A twenty-year-old case in Glasgow that coincides with this. *My* case,' she added. As though to remind him. 'Just because your victim had red hair?'

'It was the way they'd both been secured,' Lorimer insisted. 'Same sort of twist to their limbs. I keep thinking about that other boy and how similar he was to the one I found here.'

Perhaps you keep thinking about how you never solved that case, Detective Superintendent Lorimer, Stevie thought inwardly, fists clenched by her sides. *Or are you looking for a way to lever me out of this one?*

'Well, I have something to tell *you*, sir. I intend to find Rory Dalgleish's killer and I am not having this case muddied by anything that happened back in *Glasgow*, twenty years ago.'

Lorimer seemed to hesitate for a moment as though deciding how to reply then he gave her a crooked smile and shrugged his shoulders.

'So be it, Detective Inspector. I just wanted to see if you thought there might be some sort of connection . . . ' He broke off and gave an audible sigh, his eyes returning to the patch of grass where the young man's body had lain.

She looked at him thoughtfully for a long moment, wondering just what he was seeing. Was it the recent body he had discovered? Or a missing person from long ago?

Stevie stood waiting for him to speak but he did not seem inclined to turn to face her again, leaving her feeling as though her presence was no longer wanted. Was that it, then? Had he been about to pull rank and try to take over her case here on Mull?

'If there's nothing more to tell me then I'll be off, then, sir,' she said, and turned back along the track, irritated but also confused that he had brought her all the way down here to consider . . . what? Okay, the tide problem was relevant, Stevie told herself grudgingly, but this cold case was a piece of complete nonsense. Probably just a way for him to stick his nose into her case, she thought angrily, slamming the car door and yanking on her seat belt.

Lorimer watched as the silver car gathered speed and disappeared along the tree-lined road towards Salen. He hadn't expected her to be pleased, had he? And, to give Crozier her due, she was SIO in a murder case that was complicated by a senior detective having found the body. He'd wanted her cooperation, of course, hoped that she might ask him about that twenty-year-old case. Still, there was nothing to stop him from going back into the records himself, was there? Asking the right sort of questions might produce the right sort of answers. And there was one question that was like an itch in his mind: who were the people who had come to live on this island from Glasgow twenty years ago?

'You have to tell him, Aunty,' Fiona protested. 'You cannae just see something and no' let on, eh?'

Jean Erskine folded patient hands across her lap and looked at her great-niece. 'I haven't even told *you* what I saw and heard, Fiona,' the old lady said. 'And yes, of course I must speak to a police officer first. Jamie Kennedy will have to come up and see me, that's all.'

'No, Aunty, it doesn't work like that,' Fiona insisted. 'You're supposed to go to the wee caravan and tell Jamie Kennedy yourself,' she said. 'They need to get your statements, like,' the girl explained.

'Go all the way along the street?' Jean Erskine raised her sparse white eyebrows in mock surprise. 'An old woman who can hardly get out of her chair?'

'Och, Aunty!' Fiona giggled. 'You're no' as bad as a' that! See if I help you down the stairs, take thon wee zimmer that's in the close? Surely you can manage a walk along the street?'

'Well now,' Jean replied, eyes twinkling. 'Perhaps it would be better if the constable were to come up here and visit me. Then he'd be able to see the view from my window.' She smiled, waving a tiny hand, its paper-thin skin showing a tracery of blue veins.

'There is that, right enough,' the girl said doubtfully. 'Will I see if he can come up, then?'

Jean Erskine smiled fondly at her. She was a bonny girl, pretty and curvaceous like one of the old-fashioned movie stars of Jean's youth. Fiona Taig had never been particularly ambitious at school but she was a well-liked lass with a good heart and would ensure that the young Kennedy boy came up these two flights of tenement stairs to see the old lady who had known him all his life, not to mention his father and grandfather before him. She nodded her acquiescence. 'You do that, pet. That's a good girl.'

Fiona was no sooner out of the parlour door than the smile fell from the old woman's face. She hadn't wanted to see that little scene on Main Street, had she? But there was no denying that Fiona was right. And it might really matter to the police to share what she had seen.

CHAPTER TWENTY-ONE

Jamie Kennedy groaned inwardly as he caught sight of the girl coming along the road, a purposeful look on her face. It had been awkward bringing in Fiona Taig to make her statement but the look on Crozier's face had brooked no opposition. The young police constable had been all too aware of the girl's blushes as he'd posed the standard questions to her, uncomfortably aware of her darting glances at his face. It was no secret in the town that wee Fiona had fancied him since their schooldays and that her feelings towards him still lingered. Was she just seeking some sort of an excuse to engage him in conversation? Jamie wondered, watching her cross over to the town clock and the space where the caravan sat, its door open to the public coming and going along the main street.

Crozier had insisted that they positioned the vehicle in this way to encourage people to come in but it made the police constable feel as though he were sitting in a goldfish bowl, the continual greetings of the townsfolk interrupting the air of solemnity he was trying to conjure up about this case. And now here she was coming straight up to the caravan, his old school pal, Fiona Taig, one hand up to smooth the unruly curls that sprang back the moment she let them be.

'Fiona.'

'Jamie.' The girl blushed. 'PC Kennedy, I mean.' She tilted her head to one side, considering. 'Is it not awfie hard being two people at once?'

'How d'you mean?'

'Well. Everyone knows who you are, eh? Johnny Kennedy's lad. But you're someone else in that uniform, aren't you?' she continued, screwing up her eyes.

Jamie attempted a smile. He knew what she was trying to say and he felt it too, especially now that he was part of a team dealing with a murder inquiry.

'I've come to ask a favour,' Fiona went on. 'It's no' for me. It's Aunty Jean.'

'Oh, is she all right?' Jamie's face fell in alarm. Old Jean Erskine was a well-loved member of the community, a woman whose words of wisdom had been passed from one generation of children to the next as she taught the Primary Ones. How long had it been since she'd retired? Jamie wondered. She must be a good age now, at least in her nineties. His own mother and father had spoken highly of their schoolteacher, a lady who had instilled the basics of reading and writing along with good manners into scores of Tobermory children. They'd seen her six days a week, her welcoming presence in Sunday

School no different from her Monday to Friday manner, his mother used to tell him. And Jamie still remembered the old lady handing out the prizes at the end of the Sunday School session, her handshake firm and her smile warming each child as they came forward.

'Aye, she's fine,' Fiona replied. 'Well, she's got something she wants to tell you. It's about the murdered boy,' she whispered conspiratorially, leaning towards him so closely that Jamie could see too much fleshy cleavage escaping from her nylon V-neck top. He retreated slightly on the pretext of picking up his hat. Fiona's great-aunt Jean hadn't been seen on the street for a long while now, the rheumatoid arthritis having imprisoned her in that top flat above the Clydesdale bank.

'She saw something that night,' Fiona went on, the drama in her voice matching her wide-eyed stare. 'She needs you to go up and talk to her. Can you come up, Jamie?' There was a wheedling note in the girl's voice that set off alarm bells. Was Fiona at it? Was this just an excuse to lure him up the stairs behind the bank?

PC Kennedy stepped down from the caravan and glanced back towards the buildings where the street turned a corner. Jean Erskine's parlour window was in a turret looking down onto the street at an angle where she might see a lot of comings and goings, he thought. Maybe this was a genuine request after all.

'I cannae just leave this place the now, Fiona,' he said at

last. 'But tell her I'll come up when the other fellow's back, all right?'

'I suppose so.' Fiona Taig traced an invisible line on the stones with her shoe. 'D'you want me to wait here till you're ready?' she added hopefully.

'Your aunty keeps her door open,' Jamie said. 'Everyone knows that. I'll be up to see her when I can. Okay?'

'Aye, I'll tell her, then,' the girl replied, turning away reluctantly and slouching off, not attempting to hide her disappointment.

Jamie shook his head. Oh Fiona, he thought, I wish you'd find another lad to set your heart on. He watched as she disappeared back along the street, stopping to talk to one of the locals. She wasn't a bad-looking lassie, he told himself, watching the sunshine bounce off her curls as she turned back to point at the caravan. If only she didn't make her feelings for him so obvious. But Fiona Taig had never been one for the sort of subtlety so many girls seemed to employ around lads. He heaved a sigh. Fiona was the sort who seemed to like everybody, even the loud boy who'd disappeared after the ceilidh. He'd seen her shed a tear for him during the half-hour when she had given them her statement. But she hadn't fancied him, Fiona had said. *Not my type*, she'd added with a wee grin that Jamie had taken for a spot of mild flirtation.

It was a phrase that PC Kennedy suddenly remembered with a frown. They needed to find out which girl the red-haired lad had taken home after the dance but so far none of the local lasses had claimed that distinction. And maybe now he'd have some time to trawl through the boy's laptop to see if there were any clues in his previous life that might help uncover reasons for his death.

Fiona wandered along the street, wishing that Jamie Kennedy hadn't been so busy. Still, she was glad that the hotel where she worked as a chambermaid wasn't doing much business; why should she care if folk didn't want to stay in the crummy old place? There had only been three beds to change yesterday and Freda Forsyth had told her not to bother coming in till tonight. Okay, she'd miss the extra cash, but it was nicer hanging about the town for a while than having to find jobs to do at Kilbeg Country House Hotel. Besides, Fiona thought, casting a backward eye past the town clock, she could always look in again on Jamie Kennedy, now that he was ensconced in that caravan, before it was time to catch the last bus back to the hotel.

It was one of those rare July days when the wind had blown the sky clean of clouds, sunlight sparkling on the water. There were lots of boats in the bay, many still moored after the annual race from Crinan to Tobermory, and the girl dawdled by the quayside, admiring the bigger yachts at anchor. The faint clinking sounds from the rigging and the squawks from young seagulls were sounds that Fiona had grown so used to that she hardly heard them any more; they were summer sounds, part of the landscape as much as the main street crowded with tourists. She smiled as one family approached, a wide-eyed toddler hanging onto his pushchair, the mother and granny shepherding him along the pavement. They were strangers, no doubt here to explore the town in its guise as Balamory, its television counterpart. Some of the locals were heartily fed up with being asked the whereabouts of the characters' houses, but Fiona enjoyed pointing out Josie Jump's big yellow house on the hill and directing people to Breadalbane Street where the fictional PC Plum was supposed to live. It was nice being asked things like that, not swept aside as she had been with Jamie, she thought, pursing her lips in a scowl.

'Hey, who's stolen your scone, wee yin?'

'Oh, hiya, Jock.' Fiona stopped as the man in the battered panama hat patted her shoulder.

'Not like you to lose your smiles, Fiona.'

'Och, I'm just fed up with Jamie Kennedy, that's all.'

'How's that? What's he done to make your bonny face the colour of sour milk?'

Fiona shook her head. 'It's what he's *not* done yet, that's the problem.' She drew aside as a couple with a large hairy dog passed them by.

'He's to go and see Aunty Jean,' she explained.

'Oh?' Jock cocked his head to one side. 'Why's that then? Old lady not paid her TV licence? Dearie me, she'll no' like being kept in the cells, eh?' He made a long face and rolled his eyes.

Fiona gave a smile, despite herself. Jock Maloney could always make her laugh.

'No, nothing like that.' She beckoned him closer. 'Tell you what it's about.' She glanced around as though to ensure they were not being overheard. 'It's that laddie that died; Rory, the one at the hotel.'

'What about him?' Maloney's eyes narrowed.

'Aunty Jean reckons she saw something that night. Or rather some*one*,' she added dramatically. 'With Rory Dalgleish. She wants to talk to Jamie about it.' She made a face. 'But *he's* so busy taking statements from folks. Says he cannae just up and leave the caravan.'

'Who did she see?' The older man stiffened up, his expression suddenly serious.

Fiona shrugged. 'Don't know. She wouldn't tell me. Said it was better to talk to a local policeman first.' She was about to move on but Maloney seized her arm and gave it a shake.

'The night the boy disappeared, you say?'

'Aye.' Fiona frowned, pulling her arm out of his grasp. 'She's never a good sleeper. Sits up sometimes to all hours in that window seat. Sees all the comings and goings,' she said darkly.

'Well, I'm sure young Jamie will go and see her whenever he has a moment,' the man said shortly, stepping back into the middle of the street.

'Aye, I guess so,' Fiona said absently, letting the man stride away, rubbing her arm where he had grasped it so violently.

Strange bloke, Jock Maloney: happy to stop and blether one minute then as brusque as everyone else who passed the time of day with 'the Taig girl'. Fiona frowned: she knew some folk called her that in tones of disapproval ever since she had refused to follow her parents abroad, preferring to live here in Tobermory with her old aunty, and for a moment she wondered if Jamie Kennedy was one of them.

Her face brightened, though, as she recognised Eilidh McIver, an old school chum who was coming towards her.

'Aye, aye, chatting up the old men now, are we?' Eilidh joked.

'Jock Maloney? He's old enough to be my father!' Fiona protested.

'Just kidding,' the girl laughed, slapping Fiona's shoulder affectionately. 'Here,' she nodded at the Island Bakery a few paces along the street, 'fancy a coffee and a sticky bun?' She nudged Fiona's elbow. 'Give you a chance to tell me all the latest gossip, eh?'

'Aye, why not.' Fiona tossed her head. There was something rather thrilling about being so close to the whole murder case, taking messages from her aunty to Jamie Kennedy in the official police caravan. And it wasn't every day that she had the chance to be the first to relate a tasty bit of news to her pal.

'Aye, Fiona.' A few faces looked up as the girls entered the bakery. 'All right, lass?' someone asked.

The girl's smile widened.

For once in her young life Fiona Taig was the centre of attention instead of the local girl in the corner of the dance hall that all the boys took for granted.

She lifted the Perspex lid of the cake display, mouth watering in anticipation. Another few calories would make little difference to her waistline and besides, Fiona persuaded herself, she needed cheering up after that strange encounter with Jock in his panama hat.

CHAPTER TWENTY-TWO

'I think Rory Dalgleish was gay,' Lorimer said, moving the binoculars upwards as he followed the skylark's progress.

Solly pursed his lips but said nothing. The women had taken Abby up to Tobermory on a pilgrimage to Balamory, something that the two men had managed to avoid on this glorious July day. Maggie had been ecstatic about having Abby with them for a whole day and her little goddaughter hadn't seemed to mind leaving Daddy and Uncle Bill behind at the cottage. The family had slept in the spare bedroom the previous night, Abby tucked into a Z-bed in the lounge, the adventure of sleeping away from home keeping the child awake far past her usual bedtime.

Lorimer lowered the glasses and shot a glance at his friend. 'Aren't you going to ask me why I think that?'

Solly smiled his slow, easy smile, one hand smoothing the bristly beard. It was a gesture that made Lorimer think of the psychologist as some Old Testament prophet, considering how he was going to phrase his words to the waiting throngs.

'No, I wasn't about to ask you that. However, as you seem to wish to tell me . . . ?'

'It was something the press chap asked his parents. About having a girlfriend. It wasn't anything they said, just a look that passed between them as though there was some taboo there, something that was not to be spoken aloud.'

'And you imagine that it's about his sexuality?'

Lorimer nodded. 'Yes. It was as though they were afraid and ashamed at the same time.'

'Not every parent of their generation is able to accept the diversity of sexual orientation,' Solly remarked mildly. 'I know my own parents would have been appalled if I had suggested that I was gay. Though I'm sure they must have wondered about it at times,' he grinned.

'You?'

Solly chuckled. 'I was rather too engrossed in my work to make time for romantic interludes. That all changed the day I met Rosie, of course.'

Lorimer smiled back. He remembered the very night the three of them had been in that Glasgow flat, its owner lying dead on the floor. Solly had turned pale, his weak stomach unable to cope with such a sight. It had been something so diametrically opposed to Rosie Fergusson's brisk profession-alism that it was almost laughable now. It was a funny old world, Lorimer mused, remembering how the on-duty pathol-ogist had taken Solly home in her car. Theirs had been the start of such an unlikely relationship, yet it had blossomed

170

into love and marriage. Solly was no better now at scenes of crime than he had been back then, nor had he learned to drive a car, but he had different sorts of strengths to bring to the marriage, intangible things that undoubtedly gave Rosie a sense of security and belonging.

'So do you think they'll be looking for a young man rather than a girl who accompanied the Dalgleish boy after the dance?' Solly asked.

'That's just it,' Lorimer said. 'It needs to be taken into consideration. But I don't know whether Crozier and her team have any inkling about this. And I'm not at all sure I can feed the DI any more information without annoying her.'

'Tell your friend, the big chap from Craignure. What is it you call him?'

'Calum Mhor. Big Calum. I suppose I could,' Lorimer sighed. 'But I would rather one of Rory's parents had actually said something to Crozier herself.'

'Can you talk to them about it?' the psychologist asked.

Lorimer gave him a long look, his head tilted to one side enquiringly.

'Oh, no, don't even think it! I'm not even supposed to be here, never mind interfering with someone else's case,' Solly protested. 'Besides, you're the one the Dalgleishes seem to have taken to. I'm a total stranger to them.'

'But you're so good at getting people to open up to you,' Lorimer wheedled. 'And they're the sort of people who would trust a professor of psychology.'

'Even though it was his wife who cut up their poor boy?' Solly shook his head slowly. 'No, my friend, I think not. If none of the police have any knowledge about Rory's sexual orientation then I think there have to be other avenues to follow.'

'You mean closer to home?'

Solly lay back against the soft grass, the mingled scents of meadowsweet and bog myrtle wafting beside them, the lark all but forgotten. 'If it had happened in Glasgow you'd be talking to all his friends back there, wouldn't you?'

Jamie drew a deep breath as he reached the top stair. Crikey, he was out of condition, he thought. Too many of his mum's cakes and not enough exercise. Any day now he'd be sporting a gut like Calum Mhor! He fingered the memory stick in his pocket, wondering what the big police sergeant, DI Crozier and the rest of the team would make of it when he showed them what it contained.

He knocked at the door then pushed it open.

'Mrs Erskine? Jean? It's me, Jamie Kennedy. Can I come in?'

'Come away through the house, Jamie,' a distant voice called out.

Wiping his booted feet on the doormat, Jamie entered the flat and closed the door behind him. It was a strange place, he always thought, full of weird objects, like the two big dark screens covered in mother-of-pearl birds and flowers that Charlie Erskine had brought home from his voyages in the

South Seas. And pictures, loads of them covering up the flow-ered wallpaper; some faded sepia, of people from a previous century whose names Jean Erskine could give in an instant before commencing a little history about each and every one of them. That sort of knowledge would die with her, Jamie thought sadly. He'd urged Fiona often enough to get her great-aunt to commit these tales to paper or even a Dictaphone. But it never happened. Fiona wasn't too both-ered about the past, she only seemed interested in her own future; a future she kept hoping that he'd share, he thought with an inward groan.

'Come away in, Jamie,' Jean Erskine said, smiling at him from the high-backed chair that always sat in the recess of the big bay window. 'Come and sit beside me.' She indicated a smaller chair with a patterned cover of roses done in cross stitch, something that the old lady might have made herself in days before the rheumatism had seized her poor joints.

'You think I'm a right old nosy parker, do you, Jamie?' she twinkled at him as he sat down. 'But sitting here and looking out at everything makes me feel I'm still a part of the town.' Her words were not spoken with any wistfulness or bitterness for her condition, more in a simple matter-of-fact tone that the young officer admired.

'And who would ever tire of that view?'

He followed her gaze out of the window. The tide was in, right up to the edges of the old pier, and there were numerous boats at anchor in the shelter of Tobermory Bay. To one side the wooded hills rose above Ledaig, towering over the distillery and the garage plus the newer buildings that had emerged in Jamie Kennedy's own lifetime: the tourist office and the pub where folk spilled out into the sunshine with their drinks and food, the old jetty having been enlarged to encompass a decent-sized car park. Calve Island lay like a beached whale between Tobermory and the Sound of Mull, providing protection for the yachts that sheltered within this most sought-after of anchorages. Looking down, Jamie could see people walking along Main Street, locals stopping now and then for a blether, tourists more intent on examining the numerous shop windows that displayed a variety of crafts and gifts. His eyes took in the length of the street towards the old pier and beyond, then he turned to glance left and saw that Jean would only be able to follow a person's progress as far as the corner where the road took a sharp turn up the Back Brae.

'I want to tell you something, Jamie. I've told nobody else at all, not even my Fiona.' She cast a sly glance at the young policeman but he was still gazing out of the window as though only half listening to her words.

'I saw that young man,' she said softly, breaking into PC Kennedy's reverie. 'The boy who was found dead at Leiter.'

'How did you know it was Rory Dalgleish?'

'Fiona pointed him out to me a couple of times,' she said. 'What a head of red hair he had!' She smiled and shook her head at the memory. 'I could see it under that street light there.' She pointed at a lamp that stood just below the window. 'His hair looked as if it was on fire.' She laughed. 'I don't usually sit up at midnight, but it was such a clear night and the moon was shining straight into my bedroom that I couldn't sleep. I'm not the best sleeper in the world. Lack of exercise probably means I don't need so much sleep. Anyway, I was up so I made myself some cocoa and took it to the window. There's always something to see in the street after a Saturday night ceilidh.' She smiled.

'And was there anything in particular that you witnessed, Mrs Erskine?' Jamie asked, fiddling with his police cap, hoping he was sounding suitably official.

'Yes there was, PC Kennedy,' she countered, the sudden smile fading almost at once. 'I saw something that was a little disturbing.'

Jamie Kennedy sat quite still, letting the old lady gather her thoughts as his eyes turned back to the street.

'There were two of them there,' she said slowly, nodding towards the street lamp as though seeing the images in her mind. 'Rory and the other man. They were having quite an argument. I couldn't hear what they were saying, of course, even though the window was open for fresh air. Oh, hasn't it been a hot summer!'

Jamie nodded, hoping she wasn't going off at a tangent.

'I could see the boy was upset. The other one was shouting at him, pointing a finger at his chest, waving his hands in the air. Then he stomped off along the street, leaving Rory standing there looking quite miserable.'

'You could see Rory Dalgleish's face?' Jamie looked sceptical.

'I saw his bowed head and the way he stuck his hands into his jacket pockets,' she said briskly. 'Then he walked along the street. I watched him till he disappeared past the town clock.'

'And the other man . . . ?'

'Did I not say? I know fine who *that* was,' Jean Erskine said firmly. 'No mistaking *him*.'

Jamie took a deep breath. 'And who was it, Mrs Erskine?'

'It was Jock Maloney. Even on a dark night there is no mistaking that silly old hat that he always wears.'

Jean Erskine sat smiling into the twilight. It was her favourite time of day: everything was quiet now, the shops long since closed, the tourist buses away back to the mainland, leaving Tobermory to breathe its sigh of relief. Evening shadows deepened over Main Street, deserted now that locals and holidaymakers had ambled along towards the pubs and hotels.

The sound of footsteps coming along the corridor outside her sitting room made the old woman turn awkwardly in her chair. It would be Fiona, no doubt, coming to tell her all the latest news. Jean Erskine's front door was never locked, allowing the girl to come and go as she pleased.

The old woman tried to hide her disappointment as she saw that it was not Fiona after all. However, it would not do to seem inhospitable to any of the kindly folk who made their way up these long flights of stairs to pay a visit.

She smiled her welcome, though did not attempt to rise from her chair.

'It's yourself,' Jean smiled. 'Come away in and sit down.'

She turned back to the window, her back aching slightly from twisting around to identify her visitor.

'Another fine sunset,' she remarked, gazing up at the rosy-hued sky. 'It should be a grand day the morrow.'

There was no answering voice replying with a pleasant remark, only the sensation that someone was standing right behind her: sharing the view, perhaps?

Jean started as she felt the hands encircle her throat, raising her own in sudden panic.

The scream she wanted to utter was silenced.

Then the blood-red sunset turned to utter darkness as she choked against their grip, eyes bulging in her last astonished moment.

He stepped away from the body slumped on that chair, looking down at his guilty hands. How quickly they had forced life and breath from her old body! He covered his eyes and turned away, not wanting to see what these hands had done, anxious now to quit this place.

Then, unseen, the killer crept back down the stone stairs and disappeared into the darkening night.

CHAPTER TWENTY-THREE

Glasgow

Twenty Years Earlier

'It's a brown bag mo-rn-ing!' someone sang to the tune of 'Rhinestone Cowboy', the man's voice drowned in sudden laughter. Last night had been a busy one for the previous shift, the productions from several cases lying side by side in their brown paper bags. The level of humour was lost on the young officer who slid into his place in the CID room, however.

The boy's mutilated body stopped DC Lorimer in his tracks every time he came into the large room in Stewart Street. The image was pinned up on the gallery board that held various pictures of victims whose cases were still ongoing and he wondered how long it would be until someone else's fingers pulled out the green pin tacks and removed the photograph for good.

Immersion in water had taken its toll on that particular

body, of course, several underwater creatures making their small marks on the flesh. But it was the wasted face that bothered Lorimer most, the boy's eyes ravaged by marine creatures, no doubt, the way that he had seen crows peck out the eyes of dead lambs on snow-covered hillsides.

Looking at those empty sockets reminded him of the play that Maggie had been teaching to her sixth year kids. She'd taken them to see a performance of *King Lear* at the Citizens Theatre and he'd agreed to tag along. It was not one of Shakespeare's works that he knew at all and the violence had astonished him, particularly the scene where the old Earl of Gloucester had been attacked and his eyes plucked out: several pupils had visibly winced at the action on stage. The line from the play came back to him as he looked at the unnamed boy in the photograph: *Out, vile jelly! Where is thy lustre now?*

He sat down at his desk, glad that his chair was turned away from the board, though he could almost feel the image boring into his brain. The pathologist's team had done an amazing job in stitching the body back up but even their skill had not managed to repair the damage done to the boy's poor face. And so there was nothing to give to the press, no photographic image that would jolt someone's memory and give a name to the dead boy. Perhaps a clever artist might be able to simulate an image? he suddenly thought. Wasn't there a department at Glasgow School of Art that specialised in portraiture? Why not try to have an artist alter the photograph on the wall to make it presentable to the public eye? DI Phillips had more or less

179

given him the task of finding the victim's identity, so why not go down that route?

The thought was no sooner in his mind than he was gathering up his thin linen jacket and heading back out of the room. Nobody had pulled him out on another matter so far this morning and he just needed to let the desk sergeant know where he was going in case he was needed for anything else.

As he walked up towards the art school the sun slanted through the tall buildings; one minute he was in shadow, the next blinded by the morning light. It was important to look up in this city, he remembered his art teacher telling him at school, and she was right. The buildings were not just rows of tenements with shop fronts below, there were some real architectural gems to be found if you knew where to look; carvings on the edges of roofs, stained glass doors glimmering above a set of stone steps, the brass door handles lovingly polished. Glasgow School of Art was itself a testament to one man's greatness. Charles Rennie Mackintosh, one of the pioneers of Art Nouveau, may not have received the accolades he had deserved in his own lifetime but he was now revered as one of Glasgow's finest and the City Fathers were planning a worldwide exhibition of his work.

As he approached the towering building with its quirky design features – that metal arch with its dark purple eye suspended above the front steps – Lorimer felt a pang of regret. This was a place where he might have chosen to study; his grades had been good enough to try for entry rather than apply for History of Art at the University of Glasgow. Perhaps he might have completed a course here rather than dropping out and joining the police. *But then he'd never have met Maggie*, a jubilant inner voice reminded him.

Choices, he thought to himself. We make choices that can have such far-reaching consequences. What sorts of choices had led that nameless boy to his death and whose hands had bound him before strangling the life out of him then chucking the body into the river?

Less than half an hour later the detective constable skipped down the front steps of the art school, a gleam in his eye. *It could be done*, the lady in reception had told him. She'd taken him to an upper corridor where there were examples of some of the students' ongoing work, Lorimer looking suitably impressed at what the folk in the portraiture class could do. Yes, she would pass these copies of the photographs to the lecturer in portraiture when he came in, she promised.

But soon that won't be the only route you will be able to go down. One of these days we'll be able to recreate images on computers, the woman had told him. *There are all sorts of things to be found on the internet*, she had added with a smile. *Didn't the police use it at all?* Lorimer had shaken his head. He'd heard of the internet, of course, but only a select few police officers were being sent on IT courses, the rest struggling on with what other technology was at their disposal. *You'll soon be able to create a three-dimensional image of even the most wasted corpses*, the secretary had assured him and Lorimer had smiled politely, wondering just how true that might be. Still, he'd be glad of a humble pencil sketch to take to the newspapers, whenever anybody at the school could find the time to undertake that particular task.

He was just opening the back door to Stewart Street when DI Phillips came barging out, almost knocking him over.

'You, Lorimer! Come with us. Another corpse has been fished out by our friend at the Humane Society and we need to see it.'

'What . . . ?' Lorimer followed his boss out into the car park and into a waiting squad car where a uniformed officer ushered them into the back seats.

'George Parsonage,' Phillips continued, stretching out the rear seat belt as the car swung out of the police compound. 'The Humane Society officer. You know him?'

'The art teacher?'

'Ben's son, yes.' Phillips nodded. 'He's taken more bodies out of that river than you or I will ever hope to see,' he said grimly. 'A riverman, just like his father. Anyway, George has found a young man, naked and badly knocked about.' He gave Lorimer a meaningful look. 'Sounds just like the lad they pulled out. Your unknown red-head.'

There was a small group around the body when they arrived, several police vehicles already barring the way of curious passers-by. Lorimer noticed at once that some of the figures were clad in regulation white coveralls: the scene of crime officers were already in attendance, the on-duty pathologist amongst them, no doubt. Glancing at the group he was surprised to see that two of them were women, the tall figure of Dr MacMillan kneeling by the spreadeagled body and a smaller, younger one whose blonde hair was escaping from her mob cap. As she glanced up at their arrival Lorimer recognised her as the student from the mortuary who had been asking so many questions.

'Dr MacMillan, this is DC Lorimer. You'll not have met before,' Phillips said, crouching down beside the tall woman. Lorimer felt his face redden. He had watched this woman at work from his place behind the viewing screen but Phillips was quite correct, the pathologist had not been formally introduced to this lowliest member of his team.

Dr MacMillan gave him a brief smile before turning back to the dead man.

He was about the same age as their unknown victim, but instead of a thatch of red hair, this one was dark, as befitted his Asian origin, whatever that might be. Taking a step closer, Lorimer could see the fine cheekbones and sloping jaw, though at that moment he was more interested in whether the way the man's head lay on the wet grass was indicative of a broken neck rather than if he were Indian or Pakistani. The arms had been tied behind his back, the ankles fixed with twisted wires, pulling the limbs backwards so that the torso appeared to bulge outwards. He blinked, trying to remember exactly how the previous victim had looked. There had been no visible bonds left and the pathologist had hinted at some sort of twine rather than a wire. So was this a second murder linked to the first? Was Phillips's inkling correct that they were related to the gangland killings that sometimes erupted in this city?

The blonde girl stood up and took a few steps back to allow the pathologist more space for her examination, coming to stand next to Lorimer.

'Hi, are you with the SIO?' she asked softly.

Lorimer nodded. 'DC Lorimer, Stewart Street,' he replied.

The student grinned and stuck out a gloved hand. 'Yeah, I caught your name. I'm Rosie Fergusson,' she said, then turned back to the scene before them. 'That's my tutor, Dr MacMillan,' she continued, a note of pride in her voice. 'I'd like to be doing that some day.'

Lorimer raised his eyebrows then followed her gaze as the older woman went about her initial examination. The young student was quite intent on every single aspect of the proceedings, her head tilted to catch every word that the pathologist was telling Phillips. Lorimer smiled to himself. Who on earth would guess this girl's chosen profession just by looking at her? Appearance and reality did not always match up, as he'd learned from experience. Now he knew that even criminals and their ilk often appeared just like anyone else. The trick was to identify them by their behaviour and by sifting through every bit of evidence surrounding a crime. It had

184

been one of those moments of fate that had changed his own life, that day in the police line-up when he had been taken from his holiday job in the bank.

He'd been quite on his own in those days, rattling around in the small house where he had lived with Mum until her untimely death. There had been nobody then to thwart his decision to drop out of university and join these men and women who dedicated their time to catching criminals, nor any family member to applaud as he marched out of Tulliallan Police College many months later.

'Probably before you have your dinner,' Dr MacMillan was saying to DI Phillips. 'We'll give you a ring to firm up.' She turned and looked at Lorimer as though seeing him for the first time and he was struck by the twinkle in her hazel eyes. 'And you'll be bringing this young man to the post-mortem with you?'

'Aye, DC Lorimer,' Phillips said. 'We want to see if there's any link between this one and the body that hasn't been identified.'

Dr MacMillan nodded then strolled away, the girl giving Lorimer a brief smile before following in her tutor's wake, leaving the SOCOs to photograph the body and the area around it before the men who waited patiently on the upper embankment could wrap it into a body bag and transport it to the city mortuary.

'What are your thoughts on this one, son?'

Lorimer glanced at his boss who was looking at him with a faint grin.

'Could be the same perpetrators,' he began. 'But why was the first lad not still bound up like this one?'

'There's a story in there somewhere,' George Phillips agreed. 'Something for us to untangle from whatever mess these bastards leave behind them.' The DI's face was suddenly grim. The older officers were forever remarking how things had changed in the city since they had joined the Force.

'You think it's drug related?'

Phillips shrugged. 'There's always that possibility after a sudden, violent death. These types don't care what they do to people, even their own.' He kicked a stone viciously with the toe of his boot, sending it flying down the embankment to land with a dull plop into the river. 'Come on, I want to see if there's been anyone missing a young Asian family member.'

The area around Byres Road was largely populated by students, the rental flats owned by a variety of landlords, many of them second-generation Asians. Since the troubled days of partition between India and Pakistan, Glasgow had become a safe haven for many Asian families seeking a new home and some of these hard-working men had climbed the ladder of prosperity via corner grocery stores and restaurants to the heights of property ownership. There had rarely been any racial tension in the city during Lorimer's own boyhood; his classmates on the south side of the city had included several darker faces, clever kids whose aim was to become a doctor or lawyer, their quiet politeness and different religion simply accepted by their peers. Yet nowadays there was a feeling of resentment from some quarters that these successful businessmen had no right taking over swathes of property in certain parts of the city and this was something that DC Lorimer bore in mind as he walked up the hill of Great George Street to see a Mrs Singh whose telephone call had prompted his visit.

'She was a bit hysterical on the phone,' PC Winters told him. 'I heard the tape. Had to listen to it twice to make out what she was saying.' She made a face as she puffed uphill at Lorimer's side; she had only recently returned from maternity leave, her rounded curves straining under the uniform dark skirt and jacket. Thinking of Maggie's swollen belly, Lorimer felt a sudden sympathy for PC Winters. It couldn't be easy coming back to work full-time in a job as a police officer with the sort of stresses that entailed. Winters had been given the task of speaking to the family members, something that the female officers were always unfairly landed with, Lorimer knew.

'And she claims her son's missing?'

'Says he never came home last night and he has never done anything like this before. Come on,' Winters scoffed, 'a lad of nineteen staying out against his mammy's wishes? Is that so unheard of?'

'Maybe in families like theirs,' Lorimer replied quietly.

'They've got a much stronger sense of obedience than most British teenagers. Dad or Mum tells them to do something and they do it, simple as that.'

Winters raised a disbelieving eyebrow at him but said nothing more as they approached the close mouth of the tenement. The sunlight on this side of the road warmed his back as Lorimer walked up the hill, a sudden memory returning of the many mornings when he had left the subway in Byres Road and cut through Ashton Lane, climbing the steps up past Lilybank Gardens to his various university classes. It all seemed so long ago, not merely the handful of years he had spent as an officer with Strathclyde Police. And he remembered the intense Asian students from his own time; hard-working lads and lasses who lived at home, respecting the strictures of their families. No, there was something odd about this missing boy and Lorimer felt a sense of foreboding as PC Winters rang the buzzer next to the neatly typed name at the top of the list.

'Why's it always the top floor?' she grumbled, tucking a stray lock of hair under her hat. Then she yawned and blinked, making the detective constable wonder how much sleep baby Winters had allowed his mother the previous night.

'He-llo?' The sound of a woman's voice scratched over the intercom.

'DC Lorimer and PC Winters, Strathclyde Police,' Lorimer spoke clearly, his face close to the grille.

'Come up. Top right,' the voice said and then the buzzer let out a long note, releasing the lock on the heavy front door.

The close was chilly after the sunshine outside and they climbed the three flights in silence, their footsteps echoing down the stone stairwell.

The woman was waiting for them on her doorstep, a yellow and brown sari draped over one shoulder. Even before she spoke, Lorimer could see the anxiety etched on her face, making her seem much older than the mother of a teenage boy.

'DC Lorimer.' He held out his warrant card for her to inspect but Mrs Singh barely glanced at it, opening the door wider to admit them to her home.

'He's never stayed out like this before. Never,' she repeated as she led them into the front room, a large bay-windowed lounge furnished with heavy pieces of dark wood furniture, brightened by red and blue patterned cotton throws spread across the settee and chairs.

'Can you tell us when you last saw your son?' Lorimer asked, aware of the police constable sitting down next to the woman, Winters' chubby, sympathetic face turned towards Mrs Singh, her only aim right now to be a comforting presence to this distraught mother.

The questions began to draw out a picture of Desi Singh: *he was a good boy*, his mother assured them, *just a bit slow at school, not university material like his older brothers and sisters*, the anxiety in her tone tinged with regret and disappointment.

And all the while, Lorimer kept glancing at the framed photograph in the woman's hands, measuring it against his recent memory of the dead boy by the side of the river.

None of them spoke during the journey across Glasgow to the mortuary, the silence only broken by Mrs Singh's occasional sniffling into a handkerchief as she sat in the back seat beside PC Winters. How must it feel to anticipate the fact of your own child's death? Lorimer wondered. What did this woman really know about Desi that she wasn't telling them? The good boy, the one who'd been slow at school? Had he been bullied? Was he the sort of lad who was easily led astray by stronger personalities than his own? Had he ever been in trouble? She had shaken her head, refusing to admit to any more than she had already told them. Desi had been the one who helped his mother take care of the rental properties, the legacy of his late father, she had explained, trying to inject a note of latent pride into her voice and failing miserably.

And, if this boy lying in the mortuary should prove to be her son, what then? Would that open the floodgates to a different sort of story?

Later, after the screams and the tears, Lorimer managed to find the address for the eldest son, Desi Singh's brother; the mother had been unable to answer any further questions, too distraught at the sight of her dead son lying on a mortuary table.

*

Albert Road in Pollokshields was a mere ten minute drive from his own home on the south of the city and as he drew up at the flat, Lorimer recognised the area as a place where he and Maggie had attended a couple of plays in the new Tramway Theatre. He grinned ruefully; when the baby arrived such excursions would become all too rare.

Then, looking up at the windows of the top flat, the policeman's smile faded; they were here to tell a man that his brother had been murdered and to pose some difficult questions. As he turned to press the entry buzzer, Lorimer noticed that the sun had disappeared behind a bank of white cloud, the day far gone now, shadows lengthening along the grey streets.

'Mr Singh? This is Detective Constable Lorimer and PC Winters. May we come up, please?'

There was a pause then a non-committal grunt as the buzzer allowed him entry, making Lorimer wonder just how accustomed Desi Singh's brother might be to visits from Strathclyde Police.

A tall Asian man of about thirty stood on the landing outside the front door as Lorimer and his companion climbed the last of the stairs. His arms were folded across his chest, the detective constable noticed, a defensive stance that was confirmed by the mulish expression around the man's mouth, his large dark eyes hard and glittering as he watched the officers' approach.

'DC Lorimer.' He put out his hand but the other man ignored the gesture, his arms remaining folded as he stood, legs apart, in front of his door.

'The baby's just got to sleep and I'm not about to disturb my wife for whatever that stupid brother of mine's been up to now,' the man sneered. 'So just tell me why you're here and then go about your business.'

Lorimer hesitated, taken aback by the older Singh brother's words. Had young Desi brought shame on this family before? There was a wearied look about the brother's face that had nothing to do with babies or sleepless nights, more about the tedium of having to hear about his youngest brother's escapades.

'He's dead,' Lorimer blurted out. 'I've just been to the mortuary with your mother.'

The change in the man's demeanour was dramatic; the arms fell to his sides and his mouth opened in a silent O of disbelief.

'I think it might be better if we came in,' Lorimer said. 'We won't make a noise, I promise,' he added, taking a step forward and patting the man's shoulder.

The young man nodded dumbly, opening the door wider, staring at the tall detective and the uniformed officer as though unable to process the news.

Lorimer and Winters entered the flat, squeezing past an empty pram that was sitting in the hallway. It was one of the big, old-fashioned kinds with huge wheels and excellent suspension, ideal for rocking a fractious infant to sleep, or so Maggie's mother had tried to tell them when she had brought a catalogue for the prospective parents to see.

'In here.' The man ushered them into a large dining kitchen and slumped into the nearest chair, covering his face with his hands as though to blot out the world.

Lorimer sat down opposite, glancing around. The smell of something spicy was coming from a pot simmering on the stove, reminding him that it was dinnertime and Maggie would be expecting him at home. All over the city couples and families would be sitting down to their evening meal, discussing the day's events and relating whatever little new things had occurred.

'Raheem?'

Lorimer looked up to see a young woman in a pale pink sari standing in the doorway, a baby asleep in her arms.

Both men were on their feet in an instant.

'Go back into the room, Sarra. Please,' her husband entreated. 'I will explain later.' There was a note of desperation in his voice.

'Something's happened,' the woman stated, looking from one man to the other.

'Go back,' Singh repeated, this time more firmly.

She nodded reluctantly. Once the kitchen door had closed behind her, Singh sat down in his chair once more.

'Tell me,' he said. 'Tell me everything.'

There were darker clouds gathering on the horizon as Lorimer drove the last few miles towards his own home, his thoughts full of the interview with Raheem Singh. That his

193

youngest brother was dead seemed to be a complete shock, the man repeating over and over that *Desi wasn't a bad lad*. It was as though he had needed to persuade this stranger in his home of the dead boy's decent background. All of Lorimer's questions had been met with answers. Yes, Desi had run with a bad crowd, no, he didn't know any of their names, well, maybe one or two ... yes, they knew he had been missing from home but they hadn't thought to call the police. Desi wasn't wild exactly, just a bit wayward, easily led.

And so a hazy picture had emerged of the young man whose life had been cut short, a picture as yet incomplete and needing a lot more to give the detective some clues as to why Desi Singh had been murdered and dumped in the River Clyde.

There were no smells of cooking wafting from the open-plan kitchen when Lorimer opened the door. The place was strangely silent as if nobody had been there for hours. Had Maggie gone to her mum's? He looked round for a note then spotted his wife's handbag hooked onto the back of a chair. A sigh of relief made him retrace his steps out to the hall and begin to creep quietly upstairs.

She was lying in bed, curled onto her side, sleeping silently, a couple of pillows banked under her growing bump. It had been a rough night, he remembered now; Maggie getting up to go to the toilet several times, pacing the floor as the baby wriggled and kicked inside her, denying its mother any rest. She looked so young, he thought with a pang, dark curls framing her face, cheeks flushed pink against the pillow. They were both so young, so inexperienced in this business of becoming parents. Would they cope? he wondered, thinking of the Singh family with their fractious baby. Police hours could be brutal during a high profile case and he suddenly felt a pang of guilt that this lovely young wife of his might be left to take the brunt of caring for their child.

It was late, Lorimer thought, glancing at his watch, and she might have been sleeping here for hours. The least he could do was to go downstairs and prepare some supper for them both.

Perhaps it was the memory of the exotic scents in that other kitchen, but Lorimer was suddenly taken with a notion for a curry. It had been ages since they'd had any Asian food, Maggie's heartburn making it impossible for her to eat spicy meals. With a sigh he opened the fridge and examined its contents. He could rustle up a mushroom omelette when she awoke, put some salad on the side, but the unsatisfying thought of such bland fare made him close the door again with a disgruntled *humph*. It wouldn't take long to drive to the nearest takeaway for a chicken mushroom breast, his favourite choice. No sooner was the thought in the young policeman's head than he had picked up the car keys and was heading out of the door once again.

Asian Fusion was open seven evenings a week, a fact that

had endeared the place to the Lorimers once they'd moved to their home on the south side of the city.

'Good evening, my friend.' Mr Gill, the proprietor, flashed a toothy smile at Lorimer as he entered the shop.

'Hi, Sardar, how's it going?' Lorimer nodded to the grinning man who was standing behind the counter.

They had struck up a companionable friendship over the past few months and Lorimer had learned that Sardar Gill, a second-generation Pakistani whose parents had come over from Lahore, shared the Glaswegian passion for football. He and Lorimer had enjoyed many a post-match discussion on a Saturday evening after a Kelvin FC game when their favoured team had been beaten, Sardar's strong Glasgow accent expressing his disgust at the run of play.

'Ah, no' so busy the night. Too warm for curries maybe?'

'Not for me,' Lorimer declared. 'Chicken mushroom breast and a portion of fried rice, please.'

'Just the one?'

'Aye, my wife is expecting our first baby.' He wrinkled his nose. 'Not partial to curries right now, I'm afraid. But I've been getting withdrawal symptoms.'

Sardar Gill chuckled. 'Thought I hadn't seen you for a while.'

He took the order and disappeared through a narrow door that led to a kitchen, leaving the fragrant scent of spiced onions in his wake.

There was a television set at an angle on the wall for

customers waiting for their food orders and Lorimer glanced up, interested to see a new feature at the foot of the screen: the slow unfolding stream of news from around the world as it was bounced off a distant satellite.

It seemed no time at all till Mr Gill was back, a neatly wrapped parcel tucked into a blue polythene bag.

'Great thing, that,' Lorimer said, pointing at the newsreel.

'Ach, it tells you what you want to know, I suppose,' the man agreed. 'But it doesnae do the local news.' He shook his head and sighed. 'Some terrible things going on in this city, so there are. The wife's nephew ...' He drew a hand across his eyes. 'Terrible, just terrible. Found in the river. Just a boy ...'

'Desi Singh?' The words were out before Lorimer could stop himself.

Gill took a step back, the parcel still in his hands. 'How do *you* know ...? Oh, of course, you're a polis, aren't you?'

He leaned forward, the bag clasped to his chest. 'Well, maybe you can explain how a nice wee boy from a good family comes to a sad end like that?'

'I shouldn't really be talking about the case,' Lorimer apologised. 'My boss would have my guts for garters.'

'See young Desi?' Gill shook his head as though remembering. 'He was an okay wee boy. No' very many brains, know what I mean? But a harmless wee fella.'

'Ran about with the wrong crowd, I hear,' Lorimer said, trying not to show his sudden interest.

'Aye, I blame that school he went to.' Gill made a face.

'Nae idea how tae keep control of thae kids. Wee Desi was beat up wan time too many, if ye want tae know the truth.'

He rested his elbows on the counter, placing the blue bag to one side. 'Started tae run aboot with the wee hard men. Thought that would protect him, I suppose.'

'Asian lads?'

Gill shook his head. 'Naw, mair's the pity.' He edged closer to the tall policeman. 'I heard tell he was runnin' aboot wi' wan o' the McKerrell twins. Bad wee rascals, baith o' them. These boys got away wi' murder, so they did.'

Sardar Gill straightened up, his mouth open in a moment of alarm. 'Oh, I didnae mean ... shouldnae have said that,' he muttered, glancing around the shop as though fearful of having been overheard, even though there were no other customers in the shop.

'Why not?' Lorimer picked up the bag from the counter. 'Maybe it would help to talk to anyone who knew Desi well. These McKerrells? I guess we're talking about the same family that's well known to Strathclyde Police?'

The man gave him a curt nod and turned away, his face showing signs of regret at having already said too much.

The curry was barely warm by the time he had put it on a plate but Lorimer hardly noticed, so absorbed was he by the recent conversation. Glasgow was a village, folk said, and the Asian community was a close-knit part of that village, so hardly a surprise that the proprietor of his local Asian takeaway should be related in some way to the dead boy. Word of this would be spreading throughout the south side of the city by now, he mused; but would news of Desi Singh's death have travelled as far as the wider community that included the notorious gangland family?

CHAPTER TWENTY-FOUR

The lurid images on the dead boy's laptop had been at the forefront of PC Kennedy's mind all morning. *City boys!* Calum Mhor had exclaimed in tones of disgust as Jamie had flicked through the images of sexual bondage.

'BDSM,' Crozier had declared, all the men's eyes turning to her with a renewed interest. 'Explains why Rory was tied up. He was restrained,' she offered, looking at the big police sergeant who turned away, Kennedy noticed, his eyes to the ground as though unwilling to be hearing such things. 'Bondage and discipline,' she shrugged. 'Two guys having some fun until something goes wrong.'

Jamie shuddered now as he thought about what might have happened to the victim. Someone had overpowered him, taken his life when he least expected it and then, as though he were so much rubbish, had tipped him into the water, *removing the bonds first.* That had been the thing that Crozier had stressed. Evidence had been disposed of.

'Maybe they had dressed up, too,' the DI had suggested, to

Calum Mhor's obvious discomfiture. 'Would explain why he was found naked as the day he was born,' the woman had added bluntly.

The thought that someone from his beloved island home could be responsible for these acts of sexual aggression made Jamie Kennedy's blood run cold. And yet, here he was at the local garage, tasked with finding the whereabouts of a man he had always considered to be one of the town's most amiable characters.

'He's no here. He'll be at the Mishnish, more than likely.' Jimmy Beag looked up at the young policeman from his prone position under the lorry. Wee Jimmy, or Jimmy Beag as he was known, made a face. Jock Maloney might have been part owner in the garage once upon a time but he had drunk away his share of the profits long ago and it was days since he had put in any time at all in the business.

'Aye, well, I'll see him there, then,' Jamie grinned.

The policeman straightened his shoulders as he walked away from the garage. It was a fine day still and a stroll along the main street as far as the Mishnish Hotel would do no harm. He'd likely be stopped and quizzed by a few locals; no harm in that, the young man thought, especially if they came up with any titbits of information that they were reluctant to be seen sharing at the caravan on the pier. None of them would include hints about sadomasochism though, of that Kennedy was pretty certain.

It would be no surprise if Jock Maloney were to be found in the hotel bar. The man's drinking had worsened over the years since his wife had upped and left him for an Italian waiter who'd been working at the Western Isles Hotel, the magnificent nineteenth-century, turreted building that dominated the view at one end of the town. Mrs Maloney had left the boys behind as well, Jamie remembered. Keith was away at the fishing now but Richard was still at home. Was he not meant to be going to college after the summer? Jamie wondered. Surely the boy had left school now? He shook his head. It seemed years since he'd been at Tobermory High School himself, a laddie with big dreams of his own about university and travel. Well, he'd been away right enough, even though Inverness was hardly the end of the world, and he'd made his mark by becoming a police officer, he thought proudly, nodding and smiling at a wee lassie whose wide-eyed gaze followed him as he passed. No doubt another holidaymaker thinking she'd actually seen the original PC Plum out of Balamory, he grinned. It wasn't something Jamie minded; he was fond of bairns and sometimes bent down to talk to the wee ones who had stopped to stare at him. But not today. His pace quickened as he thought of what the old lady had told him. Jock hadn't said a word about a quarrel with the dead lad. Why not? Was there something that he had he been hiding?

'Aye, Jamie, in for a quick one?' Rab the barman gave a smile as Jamie entered the bar of the Mishnish. He stood for a moment in the darkened interior, its contrast with the blinding light outside making him blink.

'No thanks, I'm still on duty. Has Jock Maloney been in?'

'No.' Rab shook his head. 'Haven't seen him today, Jamie. Will I tell him to give you a call if he comes in?'

'Aye, do that, will you? Thanks, Rab.'

Jamie wandered back out into the sunlight. There was no great hurry, but he would like to talk to Maloney if he could. Perhaps he was up at the house, he thought, glancing up at the steep hillside that overlooked all of the harbour.

Tobermory had been built as a fishing port and the colourful houses along the main street had seen centuries of comings and goings as the town grew and thrived, houses climbing further and further up the slopes above, the winding braes encompassing rows of terraces. Jamie's own home in Rockfield looked out onto a grassy field and the roads that led to Salen and Dervaig. There were lots of incomers now, folk who were tired of city life and wanted to breathe clean, fresh air, their enthusiasm for their new home bringing a sense of renewed vigour to the place. There would always be the grumblers, moaning about the holiday cottages that lay empty during winter months, but on the whole the townsfolk were well integrated, accents from south of the border and elsewhere mingling happily with the local drawl.

Jamie's thoughts had accompanied him along the Back Brae and past the Western Isles Hotel to a row of neat terraced houses that lay between woodland and the nearby golf course.

He slowed as he came to the Maloney house. There was just an empty space where Jock's ancient pickup usually sat in the driveway but he walked up the moss-covered path to the front door anyway and knocked loudly.

There was no answer so he knocked again then bent down and opened the letter box. Only dust motes floated past his eyes as he scanned the hallway.

'Anybody home?' Jamie shouted.

There was no response. He tried the door handle but the place was locked up. Jamie frowned. This was Tobermory, where nobody locked their doors, even when they were out for a while. Odd, he thought. Why lock up?

A quick glance upwards showed that the bedroom windows were also shut fast.

'He's gone,' Jamie whispered to himself, a sense of foreboding filling the police constable's mind. What if . . . ?

He shook his head, already thinking of the need to contact the MacBrayne ferry ports to check if Maloney had left the island. Perhaps he should have been more vigilant, acted on Jean Erskine's words a lot sooner. It was time to speak to DI Crozier and share the old lady's observations – Jamie Kennedy was already dreading what the SIO would say.

Jamie knelt down, hands searching beneath the pot plants and several old metal floats beside the door that were tied together with pale orange twine. His fingers closed on a small, hard object. Yes! he thought, eyes shining as he fitted the key in the lock. It took several attempts as though it had not been used for a long time but eventually the door swung open and Jamie stepped inside to the shade of the hallway.

'Jock? Richard?' he called, but even as his voice fell dully in the silence he sensed that there was nobody in the house.

Jamie walked through to the kitchen where the breakfast dishes were still piled in the sink. Had they intended to return, then? He went back to the hall then took the stairs, slowly, keeping as quiet as he could.

There were two bedrooms on either side of the house, one with a neatly made single bed (Richard's, Jamie supposed) and the other with a duvet crumpled upon the larger bed. Drawers had been pulled out and the wardrobe door was lying open as though someone had made a hasty packing. He really should have a warrant to search the house, he realised, pulling back his hand as he reached out to open a bedside cabinet. He couldn't have his fingerprints all over this place. That would mean big trouble.

Instead he went back downstairs and entered the lounge, a square-shaped room with one large window that looked down towards the bay. It was an ordinary enough room with an old-fashioned brown three-piece suite in uncut moquette that looked as if it belonged to an earlier generation and a large-screen television that dominated most of one corner. Photographs had been placed on the mantelpiece, Jamie noticed, as his eyes travelled around the room.

Then he stopped and stared. A long wooden cabinet lay open, its contents missing. It was a gun cabinet, Jamie knew, and wherever Jock Maloney and his son had gone, it looked like the firearm had gone with them.

'You've got what?' Stevie Crozier clapped one hand against her left ear as the car ascended the steep brae above a scattering of white-painted cottages.

'I can't hear you,' she shouted, glaring out of the window as the big car passed a rocky embankment.

'Lost the signal,' she said in disgust, turning to the man at the wheel. 'Kennedy,' she continued, tossing the mobile onto her lap. 'For a moment there I thought he said he had a suspect, but the line broke up, so maybe that wasn't it at all.'

A few yards further on, past the entrance to Lettermore Forest, the road wound along by the coastline once more and Crozier's mobile beeped back into life.

'Yes? PC Kennedy?'

The woman's face hardened as she listened to the police officer's voice. It was typical of the lackadaisical attitude in these parts where everything moved at a snail's pace. Now it looked as if they may have lost someone who could be regarded as an important part of this investigation.

'She said they'd quarrelled?'

'Aye, that's right. Saw Maloney with the deceased after the dance, said they were having a heated argument,' Jamie agreed.

'And when exactly did you receive this information?'

A moment's silence met her acid tone. 'Never mind,' she

snapped. 'We're on our way back to Tobermory now. Check with the ferry terminals here and on the mainland. Put out a call to Oban to apprehend Maloney's vehicle.' She paused, thinking hard. 'Where exactly does this old woman live? I need to talk to her, find out *exactly* what she saw going on.' Her tone had an edge to it, suggesting that she was already doubtful about the local officer's capabilities.

'Move it,' Crozier told her driver, stretching out her legs and willing him to drive faster, biting her lip impatiently at the constraints of this single-track road and the oncoming vehicles sidling into passing places.

Jamie Kennedy stood in the shadow of the caravan, wishing for once that he had stayed in Inverness, far away from his home town of Tobermory and the dubious excitement of a murder case. There was an acid pain deep in his stomach, the knot of stress making him feel suddenly sick. If only he'd acted sooner on Fiona's message, made a better effort to locate Maloney. At least the folk at the ferry terminals at Craignure and Lochaline were now on the alert for any sight of Jock's van. Jamie heaved a sigh. He simply wasn't used to this rushing about everywhere: he'd become accustomed to the unhurried pace of life here, he realised, and now he was about to pay for these shortcomings. And, he thought guiltily, he hadn't even been able to tell Crozier about the missing gun.

As soon as he caught sight of the sleek shape of the Mercedes, Jamie pushed his way past the fish and chip van and walked smartly across the street, one hand in the air to draw their attention to a rare parking space outside the Mull Museum.

Crozier barely looked at him as she slammed out of the Mercedes.

'Which house?' she snapped.

'Top flat,' Jamie replied, pointing at the slate-roofed turret above the Clydesdale bank. He followed his senior officer along the dark passage between the tall buildings, glancing sideways at the ATM machine on the bank wall. No CCTV was positioned overhead, no silent eyes to record the comings and goings of people who walked away from the brightness of the main street.

Stevie Crozier tried to swallow her anger as she climbed the narrow stairs. There was no point in taking it out on an old woman, after all.

There was one door at the top, left ajar as though someone had recently entered, the evening light filtering from a sky-light window in the hallway.

'Mrs Erskine?' Crozier called out, pushing the door wider. 'Are you home?'

'Just go in,' Jamie suggested. 'She won't mind.'

'The door's open.' Crozier turned and frowned. 'Doesn't that suggest she's popped out for a moment?'

Jamie shook his head. 'She doesn't go out these days,' he replied. 'She'll be in the front room. Maybe Fiona left the door like that.' He shrugged. 'She's in and out to see her great-aunt all the time.'

Crozier stepped into the hallway, a look of doubt still on her face.

'Mrs Erskine?' she called out again, louder this time in deference to the frailties of old people who were invariably deaf.

'In here,' Kennedy told her, indicating a closed door at the end of the corridor. 'She's always in here.'

The DI rapped the door politely before grasping the door handle and pushing her way inside.

The old lady was sitting with her back to them, wisps of white hair escaping from a tortoiseshell clasp, her head to one side.

'She's asleep,' Kennedy whispered, seeing Jean Erskine apparently slumbering deeply on the winged chair.

Stevie Crozier took a step forwards then froze.

There was something about the unnatural angle of the old lady's head that made her put out a hand to stop the young policeman coming nearer.

She turned to catch his eye.

'What?' Jamie Kennedy looked from the expression on DI Crozier's face to the figure sleeping in front of her window.

Crozier moved slowly around the chair.

The old lady's hand had fallen to one side, thin fingers bent, holding on to nothing.

Jean Erskine's mouth was open, a gaping gasp that looked like it might have ended in a choking cry for help.

'What's wrong?' Kennedy was coming forward now, his young face puzzled.

Crozier shook her head, unable to speak for a moment.

'Oh, no!' The young policeman fell to his knees in front of the old lady. 'Oh, no! Oh, Jean!'

'Don't touch anything!' Crozier barked. Then, catching the officer by the shoulders, she hauled him to his feet.

'Don't touch her,' she said, more softly this time as she felt the policeman's body begin to tremble beneath her restraining hands.

'This may well be a crime scene, Jamie,' she reminded him quietly.

For a moment they stood together, looking down at the old woman.

Her lifeless eyes were wide open in an expression of horror that made Crozier shudder.

She had seen violent death before, but had never thought to find it here.

It did not take long for a small crowd to congregate around the corner of the pavement, the crime scene tape preventing further access into the lane that ran behind the bank. Masses of sweet-scented scarlet roses tumbled against the granite wall, the blue-and-white tape tied to their metal wires, a grim reminder to anyone who stood there of how shocking it was that a pretty place like this could conceal some dreadful crime.

'Has there been a robbery?' was a question on several lips. The front door of the bank was shut fast, opening hours long past, giving no apparent clues to the curious passers-by.

Detective Sergeant Calum McManus stood, legs apart, barring the way into the narrow lane that led to the rear of the bank buildings, his face impassive. It was times like this that he needed to be strong, he told himself. It was just the same as being in the lifeboat crew in a winter storm: there was no room for a consideration of self, just a grim determination to carry out one's duty.

The small team had been gathered together hastily after the discovery of the body, Crozier barking out orders, determined to find the man who had suddenly disappeared from his home. Kennedy had been dispatched to Kilbeg where Fiona Taig was working. DS Langley had been there today but he was sticking to Crozier's side like a limpet, Calum Mhor observed, as if to remind the uniformed officers that CID was in charge.

He looked up as a slight blonde figure approached, ready to ward her off.

'Sorry, madam—' he began, then stopped as she held up her hand.

'Dr Fergusson, pathologist,' she told him with a nod and Calum stood aside to allow the woman to duck beneath the plastic tape.

He glanced at her as she disappeared around the corner, his eyebrows raised in mild astonishment. So that was the famous pathologist from Glasgow, was it? Such a young-looking wee slip of a thing. Calum turned back with a sigh. That was a sign of becoming old, he reminded himself, and it was just a few years now until he reached retirement. He'd never thought too much about being away from the police – it had been a job he'd loved all of his working life – but right at that moment it was something that the big policeman desired with all of his heart.

The call had been as unexpected as any she had ever received. To come to a scene of crime like this, *here*, in lovely Tobermory, was far worse than if it had happened back in Glasgow. Island life was peaceful, she had been assured by the Lorimers; it was a welcome contrast to the city's high crime rate. Nothing bad ever happened there, she'd once heard Lorimer proclaim. Well it had now, she thought, as her feet ascended the last turn of the stone stairs and she caught sight of a uniformed officer standing at the door.

The old woman was still in the chair where she had died, Rosie saw with a spurt of satisfaction. Crozier knew what was needed here at the scene; although they lacked the immediacy of a scene of crime team with photographer and other forensic officers, the DI was determined to carry out the correct procedures. Rosie laid down the digital camera she had brought with her. It already contained photos of Miss Hoolie's house from *Balamory* and several of Abby, posing with a smile on her little face. Soon these happy family pictures would be joined by the sombre images of a dead woman, her body videoed from various angles in an attempt to tell the unknown story of just what had happened in the old lady's home.

Lorimer was waiting for the DI as she emerged from the building.

'Thanks for coming,' she said stiffly, looking up at him.

Lorimer nodded. It must have taken a lot for the woman to swallow her pride and call him. She had made it pretty clear that she didn't want him interfering in her case but now, with the discovery of a second body, things had changed completely for DI Stevie Crozier.

'Has Dr Fergusson finished her examination?' he asked.

'She's still up there,' Crozier sighed. 'You'll want to have a look, I suppose?'

She pulled a pair of surgical gloves from her pocket and handed them to him wordlessly. This was as much as could be expected, he mused; no white-suited figures up here, just the minimum of precautions against contamination.

'I've called for a forensic team to come over as soon as they can,' she said, a defensive note creeping into her tone as if guessing his thoughts.

'Good,' he replied, gesturing her to lead him up the winding staircase that led to the top flat above the bank. The detective inspector's hostility was almost palpable and for a moment Lorimer felt sorry for her. It couldn't be easy having him here, a senior officer who had experienced so many violent deaths in his career. Yet she had had the courage to ask for his help, knowing perhaps that his presence here was fortuitous.

'We've put out a call to the mainland to find Maloney,' she told him. 'His sudden disappearance makes him a prime suspect.' She turned to face Lorimer at the top of the stairs. 'His son's gone as well. God knows why.' She hesitated, frowning. 'We know now that they took the smaller ferry from Fishnish to Lochaline,' she continued. 'So they might be anywhere in the wilds of Morvern.'

'Or heading back down towards Oban?'

Crozier made a face. 'There are several ways they might have gone,' she agreed. 'Oban, Fort William, even further west into the peninsula. But nobody's seen hint nor hair of them yet. We'll find the pair of them, never fear.' Her words were belied by the way that the DI turned her head away from Lorimer's gaze. The Ardnamurchan peninsula was one of Scotland's last wild places, single-track roads winding around lochans and forests into miles of untamed wilderness.

The door to the flat was only slightly ajar and Crozier pushed it open with her gloved hand.

'Room at the end of the corridor,' she said, standing aside to let him pass.

Lorimer walked slowly along the hallway, noting the old-fashioned furnishings. He paused beside an ancient mahogany dresser that had numerous framed photographs displayed on its polished surface; a veritable rogues' gallery of

214

family portraits, some faded through time. He picked up one that showed a couple standing side by side, the young woman dressed in a fitted suit holding a posy of flowers, her hat placed at a jaunty angle; the man in a dark suit, the carnation in his buttonhole a dead giveaway. A wartime wedding, Lorimer realised, when coupons did not stretch to long white dresses, a happy couple tying the knot with no certainty of what their future might hold.

The pictures told a story of their own about Jean Erskine, plus what little Lorimer had been told. She'd endured the strictures and fears of wartime, the loss of her husband and all the changes that time had brought. And now her long life had ended abruptly.

It was wrong, he told himself as he entered the room where the body lay slumped on her favourite chair opposite the bay window. She ought to have breathed her last in the quiet of her own bed, a long deep sigh taking the former school-mistress from this life, with all its troubles and pleasures, into eternity.

'Ah, you're here.' Rosie stood up. 'I've just finished taking these.' She pointed to the small silver camera in her hands. 'Not what we'd use back in Glasgow but better than nothing, I suppose,' she whispered, aware that the DI was standing out in the corridor talking to one of the uniformed officers. 'She called you, then.'

'Did you ask her to?'

Rosie grinned suddenly. 'Well, I might have mentioned

that you and I had worked a lot of cases together. Maybe hinted that another pair of eyes could be useful.'

'So, no pressure from the chief constable?'

The pathologist shook her head. 'I think Crozier wanted you here, even though it might hurt her to admit it. She asked me for your mobile number and I saw her key it into her own phone,' she told him, eyebrows raised. 'Guess she really means to have you onboard.'

'Well, we're here for another ten days at least,' Lorimer whispered. 'I can help in whatever capacity she chooses, official or otherwise.'

'Seems a shame to break into your precious holiday,' Rosie observed.

'I didn't know I was going to find a body down on the shore,' Lorimer said. 'I think the holiday came to a bit of a halt from that moment on.'

'Anyway, allow me to introduce you to the deceased,' Rosie gave a grim little smile, 'the late Jean Erskine.'

Lorimer walked around the high-backed chair and squatted next to the old lady.

There was something about a dead body that robbed it of any sort of sadness: the act of putting an end to its life was over, the pain long gone and all that was left was the husk of the person who had once breathed life into the mere flesh and bones that remained. The corpse was there now to tell whatever tale it could: the wide-open eyes glazed in death had seen their killer in those last frantic moments; the marks around her scrawny neck had been made by the hands of a much stronger person, he guessed. Death would have been sudden and swift: a shock, a gasp for breath that ended in blackness. Where was she now, an old woman twice his age whose eyes had seen so much over her life? Was there a hereafter where she floated oblivious to pain or to the troubles of this world? Was she reunited with that young man in the photograph, clasping his hand once again in some other world where the spirit continued its existence, leaving the shell of its body behind? He hoped so, though such questions were never without their doubts.

'She wouldn't have put up much of a struggle,' a voice told him, and he looked up from where he knelt in front of the old woman's body to see Crozier staring at him, a questioning expression in her eyes.

'Maybe not,' he agreed. 'Wonder if she knew who her killer was?'

'We've spoken to her great-niece, Fiona Taig,' Crozier said. 'She's in a right state as you may imagine. The old lady was her only relative here. Her folks emigrated to Australia some time back but the girl stayed on, PC Kennedy tells me. God knows why. There's precious little work for youngsters on the island these days.'

Lorimer did not reply. If he had been born and raised in a special place like Tobermory, would he have wanted to travel to the other end of the globe?

'Any chance I can talk to her?' he asked.

Crozier nodded, her lips in a tight line. 'She's staying with a friend, Eilidh McIver. The hotel folk have told her to take as much time off as she needs.' She drew a piece of paper from her pocket. 'Here, that's the address.'

Manor Gardens was a small crescent of bungalows recently built on the outskirts of the town, its squares of gardens planted out with clumps of annuals and a few windblown young shrubs. Number nine was at the far end a little set back from the rest. A narrow lane ran down one side of the house, tapering away towards a building site where several other homes were under construction, their dark grey breeze blocks contrasting with the dazzling white of the occupied houses.

The door was opened seconds after Lorimer rang the bell, as though someone had stood watching for his arrival. A tall, spare man stood there, his open-necked shirt and thick socks making him appear as though he had been caught in the process of undressing.

'Hugh McIver. Come away in.' Eilidh's father stood aside for Lorimer to enter the house.

The short hallway opened into a lounge-cum-dining room where three women sat huddled together on a settee. One of them immediately rose to her feet and came towards him, casting an anxious glance at the two young women behind her.

'Oh, you're the superintendent,' she said in a breathy lilting voice that Lorimer recognised as native to the island of Lewis. 'Fiona, shall we leave you two in peace, lass?'

Lorimer looked at the young girl sitting on the settee, her hands clutching an oversized handkerchief. Her face was blotchy from weeping as she looked up at him.

'Fiona, I am so sorry for what's happened.'

She nodded as though such a statement was only to be expected, then he saw a quivering sigh shudder through her body.

'Think it was my f-fault,' she gulped. 'If I hadnae told—' She broke off, biting her lip to stop a fresh bout of crying.

'You mentioned something to Jock Maloney?'

The girl nodded. 'Told him Aunty Jean . . . ' There was another pause while she blew her nose.

'I mentioned that Aunty Jean had seen someone quarrelling with the lad who died.'

She looked up at him in mute appeal.

'Did you have any reason to suspect that it had been Maloney himself?'

Fiona shook her head, great eyes turned to his own.

'Well then, stop blaming yourself. Okay?' His tone was as gentle as he could manage.

'It wasn't just Jock I told,' Fiona said at last, a small defensive note in her lilting accent. 'I told loads of folk down the town. And Lachie, of course. Had a blether with him outside the garage before I caught the bus back to the hotel.'

'Lachie?'

Fiona nodded. 'The gardener at Kilbeg. I often get a lift

from him if he's going back home after a shift. He stays with his sister here in Tobermory.'

Lorimer stifled a sigh. The number of people who had shared Jean Erskine's supposed secret had probably multiplied considerably in a small place like this; a murder was such a rare event that any gossip about the boy, Rory, would have been a big deal and he could imagine the girl sharing her news about her aunt's sighting with a sort of relish. It was only human nature, after all.

'Did Jock Maloney seem upset when you told him about what your great-aunt had seen?'

Fiona's eyes slid away from his for a moment as she considered.

'I don't think I'd call it upset,' she began, a frown creasing her brow. 'But he suddenly seemed a bit less friendly, if that makes sense. I thought he was just being moody.'

'Is that normal for him?'

'No, not really. He's usually a good laugh,' she said. There was a pause as she blew her nose again then gazed into Lorimer's eyes. 'I can't imagine Jock doing anything bad, honest I can't. He's a nice man, even when he's fu' of the drink. Some guys aren't.'

Lorimer nodded, wondering just who had soured this young woman's attitude. Had she seen belligerent drunks at the hotel where she worked? Or, more likely, had she witnessed the unpleasant side of drunkenness after some of the late-night dances in the town?

'Okay, Fiona. It looks as if the McIvers are looking after you well here. DI Crozier will let you know when you might go back to your aunt's house.'

Fiona shook her head. 'Don't think I'll ever be able to face being there without her,' she whispered, reaching out and clutching the policeman's hand.

Jock drove along the narrow road, his eyes glaring furiously at the twists and bends. The forestry turn-off ought to be somewhere just along here, and then, hidden in the depths of the trees, the old woodman's hut where he and Richard could hide out. He cast a quick glance at the young man hunched on the passenger seat beside him. It wasn't his fault he'd turned out the way he was, Jock supposed, eyeing the dark hair falling into his face and the soft skin on his son's curving jaw that rarely needed a razor. He'd been proud of his boys once, he reminded himself. His Keith and his Richard, named after one of his ex-wife's favourite rock musicians.

He'd had such hopes for his boys, dreams that they'd make their own names out in the world, away from the restrictions of small island life. Keith had done all right but Richard ... oh what had happened to make Richard turn out like this? How had it happened? Was it something that had gone wrong before he'd even been born? Or had the boy turned away from normal heterosexual behaviour for some other reason? And could he be to blame for that, somehow?

The questions chased each other round and around Jock's

brain as he slowed down to take the next bend on the road, his heart thumping as he gave a quick glance in the rear-view mirror just in case they were being followed. If only the old woman hadn't seen him on the street that night . . .

Now they were running from the forces of the law, two fugitives who were mixed up in a boy's untimely death.

CHAPTER TWENTY-FIVE

Glasgow

Twenty Years Earlier

The pains began as she rolled over onto her back, something that the midwives at the antenatal clinic had told Maggie to expect. Sharp pains, between her legs, as though a muscle had suddenly gone into spasm. It would pass, she told herself, like the intermittent heartburn that seemed to come on a daily basis now.

Maggie wiped her brow, surprised to find beads of sweat coming off on the back of her hand. It was a hot afternoon and she had decided to lie down for a nap, the previous night's sleep having eluded her. A quick swallow of water from the glass at her bedside did nothing to help a faint sense of nausea. Was she coming down with something, was that it? Nothing at all to do with the pregnancy? She lay back with a groan. Everything was to do with the pregnancy; her bladder and stomach were all being squashed any old way by the baby, weren't they? No wonder she was feeling sick.

Well, at least the wee one had finally stopped kicking her like a football and gone to sleep. Typical, Maggie thought with a smile, the baby deciding to drop off in the daytime after a night of rumbustious activity. It had to be a wee boy, she thought, affectionately running a hand across her belly; they were such restless creatures, always on the go. She thought of the boys in her first year class, untidy wee tykes, most of them, although they had begun the academic year smartly dressed in their uniforms, ties neatly knotted, shirts clean. But by the end of the session, most of them had copied the older lads, got into scrapes, gathered up enough courage to whisper cheekily behind their hands when the teacher wasn't looking – she always knew, even when her back was turned as she wrote something on the blackboard. But then the last day of term had come and these same little scamps had surprised her by shyly presenting gifts and cards to wish her well. Maybe a boy wouldn't be so bad after all?

The next pain made her cry out, then a hot, wet feeling on her pants made her sit up and pull aside the sheet.

Maggie stared in horror at the blood trickling down her pale thighs.

Was this what they called a *show*?

It couldn't be happening so soon. Her due date was still weeks away. Unless there had been some mistake with the doctor's calculations? That could have happened, couldn't it?

Heaving herself up into a sitting position, Maggie stretched out one hand for the telephone that lay on her bedside table. With trembling fingers she dialled the number of the surgery, wondering already if her next call ought to be to her husband.

'I'll let him know, Mrs Lorimer,' the voice said, leaving Maggie with the panicked feeling that she was on her own with whatever was happening. Another spasm hit her lower abdomen and she cried out, real tears stinging her eyes.

'Mum,' she moaned, remembering that her mother was away in Edinburgh today, a visit to an elderly cousin whose number Maggie didn't have. And Mum had never expressed an interest in having a mobile phone of her own. *I'll be there if you need me*, she'd said, only a day or so ago. But now she was somewhere that Maggie couldn't reach her and tears of self-pity began to roll down her cheeks.

She struggled to the edge of the bed, dashing them away with the back of her hand, angry with herself for the sudden weakness. People had babies all the time, she told herself. She'd just got the dates wrong, that was all, she reassured herself. It would be a late July baby, not a September one after all.

But when she looked back down at the red stain spreading below her thighs, Maggie felt a sudden fear grasping at her heart.

He didn't deserve that glorious rainbow arching across the fields. A stand of birches obscured the sky for a moment as the train swung around a bend on the track, then it was there once more, faint hues from crimson to orange blending past the rain-streaked window of the railway carriage. None of the people in the seats opposite him seemed to have noticed, heads down in newspapers or magazines, a few already tucking into their sandwich lunches. He hadn't eaten anything for two days, stomach heaving at the very thought of food.

The man staring out of the window licked dry lips, wondering how to explain his lack of hunger to the folks back home. A gastric bug, he'd pretend. Hadn't he always been good at pretending, conning the women in his family into letting him play hookey from school when all he'd really wanted was to watch the children's programmes on television?

His head was deliberately turned away from his fellow passengers, a strange reluctance to let anyone look at his face lest they see what he had seen in the mirror: the face of a killer.

The train rocked steadily along, pine trees fringing sky that was a shade of heavenly blue behind grey and threatening clouds. The weather might change several times over before they arrived at the ferry terminal. Would the sea be calm or choppy for his crossing? The hills clear or blotted out by mist? Did it matter? Once he had played a game with himself, trying to see if there would still be that frisson of joy as the bus turned the corner at the top of the Guline Dubh, the distant town glimpsed for a moment.

But now, despite the hasty flight from the city, he was not even sure that he ought to be going back to Tobermory again, a place that would surely be darkened by his very presence, contaminating the town with a shadow of evil.

CHAPTER TWENTY-SIX

Glasgow

Twenty Years Earlier

'Get yourself home, Lorimer,' DI Phillips ordered. 'Sounds like you'll be wetting your baby's head pretty soon, eh?'

The DI slapped him on the shoulder and Lorimer returned a weak grin. They all knew in a vague sort of way that his wife was expecting their first child but the day-to-day business at A Division took precedence over even the most important family events. Or at least until now, Lorimer told himself, taking the stairs two at a time. George Phillips had been decent in telling him to push off, hadn't he? He was a father himself, of course. Had he been at the birth of either of his two girls? It was something he would ask him later, he thought, hurrying out to the car park, once everything was over and they were celebrating with him.

The nurse at the hospital had been fairly brusque on the

telephone, letting him know that his wife was in the labour suite and wanting him to come as soon as possible. Every light seemed to change to green as though Fate were urging him on as he sped across town, foot on the accelerator of his old Toyota, desperate to be at her side.

Maggie stared up at the ceiling, its bright lights making her blink. She had been given this hospital gown, a thin cotton affair that hardly covered her, but none of that seemed to matter now. All she was concerned about was what was happening in her body, the pains increasing so that she cried out, unable to help herself. The doctor had hurt her, his fingers probing in the secret cavities that seemed not to belong to her any more. He'd nodded towards the nurse, both of them making eye contact above their green masks, their heads shrouded in surgical caps.

It wasn't what she had expected. Birth was supposed to be a joyous affair, wasn't it? Painful, yes, the midwives hadn't minced their words about *that* aspect. But the mess left on her bed at home, the two paramedics shuffling her onto that stretcher, covering her with a blanket and strapping her body down, that wasn't what Maggie Lorimer had anticipated at all.

And where was Bill? Would he get here on time? She felt another contraction, a wave of pain shuddering through her body.

'Here, breathe in through this,' a voice told her, and

Maggie saw a pair of deep brown eyes above the nurse's mask as she handed Maggie a black rubber device.

'Gas and air,' the nurse told her. 'It'll ease the pain,' she added, placing the bulbous thing over Maggie's nose and mouth. 'Deep breath, that's good.'

Then the thing was taken off and Maggie gasped, simultaneously glad to be rid of the horrid thing yet relieved at the respite from pain that it had produced.

'A wee bit early, aren't we?' The nurse patted her hand. 'Never mind, soon be over.' The woman's eyes crinkled in a tremulous smile above her mask then Maggie watched her glance over at the doctor who had taken his stethoscope from around his neck and was listening for the baby's heartbeat. Maggie felt the cold steel go from one part of her belly to another, her eyes seeing only the top of the doctor's head as he bent to his task.

Then, as he rose, there was a moment of utter silence when he looked across at the nurse and gave a tiny shake of his head.

'What? What's wrong?' Maggie struggled to sit up, frantic now that something bad was happening to her baby.

'Shh, don't get upset now.' The nurse was at her side, holding her hand. 'Lie back, there's a good girl.'

'Just going to give you something that'll help things along, Mrs Lorimer,' the doctor was saying and there, in his gloved hands, Maggie saw the syringe and a faint arc of moisture catching the light as he approached the bed.

*

'William Lorimer. My wife's having our baby. Margaret Lorimer,' he gasped out as he reached the reception desk.

'Up to the third floor. Lift's just along there.' The woman pointed out before looking back down at her paperwork.

Lorimer waited as the lift slowly made its descent from an upper floor, watching each lighted numeral as it changed. Then, with a *ping*, the doors were open and several people pushed past him on their way out.

He was alone in the lift as it rose smoothly and silently upwards, his heart still thudding after the mad dash across the crowded hospital car park. Then the doors opened, light flooding into the corridor as he gazed frantically at the signs on the wall that indicated directions to different wards. The labour ward: that was surely where she would be? he thought, his long strides taking him down another corridor.

'Can I help you?' A curly-headed nurse behind a U-shaped desk looked up as he approached the end of the corridor.

'Margaret Lorimer? I'm her husband. I got a call ...' Lorimer was suddenly lost for words.

'Just take a seat there, Mr Lorimer, will you. I'll find out how she's doing,' the nurse said, her eyes not meeting his own. And her tone was gentle, the sort of voice that PC Winters, the female police officer, might put on when she was talking to a grieving parent.

Lorimer stood, watching as she disappeared through a doorway, a feeling of utter helplessness washing over him. Something was wrong, he knew that, had known it from the

231

time the desk sergeant had found him to say Maggie was on her way to hospital. It was too early, far too early. Could a little baby survive being born eight weeks prematurely? He didn't know.

It was true what they said, he thought, this pacing up and down might be a cliché but who could possibly sit still when the life and death of his family were happening somewhere beyond that closed door?

'I'm sorry,' somebody was saying. 'So sorry.' Whose voice was it? Was it someone she knew?

Maggie drifted on the hazy waves of a drug-induced sleep, the voices coming and going. Bill was there, she knew that now, could feel his hand stroking her face. A great sigh trembled through her as she remembered where she was.

Then her mouth opened in a silent cry.

The baby was gone. Born before his time.

'Oh Maggie, my love, my love,' she heard her husband whisper just as the waves of sleep engulfed her once more, pulling her under the blankets of darkness.

CHAPTER TWENTY-SEVEN

Glasgow

Twenty Years Earlier

'Take as much time off as you need,' George Phillips's voice was gruff with emotion.

Words not said, thought Lorimer, words felt inside but never uttered: wasn't that just typical of a policeman? We duck out of confronting our own horrors, he told himself, so beleaguered are we with the awful things that other people do to one another.

'Thanks, boss,' he replied. 'I'll be back soon.'

'No need to hurry.' There was a pause. 'That nice wife of yours needs you there more than we do right now.'

He put the telephone down at last, heartened by the concern in the DI's tone. Phillips wasn't one for flowery speeches at the best of times; he told it as it was, giving his officers the facts to work with and expecting them to deal with the fallout from criminal cases and the messes that human beings made of their lives. So he hadn't been surprised by the terseness of the phone call. Phillips had said everything he'd needed to hear.

'Who was that?' Maggie asked, walking slowly from the kitchen, her hands clasped round a glass of water.

'DI Phillips,' Lorimer replied, looking up at her pale face, a pang of sympathy washing over him at the sight of the unwashed hair tumbling around her shoulders. 'He's told me to take some time off.'

Maggie nodded, eyes downcast as she shuffled past him on her way to bed once more. Lorimer caught her arm and shepherded her gently up the stairs, feeling her wince as something inside caused her discomfort. What had she been through? His mind refused to go there; he would not try to imagine the labour suite and the cries of anguish she must have uttered.

'Here,' he said, helping her into bed. 'Want some company?' He smiled crookedly, the edge of the duvet in one hand, an invitation to lie down beside her, warm her body with his own.

But Maggie said nothing, just shook her head, looking away from his face as though afraid to see the tenderness in his eyes.

She had been sent home after one night in hospital, a lonely night when he had stared at their bedroom ceiling, unable to sleep for the knot of pain in his chest; *why?* The question that could never be properly answered thudding in his brain.

*

'I should have been here,' Mrs Finlay wept, hugging her son-in-law, patting his back as if she knew how much it affected him too.

'I don't think that would have made any difference, Alice. They say the baby had stopped breathing before ...' He broke off, swallowing hard.

'I know, I know.' She tried to smile through her tears. 'It's just so sad, all those months she's been carrying it ... *him*.' She shook her head, unable to continue.

'We'll have other babies,' he assured her. 'Just wait and see. Whole tribes of little Lorimers will be running around making your life hell before you know it.'

She laughed. 'Give her a chance, she's only just home.'

They smiled at one another then, Lorimer catching her hand lightly in his own.

'Cup of tea?' Alice gave a sigh then sniffled into her hand-kerchief, the tears coming once again. 'S-silly old woman that I am,' she gulped.

'Hey, don't say that,' Lorimer protested gently, catching her arm before she moved away towards the kitchen. 'We're all grieving for our little boy. What's so silly about that?'

'I know,' Alice nodded. 'But it doesn't seem as though he was ever really here, does it?'

He let her go, watching as she comforted herself with the familiar routine of filling a kettle at their sink and switching it on, taking mugs from the cupboard and setting them on a tray. It was the little things that were keeping this good woman going, he realised. She had already filled their washing machine with laundry and would probably peg it out later on the line if the day remained dry.

Lorimer looked around the kitchen area. There had not been enough money to make any changes since they had bought this house and the cupboards looked tired, grey marks showing where countless fingers had opened and closed them over the years. Maggie had scrubbed the place till it had shone but there was no denying that the kitchen needed more than that. Perhaps if he could refit the place? Make it into something that they had both chosen? He tried to imagine the sort of kitchen that Maggie would like. A light oak, perhaps? Something solid that would last for years to serve the needs of a growing family. He wandered around, seeing it in his mind's eye: a run of worktops in a paler colour, perhaps, to contrast with the timber; new appliances to replace the old stuff left by the previous owners. His salary had increased this year and so maybe they could afford to put a bit more onto the mortgage. Would a suggestion like that help take her mind off the awfulness of the past two days?

'Here.' Alice Finlay shoved a mug of tea into his hands. 'I'll take Maggie's up to her.' The older woman bustled off, the tea tray lined with a linen cloth, a small feminine touch that made Lorimer feel suddenly inadequate. Alice was doing a grand job of looking after her daughter while he sat here staring into space.

'Why don't you go down to the shops for the papers?'

Lorimer turned with a start, hardly realising that his mother-in-law had come back downstairs again.

'We could do with some more bread and milk,' she added. 'And if you could buy a chicken and a leek I'd make you both a pot of soup. There are some carrots in the fridge.'

'Sure,' he agreed, setting down the half-finished tea and glancing around to see where he had left his jacket after they'd returned home from the hospital, the car keys still in its pocket.

'Oh, and don't forget a bunch of parsley, will you?' Alice called out as he headed for the front door.

It was a ploy, of course, something to make him feel useful, he supposed. He liked Alice; she was a good sort to have around, her natural humour and non-stop chatter a boon to them right now. Though there was little to laugh about, Alice still managed to carry on with a bright, brave smile as though everything would be fine again. And it would, Lorimer told himself as he eased the old car away from the drive. *Everything passes*, she had said, giving him a quick hug when they had met in the hospital corridor. And it was true. Alice had survived the loss of her husband, Maggie's father, and they would overcome the loss of this tiny baby. It would just take time; that was all.

'Another cuppa? Coffee this time?' Alice asked him, setting down the empty laundry basket. 'In fact, why don't you sit down and give yourself a chance to read the papers? Maggie's sleeping,' she added, before he could protest, dropping her voice and giving a meaningful glance upwards.

And so he found himself sitting down in the middle of a summer's morning, the papers by his side. Alice had left the back door open and Lorimer's eyes caught the shaft of sunlight spreading its yellow light across the kitchen walls. For a moment he sat quite still, listening to the sound of a blackbird singing from the shrubbery outside. The world still turned on its axis, nature oblivious to the hurt that was happening inside this particular house. It was a comforting thought, somehow.

'Thanks, Alice,' he said as the older woman set down a mug of black coffee and a plate of chocolate digestive biscuits on the table by his side. 'You're spoiling me.'

'Maybe you need a bit of spoiling,' she huffed, turning back and busying herself with the vegetables for the soup. 'Put your feet up. Never know when you'll get the chance again,' she added darkly. 'All those hours you put into that job.'

It was only minutes later, skipping past the main headlines, that he found it, a small paragraph letting the world know that an arrest had been made in the case of the young Asian man whose body had been pulled from the river. McGarrity, he supposed, though there was no name given by the *Gazette*'s crime reporter and no mention of that other one, the red-haired boy. He could call the station, he supposed, but talking to a fellow officer was suddenly the last thing that he wanted to do. Instead a feeling of inertia swept over him, making him lay down the paper and close his eyes, blotting out the world for a few sweet moments.

Alice Finlay looked over her shoulder and sighed. Poor lad probably hadn't slept a wink for these past two nights. Her mouth trembled for a moment as she thought of her daughter lying upstairs. It wasn't fair. It shouldn't have happened. Alice covered her mouth with a hand still damp from rinsing the leek, stifling the sobs that threatened to come. She wouldn't wake him, she told herself, biting her lower lip to stop any chance of weeping. There would be a time to indulge in tears later in the quietness of her own home but for now she had things to do that would make life a little easier for them both.

Later, in the darkness, Maggie slept by his side, oblivious to the sound of rain drumming against the roof tiles, tired out with weeping and still groggy from all the drugs they'd pumped into her system. *You'll have other babies*, the nurse had assured them as Maggie was discharged. *These things happen*. And it was probably true. But they would have to wait a while for Maggie's body to recover from the trauma. Would every act of love now be seen as a possibility for conception? He rolled over on his side, wishing he could take her in his arms, hold her tightly as though to shield her from the world. But he had seen how Maggie had flinched from any physical contact and he'd tried not to show the hurt he had felt.

Lorimer heard her stir by his side and suddenly felt her

239

small hand search for his own. They met under the bed-clothes, these two hands, clasped together, and he breathed a long sigh of relief.

It would be all right in time, just as everyone had reassured him. There would be other babies, lovely healthy ones coming into the world. And, one day when they were old enough, they would tell their children that they might have had an older brother, little David Lorimer, who had not managed to draw his first breath in the world.

CHAPTER TWENTY-EIGHT

M rs Forsyth was out there again.

Maryka's eyes narrowed as she looked out of the caravan window. Her employer was standing at the jetty, wind blowing her grey hair upwards, making her look like some mad creature. She was wearing the same faded beige cardigan that she had worn for the past two days; Maryka had noticed the food stains spilt down the front and her hands had itched to take a cloth and sponge them off. But she couldn't do anything like that, could she? Instead she had tried to look away but these greasy marks (a splash of Archie's lentil broth?) had drawn her eyes back as though fascinated by the woman's disarray. And now, here she was, up at the crack of dawn as though she had slept in these same clothes. *Perhaps she had*, a small voice suggested and the girl shivered to think that Freda Forsyth might really be suffering from some mental disorder. She couldn't have ... ?

Maryka dismissed the thought at once, picking up her hairbrush and beginning to sweep away the tangles of the previous night. The woman's slight figure was far too frail to have manhandled a big lad like Rory. Rumours were flying around the island and one of them had hinted that the dead boy had been tied up before being flung into the water.

Who would do a thing like that? He'd been a harmless enough soul, Maryka admitted to herself. There hadn't been any badness in him. Okay, he was a loudmouth, but she'd never heard him say anything unkind about other people. She stopped brushing her hair, sudden tears filling her blue eyes; it *was* a shame what had happened, really. He was just a young lad, someone of her own age. Maybe he'd have become less of a blowhard as the years continued to shape him? She sighed. That was impossible to guess.

The older woman had turned away now from the jetty and was walking back through the wet grasses, head bowed. Was she actually muttering to herself? Maryka wondered, seeing her lips move. Mad, she told herself. Just mad.

But what had happened in her life to make her like that? And why did she stand there so often? It wasn't even as if she visited Archie Gillespie's boat to talk to the chef about anything. Just as well, the Dutch girl told herself; what she'd find in there would probably send the chef packing. Yet the ancient wooden cabin cruiser might as well not be there, bobbing on its mooring, for all the notice her employer took of it. Maryka's pretty brow furrowed as she tried to make sense of it. The grey-haired woman had gone to the edge of the water so often, even before the boy had gone missing, staring out past the jetty as though she was waiting for something to arrive.

Maryka shook her head and turned away from the window. It was none of her business. She was being paid until the end of the season when she would return home and think what to do next, leaving all those unexplained things behind her.

Hamish Forsyth groaned as he opened the curtains. She was out there again looking like some tinker woman, her hair unkempt and those dowdy clothes making her seem years older than she really was. What started as a sigh ended as a huge burp, the released wind making him recall the previous night's drinking session in the hotel bar. The craic had been good, two of the guests staying up to regale one another with stories about their travels, their host happy to ply them with malts.

Letting the curtain fall, Hamish turned back into the room, picking up his clothes, pulling open a drawer to rummage for clean underpants. He missed the red-haired boy from Glasgow; Rory had often been included in these late-night conversations, the older residents asking him questions about his future, the boy happy to respond at length. He'd been a polite chap, knew his wines too, Hamish thought, remembering the boy reeling off a list of his favourite vintages. Old man Dalgleish must have kept a decent cellar at their place in Newton Mearns. Hamish buttoned up his least-creased shirt, slipping the tails into his trousers, images of Rory Dalgleish flitting in and out of his mind. The world was so different these days, he told himself, banishing the guilty feeling that had risen to the surface of his mind.

He pulled a tweed jacket from its peg on the back of the bedroom door with a grimace. It was time to play the role of Mine Host for another day, a genial smile pasted onto his face. Hamish glanced once in the wardrobe mirror, seeing the fine red veins spreading across his nose and cheeks. Once upon a time he had laughed about that face, boasted about being a double for Father Christmas, but now all he saw was a complexion ravaged by time and booze.

'When's your aunt's funeral?' Maryka whispered, unloading the big dishwasher and handing plates and glasses to the girl by her side to put away.

Fiona shook her head. 'I don't know. Jamie ... that's my friend who's a policeman ... he said it couldn't happen yet.'

Maryka nodded, as though wise beyond her years. 'They maybe have to do, what is it called? Au-topsy?'

'A post-mortem,' Fiona agreed with a sigh. 'I hate the thought of ...' Her lower lip trembled and she clasped a pint glass to her bosom as though it were something utterly precious.

'You shouldn't have come back to work so soon,' Maryka protested, wrapping an arm around the other girl's shoulders. 'Wouldn't the Forsyths allow you more time off?'

'It – it's not that,' Fiona stammered. 'What was I going to do up there?' Her large eyes turned to the other girl. 'You

244

don't know what it's like, Maryka. Tobermory's a small place, not like Amsterdam.' She sighed. 'Everywhere I turn someone wants to ask me things. And the sight of that corner of the street ... the police tape ...' She set down the glass on the counter and rummaged in her pocket for a handkerchief.

'How about your mum and dad?' the girl asked, bending down to retrieve more glasses from the dishwasher. 'Won't they come back from Australia?' Fiona made a grunting noise that was half derisory, half a sob as she crumpled the hanky in her fist.

'They're not coming back?' Maryka gasped, standing up, forgetting the chore in hand.

'Well, once they know about a funeral ...'

'Have they left *you* to arrange that?' Maryka's indignation was almost palpable. 'Well!' she exclaimed.

'It's been a terrible shock for them too,' Fiona continued, her voice trembling. 'Mum wouldn't believe it when I phoned. I had to get one of the police officers to help me. They've been good, haven't they? That big tall one from Glasgow, the one who found Rory, he was nice,' she said, staring into space as though remembering the visit from Detective Superintendent Lorimer.

'Oh, I met *him*,' Maryka answered with a twinkle in her eye. 'Bit of all right, eh?' She nudged Fiona and the two girls began to giggle nervously.

'Come on, let's finish this and see if there's a drop in one of last night's bottles,' Maryka grinned.

'You're getting as bad as Rory,' Fiona laughed, then stopped, her hand across her mouth. 'Sorry, I shouldn't have said . . .'

Maryka shrugged. 'He started it, didn't he? Bringing us what the guests hadn't bothered finishing after their dinner. It was amazing what that boy managed to get off with. The Forsyths treated him like he was one of their family or something.'

'Poor Rory.' Fiona exhaled a huge sigh. 'He wasn't that bad really, was he?'

The Dutch girl made a face. It wasn't good to speak ill of the dead and Fiona was so emotional after what had happened to her old aunt.

'Here, last one.' Maryka passed over a wine glass. 'Don't bother to put that one away,' she managed a conspiratorial grin, 'I'll go and see what's left. Unless Hamish has got there before us,' she added with a wink, pleased to see that Fiona Taig had wiped her eyes again and put the handkerchief back into the pocket of her apron.

The dining room was empty now, the breakfast tables cleared of cutlery and glasses, last night's candles snuffed out long since. On a sideboard against the wall several bottles still stood, ready to be taken back to the kitchen, a job that had fallen to Rory Dalgleish. Hamish Forsyth had let things slip, Maryka thought with a moue of disgust. Most of the bottles of wine were unopened, labels turned outwards to display their provenance. But there were still a few left from the previous

246

evening's dinner, ones that the guests had not finished before quitting their tables and moving through to the big lounge where they could have coffee and more drinks, supplied by Hamish and his wife.

Maryka lifted a couple of dark green bottles, tilting them to see how much was left. It had to be the reds, Rory had explained. Unless they'd left them in ice buckets, the white wines weren't worth drinking.

Medicinal purposes, she'd heard him say the first time he had entered the kitchen and handed a bottle over to the girls. He'd been pretty rude to Archie the night he'd spotted the chef rolling a joint though, hadn't he? *I'll tell the Forsyths*, he'd said with a laugh. But Archie had sorted him out pretty fast. What was it he'd said as he'd caught the student by his shirt collar? *Try that on, lad, and you'll find yourself feeding the fishes.*

They'd all laughed at the time but now, recalling these words, Maryka shivered. Even Rory hadn't taken the man's threat seriously, though he'd grumbled loudly once the chef was out of earshot. She could almost hear his voice, that loud sound that had grated so much.

The sudden sob in her throat surprised the Dutch girl. She understood Fiona's tears for an old woman she'd loved.

Why should I begin weeping for a boy I hardly even liked? she asked herself as she walked back into the kitchen, a wine bottle in each hand.

'Hey, whit're youse two up to?'

Maryka started at the sound of the man's gravelly voice.

Archie Gillespie stood in the doorway, arms folded, a scowl on his weather-beaten face.

'I just—' she began.

'We wanted a drink,' Fiona butted in, coming to stand beside the Dutch girl. 'Care to join us, Archie?'

The chef stood for a moment, arms folded, the look of indignation fading as he regarded the girl from Tobermory. 'Aye, well . . .' He broke off as though suddenly embarrassed. 'How are you, Fiona?'

'In need of a drink,' the girl answered tersely. 'Here.' She took the bottle from Maryka and handed it to the chef.

Gillespie gave a faint grin. 'Ach, ye're a right pair, so youse are,' he chuckled, his Glasgow accent cutting like a blunt knife.

'Here.' He took three glasses from the shelf and set them down on the table then lifted the wine bottle to his nose and sniffed.

'Nah,' he declared, then walked away from them and began to pour the contents into the sink.

'Hey! We were going to drink that!' Maryka protested.

The chef gave a grin as he looked back over his shoulder.

'Think we c'n do better'n that, hen,' he said. Then, strolling back to the dining room, he left the two girls staring at one another with puzzled looks.

'Right.' Gillespie raised the bottle triumphantly in one hand. 'We deserve a bit better than leftovers. Whit' d'ye say, ladies?'

Maryka's eyebrows rose as she glanced at the bottle; a Grand Cru Classé, one of Hamish Forsyth's most expensive wines, reserved for only the most affluent paying guests.

'Aye, why not,' Fiona said tiredly, sitting at the kitchen table. 'Go on, Archie. Let's have it.'

Minutes later the chef was pouring the red wine into three clean glasses.

'Rory would've complained about not letting it breathe, wouldn't he?' Fiona sighed. 'Here's to him, poor laddie.' She raised her glass and Maryka did the same, a feeling of guilt suffusing her cheeks with warmth.

The Dutch girl looked at the chef who was staring down into his wine glass.

'Archie?' She looked at him sharply, wondering why he had not responded to Fiona's impromptu toast.

Then, without looking at either girl, Gillespie downed the wine as though it were a glass of lemonade, set it down on the table with a thump and rose to his feet. In a moment, the chef had turned on his heels and disappeared through the doorway once again.

'What was that all about?' Maryka whispered behind her hand.

But Fiona merely shrugged and lifted her glass.

'He never liked Rory. *You* know that,' she said at last, then took a sip of her wine. 'Called him a wee snob. Specially when Rory was showing off about the wine.'

She stared at Maryka as though remembering.

'But you'd think he'd show a bit of respect for the dead,' she muttered darkly, looking at the empty doorway.

There were only two parties left in the hotel and both would be gone by the end of the week. The knowledge made him want to grind his teeth but Hamish Forsyth had to continue to play the part of cheerful host, plying his few remaining guests with drinks whilst a gnawing at his guts reminded him of the problems that lay ahead. There were no bookings at all now that the final cancellations had come in. The newspapers, he told himself, pouring a large dram from the last bottle of twelve-year-old Deanston. They were to blame. Splashing pictures of the hotel over the front pages, the boy's face smiling out from an adjacent photograph. And to think how helpful he'd been to that mild-mannered fellow in the tweed jacket! Turned out to be a bloody reporter!

Hamish downed the tumbler full of whisky in one gulp, unaware of the man and woman who were staring at the hotelier as they hurried past the entrance to the lounge.

'Off for the day, are we?' Hamish called out as the couple passed the bar.

'Just picking up Janet's cardigan,' the man answered, not stopping, but taking his wife's elbow and propelling her through the doorway. 'We'll see you later,' he murmured, ducking his head to avoid the hotelier's glance.

The other couple had already checked out and the lounge was empty now, the glare from the morning sun casting shadows across the empty tables. He should go into the kitchen, hurry the girls to begin cleaning up this room.

What was the point? Hamish asked himself, sitting down heavily on one of the bar stools, seeing the place for what it really was: the unmerciful sunlight revealing the stains on the ancient carpet, the dusty windows ...

It was over, he thought suddenly. There would be a winding-up process, he supposed. Receivers, probably, seeing what they could salvage from the wreck of his business. He turned to look for his wife, but she too was nowhere to be seen.

That would be a bigger problem, he knew, as his hand reached across the bar to take hold of the whisky bottle; taking her away from this place where she had been haunted by the ghosts of their past.

CHAPTER TWENTY-NINE

'And that's what happened?' Solly looked at his friend, trying to catch his eye, but Lorimer was gazing past him towards Fishnish Bay and the hills of Morvern.

'Aye,' he replied. 'Came back to the division and everything had changed. They'd charged both the McKerrell brothers with the Asian boy's death. Each of them swore blind that they'd had nothing to do with the first one. That red-haired lad.'

'And?'

'And what?' Lorimer asked.

'Were they convicted? Of either of the crimes?'

'Just the Singh boy's death. Poor wee lad had got himself mixed up with some drug dealers. Got ripped off by a junkie and lost the McKerrell clan a shedload of money. Their way of solving that particular problem was to . . . ' He shook his head. 'You don't want to know the details, Solly.'

The psychologist winced, his imagination filling the blanks in Lorimer's story. The policeman had talked about several things this morning as the two men sat outside Leiter Cottage: how Maggie's sadness at being unable to bring a baby to full term had affected them both, the old wounds opened up by the death of this boy practically on their own doorstep. He had known this man for years now, guessing many things about his past and his life, but until now Lorimer had never spoken about the tragedy of losing that first baby.

'And the boy you never identified? Were they tried for his murder?'

'Ach, there wasn't sufficient evidence to charge them with that. Besides, they had a lawyer who wouldn't countenance it being brought to trial.'

'So, you never found out who he was?'

Lorimer shook his head. 'No.'

There was a pause as both men looked at the view. From where they sat side by side on the wooden bench the entire scene appeared to be framed by the ancient oak trees and the row of silvery green willows that bordered the garden. Earlier, Solly had taken a walk beyond the extensive grounds, stopping to listen to the little burn trickling over the brown stones, its margins fringed by reeds and meadowsweet. The sound of chuckling water had raised his spirits, making him smile. Such elemental things, he had mused. The immutable forces within nature guaranteed to give us a different perspective upon life.

'Do you still think these ... who were they? The McKerrell brothers?'

Lorimer glanced up and nodded.

'Did you think they knew who the boy was?'

Lorimer made a face. 'By the time I got back after Maggie had lost the wee fellow it was in other hands. I wasn't even given a chance to talk to them. Och, everything was so different back then, Solly,' he said, shaking his head. 'There were no crime scene managers and we didn't have such a big liaison with the fiscal as we have nowadays.' He gave a hollow laugh. 'We didn't even have encrypted radios, for goodness sake! Anyone with a mind to do it could listen in to police calls.'

'What about George Phillips? He was a decent sort, as I recall from the few times we met.'

'Aye, he was,' Lorimer replied shortly. 'But you have to remember I was pretty much at the bottom of the food chain in those days. A lowly detective constable.' He gave a rueful grin. 'I did make a bit of a nuisance of myself, though, and poor old George put up with me. The case is still officially open.' He smiled at Solly in a meaningful way.

'And the McKerrells? Are they out now?'

Lorimer shook his head. 'One of them is back inside. Assault to severe injury on his common-law wife. The other one was gunned down in Sighthill. Never found out who the gunman was. We always suspected it was the work of a rival gang.'

'So you could still talk to one of them?'

Lorimer raised his eyebrows. 'About a case from twenty years ago?' He picked up the empty mugs at their feet but lingered

254

on the bench as though reluctant to tear his eyes away from the sweep of water and the gently curving hills. 'I suppose I could,' he murmured.

Even as Lorimer spoke, Solly knew that the policeman was responding to some inner voice rather than the friend sitting quietly by his side. Would Lorimer travel back to Glasgow? Ask questions that had not been asked for all these years? And what of the lad from Newton Mearns? Could there be any possible link between Rory Dalgleish and the dreadful things that had happened in Glasgow twenty years ago? The tall man staring out to sea evidently thought that there was and Solly Brightman had learned over the years to trust the detective superintendent's instinctive feelings for such things.

'Nothing on the database,' Stevie Crozier, said, tilting her chin defiantly. She had gone through the correct procedure, had double-checked everything and still there was no sign of a similar sort of murder anywhere on HOLMES. What the hell had he expected? A flurry of red-haired corpses hog-tied and chucked into the drink? She paused for a moment. What if she were wrong? What if there was a link between that twenty-year-old cold case in Glasgow and Rory Dalgleish's murder? She'd come out of all this looking like a real fool, wouldn't she? The DI tapped a pencil on her desk, wondering, then looked up impatiently as DS Langley entered the room.

'Any word?'

The DS shook his head. 'No sign of them yet, ma'am, but the patrols are all out searching the peninsula.'

Crozier banged her fist on the desk. 'How hard can it be to spot the man's vehicle?'

'There's a lot of tree cover . . .' Langley began but a withering look from his superior officer made him close his mouth again.

'What we really need is the Eurocopter,' she muttered. 'There used to be two of them, but the one that crashed in Glasgow was never replaced.'

'I've seen them being used on TV,' Jamie Kennedy said, looking up from where he had been working through several witness statements. 'It can track a fugitive by their body heat, can't it?'

'Well our chances of having aerial support for this case aren't exactly high,' Crozier said gloomily. 'Hicks from the sticks like us aren't usually given priority.'

'Maybe if you asked Detective Superintendent Lorimer . . .?'

There was a sudden silence as the two men looked at Crozier, her face frozen in a tight mask of suppressed rage. For a few moments nobody spoke then a telephone ringing broke the tension. Jamie bent his head once more to his task as Langley answered the call.

Crozier sat still, hands clenched, fuming inwardly. Did the men think she was incapable of carrying out the necessary actions? But, she conceded, PC Kennedy was probably right.

Lorimer would carry just the right sort of clout to get things moving. Perhaps it was time to admit she needed his help. Besides, there was a man with a shotgun who might very well be a dangerous killer running about the countryside – surely the detective superintendent would be able to make a case for the EC135 helicopter to be scrambled?

'You okay, son?'

There was no answer from the shape beneath the grey blankets but Jock Maloney could see Richard's head moving in what he took to be a nod.

They had driven all day and half of the night, down tiny farm roads, doubling back through forest tracks in an effort to cover their tracks. It was like being on patrol again, Maloney thought, recalling his younger days in Northern Ireland when he had been a soldier with the British army. He'd seen plenty in the few years he'd been garrisoned there, explosions that had killed military personnel as well as civilians; nothing like the bad old days of the sixties when the IRA had held the country in thrall, but bad enough for a raw recruit whose only desire had been to handle a gun.

His eyes shifted to the shotgun leaning on the chair by his side. It was a long time since he had taken aim and fired at a living human being but he would do it again if he had to.

They were safe enough here for now, he told himself, looking around the room. The bothy he had found was pretty remote and they had spent hours sealing the entrance to the forest trail and covering the roof with pine branches to conceal it from prying eyes. Apart from a few birdwatchers and wildlife photographers, the bothy was rarely used, or so the Forestry Commission online guide had informed him. He'd switched off his phone before leaving Lochaline, aware that any signal could bring the police hastening after them and now, sitting in the half darkness, Jock Maloney felt the twitchiness that came from being out of contact with the rest of the world.

What do we do next? Richard had asked when they had closed the door behind them, his eyes looking accusingly at his father. And Jock had looked away, unable to answer his son's question. What was he to do? He'd fled Tobermory with Richard, terrified that the police would come for them.

The man looked down at the slumbering form of his younger son. Why had he got mixed up with that red-haired boy? If only he'd never set eyes on Rory Dalgleish ... But all the *if only*s in the world wouldn't change the facts, would they?

Thank God wee Fiona had told him about the old woman! He'd had to get them away fast. And all because Jean had looked out of her window that night and seen him quarrelling with the boy. That particular bit of gossip was guaranteed to bring Jamie Kennedy and his lot straight to their door, wasn't it? And somehow Maloney knew that Jean Erskine's words would have the police scouring the countryside for them, even now. He drew a breath, silently cursing all old women and their spying eyes. Perhaps they were already near at hand, ready to pull him and Richard from their hiding place, take them away ...

Jock fingered the gun. He wouldn't let that happen. So much had been lost already, he wasn't going to let them take Richard from him too.

CHAPTER THIRTY

'We'd have to locate them first,' Lorimer explained as he stood beside the detective inspector's Mercedes that was parked in the lay-by near Leiter Cottage. 'Have the patrol ask at every cottage and farmhouse on the peninsula if they've seen his pickup.'

'And if we do . . . ?' Crozier looked at him but she failed to see the expression in her eyes behind the large designer sunglasses.

'I think that would merit the Eurocopter being flown in,' Lorimer agreed. 'Better at night, though, when he isn't expecting anyone to come.'

'And the thermal imaging camera would be able to follow him if he caught sight of us?'

Lorimer nodded. 'I've used the 'copter before in night cases when a fugitive was holding someone hostage,' he explained. 'It's a wonderful bit of kit. Can be scrambled in four minutes and keeps radio contact with the units on the ground.'

'Even in a remote part of the country like Ardnamurchan?' Crozier risked a doubtful smile.

'Even there,' Lorimer agreed. He looked up at the sky. It was one of those rare Hebridean days where the sun had burned off an early mist leaving a panoply of blue stretching from the hilltops; a pair of buzzards mewed faintly overhead, mere specks against the unseen thermals. A helicopter would easily be seen on a day like this, he thought. 'There's no way they're going to sanction its use until we have a better idea of Maloney's whereabouts, though.'

Crozier made a face. She'd already told him about the patrols from Oban spread out from Lochaline to Kilchoan, explaining that the network of single-track roads and remote trails on the Ardnamurchan peninsula made it slow work for the officers involved.

'What can you tell me about the man?' he asked. 'I only know him from his work at the garage. Always struck me as a particularly pleasant man, I must admit. Bit of a blether, but seemed a decent type.'

'Originally from Northern Ireland. Came to the island from Glasgow twenty years ago,' Crozier told him. 'Ex-army, works as a mechanic in the garage in Tobermory as you already know. Was married but the wife ran out on him some years back, leaving him to raise his two boys. Got a drink problem, but that's not a secret apparently.'

'What about his sons, they're both still at home?'

Crozier shook her head. 'The older one lives on the

mainland, it's just the younger one, Richard, who lives with his father.'

'And the ferryman at Fishnish reckons they were both in Maloney's pickup when he left the island?' Lorimer nodded towards the dark outline of the forest across the bay; somewhere, hidden from their sight, the Fishnish ferry was accessed by a road that snaked through these trees.

'Correct,' Crozier said. 'We've had officers around the older boy's place but he hasn't seen or heard of his father or brother in months. Or so he says,' she added darkly, shifting her weight from one foot to the other.

'And the mother?'

'Lives in Edinburgh, Keith Maloney thinks. They've had no contact with her since she ran off with her Italian boyfriend. He's a waiter in one of the big hotels there. We checked.' She tilted her chin upwards as though to assure the detective superintendent that she had left nothing to chance.

'So intelligence has it that he's holed up somewhere in the wilds of Ardnamurchan.'

'Aye, and I hope the midges are eating him alive,' Crozier muttered, waving a hand across her face as a swarm of the tiny insects swooped towards them. The lay-by was close to a burn that trickled underneath the road, a haven for insects brought to new life by the unexpected warmth.

Lorimer risked a smile. DI Crozier had moderated her appearance since coming to the island. Gone were the high-heeled shoes and dresses. Today she was wearing a pair of light camel-coloured slacks and sturdy flat loafers, a checked shirt rolled up past her elbows. She'd made time to make up her face and put on tiny silver earrings though, he noticed, a concession to her feminine side. And possibly some sort of hairspray or perfume that was beguiling these tiny biting insects?

'Do we know if Maloney has a licence for the gun?'

'No.' She shook her head, swatting away the midges and turning sideways to avoid the small cloud that seemed to be attracted specially to her. 'I mean, no we don't *know* if he has one or not. That's still being investigated.'

'But he kept it under lock and key in a proper gun closet, that suggests it was legit.'

'Or maybe he was simply not bothered who knew he had one,' Crozier countered. 'He was ex-army, remember. Might just have been careful not to let his boys near it. We'll know soon enough. Point is,' she sighed, waving a finger at the detective superintendent, 'he's got it with him and we suspect him of being a killer.'

She took off her sunglasses and looked up at Lorimer. 'See, what I'm thinking is: Maloney killed Rory Dalgleish, heard that he'd been spotted quarrelling with the boy beforehand and so tried to bump off the old woman before she could tell the police what she'd seen.'

'Any reason why a man who had lived quietly in Tobermory for twenty years . . . ' He paused, gazing into space for a moment. 'Peaceably with his neighbours, by all accounts,

263

no hint of any trouble with the police ... why would someone like that suddenly kill a young chap from a nice part of Glasgow, someone he could scarcely have known? And Jean Erskine? It takes some sort of nerve to murder a person in cold blood,' he said, looking Crozier in the eye.

She glared back then dropped her gaze, shaking her head slowly.

'It's him. Got to be. Why else has he gone and done a runner?'

Lorimer watched as the Mercedes turned slowly back towards the main road. He lifted a hand in a perfunctory wave but the car sped past, its driver not even looking his way.

Could she be right? he thought. Could it be Jock Maloney who had committed these terrible crimes? The Jock Maloney he remembered didn't seem to fit the frame somehow. Appearance and reality had lulled better persons than William Lorimer into thinking a man was incapable of murder. And, a little voice murmured in his ear, Maloney had come to Mull twenty years ago; perhaps just at the very time Lorimer had been investigating another death back in Glasgow. Yet there had to be a reason, another, more persistent voice insisted. Nobody simply killed at random unless some serious mental illness took over their behaviour. So, what reason had Jock Maloney for killing the lad from Newton Mearns? And why had he become a fugitive from the law?

He remembered then what Solly had said when they had

discussed the Irishman's flight from the island. *Perhaps he's not running away from anything*, the psychologist had remarked quietly. *Maybe he's running* to *something*?

'I want to go home,' Richard mumbled.

They were sitting in the hut, the door firmly closed against the sunlight outside, the boy sitting on the edge of his bunk, head dropped into his hands.

'You want to give yourself up to the polis?' His father gave a short laugh. 'Know what'll happen if they find you? Off to the nick and then on remand somewhere like Barlinnie or Peterhead.' He leaned over his son, one hand on the back of his neck. 'And you know what they do to pretty boys like you inside, don't you?'

Richard looked up, his eyes large with fear. 'But why would the police want to put *me* in prison?'

Jock let go of his son's collar and took a step backwards. 'You know fine,' he said, looking into the boy's grey eyes. He gazed hard at his son as though searching his face for some hidden thing. But Richard Maloney continued to stare his father out, unblinking, and so it was Jock who was forced to look away, sudden doubts clouding his mind.

'You tryin' to tell me you had nothing to do with that boy?' Maloney muttered, looking at the dusty floorboards beneath his feet.

'What do you want me to say?'

'I want the truth, Richard, just the truth!' Maloney

snapped, grasping his son's shoulders with both hands and shaking him till he fell back against the wall behind the bed.

'No you don't!' the boy yelled. 'You don't want that at all. You just want me to be different from how I am, don't you?' He cringed away as if expecting his father to rain blows down upon his head but Jock Maloney staggered to his feet and strode towards the door.

'Where are you going?' The boy pushed himself into a sitting position. 'Dad? Don't leave me here . . . ' he whined.

'Just getting something from the car,' Maloney muttered. 'Stay here and don't make any noise, okay? They're out there somewhere and we need to lie low until I can be sure they've searched and given up. Okay?'

He looked at the pale face of his younger son as the boy nodded, a wave of compassion washing over him as he reached for the door handle; it wasn't Richard's fault, was it? These things just happened and there was nothing that Jock Maloney could do to change them now except hide them both away for as long as he possibly could.

If George Phillips was surprised to hear his former colleague's voice on the telephone then he did not show it.

'Lorimer! How are you? Still giving the Glasgow criminals sleepless nights I hope?'

'George. Hello. Actually I'm on holiday up in Mull. Or supposed to be,' he added with a hollow laugh.

'Oh, aye? I read about that lad's death in the *Gazette*. Didn't see your name on that one, though,' he added shrewdly. There was a pause and then former Detective Superintendent George Phillips asked, 'What can I do for you?'

'Well, I want to pick your brains, George. Can you cast your mind back twenty years to that missing person we pulled out of the Clyde?'

'Good lord! That was a while back. Nineteen ninety-five, eh? Lot of changes since those days.'

'We never made an identification,' Lorimer continued. 'Or connected the young man's death to Desi Singh's.'

There was another silence as Phillips digested Lorimer's words.

'You went off on compassionate leave,' he said slowly. Then Lorimer heard him sigh. 'Aye, that was a hard time for you and Maggie. Always thought you two had been given a raw deal by Mother Nature. How is she, by the way? Maggie, I mean.'

'She's well, thanks. A bit upset that I had to find a body down on the shore, of course.'

'Ah, that's how you're involved.'

'Initially,' Lorimer replied. 'The SIO has asked me to help out in other ways, though.'

'And do they include raking over a cold case?'

It was Lorimer's turn to pause now before answering. 'Not really,' he confessed, 'but there are points of similarity. Both boys happened to be red-haired, a possible coincidence, but what's more startling is the way they were both bound up then released from their bonds post-mortem before being thrown into the water. Crozier reckons from the data on the more recent victim's laptop that it was a case of BDSM gone wrong.'

'Strangled first?'

'Exactly. Both boys approximately the same age.'

'And your SIO hasn't made any links on the database?'

'No. However there is something I wanted to find out. Did a chap called Maloney ever come under our radar at that time? John Maloney, calls himself Jock though he's originally from Northern Ireland.'

'Don't recall that name at all, Lorimer.'

The detective superintendent gave a sigh – his old boss's memory for names and faces was legendary.

'Just a long shot. Thought I would see if there was any link. Oh, well.'

'No, sorry. Don't suppose we'll ever find out who that poor lad was. Sometimes it's better to let these old cases go, Lorimer,' his old boss told him gently. 'Concentrate on the here and now.'

'Lachie? Can you give me a lift back to Tob?'

Fiona stood at the edge of the kitchen garden, watching as the handyman-gardener raised his head.

'I'll be off in about half an hour. That do you?'

'Aye, thanks. I'm staying at Eilidh's for now,' Fiona told him. 'Can you just drop me off at hers on your way?'

'Aye.' The word was dropped carelessly as the man turned back to his work, apparently weeding between rows of vegetables. The hot summer had made most of them shoot far too early, Fiona noticed. Lachie hadn't been vigilant enough to prevent that happening. Och well, she thought as she gave the garden a last backward glance, he's always at the beck and call of Mr Forsyth for all these wee inside jobs. How can Lachie be expected to carry on two jobs at once?

It was fair handy having the older man to give her lifts back and forth. Lachie spent most nights at his sister's place in Tobermory, when he wasn't away on one of his fishing trips, and Fiona had taken to travelling with him more and more since the death of her great-aunt. Okay, she could have taken more time off, but being back in Tobermory under the scrutiny of everyone's sympathetic smiles had made the girl decide to return to her work at the hotel. And it was peaceful down here at Kilbeg, especially now that the hotel was so quiet.

It was funny, she thought, glancing back at the gardener; Lachie had never said how sorry he was about Aunty Jean. Morose old bugger, she told herself as she walked back inside the hotel. Hasn't got much to say to anyone at the best of times. Still, he'd never refused any of them lifts in his old van, had he? She couldn't fault him on that.

The gardener bent once more to his work, a hand fork easing out the intruders to his rows of beans and cabbages, mostly buttercups whose runners had spread all across the rows, their bright yellow flowers blowing in a breeze that came straight off the sea. Beside him sat a large plastic trug, almost full of dead and dying weeds. It was painstaking labour but the man seemed not to notice, steadily clearing more and more of the dusty earth, his eyes shielded by the brim of the old hat he wore.

It was not until a shadow fell across the ground that Lachlan Turner looked up.

Hamish Forsyth stood looking down on him, hands clasped. Lachie rose slowly, noticing the way his employer was fidgeting, his fingers moving round and around. Something was wrong, he decided.

'A word, Lachie,' Forsyth said, moving away and indicating that the gardener should follow him to the side of the house where there was a patch of shade.

'Won't be needing you after this week, old boy. Can't be helped, I'm afraid. But I've decided it's time to call it a day here.'

Lachie nodded. The news hadn't been totally unexpected but he wondered why the man was avoiding his eye. Embarrassed at having to fire one of his staff? Worried that Lachie might make a fuss?

'What do we owe you?' Forsyth continued.

Lachie shrugged. 'Just this week's wage, Mr Forsyth. And a nice reference, maybe?'

'Of course, of course. See to that right away.' Forsyth

looked over Lachie's shoulder at the wreck of the garden. 'Bit much for one man to tackle, I suppose,' he murmured. 'Doubt if anyone will want to take that lot on this season. Still,' he turned to the gardener and clapped his shoulder, 'may as well do what you can till the end of the week, eh? Might get a buyer for it if the place is tidier.'

Hamish Forsyth turned and walked back around the corner to the entrance of the country house hotel, leaving Lachie to stare at the garden.

Tidier, was that what he wanted? There had not been one word of thanks, Lachie realised. No *sorry to see you go*, no matter how insincere such a platitude might have sounded.

He looked down at his hands, lined and marked with dirt. What had he been doing with these hands? Making this huge bit of land a wee bit neater for a man who'd drunk away all the profits of his business? The time spent creating a design for these gardens had been completely wasted on a man like this. The gardener clenched his fists then looked at the tub full of weeds. Aye, he'd give him tidier, he thought.

Taking hold of the two handles, Lachie tipped the weeds back onto the soil then, lifting up the rake that lay on the path beside him, he carefully swept the dead weeds back along the rows, making sure they were spread out as evenly as possible. He stood back at last, a faint smile of satisfaction on his face. The rows were filled up with dead foliage now, but looked ... *tidy*. The smile spread to a grin but it did not reach his eyes. Had there been anyone there to notice, they might have remarked on the expression of misery behind the hooded eyes.

End of the week, Forsyth had said. Aye, well, he'd collect his wages and the written reference and push off back to Tobermory. He spat on the path, aiming right at a slug that had crawled out of the pile of weeds. The slug seemed to hesitate, the gob of saliva confusing it. Then, with one swipe of the rake, the gardener mashed the slug against the hard-beaten earth, his face a mask of sudden fury.

'Did he say anything about paying *us* off?' Fiona wanted to know. She was sitting in the front seat of Lachie's van as they headed up past the forestry cottages, the road climbing ever upwards from the still waters surrounding the ruins of Aros Castle. Lachlan Turner had been in one of his moods, Fiona had noticed, and the girl had asked him right out what he was mad about this time. His curt response had been to tell her of the meeting with Hamish Forsyth.

The man shook his head.

'Won't be long till they get round to sacking us though,' Fiona remarked gloomily. 'How can they afford to keep *any* of us on once all the guests have left? Archie included.'

Lachie did not reply. 'I wonder what Maryka will do,' she thought aloud. 'She told me she was on a summer contract.'

'Folks like them,' Lachie snorted. 'They make and break anything they like.'

'Rory was on a summer contract too,' she nodded, looking

idly out of the window at the fields where Highland ponies grazed, their tails swishing to keep off the flies. 'Wonder if the Forsyths paid his parents whatever he was owed.'

Lachie looked at the girl by his side, taking his eyes off the road for just an instant.

'Hey! Watch out!'

Fiona grabbed at the handle of the door as the van swerved, a sheep and its half-grown lamb bounding out of the way.

She opened her mouth to say something, to protest at the gardener's sudden carelessness. But something in the man's glare as he accelerated around the corner stopped her. Lachie's sudden anger made the girl shrink back in the passenger seat. It must be hard being paid off at his age, she decided, noticing the red flush that had crept over the man's unshaven face. Well, she thought, at least he wasn't going home to a wife and kids to break the news. Lachie Turner had never been married, something that didn't surprise the young girl. Who'd want a surly old git like him? She sneaked a glance at the man again, silently appraising him. He wasn't really that old, maybe ages with Donald Taig, her father. That scowling expression made him look like an old man, though. Mid-forties, maybe? Like Archie, the chef, she thought suddenly. Another man who never seemed in need of a woman by his side. Both of them past it, she decided, well past it for any notions of romance.

The remainder of the journey continued in silence, Fiona staring out of the window as the familiar landscape passed them by; the van protesting as they climbed the steep hills past Ardnacross to the Guline Dubh, Lachie noisily changing gear. Then they were heading down the two-lane road towards Tobermory.

Fiona Taig sighed. It was all very nice at Manor Gardens and Eilidh's folks were more than welcoming, but the time would no doubt come when she had to take steps to visit the flat above the bank that was to become her own home. It had never been a secret that Jean Erskine was leaving the property to her great-niece.

You'll have it when I'm gone, she used to say with a twinkle in her eyes. *It's been your home a whiley now anyway.* But, she wondered, with the ghosts and memories that place now contained would it ever be a place that she could live in again?

CHAPTER THIRTY-ONE

Calum Mhor strolled across the grass verge and opened the big gate. He'd seen Lorimer's silver Lexus parked on the driveway and, on a sudden impulse, had decided to stop off and talk to the detective superintendent. The fact of it being eleven in the morning when some folk broke off for coffee and scones was a secondary factor, Calum tried to assure himself.

The front door was open and from somewhere inside he could hear the gentle refrain of classical music coming from a radio. It was a melody he knew but could not put a name to; one of those popular tunes that had been used as the theme for one of his wife's favourite television programmes. But better than the music wafting out was the smell of something freshly baked from the oven.

'Hello? Anyone at home?' he boomed, knocking the door as he stepped onto the doormat.

'Oh, hello, Sergeant.' Maggie appeared from the kitchen, wiping her hands on the apron tied around her waist. 'I was just putting some scones on the rack to cool. Don't suppose you'd like a cuppa?' She smiled mischievously as though discerning his intentions.

'Well, now, that would be very nice, very nice indeed.' Calum paused. 'Is the man himself at home? I saw the car . . .' He turned and jerked his head towards the Lexus.

'He's been down at the shore,' Maggie said. 'Back any minute. Just come through, won't you? Tea or coffee?' She turned back into the kitchen.

'Oh, a mug of coffee will be grand,' Calum said. 'Two sugars and milk, thanks.'

The big police sergeant sat down, relishing this break from his routine. He had spent most of the morning going over witness statements with several of the townsfolk from Tobermory, endless cups of tea proffered by the well-intended householders. Nobody, it seemed, had any clue why Jock Maloney had fled nor, for that matter, why Richard should have gone with him. Only that poor lassie, Fiona Taig, had given any hint about the boy's hasty departure with his father.

Wasn't Richard a pal of Rory Dalgleish? she'd asked innocently. *They hung about together.* She'd shrugged. He'd written that up in his latest report for DI Crozier but something was gnawing at the back of the police sergeant's mind, something he preferred to discuss with the tall man from Glasgow. And, seeing the big silver car sitting out beside the cottage, Calum had decided that a visit was in order.

'Calum. How are you?' Lorimer stepped into the room and Calum stood up, hand out to offer a firm handshake. 'I was down at the shore. Having a look for seabirds.' He gave a crooked smile, tapping the binoculars around his neck.

'Anything interesting?'

'No, just the usual. Oystercatchers and a few hooded crows. Some black-headed gulls.'

'No bodies, then?' Calum gave a tired smile.

Lorimer shook his head. 'Finding one is enough,' he replied. 'How's the search going?' He sat down opposite the policeman.

'No sign of them yet,' Calum answered. 'But we've got a map of the region with all the old bothies marked out. That's where we'll be looking next.'

'Once they're located we can have the Eurocopter scrambled.'

'Aye, just so. DI Crozier mentioned that.' Calum nodded then stood up, a mark of old-fashioned politeness, as Maggie entered the lounge bearing a laden tray.

'I made coffee for us all.' Maggie set down a tray with three steaming mugs and a plate of newly buttered scones, a pot of home-made jam by their side.

'Oh, my, that's a treat right enough, Mrs Lorimer,' the sergeant said, taking hold of a mug with one hand and reaching for a scone. 'Freshly made scones; better with just the butter, I always think,' he murmured, sitting back down. He sank his teeth into the scone, eyes shut as though to savour the initial

277

mouthful, as Maggie exchanged an amused smile with her husband. The policeman's predilection for cakes was well known and it was not the first time in all their trips to Leiter that he had dropped in for a mid-morning snack.

'Well, now,' Calum said finally, wiping the last of the crumbs from his uniform. 'I've been talking to a lot of people back in Tobermory, trying to find out why the Maloneys left in such a hurry.'

'Yes?' Lorimer raised his eyebrows.

Calum sighed, settling his bulky body further into the armchair. 'It was something Fiona Taig said,' he began. 'About Richard Maloney and the Dalgleish boy.'

Lorimer nodded slowly, wondering what was coming, half suspecting that he knew already.

'She seemed to think they were pals,' Calum said, frowning. 'But how could that be when Rory worked down at Kilbeg and Richard was up in Tobermory?'

'Didn't Rory go up to Tobermory for a bit of a social life? He'd been at the dances, hadn't he?'

'Aye, but how had he become so chummy with a local lad?' Calum shifted from side to side, visibly uncomfortable with what he was saying.

'Is Richard Maloney gay?' Lorimer asked abruptly.

Calum folded his arms and looked down at his feet. 'Well, now. That's a big question to ask, isn't it? Not sure if I'm qualified to answer it.'

Lorimer looked at him for a long moment. It must be hard

for a man like Calum to have to consider that someone he knew from this island might have been mixed up in a sado-masochistic relationship. These were things that the gruff police sergeant would wish to leave to others on the team, of that he was certain.

'I have good reason to think that Rory Dalgleish was gay,' Lorimer persisted, despite the obvious embarrassment the big policeman was suffering at his words. 'Could Richard's disappearance have anything to do with his relationship to the dead boy?'

The police sergeant twisted his mouth in a moue of uncertainty. 'I think,' he began, 'that the best person to ask would be Jamie Kennedy. He knows all the locals in Tobermory a lot better than I do. And he was at school with Keith, Richard's older brother, so he'll know the family all right.'

'It did worry you, though, didn't it? What Fiona Taig told you?'

'Aye,' Calum replied gloomily. 'And that … what you said … crossed my mind. Richard's a quiet sort of lad, by all accounts,' he added thoughtfully. 'Oh, well, takes all sorts I suppose.' He sighed, rising to his feet. 'Thanks for these delicious scones, Mrs Lorimer. Your wife's a real treasure, Detective Superintendent,' he nodded, smiling broadly at Maggie.

They stood side by side as the police sergeant made his way out of the gate then Lorimer stepped forward to swing it shut.

'Well,' Maggie remarked, 'he seemed very coy about the idea of homosexuality, didn't he?'

'Didn't want to voice his innermost thoughts to DI Crozier, I expect. Especially after they found those images on Rory's laptop. Just simple embarrassment.' Lorimer sighed. 'Not homophobic, as such,' he added thoughtfully, 'just part of a different generation.'

'Will you speak to PC Kennedy?' Maggie looked up at her husband as they strolled back to the cottage door,

'Fancy a wee trip to Tobermory?'

'Solly and Rosie are still there,' Maggie said. 'And they did mention a picnic trip to Calgary Bay.' She grinned, taking her mobile from her trouser pocket. 'Maybe we can salvage something out of this holiday after all,' she added with a rueful glance at her husband.

'Better look out your swimming costume, in that case,' Lorimer said, slinging an affectionate arm around his wife's shoulders as they made their way back to the cottage. 'I know one little lady who'll love paddling with her Aunty Maggie.'

The dry twig cracked ominously under his boot as Maloney stepped off the track.

He froze, hands by his sides, not daring to make a move. Images of crouched figures watching him through the darkened undergrowth, their weapons loaded and ready to fire, crowded his brain, pictures from the past; but those days were long gone. Now the threat was not those menacing silent men from the IRA but British police officers, people he had believed were on his side.

The sound of a vehicle in the distance made him lift the heavy field glasses and look towards the road end. There was no sign of anything stirring, no single movement within the trees. Nothing.

Had they stopped further along the track? And were they even now coming towards the bothy? Or had it just been a passing car, a farmer's wife visiting a friend nearer to Kilchoan? There was a farm a couple of miles along the road. He had seen it before they had driven off the track. But he was certain the engine noise had ceased close to where the trees opened out at the road end. Not a local, he grimaced, the hairs standing up on the back of his neck, some sixth sense warning him that their hiding place was no longer safe.

He hurried back to the bothy, eyes straining for any treacherous twigs, back bent as he ran. Keeping low down had been second nature to him once. Memories of those dark nights came unbidden, nights when he and his fellow squaddies had moved along the roads of Northern Ireland, half fearful that an incendiary device would blow them all to smithereens. But this was daytime and the light filtering through gaps in the thick pine trees made him blink suddenly.

Maloney stopped once more, listening, but there was only the heavy brooding forest all around, not even the cry of a bird. He moved forward again, creeping on careful feet until he reached the place where he had left the pickup. They'd find it easily enough, Maloney thought, despite the attempt to camouflage it with foliage. And driving on the open road would be like saying *Here I am: come and get me.* No, they'd be better off on foot from now on.

But first there were certain things that he needed to retrieve from the hidden vehicle.

When the door opened, Richard looked up from where he was sitting, hands clutching the sides of the makeshift bed. There was an unspoken question in the boy's eyes as he saw the shotgun in his father's hands.

'We're getting out,' Jock said. 'Now. Come on, quiet as you can.'

Richard opened his mouth to protest but a glare from his father silenced him before he could utter a single word.

'Will you move!' Jock hissed, grabbing the boy's shoulder and pulling him to his feet.

'Where are we going?' Richard whined as his father closed the wooden door behind them.

'Just follow me and keep quiet,' Maloney hissed. 'Understand?'

Richard looked up at his father's face. Ever since he had been picked up on the Back Brae and swept away from the island he had been wary of the older man. There was no smell of drink on him, nothing to account for Jock Maloney's strange behaviour. Nor had there been any explanation about the necessity to quit the island, just some curt commands to do as he was told or the police would come after them. Gone was the cheerful man whose speech was full of jokes and wisecracks. The laughing eyes were dulled now and Jock hardly spoke at all except to bark an order at his son.

Something had happened to change his dad. And Richard Maloney was afraid to think what that might be.

The boy nodded and fell into step with his father. He looked round once at the track: he too had heard the sound of a car engine. Yet at this moment he was less afraid of the police officers searching for them than he was of this man carrying the gun striding out in front of him.

CHAPTER THIRTY-TWO

'Where are you?' Crozier's voice came over the telephone as Lorimer drove past the entrance to Kilbeg Country House Hotel.

'Just approaching Salen,' he replied, the hands-free telephone allowing him to respond.

'Can you meet us at the ferry terminal? At Fishnish? They're on Maloney's trail and I've got orders to bring you with me.'

'Be there in less than twenty minutes,' Lorimer replied, his eyes already seeking out a place to turn the big car.

'I'll leave you the car,' he told Maggie after he'd cut the call. 'Go with Rosie like you planned.'

'What are you going to do? Is it safe?' Maggie looked at him, sudden anxiety in her face. 'Do you *have* to go?' The sigh that left her lips seemed to express all of her pent–up frustrations and fears.

He placed a reassuring hand over hers. 'I'll be fine. They probably just want me along to have the Eurocopter scrambled. That's all.'

Maggie nodded but the fine lines around her eyes had deepened. There was a gunman on the loose in the wilds of
Ardnamurchan; that much she knew and she was not one bit
reassured by her husband's words.

'Keep down!' Maloney hissed, waving his hand at Richard.

The boy squatted beside a tree, the bark chafing his cheek
as he huddled in the shadows. The darkness within the forest
was like a cloak, softening every sound. Even their feet had
made no noise on the carpet of pine needles as they had crept
away from the safety of the bothy, venturing deeper and
deeper into the mass of trees. Somehow his father led the way,
winding through small tracks, ducking beneath the massive
branches, the scent of pine heavy in the gloomy air. Several
times he had been signalled to halt, Jock raising a warning
hand, his head up to listen for their pursuers. But Richard
heard nothing at all, only the occasional dull snap of an aged
twig beneath his booted feet.

He was thirsty now and eyed the pack on his father's back
with resentment. *Have to ration it till we find another burn*, Jock
had whispered, snatching the water bottle from his son and stuffing it into the bag. *Where are we going?* Richard wanted to ask. *And
when will we be able to find something to eat?* But he was afraid to ask
such questions, dreading what the answers might be.

The ferry crossing took just over fifteen minutes, time enough
for Lorimer to call the Glasgow Division and talk to the pilot of

the Eurocopter where it sat in its stance by the River Clyde, preparing for take-off. Beside him he saw Crozier drum her fingers on the dashboard as though to hurry the small car ferry along. He let his gaze travel away from the green ramp that separated them from the waters ahead and the sides of the boat blocking out any view. Looking upwards to the clouds wheeling above them, the detective superintendent realised that the ferry was making its turn towards the shore at last.

'It should be with us by the time we reach the road end,' Crozier said, looking at her wristwatch. 'It's mostly single-track roads from here on,' she muttered as the ferry began to lower the dark green ramp at Lochaline, its yellow painted footprints to one side indicating the pathway for foot passengers. But for once the pedestrians would be made to wait until the police left the ferry first; every moment of delay was giving more time for Maloney to disappear further into the wilds.

Lorimer nodded. He was seated in the rear of a Police Scotland Land Rover; Crozier's Merc had been left at Tobermory and his own Lexus was probably halfway to Calgary by now, Maggie driving towards their friends and a picnic with their little goddaughter. He should be with them, he thought, a strange resentment filling him, not chasing after the man who had fixed his old Lexus. He ought to be having some fun, taking off his socks and shoes, paddling in the shallows with little Abby. But the holiday had been soured the moment that Lorimer had seen the gulls and crows at the edge of Fishnish Bay.

*

DS Langley was at the wheel of the vehicle, Crozier sitting in the passenger seat beside him as they bumped along the pitted road. Time and again they came to a halt, their progress impeded by an approaching vehicle or contrary sheep deciding to dash across in front of them. Glancing out of the rear window, Lorimer half expected to see the Eurocopter against the clear blue skies but, even if it had left Glasgow by now, it was still some time away from Britain's most westerly peninsula. The Morvern hills loured over this winding road, massive and brooding as though to remind the occupants of the vehicle that here was a far greater force than the one presented by mere humankind.

Then, as if the twisting road had finally decided to give up, a vista appeared below the trees: Loch Sunart and the mountains beyond, sun and shadows etching their peaks against the blue skies.

Lorimer bent forwards as they reached a T-junction. 'Are they sure he drove left?' he asked, glancing at the sign for Strontian.

'Yep.' Crozier did not even turn her head so he sat back down, resigned to the narrow road that hugged the shoreline for many miles more as the Land Rover hastened ever westwards. Even now, in high summer, there were not so many vehicles on the road so perhaps that earlier sighting of Maloney's pickup had been genuine. Where were they now? he wondered, glancing through the trees at the waters on their left, this grey ribbon of road leading them further and further into the wilderness.

*

'Listen!' Richard halted, tugging at his father's sleeve to make him stop. 'What's that?'

Jock Maloney stood still, his eyes turned towards the rhythmic noise high above the treetops.

'Helicopter,' he said at last, his mouth closing in a thin line of resignation.

Richard followed his father's gaze. 'They'll find us now, won't they, Dad? Dad?'

He struggled against the hand that was dragging him further and further into the depths of the forest. 'What're you doing? It's no use!'

'Get a move on,' Jock snarled, dropping his hand and nudging his son with the tip of the rifle. 'Damned if I'm going to let them get us.'

'But why? What's going on, Dad? Why won't you tell me anything?' Richard stumbled away from his father, his hands raised in alarm.

'You know fine why we're on the run,' Maloney retorted. 'Now, move!'

Richard felt the gun against the small of his back as he staggered forwards, all the questions he wanted to ask tumbling around his brain as they moved deeper and deeper into the shadowed quiet of the woods.

The EC135 was like a giant wasp in the air, its yellow and black livery vivid against the cloudless skies.

'Sierra Papa Seventy,' the uniformed officer in the rear

spoke into the mouthpiece, his voice battling against the din from the aircraft's propellers.

'Sierra Papa Seventy, we read you,' a female voice called back.

'Four minutes from you, west-north-west,' the officer replied. Heading towards our target now.'

Down below, leaning against the side of the Land Rover, Lorimer watched as the Eurocopter shifted its position and headed slowly over the treetops. They had been in contact with the officer for the last half-hour, his pilot and police observer sitting up front so that they might make eye contact with any running figures on the ground. Given the thick forest cover, that would be impossible, Lorimer knew. However, they did have one advantage over their quarry: there was a special surveillance camera fitted in this craft, one that could detect human fugitives in any conditions. Normally used as a night-time device, the thermal imaging camera could pick out anybody hiding in these woods, images being recorded as the men fled through the trees.

He craned his neck as the helicopter disappeared over the dark green mass of pines, the sound of its rotor blades drumming in the air. There was no way that Maloney and his son could escape them now.

Lorimer looked round as a white van drew up beside them, armed officers in protective clothing scrambling out.

'Detective Superintendent Lorimer?' A police officer

stepped towards them, his eyes glancing briefly over Crozier before he smiled warmly, putting out a hand to Lorimer.

'Chief Inspector Pinder. Didn't expect to see you up here,' Lorimer said, his eyebrows raised in surprise.

'Oh, I get around,' the man replied laconically.

Lorimer nodded, recalling a previous case on which they had collaborated. The uniformed senior officer had some links to MI6, his role in Police Scotland being to liaise with intelligence and counter-terrorism amongst other things.

'This is DI Crozier, our SIO up here,' Lorimer said, turning to face the woman who was standing a little apart from them, her arms folded.

'Pleased to meet you,' Martin Pinder said, giving her a perfunctory nod. 'Glad you brought this fellow along, DI Crozier.' He tilted his head, giving Lorimer an appraising look.

'Lorimer, we want you to come along with us. Chief Constable asked specifically that you be in on this one.' He shrugged, giving the blonde woman an apologetic smile. 'Grab a spare stab vest and stay with me,' he added, patting his bulky chest to show that he was already prepared with body armour beneath his jacket.

Stevie took a step forward. 'You don't want me to come with you?'

'I think your role as liaison with the officers is more important,' Pinder replied. 'We need you to be out here in constant radio contact with the 'copter.'

'Yes, sir,' she nodded. If she were disappointed at not being kitted up to join the armed officers, Stevie Crozier did not show it. If anything were to go wrong inside this wooded area she would carry the responsibility of reporting it all back to base.

'We'll keep in touch with you both as we approach the target. All right?' Pinder patted Lorimer on the arm and indicated that he should follow.

'They're coming closer!' Richard stumbled on a tree root, losing his footing as he looked upwards. 'Dad! They're going to find us!' he screamed.

'Shut up and stay down,' Jock commanded. 'Make yourself as small as possible.'

He crouched beside his son, holding his arms to prevent him from getting up and making a dash through the woods. 'They're looking for two figures running. Let's not give them that, eh?'

Richard looked up. There was a grim smile on Jock Maloney's face and for a moment Richard wondered if it was really possible to outwit the might of the police force. He had trusted his father this far, he thought, crouching behind the trunk of an immense pine tree. Surely he could trust him for a little longer?

The sound of the Eurocopter was like a droning insect high above them as Lorimer and Pinder stepped into the forest, a line of darkly clad officers ahead of them. Pinder touched the headset he was wearing and glanced at the tall man at his side.

'They've located them,' he said, nodding. 'Two persons on the right-hand side of the forest seen on the thermal imaging screen. Your friend out there knows it too,' he added. 'Hopefully we'll bring them both back without any fuss.'

'Are you anticipating any trouble?'

'He's got a gun. Was an ex-sniper. Wanted for a possible double murder. Isn't that trouble enough?'

Lorimer did not reply. There were several things that didn't seem to add up, to his way of thinking: mostly a motive behind the deaths of a young man and an innocent old lady. And, he reminded himself, the body of Rory Dalgleish had been dumped from a boat and Jock Maloney was neither a sailor nor a fisherman. A body dumped off the shores of Tobermory wouldn't have come ashore at Fishnish Bay, surely? Even given the strange high tides that had been in force that particular morning. It just didn't make any sort of sense to see the man from the garage as a killer.

Jock Maloney crouched closer to the tree, his son huddled beside him. Richard had his head down and eyes closed. Was he praying? The thought came to Maloney's mind. And if so, what exactly was he praying for: a sudden release from this awful situation?

For a moment he looked at the boy, remembering him as

the wee lad he had been not so very long ago, a toddler stumbling about, always cheerful, an eager schoolboy with pals coming constantly to their door. And, even when his mother had left, Richard had kept the same good-natured outlook, a smile for everyone. *Jock's lad*, they'd called him, *chip off the old block* whenever Richard had cracked one of his daft jokes. But appearances belied the realities of this young man's life and as he stared at the back of his son's head, Jock raised his rifle.

'Maloney!' The shout seemed to fall and die in the dense tree cover, despite the loudhailer that Pinder held to his lips. 'You're surrounded by armed police officers!' he called. 'Come out and give yourself up!'

Lorimer glanced around him: it was true enough, the officers had spread around the point where the thermal imaging had shown the presence of two live bodies, hunkered down beside a giant Caledonian pine.

They waited for a moment, all eyes focused on the spot, weapons aimed towards their hiding place. There was no movement from any side, every single police officer maintaining complete silence. Nor was there any sign of a stirring from the depth of the trees.

'Maloney!' Pinder barked the name out once more. 'Drop your weapon and come out!'

'Dad!' A muffled cry came from the shadows, and the unmistakable sound of running feet.

Then a single shot rang out, followed by an unearthly scream that made shivers run down Lorimer's back.

The armed unit was moving now, closing in on the gunman, Pinder and Lorimer at their rear.

'Let me speak to him.' Lorimer pulled at Pinder's sleeve. 'He knows me.'

Pinder stared at the man by his side for a moment then nodded, handing over the device without a word.

Lorimer raised the loudhailer to his lips, its white arc suddenly incongruous against the deep green darkness.

'Jock!' he called. 'It's me. Lorimer. Can you just stand up and move forward? Here's what I want you to do, all right?' He spoke calmly, years of experience dealing with dangerous and frightened men making him keep his voice low and steady. 'I need you to drop the weapon, Jock. D'you hear me? There are several rifles trained on you right now, Jock, and I don't want you to come to any harm. Okay?'

He lifted the loudhailer away from his mouth for a moment, taking another deep breath.

'Throw the gun out where we can all see it, Jock,' he commanded.

Once more he let the loudhailer drop as they watched and waited, the silence almost tangible.

The rifle dropped onto the forest floor, a quiet thud as it hit the carpet of pine needles.

'Come forward, Jock,' Lorimer continued, keeping his eyes on the great pine tree. 'Hands in the air so these armed officers can see you are no threat to them. Got me?' He spoke in a matter-of-fact tone as if he issued instructions like these every day.

There was a pause and he glanced sideways, catching Pinder's eye. The senior officer was in charge of these men now and could order them to open fire with one sweep of his arm should Maloney prove to be a threat.

Lorimer held his breath as the figure emerged from the shadows, stumbling slightly. Jock Maloney came towards them, his hands high above his head, the khaki jacket riding up over his dark blue shirt, a triangle of pale, fleshy stomach showing above his waistband.

'That's good, Jock, nice and easy now.' Lorimer stretched out a welcoming hand, encouraging him to keep walking forwards.

Then in a moment the garage mechanic was surrounded by armed officers, his wrists bound behind him in metal cuffs.

It was fleeting, that expression of bewilderment on Maloney's face before his head dropped and the eyes became shuttered against his captors, but Lorimer had noticed it and it made him wonder.

'Where is Richard? Where is your son?' Pinder was face to face with the man now but Maloney's mouth was a closed narrow line as he looked down at the dusty earth.

'Over here!' The cry came from the trees behind them. 'Call an ambulance. The lad's hurt,' someone shouted.

'Jock, what have you done?' Lorimer shook his head. Had

this man actually tried to take his own son's life? Had that been the shot they'd heard?

'It wis me,' Maloney grunted, his eyes flickering upwards to the tall man standing before him. 'I did the lad from Glasgow.'

'And Jean Erskine? Did you kill her too?'

'*What?*'

The word was out before Maloney had time to think, his mouth open, eyes widening in astonishment. Then, licking his lips and darting a look at the figures stamping through the trees, he nodded. 'Aye, aye, that wis me an' all. Course it wis,' he agreed. Though now his eyes were downcast once more, refusing to meet Lorimer's own.

'Take him away,' Pinder ordered. 'See what shape the boy is in.'

Lorimer watched as the father was led away along the narrow path that cleft this dark mass of trees, a gaunt figure, drooping between two armed officers.

The man had just admitted to a double murder. That would please DI Crozier, no doubt, he thought grimly. But Jock Maloney's reaction to the news of Jean Erskine's death had shown something quite different from guilt or remorse: it had shown the detective superintendent that it was news to the Irishman. And, at that moment, Lorimer was beginning to wonder if Maloney's mumbled confession had any grain of truth in it at all.

CHAPTER THIRTY-THREE

Jamie Kennedy took off his chequered hat and tossed it onto the passenger seat. Smoothing his hair, he glanced in the car mirror and made a face at his reflection.

'Aye, you'll do,' he told the young man nodding back at him. Was it so strange to see his hand trembling as he lifted the file from the seat beside him? The events of the past twenty-four hours had left them all a bit hyper, he told himself, biting his lower lip. Or, an inner voice suggested, was it the thought of having to face Fiona and how she might react to his news?

Manor Gardens was not a place Jamie had driven around before though he'd passed the half-built estate plenty of times. Like everyone else from the island, the police constable had watched for months as the builders constructed houses on the field of tawny grasses that were now barely remembered. The new homes were going up fast, and quite a few of them were occupied, like the one he had come to visit.

He swung out of the car and closed the door, not bothering

to lock it: that was a mainland habit PC Kennedy had given up months ago.

Fiona had told him about the bungalow where she was staying with Eilidh and her folks and Jamie's eyes moved along the row of pristine white houses until he came to number nine.

'Jamie!' Fiona was at the door before the officer could even press the shiny brass bell set into the varnished doorframe.

She's lost weight, was his first thought, a wave of shame washing over him as he regarded the girl he had known since childhood. What sort of pain had wee Fiona suffered in the days following Jean Erskine's death? Her face had lost its customary bloom and he felt a pang seeing the sharp cheekbones that gave the girl a drawn, haunted look.

'Thanks for coming by,' Fiona said, standing aside to let him enter the house. 'D'you want a coffee? I'm on my own but they've told me just to treat the place like home.' The girl stopped, her large eyes turned to him. 'Don't know what I'd have done without the McIvers,' she added, huskily.

'Aye, they're nice people,' Jamie agreed, following Fiona into a large bright kitchen at the back of the house, its white-painted walls mellowed by the morning sun streaming through the windows.

'I like this,' he remarked, moving towards the double-sized windows for a closer look. 'You can see the hills from this angle.'

'You haven't been up here before, then?'

Jamie shook his head, still staring at the view from the back of the house. 'Didn't think they'd be like this,' he confessed. 'A decent outlook makes all the difference, eh?'

'Coffee?'

'Aye, thanks.' Jamie turned back and watched as the girl busied herself opening cupboards and taking out mugs and plates. Her blonde hair looked newly washed, the sunlight glinting on strands, and for an instant Jamie wanted to reach out and touch it, to feel its softness the way he had done when Fiona Taig had sat in front of him in Primary One, her long golden curls a temptation for a curious small boy.

'Still milk and two sugars?'

Jamie smiled and nodded as Fiona handed him the mug.

'Let's just sit in here, eh?' he suggested as the girl made a move towards the kitchen door.

'Okay.' Fiona pulled out one of the wooden chairs around the kitchen table.

'You said you'd something to tell me,' she began.

Jamie nodded, seating himself opposite. 'A lot to tell,' he agreed, tapping the file that lay unopened on the table.

'First of all, though, I want to say I'm sorry for taking so long to go and see your Aunty Jean. If I'd gone up sooner . . .'

'Hey.' Fiona stretched out a warm hand and placed it on his. 'That was never your fault. More mine for gabbing all over the street,' she sighed.

'No, it wasn't. You mustn't think that, Fiona,' he said seriously, looking at her intently. 'Anyway,' he took a sip from his mug, 'looks like it's all over now.' He leaned forward. 'Jock Maloney's in custody and has confessed to both of the murders.'

'Jock?' Fiona sat back suddenly, frowning. 'But why . . . ?'

'I know, it's a shock, isn't it? But that's not the half of it, Fiona.' Jamie shook his head. 'See, he must've taken a real mad turn. They say he tried to take a shot at Richard.'

'What? *Richard?* Bloody hell! Is he all right?'

'Not sure just what damage was done. Last I heard he was going into theatre to have a bullet removed from his shoulder.'

'Good God! You mean Jock tried to kill him?' Fiona's eyes widened. 'What possessed the man?'

'Goodness knows. Anyway, Richard's in Glasgow Royal Infirmary and his dad's somewhere down in Glasgow too, being questioned by the police.'

'Jock.' Fiona sat, staring past her old schoolfriend. 'Jock Maloney. I can't believe it. Can you?' She looked at Jamie again.

'Well he's told them it was him.' He shrugged. 'Look, that's not the only reason I wanted to see you, Fi,' he said, the name he'd called her in childhood slipping naturally from his lips. 'We've asked the procurator fiscal if he'll release your aunt's body for burial.'

Fiona sniffed suddenly and blinked.

'Oh, Fi. Here.' Jamie bent across the table, a clean white handkerchief in his hand.

She sat very still as he wiped away the stray tear that had

trickled down one cheek, reminding Jamie Kennedy of the child she had been, the little girl who had tagged along behind him every day after school until, in his older teenage years, he had chased her off, embarrassed by her attention.

'I also wanted to say,' he began quietly, 'if there's anything I can do to help. With the arrangements . . .'

Fiona nodded, a tremulous smile on her face. 'Thanks,' she replied, swallowing hard. 'Times like this you know who your friends are, eh?' She laid her hand on his arm, giving it a squeeze. 'And I won't broadcast the news about Jock all over the town.'

'It'll all come out soon enough,' Jamie sighed. 'That newspaper man from the *Gazette*'s already been talking to DI Crozier this morning. And I expect the *Oban Times* will have a field day. First murder in these parts in living memory. *My* living memory anyhow,' he added. 'And yours.'

Later, as he slowly circled the crescent of houses to make his way back to the town, Jamie Kennedy looked across at the homes still under construction, the scaffolding bright against the dark grey breeze blocks. His eyes travelled along the building site. There were some bigger villas, family homes that were set up a little higher from the rest, a line of trees framing them to one side, gardens that were big enough for kids to play.

This would be a good place to live, he suddenly thought. A grown-up place; somewhere to raise a family.

CHAPTER THIRTY-FOUR

The smell of hospitals never changed, thought Lorimer, as he pressed the lever, sending a stream of antiseptic fluid onto his hands. There was still that faint tang of cleaning products mixed with the whiff of cooked onions that seemed to permeate even the most pristine of hospital corridors. He was in the old part of the Glasgow Royal Infirmary in Castle Street which, despite the recent sandblasting of its sandstone exterior, was still a formidable building towering above the road system as though to tell the denizens of this city that it brooked no nonsense with any of them. Walking through the gatehouse entrance had been like passing into a different era, reminding Lorimer of a time long past when only the well-to-do could afford treatment by doctors in this infirmary.

He had been advised that Richard Maloney was in a side room off the orthopaedic ward, a precaution insisted upon by the senior officer. Crozier had agreed that it was a necessary action to keep the young man safe from media intrusion as well as allowing the police access while he was recovering from surgery. He nodded to the female police officer by his side, a woman ten years his senior, who had been trained in family liaison situations and was well used to dealing with sensitive issues. 'All right, Emma-Grace?' he asked.

'Yes, sir. Poor lad,' she said. 'Wonder what he'll make of your visit.' Her tone was a mixture of genuine sympathy tempered by a brisk no-nonsense shake of the head.

Lorimer raised his eyebrows speculatively. Just how Richard Maloney would respond to an unheralded visit would be interesting to say the least. He glanced briefly at his companion. Police Constable Emma-Grace Branson had chosen her profession over an early desire to become a concert violinist; only a small number of talented souls really made it to the concert platform and PC Branson had not been amongst those lucky few. He reflected for a moment; who would guess looking at the hands folded so neatly in front of her that they were capable of playing some stunning music? It was yet another instance, Lorimer thought, of appearance belying a hidden reality.

A nurse came forward, smiling at Lorimer, but as soon as he held out his warrant card, her expression stiffened.

'Detective Superintendent Lorimer. PC Branson. We're here to see one of your patients, Richard Maloney.'

'He's not to be upset,' she began. 'The doctor's given him medication to calm him down.'

'Is he asleep, then?'

She shook her head. 'I just took his blood pressure a few

minutes ago,' she admitted. 'He'll still be awake, I imagine. Room twenty-four, just along there,' she said, indicating the right-hand side of the corridor.

'Thanks.' Lorimer gave the nurse a lopsided smile and was gratified to see her give them a friendly nod in return.

There were two names attached to the door: the patient's and his doctor's, Mr Wang, the orthopaedic surgeon who had spoken to Lorimer earlier in the day.

He gave a couple of raps on the door, even though it was already slightly ajar, then entered the room.

Richard Maloney was propped up against a bank of snowy white pillows, his shoulder and left arm swathed in bandages, a drip to one side feeding medication into his system. Curious eyes swept over the detective, widening into a look of alarm as he presented his warrant card.

'Richard, I'm Detective Superintendent Lorimer,' he began. 'And this is PC Branson. Mind if we sit down?'

The young man continued to stare at Lorimer for a long moment then nodded his assent. His face was pale and drawn with dark circles under his eyes that made the detective feel a sudden pity for the lad. He was, what? Eighteen? Just a boy, really, on the threshold of adulthood, his formative years guarded by life on the island.

'Do you feel strong enough to talk to me, Richard?' Lorimer asked gently.

A sigh followed. Then, 'Aye, I suppose so.'

The boy's voice was soft, his mellow accent so familiar to

Lorimer now after years of visiting Mull. It reminded the detective superintendent of the warmth of the local people and the feeling of pleasure that each successive visit to the island had brought to Maggie and himself. Once more the sensation of anger against a cruel fate that had caught him up in a murder case washed over him: nowhere was more special than their safe haven in Mull. It was a place that ought to have remained free from all the evil and darkness that dogged his footsteps here in the city. But nowhere was sacrosanct; wherever people lived, loved or vented their hate gave rise to the possibility of terrible deeds. Not even the calm, slow pace of life on that island could keep the midnight out.

'We need to know what happened,' Lorimer explained. 'There will be time later on when you feel up to it that we need to take an official statement. But for now, I thought we'd have a wee chat.'

'I've met you before,' Richard said suddenly. 'A few years back. When you had that dark blue Lexus. Dad fixed it up for you.'

'So he did,' Lorimer agreed. 'Gave it a new lease of life for a while. Did over two hundred thousand in that old car, would you believe.'

'He's a good mechanic,' Richard said, a defensive note in his voice.

'And a good father?'

The boy looked away, his eyes closing.

'Richard, we need to know what happened back in

306

Tobermory,' Lorimer said, gently. 'Why did your dad take you off the island?'

The sigh that escaped from the boy was joined by a gasping sob and a silent shake of the head.

'Richard.' Lorimer's tone was sterner now, making the boy turn to look into his eyes. 'Your father has confessed to killing Rory Dalgleish. And Jean Erskine.'

'No! That's not right!' The words escaped from the boy's lips, two angry spots of colour appearing on his cheeks. 'He couldn't have done that, he just couldn't!'

'Now, how's that, Richard? Can you tell me?'

The boy's own eyes were blazing for a moment then he turned away, unable to withstand the piercing blue that had pinned many a suspect within the confines of an interview room.

'Tell us what happened the night of the dance,' Lorimer said, changing tack, his tone gentler once again.

'We were having a nice time,' Richard began slowly. His face was still turned to the wall but now it was as though he could see the events of that fateful night as he spoke. 'Rory was in fine form,' he continued, a faint smile hovering on his lips. 'Swinging that kilt of his at the dance.' The smile deepened, the boy's cheeks dimpling as he remembered. Then it faded abruptly.

'What happened after the dance, Richard?'

The boy's head flopped back against the pillows, his eyes staring at the ceiling.

'We were going along the street. Me and Rory,' he replied.

'He had a half bottle and we were taking nips out of it when my father came along.' He closed his eyes tightly as though blotting out whatever had happened next.

Lorimer nodded to himself, watching the pain in the boy's face, a pain that had nothing to do with the wound in his damaged shoulder.

'You and Rory were more than just pals, weren't you?' he asked quietly.

The silent nod and the tear trickling from the closed eyelids told its own story. A life on the islands was not all peace and quiet, he suspected, not if you were avoiding the gossips and the wrath of a homophobic father.

'Look, lad, I have to ask you something very personal,' Lorimer began, watching the young man's troubled expression. 'You and Rory, were you into bondage of any kind?'

'What?' Richard's eyes widened then he looked away in obvious embarrassment.

'You'd not be the first young man to experiment.' Emma-Grace smiled disarmingly and shrugged as though it was something she came across on a daily basis.

'Did Rory ever suggest anything like that?' Lorimer persisted.

A silent nod and two flushed cheeks were all the answer the patient could give. Then, 'I wasn't into all that,' Richard whispered. 'Rory *said* it didn't matter. But I could see he was ... ' The lad hesitated. 'Disappointed,' he said at last, clearing his throat as though the word had lodged there painfully.

Lorimer nodded. Richard had a gentleness about him and Lorimer believed him: he did not look like the sort of boy who would submit to another man's sadistic tendencies. And, he reminded himself, it had been Rory whose body had shown signs of bondage.

'Let's talk about your father. He had a row with Rory, didn't he?'

'Aye. He ordered me along the road but I could see them arguing from where I stood at the corner of the Back Brae.'

Lorimer nodded to himself. That made sense. There had been no mention of a third person seen from Jean Erskine's window, a vantage point that did not extend to where Richard had been standing that night.

'And after that?'

Richard's eyes opened. 'I never saw Rory again. Dad dragged me off home. Gave me a right hammering.' He winced as though the blows were still fresh.

'And where did Rory go?'

'I don't know,' Richard said miserably. 'The last I ever saw of Rory was him walking back along towards Ledaig.'

'Towards the garage?'

Richard nodded his reply.

'And did you stay at home that night?'

He shook his head. 'No,' he whispered. 'I went out much later to look for Rory. But there was nobody down the town at all. Not a soul from the dance.'

'What about the boats? No sound of any parties going on?'

'No, nothing.'

'And your father? Where was he?'

'I don't know,' Richard replied. 'Thought he'd gone to bed. Thought I'd heard him snoring as I opened my bedroom door.'

'What time was this?'

Richard attempted a shrug then grimaced. 'Maybe two in the morning?'

Lorimer sat very still. If this was true, then perhaps his instinct about Jock Maloney's confession was true.

'Richard, listen to me. Your dad might have told the police a lie. What he said about being responsible for these deaths could be false. And if you were to testify that you were sure he was asleep at that time, well, that could make a real difference.'

'But *why* did he say that?' Richard's face was twisted with anguish. 'And why did he make me run away with him? Why did he try to shoot me?'

It was Lorimer's turn to shrug. 'That's something we need to find out, isn't it?' And, although the detective superintendent's words sounded sincere, they belied the suspicions that were already forming in his mind.

DS Brian Langley put down the telephone and came to sit behind the desk, his fingers hovering above the keyboard, intent on sending an email to DI Crozier. She was off again on one of her jaunts, leaving him to do all the donkey work as

310

usual. The man's face clouded with resentment: all this bloody paperwork. And now he was supposed to send on this telephone message to let her know about the change of time for her meeting in Glasgow. Her mobile had been switched off, or more likely the train from Oban had been passing through a tunnel, Langley thought, an idea forming in his mind.

His mouth twisted for a moment, then, as a thought became an action, the detective sergeant closed down the laptop.

She'd never know, he thought gleefully. Anyone could be forgiven for making a mistake, he told himself. And he would manage to cover it up somehow. But DI Stevie Crozier was in for a little shock when she finally arrived at Pitt Street.

DI Crozier hated Glasgow. She scowled at the noise of traffic as she waited to cross at the lights, people jostling at each side of her. Back in Oban she had been the one in charge of everything; here in Scotland's largest city, she was just a small fry. Yet if she were honest with herself, Stevie was angry that her suspicions had been so well founded. Detective Superintendent Lorimer had indeed managed to weasel his way into her case. Okay, it had been a decision taken by the fiscal and the chief constable at the end of the day, but here she was, ostensibly still the SIO in the case of Rory Dalgleish and Jean Erskine whose murders had occurred on *her* patch.

The train from Oban had spilled out its passengers at Queen

Street Station and now she was crossing Buchanan Street, eyes searching for a decent place to have lunch, before heading uphill to the old police headquarters at Pitt Street where Lorimer had arranged for the press conference to take place.

A tramp outside the station had waylaid her, his polystyrene cup outstretched, a mumbled plea for change in eyes that were vacant of all hope. She'd stood aside at once, avoiding the dirty mess of rags that he was sitting on as much as the poor-looking whippet nestling under a bit of grey blanket. It was typical of the city, she thought, high heels slipping on the cobbles, dodging past a black cab that roared its way around a corner. Everywhere she seemed to look there was dirt and decay, people washed up like so much rubbish. It made her suddenly long for the fresh sharp tang of Oban Bay, seagulls screeching above the fishing boats, police officers taking time to see to the needs of their community. Langley had been visibly miffed when she had told him there was no need for him to accompany her to Glasgow. In truth nobody had suggested that anyone else from the team needed to be there and she had felt a sense of pride in representing her little task force. But, now that she was actually here, all that had vanished, leaving DI Crozier wishing that she need not take part in this affair and wondering just what she would say to the journalists that awaited them.

He saw her arrive at last, raincoat folded over one arm, looking around to see if there was anyone she knew. For a moment

Lorimer felt sorry for the woman who had done so much to make her dislike of him obvious, even though he was irritated that she had failed to show up for the meeting prior to the conference.

The case was done and dusted as far as she was concerned: had she simply decided that there was no need to make an appearance to discuss their strategy in front of the cameras? And, Lorimer wondered, how would DI Stevie Crozier react when she saw proof that Jock Maloney was not their killer? At least that would not be a subject aired at this press conference, thank goodness, particularly as such proof was still to be established. Meantime, there was the small matter of obtaining permission to question the man who was in custody in Low Moss Prison.

The hall was packed with reporters, their mobile phones and iPads ready to record any titbits of information pertaining to the double murder case and the apprehension of fugitives up on the Ardnamurchan peninsula. A buzz of sound came from these people as Lorimer stepped forward and nodded at the DI, ushering her to the front of the platform where the dark wooden table was already prepared with several fixed microphones.

'I've done the sound check,' he whispered behind his hand. 'It's all ready for you. What happened?' he added. 'Was the train held up? You didn't call to say you'd be late.'

'What d'you mean?' She looked at her watch. 'This is when I was asked to be here. That was what DS Langley told me.

313

Why wasn't I given time to discuss things beforehand?' she hissed back, clearly upset about being thrust into the spotlight so soon after her arrival.

Lorimer raised his eyebrows. 'But you were,' he said softly. 'Someone from upstairs called asking you to be here an hour ago.'

Stevie Crozier shook her head slowly from side to side, her eyes snapping in sudden fury. '*I* didn't get any telephone call,' she replied. 'I haven't spoken to a single person since I left Oban.'

Lorimer shrugged, his gesture saying *I don't know*, leaving the woman tight-faced and anxious as she sat down at the table. It was a matter to be discussed later on but someone's head would roll for failing to brief the DI on the arrangements for this morning's meeting.

He leaned across and spoke quietly. 'Okay, over to you, Detective Inspector,' he said. 'I'll just introduce you, then, shall I?'

Later, Stevie would recall little of the individual questions, Lorimer chairing the meeting with an expertise that showed he was well used to dealing with the media. It seemed to Stevie that lights flashed constantly, sometimes blinding her to the person who was calling out their name and newspaper, words directed towards her that she caught and batted back, all her neglected media training coming into force. There were questions about the boy. Where had he been found?

Why had Detective Superintendent Lorimer not been put in charge right away? (Lorimer had answered this smoothly, explaining that he had been on leave, that DI Crozier had conducted the murder inquiry with the utmost efficiency; Stevie loving and hating him for that reply in equal measure.) Then all those questions about Jean Erskine: Stevie had been on surer ground here, recalling the finding of the old woman clearly as she spoke. They had quickly turned their attention to Jock Maloney, his background (that was easy stuff) and the operation to capture him out in the forested area. The DI had replied as best she could, remembering the sounds coming over the airwaves as she had stood out on the open road by the Land Rover, that shot resonating through the trees.

Then it was over, Lorimer insisting on the last question coming from a reporter in the front, a pretty dark-haired young woman from the *Inverness Courier*.

'Do you have any idea *why* Maloney killed these two people?' she asked, her clear tones ringing out.

And, as Stevie hesitated, Lorimer bent towards his microphone to answer.

'Mr Maloney is still being questioned about his part in these incidents. There will be further opportunities to make contact with our press office in due course. Thank you all for coming.'

And then the cacophony of protests from the assembled crowd of journalists as they wondered aloud what was going on? Hadn't Maloney confessed to the murders already?

Lorimer's hand on her elbow quickly guided Stevie out of the hall and they headed up a back staircase then along a corridor.

Lorimer knocked on an unmarked door. A woman's voice from within called, 'Come in.'

Then Stevie Crozier found herself face to face with Joyce Rogers. The deputy chief constable of Police Scotland sat in a wood-panelled room, its walls devoid of any sort of decoration except for the old Strathclyde Police badge, its colourful thistle emblem long since replaced elsewhere by the plain blue of the current regime.

'Ma'am,' she began, feeling an absurd desire to bend her knee and curtsy. Rogers was the one woman in the entire force that Stevie longed to emulate; someone who had withstood the changes from being second in command at Strathclyde Police until the historic reorganisation in April 2013 when she had been appointed as the next most important figure to the chief constable in the whole of Police Scotland.

'Lorimer tells me that the train broke down. Such a pity. I wanted to talk to you about the progress of the case. Never mind. Perhaps you can spare a little time later today.' Rogers looked at the delicate silver watch on her wrist. 'Say about three?'

And Stevie had nodded her assent, silently blessing the tall man standing at her side for covering up the mismanagement of her arrival in Glasgow with a white lie. 'Thank you, ma'am. I'll be glad to talk to you.'

'And Lorimer, that matter we discussed earlier? Will you have spoken to Maloney by then? Can you join us?'

Stevie looked at Lorimer, bewildered. What was going on? What matter had been discussed? And, a horrid suspicion rising in her mind, had it been Lorimer who had deliberately failed to send her the correct instructions to keep her out of his way?

CHAPTER THIRTY-FIVE

Low Moss Prison in Bishopbriggs was a far cry from HMP Barlinnie where the detective superintendent had visited several prisoners incarcerated for murder. Walking through the brightly lit corridors, one could be excused for imagining that this was a further education college out in the countryside and not a high security prison full of dangerous men.

The prison officer at his side chatted happily about the recent visit of a well-known writer to their library, an event that had, according to the man, inspired an outbreak of reading, crime fiction being the prisoners' preferred subject matter. Lorimer raised his eyebrows in silence. He'd heard it all before, had seen the selection of books in several prison libraries whenever Maggie had donated boxes from her colleagues at school.

'Is Maloney much of a reader?' he asked.

''Fraid not.' The officer shrugged. 'Sits in his cell for as long each day as he can get away with. He's made to come out

318

for recreational times, of course, and he is meant to be part of a work detail.'

There was a pause and Lorimer stopped walking for a moment, turning to the man. 'But . . . ?'

'It's the same old story. Sudden withdrawal, won't communicate with any of the staff or the other prisoners, doesn't want to see anyone.'

'Yet he agreed to see me.'

'Yes, he did. First time I've seen anything like a spark of life in that prisoner since he was brought down here.' There was an expression of curiosity in the man's eyes but Lorimer merely smiled. If the visit proved successful then the prison officer by his side would hear all about it soon enough.

DI Crozier had failed to obtain much from the prisoner after his initial confession. Lorimer had read the man's signed statement after his arrest. Even then he had felt some disquiet at how easily the police had accepted Jock Maloney's version of events. And yet the DI had been thorough, there was no question about that. She had not demurred when he had suggested this visit. *I might have the inside track because of our association in Mull*, he'd reasoned. *Perhaps he'll open up to someone he knows outside of all of this?* He'd been heartened by her readiness to allow him access to her suspect. Perhaps, a cynical little voice intoned, DI Crozier had no real expectations of Lorimer succeeding any more than she had already and was simply humouring the detective superintendent.

They continued walking on up a sloping corridor where

319

light flooded in from the summer skies. It was already sounding more hopeful than he had anticipated.

'If you would just wait here for a moment, sir? They'll be bringing Maloney down to the room across there in a few minutes.'

Lorimer found himself standing opposite the pale yellow door to the room that was normally used by solicitors for meeting with their clients. There was something about this place that lifted one's mood – and it wasn't simply caused by the sun sparkling behind the frosted glass windows. Every floor surface was clean and shining, every wall looked newly painted in pastel shades, a far cry from the Victorian establishments where Maloney might have been sent.

When the three men rounded the corner of the corridor and came towards him, Lorimer looked up then looked away almost immediately, not recognising the prisoner being escorted between the two officers. When he glanced up again it was to see the thin face of Jock Maloney staring at him intently. Head bare, his grey locks thinning and with stubbled chin and cheeks, the man looked years older than the cheerful garage mechanic he remembered from Tobermory. For an instant Lorimer tried to imagine the jaunty panama hat that had been Maloney's trademark, the easy banter that they had once enjoyed whenever his car had been at the Ledaig workshop.

'In here.' One of the officers led Jock into the room and motioned him to sit at a small table that was fixed to the floor, a necessary precaution lest a prisoner become violent and decide to begin throwing furniture around the room or, worse, at any visitor.

'I'll be fine, now, thanks.' Lorimer looked each of the prison officers in the eye, his tone brooking no opposition.

'We'll be right outside, sir,' one of them said, nodding at Lorimer then giving a quick glance towards the prisoner. But Jock was staring down below the table at his hands as if he wanted to blot out everything that was happening around him.

As soon as the door was closed, however, he looked up and met Lorimer's steady blue gaze.

'Aye,' Jock Maloney began. 'It's yourself.'

'Jock.' Lorimer nodded and reached out to shake the man's hand. Jock leaned across the table, extending his right hand, the courtesy returned. It was cold and clammy to the touch but still firm; the man might have lost some of his spirit but there was still strength in these hands. Had they, Lorimer wondered fleetingly, been the hands that had stopped the lives of two innocent victims?

'You didn't request a solicitor,' Lorimer began.

'No need,' Maloney replied tersely. 'We know one another well enough.'

Lorimer studied the unkempt face of the man before him. It was every prisoner's right to have a solicitor present at meetings such as these. But, no, it was to be a private discussion between the two men and that in itself gave the detective superintendent pause for thought. He cast his gaze over the man from Mull, seeing changes that even a short time in prison had wrought: the dark circles under his eyes, accentuated by an unfamiliar pallor.

'How are you, Jock?'

There was a faint smile then Maloney shook his head. 'Aye, they're all right in here. Doing their job, I suppose.'

'Nothing to complain about then?'

Jock gave a short laugh. 'I could do with a fish supper at times.' He bit his lip as it began to tremble. 'Preferably one from the old pier.' He wiped his eyes with the back of his hand and let out a long sigh of despair.

'I went to see Richard,' Lorimer told him.

The man's head came up, his tear-filled eyes looking at the detective superintendent.

'How is he?'

'Well, his shoulder's been operated on, they took the bullet out but it will take a long time for it to heal. The bone was pretty well shattered.'

There was silence between the two men for a moment as Jock shook his head, still biting his lip to prevent himself uttering a sob.

'What actually happened, Jock? Did you try to shoot Richard? Or was it an accident? I think it would help him to know.'

For a fleeting second there was a light in the man's eyes that flickered and died as though some unspoken decision had been made.

Then a sigh that made the man's whole body slump back on the moulded plastic seat. 'I didnae intend to hurt him,' Maloney began, then looked away from the detective superintendent as though trying to blot out the memory.

Lorimer nodded. 'Our team is looking at the site in the forest,' he said. 'See if forensics backs that up.'

Maloney nodded silently, raising one arm to his face and wiping his eyes with his sleeve.

'They tell me he'll be in hospital for a wee while yet before he can travel back home,' Lorimer continued. 'Keith's been in to see him, though.'

Jock lifted his head once more at the mention of his elder son.

'But no' his mother?'

Lorimer shook his head. She had been informed of what had happened but had stated that she did not wish to become involved. Strange, he mused. How could a woman abandon her sons like that? For a moment his thoughts turned to Pamela Dalgleish and the anguish in that mother's face as she had left the hospital at Craignure, the certainty of never seeing her youngest child again filling her with such terrible grief.

'I believe Keith is going to take some leave from work to drive Richard back once he's fit enough to be moved,' he said gently.

There was the slightest movement from the man's head as he stared past Lorimer. What was he thinking? How badly had the break-up with his ex-wife affected him? Or were Maloney's thoughts directed at more recent events? And was there something in that face to tell the detective the real story? Why Jock Maloney had ended up here after confessing to the murders?

'I didn't know you had a boat, Jock,' Lorimer said, his conversational tone and change of topic designed to disarm the prisoner. It was a tactic he was used to employing; something that could provoke a suspect into letting down their guard.

Jock frowned. 'No, you got that wrong,' he replied. 'I've never had a boat.'

'Oh, is it Richard who sails, then?'

'Who's been filling your head with rubbish? We've never had boats, man! It's cars in *our* family.' He gave a hollow laugh. 'Fact is, none of us even learned to swim and we live on an island.'

'I'm thinking you didn't like the relationship between Richard and Rory Dalgleish, Jock?' Lorimer's tone had not altered, another sudden change of question thrown casually to see the other man's reaction.

'Shouldn't have . . . !' Maloney blustered then stopped.

'Shouldn't have *what*, Jock? Richard shouldn't have begun a relationship with the lad? Is that what you're trying to tell me?'

Jock Maloney covered his face with both hands and began to rock back and forward in his chair, a small sound of distress escaping into the room.

'Jean Erskine saw you quarrelling with Rory, didn't she, Jock?' Lorimer went on. 'Perhaps she had even seen the way those two boys behaved towards one another.'

Jock shook his head, a whimpering noise coming from behind his hands.

'You were ashamed, weren't you? Didn't want folk to be talking about Richard. Your son. You had to get away from all of their gossip, didn't you?'

'Bloody place!' Jock had taken his hands from his face, the tears visibly streaming down the man's cheeks. 'Couldn't walk the length of the street but someone would spin a lie about you!'

'But it wasn't a lie, was it, Jock?' Lorimer insisted. 'Richard *is* gay. But it was you who couldn't face that particular truth.'

Jock opened his mouth to protest but Lorimer slammed his fist down onto the table between them, making the prisoner jump.

'You never touched a hair of Rory's head!' he growled. 'Or of poor old Jean Erskine. Did you, Jock?'

'I . . .'

'Your confession is nothing more than an attempt to protect your son, right?'

Jock gave another groan and leaned forwards, putting his grizzled head in his hands.

'See, here's what I think happened, Jock.' Lorimer sat back and swung one leg across the other, his mild tone back once more. 'You fled Tobermory, supposing Richard to have

325

committed a terrible thing. Homosexual behaviour is something you don't understand, is it? Something you don't *want* to understand. You could not conceive of it being anything gentle or loving, could you? To your mind it was associated with violence, something disgusting and unnatural, am I right?'

The moan from that lowered head was enough to make the detective continue.

'Perhaps you thought it would be better if Richard were to be shot like a dying dog than face whatever prison could do to him,' Lorimer said softly. 'Was that what you thought as you raised that rifle, Jock?'

A sniff came from the man opposite.

'But you couldn't do it. You couldn't kill your wee boy, could you?' Lorimer went on. 'Maybe you thought you were capable of an act like that but at the last minute you changed your mind and the gun went off, injuring Richard.'

'He cannae come into a place like this,' Jock whispered. 'He just cannae.'

'Listen to me, Jock.' Lorimer uncrossed his legs and leaned forward, his eyes searching out the other man's face. 'Richard had nothing to do with Rory's death. And from your initial reaction I could tell that neither of you had an inkling about what had happened to Jean Erskine.'

'Are you ... sure?' Jock raised his head, his brown eyes fixed on the man on the other side of the table.

'I need evidence to show that it was impossible for Richard

to have carried out such a thing,' Lorimer admitted. 'But one thing I am sure of is that whoever killed Rory Dalgleish needed a boat to dispose of his body. Now. Listen to me, Jock, and I'll tell you what I'm going to do.'

Stevie Crozier lifted her coffee cup and sipped the dark liquid. Nothing had ever tasted quite so good, she thought. And it was just the two of them there in the deputy chief constable's office, women who had succeeded in their respective careers, while Lorimer was off on a fool's errand to speak to the prisoner.

'I have to commend you on the way you appear to have carried out this case to a satisfactory conclusion, Detective Inspector.' Joyce Rogers raised a porcelain teacup in a salute to the blonde woman seated opposite.

Stevie Crozier felt her cheeks burn in response to the compliment. It was hard to imagine a better outcome; a man banged up for these dreadful crimes and now the woman she admired being so generous with her praise.

'It can't have been easy having Lorimer there in the background,' Rogers commented, a twinkle in her eye.

'He didn't interfere, ma'am,' Crozier said, realising as she spoke that this was quite true. Lorimer had kept in the background as far as the process of investigation had been concerned, only coming to join the team as and when he had been required to do so. Stevie brushed aside the memory of his attempt to connect the young boy's death with a twenty-year-old cold case. Everyone had failures in their past, she acknowledged, even the great William Lorimer.

As though summoned by the mention of his name they heard a brief knock on the door and there he was, his tall figure looming over the two women, an inscrutable expression on his face.

'Lorimer, we were just discussing you!' Rogers said mischievously. 'Join us for a celebratory cup of tea?' The deputy chief constable waved her cup aloft.

'No thank you, ma'am, DI Crozier.' Lorimer turned to give the other woman a courteous nod. 'I don't think celebrations are quite in order. Yet.'

'What do you mean?' Crozier looked up, startled.

'He's retracted his confession,' Lorimer said, his hands on the back of Crozier's chair.

'What on earth . . . ?' Crozier began but a warning hand from Rogers stopped her.

'Tell us,' Rogers commanded. 'Sit down right now and tell us everything that happened at Low Moss.'

'So,' Joyce Rogers sighed as the detective superintendent finished describing the meeting that had taken place between Maloney and himself. 'What do we do now?'

'Find the real killer,' Lorimer said bluntly.

'But, Maloney—' Crozier seemed too full of pent-up emotion to continue, or else that look from the deputy chief constable cut her short.

Lorimer looked at the blonde woman; she had seemed so full of life as he had entered the room but now the figure seated beside him appeared diminished, somehow; her face had crumpled as he had given details of the reason behind Jock Maloney's confession and the new evidence that Richard claimed of hearing his father asleep as he'd crept out to find Rory Dalgleish.

'It hardly bears thinking about, that sort of attitude, but we see it all the time, don't we?' Joyce Rogers commented. 'Old-fashioned homophobia. Refusal to admit that your boy is different from the way you want him to be ... although actually wanting to have him die rather than be locked up with hardened criminals is very extreme.' Her sigh and shake of the head expressed the sadness that Rogers genuinely felt. The cups lay abandoned on the low table between the three police officers, their contents now cold.

'What do you want me to do now, ma'am?' Stevie Crozier's miserable tone made Lorimer want to put a consoling arm around the younger woman's shoulder; the DI was obviously crushed by his revelations. How must she be feeling? One minute she was a successful SIO and now her entire case had crumbled around her ears.

'Go back to Mull,' Rogers said briskly. 'And take this fellow with you.' She smiled up at Lorimer. 'He can be quite useful at times.' She raised playful eyebrows at the detective super-intendent.

'And who is to be in charge of the case?' Crozier muttered.

'Why, you are, DI Crozier. Detective Superintendent Lorimer is still officially on leave but I think I can arrange that he be seconded as your special adviser. If that's what you want?' She looked from one to the other quizzically. 'I'm sure you two have already established a good working relationship? Yes? That's fine, then,' she continued without waiting for a reply from either of them.

'We will see where the matter of Maloney's imprisonment stands,' she added. 'There will be the usual delay until the fiscal and Maloney's lawyers decide what is to be done. He is still charged with several other matters, don't forget,' she warned Lorimer. 'Attempted murder of his own son being just one of them. So I hope you haven't promised him an instant release from Low Moss Prison.'

The man from Tobermory was becoming used to the prison routine, his day punctuated by mealtimes when he could relax for a few minutes with the other prisoners. He rubbed the back of his neck as they were shepherded into the dining hall by the prison officers, feeling the tension that had been there ever since Lorimer had confronted him, his eyes roving over the tables, seeking out a friendly face.

Jock sat down opposite Eddie, the boy who had smiled at him from his first day in this part of the prison. *Ah'm Eddie*, he'd told Jock. *Ah may be gay but ah'm nae trying tae be ither than jist friendly, awright? No fear of me comin' oan tae ye, big man*, he'd chuckled.

It was hard to believe that this youngster was actually a thirty-four-year-old man. *See bein' in here? It either ages ye or keeps ye lookin' young*, Eddie had told him when Jock had voiced his surprise.

'Aye,' Jock began by way of a greeting now. 'You're still here then?'

'Ah'm oot o' here the morra,' the boy agreed, his smile revealing teeth that had been treated by several different prison dentists over the past two decades. 'Cannae wait.' Eddie jigged up and down in his seat at the dining table. 'A' these things that've changed since ah wis banged up, like. 'Sno' the same as it wis afore.' He shrugged. 'See back then? Couldnae get ma heid roon bein' gay, could ah? 'Swhat done it fur me.' He looked down and away, the memory of killing another human being a burden he would always have to bear. 'Huv tae say, if it hadnae been fur the officers and the medical staff I'd've topped maself lang since. Came tae terms wi' ma ain sexuality, so ah did. Ma mammy's okay aboot it and so's ma old man.' He shrugged and smiled.

'You're not worried about what people think, then?' The words were out of Jock's mouth before he realised. 'Sorry, didn't mean . . .'

'Ach, ye're all right, big man. See, ah've got it all sussed out noo.' Eddie leaned forward and held Jock's gaze. 'Love's love,' he said softly. 'It's that simple.'

Jock sat back and stared at the meal the passman put down in front of him.

He had tried to protect Richard, hadn't he? Wasn't that out of love?

Tears stung his eyes as he thought of his son. What he would give to hug him right now, tell him that he was sorry.

Jock glanced at Eddie who was tucking into his helping of shepherd's pie. Tomorrow this young man would be free to join the outside world and free to be himself in every way. Surely that was what any loving father would wish for his son.

It was as though the artist had painted it for him, the image burning in the young man's brain as he stood staring at it.

The Bloody Tryst *had captured both their imaginations as they had strolled around together, ever mindful of the need not to stand too closely if one of the uniformed security guards happened to look their way. At other times, an illicit handclasp, a silent brushing of lips against the other's cheek brought a familiar warmth to his loins that was always the forerunner of something sweeter to come.*

But that was gone now, for ever, the image before him like an accusation. Had theirs been a fated love affair? Was it something that was destined to end in violence and tears? As he looked at the painting, the body of the lover lying sprawled on the ground, the man remembered only the dead eyes of the red-haired boy, not the passion that had gone before.

Why had he returned to the city? And what had drawn him back to this place where so many secrets remained? It was as though the spires of the art galleries had beckoned him like a hand as he had stood outside the university, looking down past the gardens, couples sprawled on the summer grass, to that place where he had found something that he had thought to be love. Of course he had made discreet enquiries about the boy, asking after him by name. No, he wouldn't be back to finish his course, he had told his tutors up at Glasgow School of Art. Yes, he wanted to take all his folio work away, thanks. Were they still running the life classes on Saturday mornings? Was Gary going to sit for them again? No? Just didn't turn up one day. Odd, wasn't it? And, no, they couldn't tell him anything about the red-haired model. They came and went, these fey types who sat for the art students, the woman's smile seemed to say as she left him with a careless shrug.

And all the time that lump in his stomach like a lead weight, the knowledge that it was his own wilful act that had taken Gary away from them.

Nobody had missed the lad, it seemed. Even the young men who mooched about down near the playing fields at Port Glasgow had no idea where the red-haired boy had gone, nor had they displayed any interest. Want to do the business? they had asked hopefully, but he had shaken his head, too weary with his burden of guilt to summon up any notion for a sexual encounter. Gary had vanished and nobody had come forward to ask where he was. But he knew. That newspaper clipping burned in his pocket, the description of a body pulled from the Clyde and the request for anybody who had known the victim to come forward.

The man turned away from the painting, fists clenched by his side, a sudden need to be out of the building, to breathe fresh air. He almost ran down the marble staircase, feet hastening across the cold *floor of the art gallery and museum in his desperation to leave the building.*

Then he was walking past the rows of parked cars, the sun beating down on his head. Nobody would ever know what he had done. Nobody would ever care.

CHAPTER THIRTY-SIX

'Are you going out or staying in?' The woman stood, arms folded, as she regarded the ill-shaven man standing in the doorway of the house. 'Only I've the whole place to smarten up if we're to start taking in a lodger.'

'Don't know why you can't just do the B&B like everyone else,' Lachie Turner said morosely, refusing to look over his shoulder at his sister, the cigarette in his hand almost smoked down to its filter tip.

'Hm. If you were bringing in some money then we wouldn't need to offer a room to let!' Bella Ingram snapped.

'Hardly my fault that Forsyth drank all his profits away, is it?' Lachie replied, his reasonable tone making the woman humph even louder.

'Well, you can finish your dirty fag and get in here and lend a hand,' Bella retorted at last. 'If the Tourist Office phone and say there's an offer for the spare room then we cannae very well turn it down, can we?'

Her brother lifted bushy eyebrows to heaven then blew the last line of smoke from his unshaven lips.

'Don't know why you couldn't have stayed on at the fish farming,' Bella scolded crossly, her words aimed at her brother's back. 'At least there you had a decent wage!'

Lachie did not deign to reply. He took one last lingering drag on the cigarette then flicked it away into the fuchsia bushes, knowing that this small action would annoy his sister. Forsyth hadn't sent the promised reference after all and the handyman-gardener was reluctant to begin offering his services until it had arrived.

'I'm away on out,' he said, pushing himself off the doorpost and sauntering along the pathway to the garden gate. The old van sat outside, its road tax disc dangerously close to being out of date. Tomorrow was the first day of August and with it came the realisation that he would be breaking the law by his failure to pay the necessary fee.

'To hell with them all,' he grumbled, kicking a pebble off the paving stones that he had laid so carefully all those years ago for his elder sister and her husband. Dougie was gone now; drowned at sea, leaving a bitter widow and a brother-in-law whose sporadic income was barely sufficient to cover his bed and board. Dougie Ingram had left the boat to Bella yet the widow had never sold it, preferring to hold on to the memory of her husband, the gilded lettering *BONNY BELLE* on the fishing boat's prow fading over the seasons like its namesake.

He would drive back down to Kilbeg, demand the reference from Forsyth and maybe even hint about payment for the garden designs that were still in the man's possession.

Lachie stumbled as his left knee bent under a sudden pain. He swore, cursing the fate that had made him a victim to the aches of arthritis that the doctor had diagnosed. It was the *downside of outdoor work*, the woman at Craignure Hospital had proclaimed, giving his knee what was meant to be a friendly slap, the mere touch of her hand making him wince. What did she know about outdoor work, the stupid bitch? he thought, gritting his teeth against the ache. Hadn't he bent down on a kneeling pad to weed her own big garden often enough? And her with an able-bodied husband, though the man was more often on the hills lugging his photographic equipment than helping his hard-working wife.

She had been mentioned in the *Oban Times* as the doctor assisting in Rory Dalgleish's case, Lachie recalled, putting the van into gear and setting off along the street. He turned the vehicle around a sharp corner, its engine protesting as the incline became suddenly steeper. In moments he was heading down Breadalbane Street, past Miss Hoolie's green-painted house that was beloved of little children looking for *Balamory* landmarks, past the police station then heading out of the town, the van gathering speed. He would not think about Rory Dalgleish, Lachie decided. Or of any dead body lying on a cold mortuary slab. It was not a day for those sorts of thoughts.

The sun shone down on the winding road, a few clouds

drifting high above the surrounding hills. Today was a day for new beginnings; once he had a reference in his pocket he would begin to look for work and perhaps a new place to stay away from the carping tongue of his embittered sister.

Hamish Forsyth was nowhere to be seen. Lachie had wandered from the empty reception area through the residents' lounge and into the kitchens but the place appeared deserted. Even the bar was closed up, as if the owner had decided for once to keep temptation at bay. Lachie stood at the foot of the staircase, looking upwards and listening.

'Are you looking for someone?'

'Christ! Maryka. Dinna do that to a body!' Lachie yelped, putting his hand to his chest as though to protect a fluttering heart.

'Give you a fright, did I?' The girl grinned, flicking the duster she held between her finger and thumb. 'Sorry,' she added, sounding anything but.

'You still here then? They haven't given you the push yet?'

The girl shrugged, an enigmatic expression on her pretty face.

'And Elena? She still here too?'

Maryka shook her head as she stuffed the duster into her apron pocket. 'Not any more. Her cousin in Fort William told her about a job in their hotel so she packed up and off she went.'

'But did she get her wages first?' Lachie asked slyly.

'Think so,' the Dutch girl answered. 'Anyway, I'm not leaving until the end of August. And they'll have to pay me what's owing.'

'You'll be lucky,' Lachie scoffed. 'I doubt if there's enough cash left to pay any of us what's owing.'

'Oh, I don't know,' Maryka said vaguely, examining her fingernails. 'Must be money coming from somewhere. We're not starving here yet. And Archie's still here living in that old wreck of a boat of his so we're still being fed.'

'So, where are Lord and Lady Muck?'

'Out.' Maryka yawned as though it was of no interest to her. 'There's no guests left. I'm just doing out all the rooms,' she added, nodding upwards. 'Why? Did you have an appointment to see them?'

Lachie's jaw hardened visibly. Cheeky wee madam, he thought; who did she think she was, acting as if she were in charge of the place! And getting paid for a month longer than the rest of the staff. Though why Archie Gillespie was still here was a mystery.

'Tell Hamish Forsyth he needs to send me on that reference,' Lachie said, stepping forward and wagging a finger in the girl's face. 'Okay?'

The Dutch girl took a step backwards, raising her hands in a defensive gesture. 'Sure, Lachie, I'll tell him. Sure I will.'

'Aye, well, I'll expect to hear from him sooner than later,' he growled. 'Be sure to tell him that too.'

*

As the gardener slouched away through the open door of the hotel Maryka walked slowly after him, waiting in the doorway and watching as he drove off in the old van.

It was one of those sultry afternoons when all the world seemed to stand still, not even the song of a bird disturbing the heavy silence. Leaden clouds sat over the Morvern hills, stealthily gathering a blurred veil over the previously blue skies. It would thunder later, she thought, looking up. And pour with rain. Shuddering despite the close atmosphere, the girl walked slowly back into the hotel, tempted to shut the heavy door behind her.

With the departure of the gardener, Maryka felt even more alone in the big house than before. Archie had gone for a sail somewhere, the jetty strangely bare without the old boat sitting at anchor. Perhaps he'd gone for good? She had no idea.

One by one they had all left her behind, she thought, one hand sweeping her duster over the banister as she climbed the stairs. Rory with his loud voice ringing out, Fiona who would share a giggle and Elena, who had cleared out of the caravan for better prospects elsewhere.

The Dutch girl had been selective with the truth, unwilling to share certain things with Lachlan Turner. Yes, she had an agreement to stay for another month, but whether there would be more than enough for her return fare to Amsterdam remained to be seen. Still, she wouldn't be explaining to the gardener what really kept her on the island. No, that was a secret that Maryka hugged to herself.

Ewan Angus had been to see her only this morning, the fish placed hastily in the shed at the bottom of the garden, his strong arms around her, a whispered promise in her ear. The girl put a finger to her lips as if she could still feel the fisherman's stolen kisses. There was something he had to do, he had told her, a serious look on his handsome face. Then he would return and they would go off together in his boat, just the two of them.

The girl smiled, remembering his voice and the expression in those sleepy eyes that told her he wanted more than just a few kisses.

Maryka was almost at the end of the upper corridor before she saw that her feet had taken her right up to the Forsyths' own quarters. She felt for the can of polish in her apron pocket and shrugged. Well, their rooms would need cleaning too, she reasoned, turning the brass door handle and pushing open the door, a sudden curiosity to know more about the place where her employers lived. Mrs Forsyth had never expressly forbidden the girls to clean these rooms but it had been taken for granted that PRIVATE meant just that.

The first bedroom was large with dark burgundy wallpaper and a faded red tartan carpet like the ones in the public areas of the hotel. A job lot, Maryka decided, and not put down recently, that was for sure. She stepped towards the window and looked out the back of the house, seeing the long line of rhododendrons obscuring the driveway. It was Hamish's bedroom; that was obvious, the girl thought, wrinkling her nose against the stale smell of booze and the heap of unwashed clothes lying across an armchair by the window. For a moment she was tempted to throw up the sash and let some fresh air into the stuffy room but a little voice of caution reminded her to leave well alone. It was better that nobody knew she had been there.

A second door opened into an ante-chamber where an ensuite bathroom had been built, obviously to be used by the occupants of each room. Maryka switched on the light, opened the door and sniffed. At least there was a scent of pine here, something fresh. Mrs Forsyth could not be faulted for not keeping this bit of their shared domain clean. Turning, she saw that her employer's own bedroom was closed, a key in the outer lock.

A chill came as though from under the bedroom door, a draught from an open window, perhaps? Her hand stretched towards the key, yet Maryka was seized with an odd reluctance to enter her employer's room.

No, she thought, I can't go in there. That closed door held many secrets, she thought. But were they secrets that she really wanted to know? She shivered suddenly and found herself retreating hastily as though some unseen, malevolent presence were watching her.

CHAPTER THIRTY-SEVEN

E wan Angus twisted the orange twine nervously between his long fingers as he stood outside the back door of Calum Mhor's house. Mrs Calum would be glad enough of the pair of sea trout dangling from his fist, he knew, but the big sergeant's reaction to what he was about to tell him was another story.

'Come away in, Ewan.' Mrs Calum stood in the doorway, beaming. 'You know where the kitchen is, lad,' she said, taking the fish from the tall young fisherman's hands and then stepping aside to let him enter the house. 'A cup of tea? Kettle's on.'

'No thanks, missus.' Ewan Angus bobbed his head then took off the flat tweed cap he was wearing. 'Actually,' he cleared his throat nervously, 'I was wondering if Himself was at home?'

'Calum?' The woman's eyebrows rose in surprise. 'Aye, he is, right enough.' She stared at the young man for a moment then waddled off to the foot of the stairs.

'Calum!' Her voice boomed as she called out her husband's name. 'A fellow here to see you!'

There was the sound of a door closing upstairs and heavy footsteps descending then the big policeman came into view.

'It's yourself, Ewan Angus, what can I do for you, lad?'

'I ...' He glanced furtively at Mrs McManus standing watching.

'It's a wee bit private, sir ...' he said, biting his lip and nodding apologetically at the police sergeant's wife.

Calum Mhor raised his chin. 'Aye, well. Come away ben the house. We can have a wee talk through in the lounge,' he said, ushering the younger man along the hallway. 'The visitors are all away out just now.'

Ewan Angus followed the policeman into a spacious room that was light and airy; to the fisherman's eyes everything seemed very clean and bright. Glass-topped tables and a sideboard full of ornaments and silver-framed photos gleamed, a testament no doubt to Mrs Calum's work with polish and duster. He looked past the flowered curtains drawn back against picture windows that faced the pier where the *Isle of Mull* was disgorging its final stream of cars for the day from below its raised bow.

'Sit down, lad,' Calum said.

'Thanks.' Ewan Angus perched on the edge of a cream-coloured sofa as though afraid that he might somehow leave a mark on the pristine furnishings.

'There's something on your mind,' Calum observed, giving the fisherman a shrewd look.

'Aye,' Ewan Angus sighed audibly. 'We should have come

345

to you at the time,' he began, looking down at the cap and screwing it between his fingers. 'Only . . . '

'Aye?'

'Da was worried we'd lose the boat,' Ewan Angus blurted out.

'Ah, you were at the splash.' Calum nodded. 'Well. That's something between thee and me, eh, laddie?' The big man winked and grinned.

'Well, it's no' as easy as that, sir,' the young man replied. 'You see . . . I'm here to explain about that poor boy, the one that Mr Lorimer found at Leiter.'

Calum Mhor watched the fisherman walk, head bowed, back along the road towards the car park where he had left his father's van. It had taken a bit of courage to come and confess their small part in the discovery of Rory Dalgleish's body. But had old Ewan Angus known that his son was making this visit to the police sergeant's home in Craignure? Perhaps the lad was at this moment wondering how to explain his actions to his fisherman father.

Lorimer had been right after all, he thought, walking away from the window as he mentally admired the perspicacity of the Glasgow detective. The tide had been unnaturally high but even so, that had not explained why the body had been found on dry ground. But now that part of the puzzle was solved. The discovery of Rory's dead body by the two fisher-men and the old man's fear that they would risk confiscation of their boat and nets accounted for that inconsistency. He was prepared to make an official statement, Ewan Angus had agreed, his head hung in sudden shame. He'd make sure of that. And, once the old man had been told that it was a fait accompli, he'd surely agree to do the same, despite the consequences.

What DI Crozier would do to the fishermen was anyone's guess, Calum sighed to himself. He would do his best to mitigate the penalty placed upon them but keeping such information was bound to have repercussions of some kind. They'd be lucky to keep their boat but perhaps Crozier could be persuaded to see reason? He hoped so. Things had been hard for old Ewan Angus after his partner, Dougie Ingram, had died. Bella had refused to allow the older man permission to use the boat after her husband's death and they'd had to make do with illicit forays into other folks' waters. It was something that the big police sergeant and others had overlooked, the feeling that Bella Ingram had wronged her husband's partner outweighing any legal consideration.

His thoughts turned to what sorts of losses were inevitable. There was the net, for one thing. The fishing net that had caught the boy's dead body would have to be examined as soon as Ewan Angus could bring it to the incident room in Tobermory. Calum Mhor sighed. Perhaps he would talk to the tall detective from Glasgow, see if he could persuade Crozier to go lightly on the father and son.

*

347

'Courlene,' the voice on the telephone told her.

'What's that exactly?' Rosie enquired.

'It's all in my report, I've just sent it to you as an attachment,' the forensic officer explained. 'It's a sort of twine used in the fishing industry. You can read up on the whole thing once you open my email.'

'Courlene,' Rosie whispered to herself, fingers busy at her keyboard. She sat back and read the report from the man who had just called her. The severe pressure marks on Rory Dalgleish's body had been made with a sort of polythene twine, the scientist claimed. It was one of the most successful of Courtauld's commercial twines developed for the fishing industry, mainly distributed by a company called Boris Nets and now used by fishing fleets all over the world.

Great, Rosie thought. *Doesn't exactly narrow it down, then*. However the report went on to explain that the marks imprinted on the victim's wrists and ankles were not made by the fishermen's nets, which would have left a criss-cross pattern, but by lengths of the twine instead.

She scrolled down, looking at the various types of twine, her cursor coming to rest on the orange strands marked out by her friend in the forensic lab. It was a type of twine that had once been sold by chandlers but had been discontinued more than twenty years ago. That was not to say, the report went on, that some of this brand of Courlene was not still in existence, rolled up in corners of fishing boat lockers all over the globe. She read on, taking note of the scientific properties of the twine and glancing from time to time at the photographs by the side of her laptop, seeing the marks around the boy's limbs that even such long immersion in water had failed to remove.

Rosie stared past the screen for a long moment, wondering. Solly had told her all about the cold case from 1995. Had Lorimer been correct to imagine there was a connection between these two murders? Her glance fell onto the screen once again. And, she thought, a faint smile hovering over her lips, could this be the very thing to link them both together?

Detective Superintendent Lorimer handed back the book to the clerk behind the desk. It was important to sign and date any entry whenever a production was to be re-examined. Any failure to do so could jeopardise a future court case. He waited patiently while the woman went in search of the bag.

'Just a few samples,' she told him. 'Was that all the deceased had on him?'

'He was found naked in the water,' Lorimer explained. 'There were only ever the forensic samples taken at the post-mortem.'

'Sad,' she remarked, shaking her head. 'There's a story there somewhere, no doubt.'

Lorimer took the production bag from her hands and slipped it into the case file he was already carrying. Things had changed a lot in twenty years, he mused, but at least the evidence from old cases was still being preserved, even if it only amounted to the filth taken by a pathologist from under a victim's fingernails or the water weeds that had been clinging to his body. The cadaver itself had long since been buried in an unmarked grave but there were plenty of photographic records from the post-mortem still in the file. He heaved a sigh, remembering that morning by the Clyde and the young student who had risen to become Head of Forensic Medical Science at the University of Glasgow. How young they had both been back then! And how things had progressed in both their professions. Nowadays Rosie could email him with the results of toxicology and other tests so that a case could be pushed along far more swiftly than in the old days when they were both just starting out.

He pushed open the door to his office and laid the file on his desk, a surge of anticipation making him shiver suddenly. What if . . . ? He sat down and leaned forward, his hand resting for a moment on the front cover of the file, the date on its label filling his mind with so many memories.

When he opened the folder it was like turning back time itself. The photographs of the boy's dead body lying on the grass, the notes that he remembered writing as a young detective constable and the rubber stamps from the Crown Office.

He turned the pages of the file, setting the photographs carefully to one side.

The drawing slipped out from between the pages of the file, so that Lorimer almost let it fall from his fingers. It was still in its plastic bag, taped down behind to keep it clean, he supposed, turning it over.

The pencil-drawn image of a young man stared out at him. Where had it come from? Lorimer wondered, brow furrowing. Then he remembered. Hadn't he asked at the art school if an image could be created from the original photographs? Someone had done this, not an enhanced digital photo, but a carefully executed sketch. He stared at the pencil drawing of the boy as he might have looked before the murder. It had been the same day that Maggie had lost the baby. He'd gone on leave afterwards and the case had been put aside by the time he had returned. But someone had carried out his request and the drawing had been put into the case file along with all the rest of the notes. But he had never seen it, and, numbed with grief for the loss of their baby son, Lorimer had never even remembered that he had asked for such a thing to be done.

He stared at the drawing. It was a black and white pencil drawing but even so, the detective could recall the young man's flame-red hair. He sat back, a sense of loss pervading him. Someone's son, he thought. Someone's friend? And yet not a single person had come forward and this drawing had languished unseen for twenty years inside these case notes, never seeing the light of day or being copied into thousands of newspapers where it might have jolted somebody's memory.

It could still be done, he mused. *Crimewatch* might be interested in a cold case from twenty years back. *Do you recognise this man?* he could almost hear the blonde presenter ask.

Courlene, he reminded himself, picking up the file and sifting through the section where several photographs had been

351

It had begun over a cup of tea, a nice green pot set on a wooden stand, as he recalled. How such a simple object could be imbued with the bitterness that had followed!

The café in Kelvingrove had been quiet, few visitors about on that memorable weekday; the red-haired waiter had been chatty, smiling and catching his eye in a manner he recognised only too well as flirtation. It had been so easy after that, meeting along the pathway of the river, the excitement of a new clandestine relationship that was going to be just for fun, the lad had said, just for the moment. Except that he had given Rory other ideas.

There was pain, always pain, he'd told the boy as he'd pulled his bonds tighter, laughing as he'd heard his cries; that's what made everything worth it.

He hadn't expected the lad to follow up his suggestion of finding a post at Kilbeg, expecting the handwritten note with details scribbled down to be discarded after he had gone back home. And yet, Rory Dalgleish's arrival on the pier at Craignure had filled his mind with images of what they might enjoy, images that were always accompanied by the sound of Rory begging him to stop the pain. Begging, but really wanting it too. Else why would he have come to work on the island?

The summer had been hot and sticky some days and the cool of the boat had given them some respite from their day-to-day work, different though it had been. There, as the waves had lapped against the hull, he and Rory had experimented with their lovemaking, passion driving them both to seek more adventurous ways of fulfilment.

And death had been the summit of his desire. Was this something he ought to have known? He felt that twitch in his fingers as though they were somehow apart from his body, entities that had a will of their own. Should he not feel exonerated from the guilt that tugged at his heart?

There had been moments when he had thought of confessing, wondering why another had taken the blame instead. But now Jock Maloney had changed his testimony and the investigation had begun all over again.

He could feel a shadow beginning to spread over his mind, blotting out the way his hands had grasped the boy's neck, the old woman's muffled cry as he had snuffed out her life. There was nothing more he wanted now than to sink back into its darkness.

CHAPTER THIRTY-EIGHT

She was standing on the edge of the jetty, staring out to sea, arms wrapped around her chest to keep out the wind. Something about the way her hair blew up from her face tugged at the girl's heart. There was deep sorrow burdening those narrow shoulders, she thought, a story left untold.

'Mrs Forsyth,' she called out, but Maryka's words were carried away by the gusts coming off the water, tips of waves turning white, crescent-shaped eddies licking the wooden timbers below the landing stage.

'Mrs Forsyth?' Maryka stepped forward and tapped the older woman's shoulder, making her start. 'It's time for dinner. Archie sent me to tell you.'

The woman looked at her, uncomprehending, as she turned back from her contemplation of the expanse of water that lay between island and mainland.

'It's dinner time,' Maryka persisted gently, tucking her arm under the woman's cardigan sleeve and guiding her along the pathway back to the hotel. 'Archie's got a nice bit of sea trout baked with a salad, you like that, don't you?' she gabbled, aware of the blankness in the woman's pale eyes and the way she allowed herself to be meekly led back to the hotel.

Suddenly, as though she had remembered something, Mrs Forsyth clutched at the girl's arm.

'Will Gary be there?' she demanded. 'Has he arrived back yet?'

Maryka opened her mouth to ask *Who's Gary?* Had her suspicions been correct after all?

'Your son, Gary?' she asked, holding her breath for a moment to see the woman's response.

Freda Forsyth wrinkled her brow for a moment then shook her head. 'He's been away for such a long time,' she sighed. 'But I think he'll be back soon.' She let the girl's arm fall then turned to look out to sea, a strange wistfulness in her face.

Maryka bit her lip. Had their son perished at sea a long time ago? Was that why she came down to the water's edge so often? Did some tragedy from years gone by explain her increasingly bizarre behaviour?

'It's just the four of us tonight,' Maryka said at last. 'Mr Forsyth, Archie, you and me.'

The woman gave no indication that she had heard, merely stepping obediently along the narrow path, eyes fixed on the daisy-strewn grass.

'I think there's a mystery here,' Maryka whispered to the chef, handing back the reefer. Their dinner was over and the

Forsyths had retired to their upstairs rooms leaving her and Archie to clear up. The chef had sparked up their usual after-dinner joint now that they were alone together and the back door was open wide to let the pungent scent of the cannabis drift into the night. They were standing side by side near the big kitchen sinks, Maryka slowly drying the last of the cooking pots, Archie Gillespie hanging them up on the metal hooks suspended from a small pulley fixed to the ceiling.

The chef gave her a look. 'Like how we get our last wages?' he grunted between tokes.

'No, not *that* sort of mystery,' Maryka huffed. 'Listen, guess what I just found out?'

The chef made a face then yawned as though anything the girl could relate was bound to be of little interest. He took one last draw on the reefer then, deciding it was finished, threw it into the sink where it sizzled and died.

'*They had a son,*' she said, forcing as much drama into her voice as she could. 'Did you know that?'

Archie Gillespie shrugged. 'What happened? Did he see the light and scarper?'

'I don't know. Only,' she leaned closer to the chef and dropped her voice, 'poor old Freda was muttering about someone called Gary. Someone she was waiting to come back here. I bet you anything it was their son. And something bad happened to him,' she added darkly.

'Och, your heid's fu' o' nonsense, hen,' the chef snorted derisively.

'No, really, listen,' Maryka said slowly, the drying cloth forgotten in her fingers. 'I'm sure that's why her nibs goes down to the dock all the time.'

Archie turned and looked down at her, his attention caught.

'See, she thinks he's coming back. But d'you know what I think?'

'Give me a clue? He went off to join the navy?'

Maryka shook her head. 'I think he's dead,' she whispered. 'And she won't accept it after all these years. I *think*,' she continued, 'that Rory's murder has brought it all back to her. Maybe we should tell the police?'

For a long moment the chef glared at her, a dark frown tugging down the corners of his mouth.

'Know what I think?' he growled, jabbing a reddened finger towards Maryka's face. 'I think you want tae leave that poor woman alone. You think too damned much for your own good.'

He banged down the grill pan on the kitchen counter and, without another word, stalked out of the back door and into the gathering dusk, leaving the girl to stare at his retreating figure and wonder at the venom in his tone.

CHAPTER THIRTY-NINE

Talking to parents who had lost their child was one of the hardest things that Stevie Crozier had ever done. And having the tall detective superintendent standing by her side did not make it any easier. She shifted from one foot to the other as they stood in the wide entrance porch of the house on Glasgow's affluent south side. It was a large, solidly built home dating from the earlier part of the twentieth century, its grey stones looming up before them as they had walked from the car to the front steps of The Pines, the place doubtless named for the stand of conifers that screened the façade of the house from the main road beyond. It was, Stevie had been informed by DS Langley who knew Glasgow well, one of the most sought after locations in Newton Mearns. And, driving along from the roundabout that separated Kilmarnock Road from the Ayr Road, Stevie had to agree with that.

Stevie glanced behind her, noting the extensive lawns to the front. This garden showed someone's careful hand, the edges deeply trimmed and not a weed in sight. She sighed longingly, remembering her own little patch of garden back in Oban, its grass left uncut far too often. Money could buy the best of gardeners to keep the place as smart as this. But, a little voice reminded her, no amount of money would ever buy back the Dalgleish's youngest child.

'You okay?' Lorimer asked, looking down at her. Stevie turned back and nodded her silent reply, inwardly cursing herself for letting her feelings show.

The DI watched as Lorimer pressed a bell that was set into the sandstone wall above the brass nameplate in bold lettering: DALGLEISH. They were expected but she doubted if either of them would be welcomed.

The door opened after a few seconds to reveal a young woman in her twenties, her trim black suit and patent leather court shoes evidence of recently having come from work.

'I am Detective Inspector Crozier,' Stevie said, proffering her warrant card. 'And this is Detective Superintendent Lorimer.'

'Hello.' The young woman looked them both up and down before stepping back. 'Come in. I'm Jennifer, by the way, Rory's sister.'

Stevie entered the house, followed by Lorimer, walking along a wood-panelled corridor and into a spacious sitting room.

'Mum and Dad will be down in a minute,' Jennifer told them. 'I had a conference at Glasgow Royal Infirmary, that's why I'm here,' she explained.

'Of course, you're a doctor,' Lorimer smiled, standing by the fireplace, hands behind his back.

Jennifer Dalgleish made a face. 'Doesn't make knowing all the details about what happened to Rory any easier,' she said, looking from the tall detective to Stevie. 'But I do try to spare the parents. Luckily my speciality is orthopaedic surgery. Don't get too many opportunities to see anything other than living patients, thank God.' She waved a hand towards the three-piece suite that faced a pale cream Georgian fireplace. 'Look, please sit down. I'll tell them you're here.' She gave a half smile and turned away, her long tawny hair swinging in its tortoiseshell clip.

Stevie perched on the edge of an armchair, taking time to look around at the room. It had been carefully designed by an expert eye, she decided. Either Pamela Dalgleish had some skill in this area or else the place had been decorated by a professional interior designer with no expense spared. Silver and blue patterned curtains screened the huge windows to one side of the room as well as the enormous bay windows to the front of the house, and underfoot were a thick sea-blue carpet and carefully placed lambskin rugs. A smoked glass table to the rear of the room held a tall vase of white regal lilies and stems of grey-blue eucalyptus, the colours in perfect harmony with the furnishings.

'Nice place,' she remarked, turning back to see that Lorimer was watching her with interest, a half smile on his handsome face. 'Good room to relax in, I would think,' she murmured.

'It's never as tidy as this in our house,' he admitted. 'Too many books all over the place.'

Stevie smiled back at him. It was a small enough piece of personal information but suddenly the man sitting across from her seemed endearingly human. Lots of books, she thought. But had he any time to read them?

The question would not be answered just then, however, as Pamela and Douglas Dalgleish entered the room, causing both police officers to stand up and greet them.

She was still showing all the hallmarks of grief, Stevie thought, as she took the bereaved mother's hand.

'Superintendent Lorimer, Inspector Crozier.' Douglas Dalgleish gave a stiff little bow in her direction but Rory's mother had come forward and was clasping Lorimer's hands as though fastening herself to an anchor. She was conscious of a spurt of annoyance. *He* was the favoured one, not her, she thought, then immediately chided herself for such pettiness.

'Detective Inspector, thank you for coming all this way to Glasgow,' Pamela Dalgleish said gravely, ushering Stevie back into the armchair and settling herself on the settee beside her husband.

'I apologise for the distress all this might cause you,' Stevie began, 'but we are reopening the case. I'm still senior investigating officer,' she continued. *Make that clear from the off*, she thought. 'But Detective Superintendent Lorimer has agreed to play a part in the ongoing investigation, given his personal contacts in Mull.'

'I'm so glad,' Pamela Dalgleish declared, a hand briefly covering Lorimer's.

'I will keep you both informed of any developments in the case, of course,' Stevie told them. 'I assure you that we will do everything in our power to find whoever did this to your son.'

'Thank you.' Douglas Dalgleish cleared his throat and nodded in Steve's direction.

'I would not have been involved at all but for my finding Rory that morning,' Lorimer reminded them.

Stevie Crozier hid a self-satisfied smile; Lorimer was certainly trying to do the right thing, she had to admit, deferring to an officer less senior than himself.

'We have to ask you more questions, I'm afraid,' she said, her tone brisker than she intended. 'First, I want to ask you about Rory's friends; who his closest pals were, where they live, if there are any connections with Mull.'

Pamela and Douglas Dalgleish looked from one to the other.

'Well, there's Jimmy Fotheringham,' she began. 'Rory's school chum,' she explained, looking back at Stevie. 'He lives in the house two along from here. Rory and Jimmy always went to school together, ever since they were little.' She stopped for a moment and Stevie saw the lower lip being bitten, a sure sign that the memory of Rory as a child had brought tears to the mother's eyes.

'Jimmy's at home just now,' Douglas continued. 'Waiting for the results of his exams.'

'He wants to go to university next year. To study law,' Pamela went on.

Stevie made a show of scribbling in her notebook. 'Anyone else who might give us personal details about Rory?'

Again Stevie saw that doubtful look between the parents.

'What about his workmates from the café?' Pamela asked her husband.

'Well, he was there long enough, I suppose,' Douglas Dalgleish answered his wife.

'The café?'

'The one at Kelvingrove Art Galleries and Museum,' Pamela explained. 'Rory worked there for more than a year. If only he had stayed instead of—' She broke off, putting both hands over her face. Stevie could hear the long sigh that became a strangled moan as the woman sought to control her grief.

'Do you have any names or addresses for his friends there?' Lorimer asked gently.

'No, he never brought any of them back here,' Douglas Dalgleish said stiffly. 'Though he did tend to go out with some of them after work. To concerts and things,' he added lamely, with a desultory wave of his hand that expressed how hopelessly out of touch he had really been with his younger son.

'There was someone special,' Pamela said, sitting up with a sniff and turning to her husband. 'You know there was,' she said, the accusatory tone of her voice making Stevie glance across at Lorimer. His slight nod was all that was needed.

'Can you tell me who this was?' he asked, turning in his chair to face the man and woman beside him.

Pamela shook her head. 'I think it was an older man,' she whispered.

'How do you know that?' Lorimer asked.

'I heard Rory speaking to him sometimes on the telephone,' she said, looking guiltily at her husband.

'You never told me this,' Douglas said gruffly.

'He used to say things like "See you later, old man," but not in the kind of cheery way he spoke to his pals,' she said, turning back to Lorimer. 'It was almost sarcastic. Gave me a funny feeling. It was as though Rory was meeting this person for something ... *clandestine*.' She shook her head as though the word didn't fit what she was trying to say.

'Do you think Rory was having a relationship with this older man?' Lorimer's tone was so matter-of-fact that it took Stevie's breath away. He could have been asking about the boy's work schedule rather than details about his private life.

Pamela Dalgleish nodded. 'He never *came out*,' she explained sadly. 'But we knew without him ever having to tell us, didn't we?' She placed a hand on her husband's arm and Stevie saw Douglas Dalgleish heave an enormous sigh.

'Have you any idea who this man might be?' Stevie asked. 'Someone from work perhaps?' she suggested.

'We never knew,' Pamela told them. 'It was something that Rory kept secret from us.'

'But *you* thought it had something to do with him going to Mull,' Douglas said.

'Yes,' Pamela agreed. 'He was excited. Said he had been given "a head's up". Those were his very words' – she smiled sadly as though remembering them all over again – 'about the job at Kilbeg Country House Hotel. We wondered if it was someone on the staff at Kelvingrove who had a contact there.'

'That's certainly something we will look into,' Stevie told them.

'This won't come out, will it?' Douglas Dalgleish asked them. 'In the papers? About Rory's preference, I mean?' His face was suffused with colour, the embarrassment of being a father to a young gay boy so apparent that Stevie wanted to shake the man. *Rory was gay, get over it!* she wanted to shout. *It's no big deal!* But, here in this stylish home in one of Glasgow's finest properties, it was clear that their son's sexuality had been more than these parents had been able to cope with.

'There is absolutely no reason at present for the press to know about this,' Stevie told them gently. 'Now, if you can give us a little more information about Rory's other friends from school and the immediate area?'

Lorimer looked over at Stevie as they drove across town. Jimmy Fotheringham had been a pleasure to talk to, a relief after the strained atmosphere at the Dalgleish home. It was an equally grand house from the outside but within there was evidence of the chaos of family life. *Yes, everyone assumed that Rory was gay*, Jimmy had said with a shrug that said 'so what?' *No, he hadn't seen him with anyone in particular.* They'd not been out with the crowd for ages, the lad had explained.

Perhaps there had been few facts that were pertinent to a murder case but the two officers had been given more of an insight into the fun-loving red-haired teenager and his boisterous manner than anyone else had yet provided. Rory had been well liked by his peers, it seemed. Perhaps those who had known him from childhood were more accustomed to and forgiving of his loud behaviour?

'I've never been here before,' Lorimer heard Crozier confess as he turned from Kelvin Way towards the dark red sandstone edifice of Kelvingrove before them.

'You'd like it,' he assured her. 'Maggie and I come here as often as we can. Which isn't nearly often enough,' he grinned ruefully.

'You're interested in art?' There was surprise in the woman's voice.

'Began a degree course in History of Art up there,' he replied, pointing towards the university building on the hill above them, its spire a jagged outline against the pale grey sky.

'You're a graduate?'

He smiled and shook his head. 'More like a drop-out,' he laughed. 'Completed my first year then joined the force. Not that I failed my exams or anything,' he admitted, 'it was just that ... ' He shrugged. 'I'll tell you about it some time. Long story,' he added, glancing at the curiosity in Crozier's eyes.

They emerged from the silver Lexus into a wind that was sweeping a flurry of early autumn leaves across the tarmac in front of wide stone steps that led to the entrance.

'We always used to come in from the other side of the building when we were kids,' Lorimer explained as they ascended one of the wide stone steps that led to the entrance. 'Through an old revolving door then across the black and white floor.' He smiled as if the memory was still fresh in his mind. 'Big changes a few years ago, though,' he admitted, allowing Crozier to enter in front of him. 'Nice modern feel to a lot of it, like the café here.' He turned to point at the sign. 'But they've kept the essence of the place, I'm glad to say.'

The café was situated in the lowest level, one part looking straight out onto the grass and pathways with trees beyond and a railing that separated the grounds from the banks of the River Kelvin. The other, larger, area held several rows of tables and chairs for visitors looking for a snack or a full meal. Several young waiters and waitresses were busily attending tables, their long black aprons sweeping past, trays held aloft.

'Who did you speak to?' Crozier enquired as they made their way to the serving hatch at the rear of the restaurant.

'Manager's name is Daisy McColl,' he replied. 'She sounded about fifteen,' he added, raising one sardonic eyebrow.

'Sign of you getting old, sir,' Crozier said, risking an impish grin.

Lorimer nodded back, glad to see that the woman by his side had thawed sufficiently towards him to crack a joke.

'Detective Superintendent Lorimer and DI Crozier to see Daisy McColl,' Stevie told the young man behind the bar area, holding out her warrant card for inspection.

'Oh, hold on and I'll get her. She's just round in the kitchen,' the lad replied, giving the two police officers a swift up-and-down glance as though curious to know why they were here.

Moments later a short, stout woman appeared, her lined face and greying hair twisted into a neat bun on the nape of her neck, giving her the look of a benign grandmother.

'Hello,' she said, extending a hand to Stevie Crozier. 'I'm Daisy.'

The woman's fluting voice did not match her appearance, Lorimer thought immediately; people usually lost that fine youthful timbre as age overtook them, but Daisy McColl did indeed sound like a teenager, now that he heard her once again.

'Thanks so much for seeing us, Ms McColl,' Stevie said, moving aside to allow Lorimer to take the woman's damp hand in his. Not nerves, she decided, looking into a pair of steady grey eyes, more likely the manageress had just dried her hands in the kitchen.

'You wanted to ask me about Rory. Can we go into my office?' she suggested, pointing at a door next to the servery.

'Now then,' Daisy McColl said briskly, showing them both

to a pair of bentwood seats beside a small wooden table that obviously served as a desk. 'What can I tell you?' She looked with shrewd eyes at the officers in turn.

'Rory Dalgleish worked here until the beginning of the summer,' Crozier stated.

'That's right. He did shifts, mostly at weekends. Had his exams to think of,' Daisy added then sighed. 'Much good they'll do him now, poor laddie.'

'I wonder, did you see Rory with an older chap on any occasion?' Lorimer asked.

Daisy's eyebrows rose. 'Older? Well, none of our waiters are what you might call older. All students,' she explained. 'I'm the old one here.' She chuckled, a merry sound that made the detective superintendent smile.

'Did you ever see Rory meeting an older man, perhaps after one of his shifts?' Lorimer persisted.

Daisy McColl folded her arms and sat back, looking into space. 'There was someone, right enough,' she began. 'Came in here regularly for a week or so in the springtime, now that I recall. It was a week of dreadful weather,' she said slowly as though dredging her memory for details. '*He* was an older man.' She looked at Lorimer then nodded. 'Rory always seemed to be the one to serve him,' she said. 'And I did see him waiting for the boy after work on one occasion. Never thought too much about it. Thought he might have been a friend or a relation.' She shrugged. 'We get so many in and out of here, it's hard to remember any faces, but I do remember this man.' She looked up into Lorimer's face. 'Medium height, dark haired, maybe a bit of grey? Not sure ... ' She tailed off, biting her lower lip in an effort to remember. 'Maybe in his late forties? I thought maybe he was an artist or something. We have lots of arty types in here, of course,' she added.

'What made you think that?' Crozier had leaned forward a little.

'Oh, the usual. Straggly hair over his collar, a bit unkempt really. Unshaven, as I recall. Designer stubble they call it nowadays,' she laughed.

'Would you be able to identify this man from a photograph?' Crozier asked.

Daisy shrugged. 'Probably. I've got good visual recall, if that's what you mean.'

Lorimer frowned. There was no image as yet for this woman to see; Crozier's remark was a bit premature. Still, it was good to know a little about Rory's mystery friend.

'Don't suppose you have any other details about the man? Name, for example?'

'No, sorry.' Daisy smiled sadly. 'And, now that you've brought it back to me, I remember that he always paid in cash so even if we kept receipts that long we wouldn't have any card details. I watch all these TV crime dramas, you know,' she added breathlessly. 'That's what you would do, isn't it? Check to see whose name was on a receipt?'

*

'Sharp as a tack, that one,' Lorimer said as they crossed the road towards the car. They had asked several of the waiters and waitresses if they had any knowledge of Rory's mysterious friend but only Daisy McColl seemed to have taken any interest in the comings and goings of her clientele.

As the silver car drove off, a figure watched from a window high above the winding terrace. Mona Daly tucked her mouse brown hair behind her ears and blinked. Daisy had told her about the visit from the police and it looked as though they had left now. Her heart thudded in her chest. The things she had seen from her office . . .

The secretary moved away from the window and crossed the room. It was a good time to break for the morning, she decided. And perhaps Daisy would have some nuggets of gossip to share.

'Come and take a seat. The millionaire's shortbread's just cool enough to go with a cuppa.' Daisy grinned as her friend's face appeared at the serving hatch.

'Police gone now?' Mona asked.

Daisy nodded. 'Nice big fellow. Woman wasn't from around here. Couldn't place her accent at all.'

'He was found dead in Mull,' Mona rejoined, the note of drama in her voice making it fall to a whisper. 'Maybe that's where she's from?'

But Daisy McColl's shake of the head was decisive. 'No, that's not where she originates. Nice voice, educated . . . ' She broke off, musing.

'Anyway, never mind that,' Mona continued, impatiently. 'What did they ask you about Rory?'

'Wanted to know about an older man.' Daisy shrugged. 'Big, dark-haired chap; arty type, I thought. Needing a shave. I'd seen them together a few times right enough but didn't think anything of it. Why?'

The woman opposite had turned a queasy shade of pale. Daisy leaned forward and clasped her friend's hands. 'Mona? What's wrong? You look as if you've seen a ghost.'

Mona Daly gave a faint groan and closed her eyes. 'Oh, dear God,' she murmured. 'I remember a man like that. I saw him with Rory, doing things no decent person should see in public ... ' Her eyes flew open in alarm. 'Oh, Daisy!' she exclaimed, one hand covering her mouth. 'I ... I think it was the same man I saw doing horrible things to another boy. A long time ago ... ' she mumbled, staring wildly at the woman opposite.

Then, choking back a sob, 'Daisy,' she cried, 'I think I've done a terrible thing.'

CHAPTER FORTY

'Mona Daly.' Crozier repeated the woman's name to Lorimer. 'She's a friend of Daisy McColl, apparently. The two of them have worked at Kelvingrove most of their adult lives.'

'And she has information about Rory?'

Crozier made a face. 'Not just about Rory,' she said. 'Some garbled story about another red-haired boy with the same man. Sounded a bit frantic on the phone. Told her she needed to come in and make a statement. Poor woman yelped right in my ear. Bit of a panic merchant by the sounds of her,' she added doubtfully.

'Is that all ...?'

Crozier shrugged. 'Whatever she needs to say, you'll hear soon enough.' She nodded towards the clock on the wall. 'She'll be over here in half an hour.'

'Okay ...' He paused for a moment and smiled. 'Mind if we have someone else sitting in on this interview?'

*

The woman waiting in the reception area at Stewart Street police station looked up as Lorimer opened the door.

'Ms Daly? Detective Superintendent Lorimer.'

'It's Miss . . .' the woman replied tartly. She began to stand, then gave a gasp of alarm as her handbag fell off her knee, scattering its contents across the linoleum floor.

'Oh, oh, I'm so sorry,' she began, immediately down on her knees, scrabbling at the coins escaping from an old-fashioned tartan purse that had sprung open. Lorimer hunkered down beside her, collecting a half-open packet of tissues, a railcard (one swift glance showing that Miss Mona Daly did indeed qualify for senior concessions), a tube of cough sweets, several biro pens and a 2015 diary from the Royal Society for the Protection of Birds.

'You're a bird lover, too?' he said, wagging the diary at her with a smile. 'We've been members of RSPB for ever.'

'Oh, yes,' the woman enthused, a smile lighting up her pale blue eyes. 'I love the wee birds. Always put out food for them in the garden.'

Mona Daly stood up, hooking the handle of her handbag across her arm in a manner that suddenly reminded Lorimer of a great-aunt, a smart, well-dressed woman who had always insisted that a lady is never properly attired without gloves and a hat. Those days were long gone, though he reckoned that Ms Daly might have adhered to those fashions had she been born in an earlier era.

Her dark grey two-piece suit and low-heeled court shoes

were smart enough, he supposed, ushering her through the double doors and towards the stairs, but a woman with her mousy colouring needed something more vivid to bring her to life. A bit of red, a scarf, say, would have helped, he decided, thinking of a painting he had seen in Solly's flat recently: it was one of the professor's favoured abstracts, swirls of charcoal and grey with one sudden burst of scarlet bringing movement to the piece.

'In here,' Lorimer said at last, indicating the open door to his office.

'This is Detective Inspector Crozier,' he said as Stevie rose from a chair to greet the woman.

'How do you do,' Mona Daly said gravely, extending a hand in Crozier's direction.

'Please, take a seat. Can we offer you something? Tea? Coffee?'

'Thank you, no. I … we … already had our morning break,' she said, looking from one to the other in a flustered manner.

'Right, then let's begin. You called DI Crozier to say you had some information about Rory Dalgleish?'

'Yes.' Mona Daly blinked, clutching the handle of her handbag with both hands as though terrified to let it out of her grasp. 'But that's not the only thing I want to tell you. I am ashamed to say that I ought to have come forward to talk to the police a long, long time ago.' She stopped anxiously, her front teeth leaving white marks as she ran them repeatedly over her lower lip.

'It was a horrid thing to see,' she said, turning to Crozier. 'Two men doing nasty things to one another.' Her voice fell as though the shame of what she had seen still lingered in her memory. 'The newspaper asked for help,' she went on, 'and I didn't come forward ...' She shook her head, eyes closed as though trying to blot out her misdeed.

'Perhaps you could explain what this was about?' Crozier looked mystified.

'Oh, the boy who was found by the river. They never knew who he was?' She turned to Lorimer.

'When exactly was this?' he asked, a frisson of something strange tugging at his emotions.

'Summer 1995,' she said, her voice more assured now that an easier question was being put to her.

'The red-haired boy that was pulled out of the Clyde?'

'Yes. There was a description in the paper but no photograph. Well there wouldn't be if they didn't know who he was,' she said, her shoulders relaxing for a moment.

'And you think you saw him?'

She hesitated, looking at Crozier then back to Lorimer. 'Him or someone very like him. I used to see them together, outside the art galleries,' she explained. 'Then, one day I was in town. It was a nice evening, summertime ...' She stopped and looked into the middle distance as if recalling the memory. 'I was coming from St Enoch's. It was quite new then,' she explained to Crozier. 'Someone had told me that there was a family of swans on the Clyde and so instead of going straight for the Underground, I decided to walk along the riverbank.' She paused, looking from Crozier to Lorimer as though to see that they were following her story. 'That's when I saw them. The man and the red-haired boy. All lovey-dovey.' She gave a delicate shudder. 'It was disgusting!' she exclaimed. 'Two men doing things like that in broad daylight!'

'And you were certain that this young man fitted the description in the *Gazette*?' Lorimer spoke firmly.

'Oh, yes!' The woman bridled instantly.

'But you didn't think to call the police?'

She reddened at that, pent-up guilt suffusing her face and neck with warmth.

'I ... I thought someone else might have seen him,' she began lamely. 'Didn't want to get involved ...'

'So why come to us now?' Crozier demanded testily.

'Oh!' Mona Daly was obviously taken aback. 'Well, that's the whole point, isn't it?' She looked from one officer to the other as though bewildered at their lack of understanding. 'It was the same man,' she said. 'The one I saw with Rory. The same man who had been hanging around with that other red-haired youth all these years ago.'

There was a silence as her words were digested, then Lorimer opened a thin file that had been under his clasped fingers. He drew out the artist's sketch that had been made almost twenty years before, the image that had never been shown to the public in the wake of the young man's death.

'Is this the boy you saw?' He held up the drawing in front of her.

Mona Daly's hands flew to her face, a sob escaping from her mouth as she nodded. 'Yes, oh my dear lord, yes. That's definitely the boy I saw.' She sniffed loudly and began to open her handbag but Lorimer passed her a Kleenex tissue from the open desk drawer at his side.

He tried to catch Crozier's eye as they listened to the woman blowing her nose noisily but the DI had picked up the sketch in its plastic covering and was staring at it intently.

'Now, Miss Daly, perhaps you might be good enough to give us a description of this other man, the one you saw more recently with Rory Dalgleish.'

CHAPTER FORTY-ONE

'It's got to be the same perpetrator!' Lorimer insisted. Stevie Crozier and Solly were sitting next to him as they pored over the original case file together.

'And what's the connection between Glasgow and Mull?' she asked.

'Well, we know from the Dalgleish parents that Rory had been persuaded by someone to take that job in Kilbeg,' he told her. 'And that is where I think we ought to begin looking again.'

'I agree,' the psychologist said slowly. 'There must be someone on the island who has information about these two boys.'

The blonde woman shook her head. 'I was wrong. Thought you were harking back to a cold case that couldn't have any relation whatsoever to Rory's death.' She smiled weakly. 'Sorry.'

'Ach, it was a long shot,' Lorimer admitted. 'But it was that unusual way they'd both been tied up. Which reminds me . . .'

He stretched behind him to pull another, thicker, file from the cabinet behind them. 'Courlene,' he said. 'Rosie alerted me to this.'

He spread the post-mortem photographs across the desk. 'Look here,' he said, placing two images together. 'This one's of our missing person, that one's of Rory. See the striations?'

'They're the same,' Crozier said, bending to study the pictures.

'Possibly made by Courlene, a polythene twine used in the fishing industry. You'd get it in any chandlery,' he told them, looking from Crozier to Solly.

'So, anyone who knew Rory and had a boat . . . ?' the psychologist mused.

He grinned at him. 'That's where we want to begin,' he said, turning to Crozier. 'Your team on Mull with me tagging along behind.'

Stevie Crozier gave him a silent look then dropped her gaze.

There was something in the way she refused to meet his eyes that gave Lorimer a frisson of concern; he could see that she was intrigued about the cold case from 1995. And, he hoped, just as eager as he was to find the killer. But something was still eating at her. He would have to tread gently around this woman or their uneasy relationship might prove to be an impediment when the case resumed.

'Will you send this to the *Gazette*?' Solly asked, nodding at the large buff envelope in his friend's hand.

'And *Crimewatch*, if they can slot it in,' Lorimer replied. 'We need to pull out all the stops now, make as much of a fuss as possible. Whoever is behind these two young men's deaths must know that we are on his trail.' He paused by Solly's side as they waited to cross the road at Kelvin Way.

'You don't expect him to come forward and confess his crimes, surely?' The psychologist's crooked smile held the tiniest hint of derision.

'What do you think, Solly?' Lorimer turned, eyebrows raised as they moved towards the other side of the road and headed into the park.

There was silence for a time as the psychologist walked by Lorimer's side. Once upon a time these lengthy pauses for deliberation had annoyed the policeman but he was used to them now and waited patiently for an answer to his question. Nobody could ever accuse the professor of being hasty; careful and considered, his pronouncements were usually the result of much thought.

They were at the pond and slowing down to look at the water before Solly spoke again.

'He has certain tastes,' he began, 'for young men willing to participate in the bondage and discipline aspects of a sado-masochistic relationship. Perhaps he paid them? Perhaps they were the submissive partners in an ongoing sexual relationship.' He stopped and smiled, watching some young coots bob their way across to the overgrown island that provided nesting sites for many of the waterfowl.

'Once he was in this city of ours,' Solly continued thought-fully, 'when he was a much younger man, possibly exploring the parameters of his own sexuality, perhaps he felt more freedom to carry out his relationship here than in other parts of the country?'

'You mean he deliberately went to Mull to try to stifle these homosexual tendencies?'

Solly turned and looked at his friend. 'As I see it, there are several possible scenarios. The perpetrator was living here in Glasgow and after the first boy's death he wanted to escape from the sort of life he had been living. Whatever that may have been. Mull offered something that he needed, perhaps? A safe haven where he could work and live without arousing suspicions. He will have *wanted* to change his lifestyle, if that theory holds water.'

'But Rory Dalgleish coming to Mull changed all of that,' Lorimer insisted. 'And we know that someone suggested the job at Kilbeg Country House Hotel to Rory. Someone wanted him to come away from the city to Mull.'

'And perhaps this someone has links with both Glasgow and Mull?'

'If the killer had a place in Glasgow, why would he need to lure Rory away from the city?'

'True.' Solly stroked his beard thoughtfully. 'Which brings me to an alternative theory. You seem to want to find a person who came to the island about twenty years ago. But what if ...' He looked past Lorimer, a faint smile on his intelligent face as though his thoughts were taking shape.

'What if ...?' Lorimer asked, a slight impatience in his tone.

'What if the person you are looking for originates in Mull? What if his initial victim was a terrible accident?'

'But what led him back to Glasgow? To Kelvingrove Art Gallery and Museum? That's where we think he may have met Rory.'

'We often revisit the scene of a place where we have loved,' Solly mused. 'Perhaps it was fate that led him to seeing Rory Dalgleish, a young red-haired lad who just happened to be gay. And,' he looked at Lorimer with pity in his eyes, 'possibly a young man who was rather lonely. From what you've told me of the parents, Rory never had the courage to come out to them. His relationships with other men may therefore have been furtive and guilty. Or,' his bushy eyebrows were raised in speculation, 'the aspect of hiding such things from them may have added to the spice of a sadomasochistic sexual relationship. The older man to whom he submitted may well have been a father figure of sorts.' He shrugged. 'I could go on in this vein for quite a while, my friend, but I don't know just how helpful my ramblings might be in helping you find this man.'

'Well,' Lorimer began slowly, 'you've certainly given me plenty to consider. We need to look at facts, of course, and evidence ... if we can find any.'

'Your killer needed a boat, you say.' Solly nodded, stooping down to pick up a crust of bread that had been dropped by a child. He began to break it into crumbs, throwing the pieces one by one onto the grass verge where feral pigeons immediately congregated, gobbling and pecking.

'There is a line of thought that Rory went off with someone after the dance. Someone who had a boat, a yacht, we don't really know.'

'And Rosie tells me that this binder twine . . . ?'

'Courlene,' Lorimer supplied.

'Yes, this Courlene was possibly the stuff used to secure each of these young men prior to their death?'

'It's a possibility, yes,' Lorimer agreed.

'*If*' – Solly stressed the word – '*if* the bonds were not removed until rigor had set in, does that not tell you something about your killer?'

Lorimer breathed in deeply. 'Yes, I think I see what you're getting at. Why did he not immediately dump these bodies after the boys had died?'

'Why indeed?' The psychologist's smile was sad now. 'Perhaps it was hard to let either of them go. And the memory of that first death must have been so difficult to put behind him.'

'So why did he allow himself to become involved with Rory twenty years later?'

'Why do any of us allow our emotions to overcome our better judgement?' Solly said, turning to look his friend in the eye. 'We had a lecturer at university. Nice man. His wife died of breast cancer. He was utterly devoted to her, spent hours at her bedside in the hospice, supported his children afterwards in such an admirable way.'

'What happened?' Lorimer asked, his curiosity piqued.

'He married again less than eighteen months afterwards. To a nice lady who very much resembled his late wife. The children loved her.' He shrugged.

'The object lesson being . . . ?' Lorimer began to walk away from the pond towards the path that led to Solly's home, the psychologist falling into step beside him.

Solly caught his sleeve and nodded. 'The object lesson, if that is what you wish to call it, is that Rory Dalgleish evoked the same strong feelings that his lover had for his original victim.'

Once more the detective superintendent found himself haunted by the image of the nameless red-haired boy. The difference now was that there was some slight possibility that someone might remember him from twenty years before.

Lorimer turned the pencil sketch around and peered closely at the writing on the reverse. P McGrain was written in dark lettering, as though the artist had been using something like a Rapidograph pen. Lorimer frowned. He had no recollection of a P. McGrain from his visit all those years ago. A sudden urge to revisit the school of art made him rise from his desk and slip the picture into a leather briefcase. He had failed to follow up this important aspect of the dead boy's identity, somehow. Nowadays their technical support would have created a digital image for the police. Things had been so different then, Lorimer mused, shrugging his arms into a dark linen jacket and heading out of the room.

The route to Glasgow School of Art was up a steep hill but the detective superintendent did not notice the slope as he walked briskly along the narrow pavements. Lorimer's mind was still on the early days of his career: so many changes had taken place. Technology had made life easier for investigating officers in so many ways: emails could send information in seconds that had taken days to arrive twenty years before; digital imagery could recreate the face and body from the remains of a person dead for many years; forensic medical science had surged ahead too, so much more detail being given by DNA samples. Aye, he thought, it was a changed world.

As he approached the staircase leading to the door of the art school, Lorimer gave a half smile to himself, glad that there were some things that had not changed – like the hallowed building designed by Charles Rennie Mackintosh. Here, he noted, seeing a boy race down the steps, clutching a huge burgundy-coloured folio under one arm, life and art were intermingled. Yes, there might be more emphasis nowadays on art installations but he hoped that the crafts of drawing and painting were still considered as vital skills.

'Hello?' He knocked on the receptionist's door. 'Detective Superintendent Lorimer, Police Scotland, here to see the principal.'

'Ah, yes, she's just upstairs. Let me show you.' The woman rose smiling from her seat behind an ancient carved desk that looked as if it might have been in the school since the heady days of Mackintosh and his cohorts themselves.

Lorimer followed, glancing at the pale statues that graced the dark corridors, survivors of the terrible fire that had threatened to destroy one of the city's best loved and most iconic buildings.

The woman knocked on a door then pushed it open.

'Detective Superintendent Lorimer to see you, Miss Hastings.'

'Hello.' A short stout woman wearing a grey shapeless dress, a mass of crazy red curls tied up in a green batik bandana, swept forward and took Lorimer's hand in hers. It felt dry and warm, making the detective glance at the principal's fingers: how many works of art had the celebrated Dora Hastings created in her lifetime? Yet she had chosen the path of teacher despite being one of the foremost painters of her generation.

'It's about this.' Lorimer drew the sketch from his briefcase. 'It was done about twenty years ago, possibly by one of your former staff?'

Dora Hastings reached for a pair of tortoiseshell over-reader spectacles and perched them on her nose.

Lorimer watched as she examined the sketch. At first she seemed to frown then the puzzled expression changed, her mouth falling open.

'Goodness!' she exclaimed. 'Where did you get this?'

'It was supposed to have helped identify a murder victim twenty years ago,' Lorimer said, a note of apology creeping into his voice.

Dora Hastings turned the sketch around.

'P. McGrain,' she said slowly, then took off her glasses and stared at Lorimer. 'That's Peter McGrain. He was one of my colleagues until his retiral a couple of years ago. So,' she popped the glasses back on and studied the sketch again, 'someone asked Peter to do this.'

'Yes. But the original victim is connected to another ongoing case,' he explained. 'And I was hoping that Mr McGrain might give us permission to publish this image.'

Dora Hastings gave a long smile that made her eyes crinkle. 'You want to find out who this boy was?'

'That's correct.' Lorimer gave her a puzzled look.

Dora Hastings shook her head, making the silver hoops on each ear catch the sunlight that poured through the window behind her. 'I can tell you,' she said, looking back at the sketch.

Lorimer sat quite still, hardly daring to breathe. Was he about to find the answer he had sought in the case that had haunted him all of these years?

'Ah, poor boy,' she said, clutching at her throat. 'We wondered what had become of him.'

'You *knew* this boy?'

'Yes,' she said, continuing to stare at the sketch. 'Peter

would have known him too. I'm surprised he didn't mention anything at the time.

'He was one of our life models, you see.' She paused for a moment, looking up as if to remember. 'There must have been any number of sketches made of this boy before ... you say he died?'

'He was a murder victim,' Lorimer replied.

He paused for a moment, desperately wanting the woman to give an affirmative answer to his next question.

'Do you happen to have known his name?'

CHAPTER FORTY-TWO

Peter McGrain was not at home when the officer from Police Scotland called at his address in Kilsyth. *Portugal, I think*, a neighbour offered helpfully. *He's got a house out there. Think he'll be home tomorrow*, she'd added.

Lorimer read the email and made a face. He had been expecting, well, hoping at least, to speak to the artist face to face today. It felt as though he were so near the end of this search that had been abandoned twenty years ago; so close to keeping his promise to that dead boy lying on the cold banks of the River Clyde. Well at least there wouldn't have to be a search for a Peter McGrain in Portugal; yet he chafed at having to wait even one more day to question the man. Why had the art school lecturer failed to reveal the identity of the dead boy all those years ago? He must have known ... was he somehow involved in the victim's death? The investigation had uncovered some facts about McGrain: to all intents he had been a happily married man, a retired lecturer and keen watercolourist who spent a lot of time painting abroad. There were no children from the marriage, Dora Hastings had informed him; Mrs McGrain had been an art teacher at a Glasgow school before she too had retired. She had died quite recently, the director had added sadly. Peter was all on his own now.

The detective superintendent heaved a sigh, recalling summer holidays spent with Maggie in Portugal. Perhaps they would return there again, he mused. Were their days in Mull over now? Maybe Mary Grant would be reluctant to let them have the cottage again after all that had passed ...? Well, he would be returning to Leiter the day after tomorrow. They were booked on the six o'clock ferry from Oban and he would be with his own dear Maggie again.

Peter McGrain ran a weary hand across his forehead as he opened the front door. He looked up at the tall man standing there and nodded. 'You'll be Lorimer then.'

'Detective Superintendent,' Lorimer replied briefly, holding out his warrant card. 'I'm glad to find you at home,' he said. 'We were here yesterday looking for you. Mind if I come in?'

Peter McGrain stood aside with a resigned shrug. 'Place is a mess already,' he said. 'Haven't even begun to unpack ...'

Lorimer inched past a pile of canvases stacked against the wall of the passageway.

'Only came back at this time because I have to curate an exhibition,' McGrain explained. 'Usually spend the entire summer in Portugal.'

The artist led Lorimer into the back of the house and the

detective found himself entering a spacious kitchen with slanting roof windows that flooded the room with light. There was an easel set up in one corner next to a scrubbed pine table covered with jars of brushes and a large cafetière of coffee with a Highland pottery mug beside it.

'It's still fresh if you want a cup ...?' McGrain offered, seeing the detective's glance.

'Thanks, but I'm fine. Just wanted to ask you some things about your time at Glasgow School of Art. It's in connection with the death of a young man who was a model in the life classes twenty years ago. Summer of 1995.'

'Aye.' McGrain shook his head and sighed. 'A long time ago now. Hoped it would always be forgotten about. I'm sorry you've had such bother finding me,' he replied, looking up, his tone full of contrition.

'Why didn't you contact us at the time?' Lorimer asked. 'You knew we wanted to find out who he was.'

There was a short silence then Peter McGrain gave another sigh.

'Things were a lot different back then,' he began. 'My wife was still alive ...'

Lorimer waited for him to continue.

'It's not something I ever wanted her finding out,' McGrain continued nervously.

'And now?' Lorimer asked.

The artist ran his hand through the mop of thick grey hair flopping over his forehead.

'Now things are different,' he said sadly. 'I've only got myself to think about.' He sat down at the table and took a gulp of the coffee. 'How can I explain it? Gary and I ... well, it was a fling, I suppose. A stupid mistake on my part, you understand. But I didn't want anyone to find out.'

'Even when you knew the boy was dead and you were asked to make a sketch of him?'

'No,' McGrain mumbled. 'I'm sorry. It was wrong of me, I know ... and Gary ... well, let's just say that he spread his favours about.'

'He was promiscuous?'

McGrain gave a short harsh laugh. 'Promiscuous? That's a generous word to use, Detective Superintendent. Gary Forsyth didn't just earn a living as a life model.' McGrain's tone was full of self-disgust. 'He was a rent boy.'

Lorimer started at the name. Forsyth? It had been twenty years ago that the Forsyths had bought Kilbeg House in Mull. Could the dead boy have been their son? Or was this just some sort of strange coincidence? But, he reminded himself, he was the very man who did not believe in coincidences.

'Nineteen ninety-five,' he said slowly. 'Can you remember the names of any students who were in that life-drawing class back then?'

'It was a long time ago. Not sure how many of them I'd remember. Can I get back to you on that? It might take me some time to trawl through my old class notes.'

'Here's my card. I'd appreciate having a list of those

students as soon as possible,' Lorimer told him, resisting the urge to remind McGrain that he had already waited twenty long years to discover the murder victim's identity. He shot a glance at the hands holding the pottery mug; strong, clever hands that could wield a paintbrush. Had they been the hands that encircled the boy's throat twenty years ago? Hiding his affair from his late wife: was that sufficient motive for murder? Lorimer wondered as he made his way out of the artist's home.

Now he had to make another journey, back to Mull where, if his suspicions were correct, the parents of Gary Forsyth would have to be told about the death of their son.

'Tomorrow will be time enough to confront them about Gary Forsyth,' Lorimer told Crozier, who was sitting next to him on the upper deck of the *Isle of Mull* as it ploughed through the waves, Solly standing only feet away from them, his dark hair blowing in the sea breeze as he gazed out over the rail. The psychologist had joined them after the boat had left the pier, his own journey having begun at Glasgow Queen Street station.

'I thought you'd want to see them right away,' Crozier replied. 'Why wait another day?'

Lorimer smiled. 'I want to have someone else there.'

'Oh, and who is that?'

'Professor Brightman.' He nodded towards the psychologist who was evidently enjoying the smell of the wind and sea.

'He and the family are staying with Dr MacMillan and her husband for a few days. Rosie and Abby will be at Craignure to meet him. Could have travelled up in the car to Oban with us, but he preferred to take the train. Said he had some thinking to do.' Lorimer smiled.

'I see,' Crozier replied stiffly. 'And this has been cleared . . . ?'

'Oh, yes,' Lorimer assured her. 'The deputy chief constable has made Professor Brightman's involvement quite official.'

'You and he have worked together quite often, haven't you?' the DI asked. 'He's made a bit of a name for himself as a profiler,' she added.

'Yes, I suppose we have. We didn't really hit it off at first, Solly and I,' Lorimer told her. 'I was a suspicious brute in those days. Didn't hold with all that psychobabble.'

'And what made you change your mind?' she asked, trying to tuck a windswept lock of hair behind her ear.

'*He* did,' Lorimer said simply. 'Oh, I did some reading. Canter's work mainly. But it was Solomon Brightman himself who showed me how useful his work could be.'

'I've never used a profiler before,' Crozier confessed, glancing at the psychologist who was now wandering further along the deck as if to obtain a better view of the approaching island.

'Well, they aren't used in every murder case and usually only in cases of multiple killings. Though there were some investigations by profilers, Canter being one of them, in the wake of Madeleine McCann's disappearance.'

'So,' she began, 'what exactly do you expect from Professor Brightman in this case?'

'Ah.' Lorimer nodded and smiled. 'How can I begin to describe the way that Solly works?'

By the time the boat had passed Duart Castle and was making its way towards Craignure pier, Stevie Crozier had learned something of the relationship between the tall detective superintendent and the psychologist. She had not paid much attention to the bearded man but now he intrigued her and she was keen to see just how he would be of help when he and Lorimer arrived at Kilbeg Country House Hotel the following morning. And, just as keen to be there when the Forsyths were asked questions about a young man who had been murdered twenty years ago.

It had been Lorimer's idea for Stevie to book into Kilbeg. Calum, her local police sergeant, would be meeting her at Craignure and driving her along the coast to the country house hotel. And DI Stevie Crozier was determined that the evening ahead would be usefully spent before the two men who had been seconded to her team began their inquiries at Kilbeg.

Maggie was waiting by the open gate when he arrived and the tension that he had felt since leaving Glasgow fell away from

Lorimer's shoulders as he drove carefully across the pebbled drive and parked outside Leiter Cottage.

'You're back,' she said simply, then he was holding her close, breathing in the sweet scent of her hair, the warmth of the evening enveloping them. Somewhere on the hills there was a baaing of sheep and out on the shore the familiar cry of oystercatchers. The notion of a trip to Portugal was already fading, the return to Leiter like a homecoming, his desire to be here with Maggie stronger than ever.

'Hey, the midges are bad tonight,' she laughed. 'Come on in and have some dinner. I've made your favourite curry.' She paused, looking up at him suspiciously. 'You didn't go and eat fish and chips on the boat, did you?'

'No chance,' Lorimer smiled, taking her hand and leading her into the cottage. 'Not when I knew you'd be cooking me something special.'

'There's the menu, miss,' the girl with the long blonde hair tied back into a ponytail smiled as she handed Stevie the leather-bound folder.

Stevie smiled back, recognising Maryka from the previous visit when she had spoken to members of the staff.

'You're still here then?'

The girl gave an insouciant shrug. 'Till the end of the season anyway,' she replied. Then, as though she had remembered exactly who this guest was, she stepped back a little and folded her hands. 'The specials today are broad bean risotto with parmesan crisps and pan-fried saithe,' she said primly.

'Saithe?'

'It's fish.' Maryka's mouth twitched at the corners. 'A white fish, I think. It's fresh and local to here, anyway,' she added. Then, bending down a little and dropping her voice to a whisper she said, 'My boyfriend caught it.'

'Hm.' Stevie glanced at the menu open at the choices for dinner. There wasn't really a lot to choose from, she saw. She was the only guest rattling around in this vast dining room so perhaps there wasn't much point in cooking very many dishes. Besides, they were probably at the stage of emptying their deep freeze before supplies ran out. It was one of the hottest topics for gossip on the island, after the murder cases, that the Forsyths were stony broke.

'Okay,' she decided. 'Scallops followed by the risotto, thanks.' She gave a polite smile, catching the girl's eye.

'Good choice.' Maryka nodded. 'Archie, the chef, dives for the scallops himself,' she said. 'They're really nice.'

As she left, the detective inspector pondered over the waitress's last words. *Someone with a boat*, Lorimer had said. *Method, means and opportunity*; the phrase came at her forcefully. It was a mantra that detectives the world over must employ, Stevie mused. And here she had been handed at least two of these ... on a plate! She smiled at her own cliché. The chef owned a boat, didn't he? And used it to dive for scallops ... Stevie itched to go down that little path to the dock and snoop around the man's boat. What might she find there? She closed her eyes for a moment and thought about the pages from the internet that she had examined so carefully, pages that contained selections of fishing tackle and that bright orange twine that so many fishermen used: *Courlene*. Would they find any of that in Archie Gillespie's boat?

Dinner was better than Stevie had expected: the scallops were probably the best she'd ever eaten and the risotto had been made with fresh broad beans. Did they have their own vegetable patch out there in the kitchen garden? she wondered. She had passed on dessert and now the waitress was returning with a small glass in her hand.

'Compliments of the chef,' Maryka told her. 'Something to go with your coffee.' She frowned. 'I ... don't remember what it was he called it ...?'

Stevie took the glass from her and sniffed at its contents. 'Kahlúa,' she told the girl. 'Lovely.'

'Will you come through to the lounge for coffee? Archie has made some of his special sweets.' Maryka turned furtively as if to check that nobody was listening to their conversation.

'Thanks, I will,' Stevie said, rising from the table. Then, noticing the girl's hesitancy, she frowned. 'Is something wrong, Maryka?'

Once again the waitress looked around her, a worried expression flitting across her face. 'I ... can I talk to you, miss? In private?'

Stevie nodded and followed the girl out of the empty dining room, past the reception hall and into a large airy lounge that looked out onto the Sound of Mull and beyond. Dusk was falling and a blue haze softened the contours of the Morvern hills. From an open window she heard the lonesome cry of a curlew, its watery call making Stevie shiver.

'Over here,' Maryka said, beckoning Stevie to a table that was set into an alcove in the corner away from prying eyes and out of earshot of anyone who might choose to enter the room. 'The Forsyths are out tonight. At the drama club's play,' she explained, sitting down next to the detective and beginning to pour coffee from the pot that had been placed on the table earlier. 'But I don't want Archie to overhear us.'

She must have expected me to listen to whatever she has to say, Stevie realised, taking a backward glance around the room.

'I wanted to tell you something,' Maryka whispered. 'It's something I saw, well, not saw exactly, more *felt*, if you know what I mean.'

'Go on.'

The girl twisted her lip as though unsure of herself. 'Promise you won't tell them I told you.'

'Okay,' Stevie agreed, while reminding herself that any promises made in a police matter were never binding.

'I was going to go into Mrs Forsyth's room,' Maryka said, glancing up lest anyone had come in to hear her words. 'I should not have been there, you see. I do not clean their private apartments, but I wanted to see ...' She gave a shrug as if to excuse her own youthful curiosity. 'Anyway,' she leaned closer to the detective inspector, 'I stood outside the lady's room, saw the key in the lock and ...' She paused, a gleam in her eyes, and Stevie sensed that the girl was trying for dramatic effect. 'I could not go in,' she said. 'I felt as if someone was there ...' Her eyes widened as she recalled the moment. 'I think it was a ghost,' she whispered. 'I felt such a strange thing, like someone was watching my every move!' She gave a delicate shudder. 'There's something in that room, miss, I just know there is.'

'Goodness!' Stevie remarked, sitting back and looking intently at the girl. 'A ghost? Now who on earth do you imagine that might be? Is there any history in the house of a sudden unexplained death?' Her heart beat just a little faster despite common sense telling her that the girl was just being fanciful.

'I *think*,' Maryka began, 'it must be their long-lost son. The Forsyth's son. Maybe he was lost at sea a long, long time ago. And that's why she goes down to the jetty and stares out at the water so much of the time.' Her voice had taken on an excited tone now and Stevie recognised the way that the girl's imagination may have woven a story around the strange woman who wandered towards the shoreline, especially in the wake of Rory's death.

She tried not to betray the knowledge that she already had as she replied. 'Thanks, Maryka. That is really helpful. And I am sure you have nothing to worry about. Ghosts can't hurt you,' she smiled, not adding that it was flesh and blood humans who could wreak the most damage.

'You won't mention me?' the girl asked anxiously.

'That shouldn't be necessary.'

She saw a wave of relief cross the girl's face as she stood up. Then, as though she had just remembered that Stevie was a guest she motioned to the coffee pot and the dish of home-made tablet. 'Enjoy your coffee, miss.'

Stevie watched her go then gave a sigh. By tomorrow everyone else here would probably know the truth behind the woman's sojourns at the water's edge. A refusal to admit that he was long dead? Or the continued hope that he might return? She picked up the Kahlúa and downed it in one long gulp, feeling the coffee-flavoured liqueur warm her throat, knowing that the news they had to impart might well destroy whatever sanity the poor woman still had.

The girl's revelation had unsettled her and Stevie looked around at the lounge as though seeing it for the first time. It was sinking into decrepitude, she realised, looking at the dusty curtains and the worn patches of carpet under her table. It was a place that was uncared for, unloved.

What had happened between Gary Forsyth and his parents? Why had they not made contact with the police twenty years ago when their son had vanished? There was something here, in this very place, she decided, that bore a closer examination, her professional instincts rising to the surface.

Stevie was glad of the soft-soled court shoes as she crept around the back of the hotel, the gravel scarcely crunching under her quiet feet. There was a light on in the kitchen and she could see figures moving within. A quick glance told her that the rooms above, where the Forsyths had their private apartments, were in darkness. Yet they were sure to come back soon, see that all was well before making their own way upstairs. In her experience of the hotel trade the proprietors were usually the last to turn in for the night.

The DI continued her walk around the building, coming at last to where she had parked the Mercedes. A small smile crossed her face as she saw that it was the only vehicle there; the Forsyths must still be out for the evening, leaving the Dutch girl and the chef in charge. Stevie glanced at her wristwatch: it was only nine thirty. How long did a play last? Time enough for a quick look upstairs, perhaps?

The hallway was deserted as she came back inside and, as though haste were needed, she ran lightly up the wide stairs and along the corridor until she came to the Forsyths' private rooms. There was the merest hesitation as she reminded herself that she had no search warrant, nothing official to allow her to poke about the couple's rooms, but a stronger feeling overcame such scruples as she walked boldly into Hamish Forsyth's room and across to the place where Maryka had told her of the eerie moment she had experienced outside that room. The door was shut tight, just as the girl had described, but the key sat in the lock. For a moment Stevie listened,

404

wondering if sudden footsteps might disturb her, but there was nothing, not even the hoot of an owl in the trees outside.

Taking a deep breath, the DI turned the key and entered the room. There was no need for torchlight here, she realised, looking out of the long windows as moonlight flooded in, illuminating the room.

It was a sad place, the woman thought, her eyes taking in a silken patchwork quilt that had seen better days, pulled threads exposing several corners of the different squares of fabric. The furniture was all dark wood and old-fashioned; it had probably suited the place at one time but, with the half-panelled walls and the picture rail that held dismal prints of Highland cattle and rainswept glens it added to an overall appearance of gloom.

There was one rather nice watercolour picture, however, its pale tints somewhat faded because it had been placed opposite a window. Stevie moved closer to examine it, giving a nod of recognition. The hills of Morvern were outlined beyond the stretch of sea, a small jetty giving some interest to the foreground: it was the view from the hotel, all right; probably painted by a former resident. There was no signature at the foot of the picture.

She walked around the room, giving the bedside cabinets a careful examination until she came to Mrs Forsyth's dressing table. A mess of hairpins and a brush that needed cleaning sat amongst various bits of make-up, screwed up paper tissues and little porcelain boxes. Wherever it was that they had gone to see this play, it was evident that the woman had made some effort to tidy herself up.

Because it was on an upper shelf of the dressing table, away from the clutter below, she did not notice it at first, the photograph slightly askew in a plain silver frame. Stevie picked it up and held it higher, letting the moonlight fall onto the image.

Then her mouth opened in a moment of astonishment.

The boy in the photograph was smiling out at her, an impish grin on his face as though he was about to say something, his hair a bright flame colour against the cloudless blue sky behind him.

'My God!' Stevie whispered, the hand that held the picture trembling. 'Rory?' Only it was not the lad whose murder she was investigating, she suddenly saw, but another person. *The boy in the sketch.* The photo was of someone who resembled the dead boy so closely that Stevie had taken him for Rory Dalgleish. Was that why Mrs Forsyth had taken such a shine to the red-haired boy from Glasgow? Had she known all this time that her own son was dead? The questions circled Stevie's mind like tigers.

The sudden crunch of tyres on gravel made her set the photograph back down exactly where she had found it, anxious now lest anyone find her snooping around.

In moments she had turned the key back in the woman's bedroom door and was across Hamish Forsyth's room and out into the corridor, her heart thumping in her chest.

What was going on in this place? Why had neither of the Forsyths reported their son missing? Lorimer's instinct had been right about the missing boy. Stevie hurried back to her room haunted by the image of that red-haired boy smiling out from the photograph, an image that was at odds with a boy's corpse, its limbs twisted out of shape by some fisherman's twine. It burned in her brain as though taunting her to find answers to her questions. And, she thought suddenly, there was one place where some of these answers might still be found.

A hasty change of shoes and a dark jacket were all she would require to sneak around that boat by the water's edge, Stevie told herself, slipping her feet into flat, rubber-soled loafers. Locking her bedroom door behind her, she crept quietly downstairs once again and slipped out of the warmth of the hotel into the chill darkness of the night.

The moon that had brightened the night, leaving a trail of silver across the water, slowly disappeared behind a bank of cloud. Its round face fell away from sight until the last arc of white was covered up, the darkness fleeing past like shadowy phantoms wrapped in ragged cloaks.

Waves licked the wooden platform, repeated small splashes as though eager to reach landfall. The figure standing by the edge looked out to sea for a long moment as though in expectation of something. Then a tiny beam of light fell onto the decking as Stevie switched on the torch of her mobile phone, pointing it at the boat ahead of her. She had heard the chef as she passed the kitchen door, the noise of pots clanging inside, his Glasgow accent mingling with another male voice that she could not identify. Perhaps she might take this chance to look at his boat, a little voice had suggested, and Stevie had followed that thought until now when her feet had taken her along the grassy path and she was standing right by the gangway.

A quick glance behind told the detective inspector that nobody was approaching. Should she dare to board the boat? It was another person's property, after all, and to enter was against every rule that a police officer had learned. But the memory of the visit to those stricken parents back in Glasgow made Stevie place her foot on the gangplank, her torch pointing towards the boat. She was determined to find out the truth, give them the answers that they deserved.

In a moment she had scrambled up. The wooden deck beneath her feet swayed side to side, the force of the tide beneath causing the vessel to bob back and forth on its mooring. Stevie walked slowly around the cabin, keeping a close watch on the path lest Archie Gillespie appear from the hotel kitchen. She had reached the stern when the pinpoint light fell upon a coil of orange twine placed neatly on top of a long wooden box.

She drew in a sharp breath. Courlene. And plenty of it, too. Crouching down, the woman felt the end of the twine; it pricked as she drew her finger across it. Recently cut, then, she nodded to herself. Could this have been the very twine that had bound that poor boy from Glasgow?

Retracing her steps Stevie came to the door of the cabin, her fingers on its handle before she had time to think about what she was going to find inside.

Steep steps from the doorway led down into the depths of the cabin. She pocketed her phone for a moment, using both hands to clutch the ropes set on either side of the entrance.

She did not hear the feet behind her.

There was no warning shout.

Only that heavy blow to the back of her head plunging Stevie into the deep, deep darkness.

CHAPTER FORTY-THREE

Lorimer parked the Lexus beside the hotel at the *Residents Only* sign. The only other cars taking up any space were the Forsyths' dilapidated Volvo estate and Crozier's Mercedes.

'Ready for this?' he asked the man sitting beside him.

Solly nodded and yawned sleepily.

'Mull air getting to you?' Lorimer joked.

Solly smiled back. 'Abby was up at the crack of dawn asking about when we were going to take her to see PC Plum again,' he said.

Lorimer laughed. 'She's taking after her Uncle Bill, I see. We'll need to get her a wee police hat before much longer.' His expression changed as he looked across at the professor. 'It's a shame, though, having to be here on business when you should be enjoying the island with Rosie and Abby.'

'And you,' Solly countered. 'Most of your own holiday has been taken up with this case. I feel for you and Maggie.'

'Aye.' Lorimer gave a sigh. 'She puts up with a hell of a lot, my good woman. Anyway, let's get inside and see what Crozier has to tell us about the breakfasts in this place.'

The two men walked around to the front of the building and entered the open doors.

Almost at once Mrs Forsyth came out, her face a picture of fury.

'Where's Archie?' she demanded. 'What have you done with my chef?'

Lorimer looked at the woman in amazement, seeing her fists bunched by her sides, her hair escaping from an untidy attempt at a pleat at the back of her head. 'And that woman's never come down for her breakfast, either. Seven thirty, she told me. And now it's nine o' clock! I can't keep things warm in the stove all morning for her!'

Then, with another glare at the two men, she turned and marched off, leaving them exchanging worried looks.

'The chef's disappeared?' Solly began.

'Come out,' Lorimer said, taking his arm and turning back to the doorway. 'Look,' he said, pointing towards the water's edge.

'What am I supposed to be seeing?' Solly asked, frowning. 'I don't see anything out there at all.'

'Exactly,' Lorimer replied. 'Archie Gillespie's boat is always moored there.' He turned to the psychologist and nodded, his mouth a grim line. 'He lives on that boat. And now it's gone.'

It was a matter of a few minutes to locate the DI's room and then to have the Dutch girl bring the spare keys to open it up.

'No one here. Bed's not even been slept in,' Lorimer said as they all stood on the edge of the room looking in. He turned to Solly, a worried expression on his face. 'What the hell's she been up to?'

'Oh,' the blonde girl cried, hovering uncertainly behind them. 'Maybe that was my fault,' she said, glancing from one man to the other, a frightened look on her face. 'I told her things last night . . . '

Lorimer waved a hand at Maryka. 'Don't go away,' he told her sternly. 'We may need to talk to you.' He took out his mobile phone and turned away.

'Craignure police station? This is Detective Superintendent Lorimer. I need to speak to Sergeant McManus.'

Stevie woke with the sensation that she was going to be sick, but there was something across her mouth that prevented the fluid in her throat from escaping and she moaned, swallowing the bile back again. There was a terrible ache in her head, a throbbing that didn't make any sense. Had she drunk too much last night?

Then, as her eyes opened at last, the detective inspector became aware of her plight.

She was lying on her side beneath some sort of long shelf, her hands tied firmly behind her. As she moved her legs, Stevie realised that her ankles, too, were bound up. Her second thought was that everything was moving up and down, the motion making her feel sick all over again. But, although she could hear the sound of lapping water, she was not imprisoned aboard Gillespie's boat, she realised, blinking against the dim light, but in some sort of shed.

A swift glance downwards filled the woman with horror.

It was that orange twine that bound her ankles together. Courlene.

Had she been left here deliberately? And was the man who owned that boat coming back for her? Would she – Stevie swallowed hard as the nausea rose in her throat again – be taken on to that boat only to be dumped overboard?

Stevie closed her eyes again, trying not to imagine the splash as her body hit the water or the sinking down and down into the depths as her lungs struggled for air. Would it be over quickly?

Tears trickled down her face as she began to sob, the sounds muffled by the boxes that were laid floor to ceiling next to where she lay.

'Fetch the Forsyths,' Lorimer told Maryka. 'We need to speak to them. Now.'

He glanced at his watch. It would take Calum only a few minutes to reach Kilbeg but in the interim there was something he and Solly needed to tell the two hotel proprietors.

'What's going on, Detective Superintendent? Where is that female officer of yours?' Hamish Forsyth marched into the lounge, his wife behind him.

413

'Sit down please, sir. Madam,' Lorimer said firmly. 'There is something that we have to tell you. It concerns your son, Gary.'

'Oh!' Mrs Forsyth put a trembling hand to her mouth then sank into a nearby chair.

'I'm very sorry to have to inform you but we have intelligence that gives us reason to believe that Gary Forsyth died about twenty years ago in Glasgow,' Lorimer told them.

'Are you sure?' the woman asked, her eyes large with sudden hope. 'Are you sure it was him, my Gary . . . ?'

'I'm afraid so, Mrs Forsyth. His body was never identified. Until recently.' Lorimer paused. How to explain that cold case? How to tell a grieving mother that her son's body had been taken for use in the university for students of pathology, its remains now in an unmarked grave.

'Mr Forsyth, when did you last see your son?' Solly asked, looking at the man's ashen face, the lips being licked as though no words could ever express what he was feeling at that moment.

'He never wanted to see his son!' Mrs Forsyth hissed. 'He wanted him dead! Didn't you?' She half rose from her seat, dashing the tears from her eyes. 'It was *your* fault that he went away!' she accused. 'My poor boy!' Then, as though a flood had been dammed for far too long, the woman began to weep loudly, tears flowing down her cheeks.

'Is this true?' Solly asked the hotelier. 'Did Gary go away because of something between you?'

But the man just looked down at his hands, a small shake of the head his only response.

'I'll tell you why he drove Gary away!' Mrs Forsyth yelled. 'I'll tell you what he told my boy. "No queers in this house!" Those were his very words! Didn't ever want to see him again. Well now you never will!' she screamed, rising up, her fists ready to rain blows down upon her husband's head.

But Lorimer's strong hands lifted her back into her chair just as Calum McManus entered the room, a look of bewilderment on his florid face.

A quick shake of the police sergeant's head was all Lorimer needed to know: Crozier was still missing. And he was certain that one particular person had been involved in her disappearance.

'Now,' he said sternly, looking around at Hamish Forsyth who had stood up at the police sergeant's arrival. 'What can you tell us about Archie Gillespie?'

The sound of approaching feet made Stevie stiffen. He was coming back to take her . . .

With an ominous creak, the door of the shed was pushed open then she saw the shadow of a tall man outlined against the pale morning light.

The gag ripping from her mouth made Stevie utter a small cry.

'Sorry, did that hurt?'

Stevie shook her head as she looked up into a pair of concerned blue eyes.

'Thank God we found you,' Lorimer said, a Swiss Army knife making short work of the binding twine that held her arms and ankles. 'Stand up slowly,' he advised, holding her arm gently as he helped the DI to her feet. 'Circulation might make your legs feel pretty painful.'

Stevie tried to muffle a yelp of pain but failed, falling into the tall man's arms, tears coursing down her cheeks as she wept into his chest, feeling a kindly hand patting her back.

'I'm sorry,' she whispered. 'I wanted to see what was on his boat.'

'Gillespie? He attacked you?'

'I don't know who it was,' Stevie answered, putting one hand to her head and squeezing her eyes shut against the pain. 'It's hard to remember exactly what happened ... '

'It's okay. You're safe now,' she heard Lorimer say. Then she was outside, being helped along the path to the waiting police Land Rover.

The detective inspector looked up into a morning sky full of white racing clouds and breathed a long sigh that ended in a sob.

Stevie Crozier had no idea how long she had been lying in that wooden pantry, fearing that her assailant might return. She took a deep breath of the fresh air, her overriding thought at that moment was how grateful she was to be alive.

CHAPTER FORTY-FOUR

'Where can he have gone?' Calum Mhor asked as he stood on the little jetty beside the tall detective superintendent.

'That's what I was going to ask you,' Lorimer replied drily. 'Has the coastguard any way of tracing him?'

'Ach, we don't have one locally any more,' Calum said in a disgusted tone. 'Cutbacks. All they can think of is saving money, not saving lives. We'll have to put out a call to the police services all around Morvern and Mull. Maybe he only went a wee bit along the coast?' he added, but there was little hope in the big police sergeant's tone.

'You think Gillespie is the man we're after?' he asked as they retraced their steps back to the hotel.

Lorimer shrugged a silent reply. Crozier was on her way to the hospital at Craignure, DS Langley by her side. He had run one hand lightly over her scalp checking for injuries before they had left, feeling the swelling and the dried blood under his fingers. Had it been Gillespie who had attacked the woman? Crozier had seen nothing, she'd confessed, remembered little about the previous night after she had come to the boat. As yet the Forsyths had not given too many details about the chef, the woman too stricken with the news of her son, the hotelier monosyllabic, when he could utter anything at all. Lorimer had left Solly with them, a promise to be back as soon as he and the police sergeant had had a look at the jetty. But the empty berth held no clues at all and it was with a feeling of utter despondency that Lorimer re-entered the hotel lounge.

Maryka had brought trays of coffee and shortbread biscuits and was pouring out a cup for Mrs Forsyth who sat slumped into her chair, a dazed look on her face. Solly acknowledged his friend's presence with a tiny nod but from the way the psychologist was crouched down beside the man's chair, Lorimer could see that he had succeeded in engaging Hamish Forsyth in conversation.

'Twenty years ago we bought this bloody place,' he heard Forsyth say, but the words were uttered with a sigh of resignation as if the news of their son's death had drained all bitterness from his soul. 'Gary was away and we needed a fresh start. *She* wanted to come here,' he told Solly, glancing back at his ashen-faced wife. 'Never knew why.' He gave a hollow laugh. 'Ask her now. Ask her why she stood at that damned jetty day after bloody day.' His voice ended on a high strained note and he picked up the coffee cup in front of him, looking at its contents as though they might be the answer to all of his questions.

'Mrs Forsyth?' Solly stood up and came towards the woman, seating himself on the arm of her chair. 'Can you give an answer to that?'

'He said he'd come here,' she said slowly, turning to look out of the window at the stretch of water that linked island to mainland. 'Gary. He said he was coming up to stay. I had a letter, you know. From Glasgow,' she added, turning to give Solly a peculiar look that made him shiver. Her eyes had a far-away stare that he recognised from years of interviewing patients at the State Hospital in Carstairs. Behind them a kind of madness festered, years of hope and longing wasting a fragile mind.

'Gary wrote to you?'

She nodded. '*He* didn't know, of course,' she muttered darkly. 'He didn't *want* to know.' A brief turn of the head indicated the father who had disowned his son. 'Things have changed now, haven't they? Even get married nowadays.' She laughed a short dry laugh. 'Who'd have thought it? But then ... ' Her words trailed off, leaving the listeners to fill in their own version of what sort of world it had been when his father had thrown Gary Forsyth out of the family home.

'He told me about a hotel. *This* hotel,' she added. 'He was going to come back and work here with his friend.'

'And do you know who Gary's friend was?' Solly asked gently, the silence around him full of expectation as the others listened for her response.

'No,' she replied sadly. 'But I had the impression it was

someone local. Someone from Mull. We bought Kilbeg and I waited for him to come back.' She smiled, her eyes flitting from Solly to the other men standing nearby.

'He isn't coming back,' Solly explained gently. 'Gary died a long time ago.'

'What about Archie Gillespie?' Lorimer came forward and hunkered down at the woman's other side. 'Was he here when you bought the hotel?'

'No.' Hamish Forsyth turned and answered for his wife. 'Archie answered an advert we had placed in the *Oban Times* and the *Gazette*. Came up here in that old boat of his and has been here ever since. Like one of the family,' he murmured, a puzzled frown creasing his bushy eyebrows.

'And was Archie Gillespie here when that letter arrived from Glasgow?' Lorimer asked, pinning Mrs Forsyth with his blue gaze.

'I can't remember.' She blinked then smiled at them all in turn, her raised eyebrows and outspread hands telling all that they needed to know. The woman had reached a point where the sorts of details that the police required had ceased to have any importance; the certainty of her son's death tipping her further over the edge. But, Lorimer reasoned, if it was found that Gillespie *had* arrived at Kilbeg after Gary's death, could that put him in the frame for the boy's murder?

CHAPTER FORTY-FIVE

'And she's all right?' Lorimer wanted to know.

'Aye, seems to be. We'll know more when she's been seen at Oban hospital. Dr MacMillan wants her to have a scan.'

'Does she know what damage has been done?'

'Fractured skull at least, the doc says.'

Lorimer drew in a deep breath. Assault to severe injury looked like being on the charge sheet, amongst other things.

'Gillespie gave her some crack on the head. If it *was* Gillespie,' Calum amended carefully. 'Must have tied her up and dumped her in the old outdoor pantry. No idea where he's gone now. Could even be across to Coll. Or Tiree, perhaps,' he added thoughtfully. 'Think we may need that helicopter of yours again, sir.'

Despite the intense pain in her head, it was amazing how much better she felt with fresh dry clothing and a hot bowl of porridge inside her, Stevie thought as she lay in the ambulance taking her off the car ferry to Oban hospital. Back in Craignure, Dr MacMillan had been kindness itself, helping Stevie into a hot shower and giving her some clothes that fitted surprisingly well. The big police officer back at Kilbeg had packed her toiletries but had not thought to bring a change of clothing.

With all that was going on there, Stevie couldn't blame him.

'Looks as if we are about the same size,' the woman had smiled, patting Stevie's shoulder as she had emerged from the shower, swathed in a fluffy towel. 'Think these'll tide you over for a wee bit, Detective Inspector.'

Stevie watched as the clouds flew past the windows of the ambulance. She badly wanted to close her eyes and sleep but her memories of the previous night were clear enough now.

There would be a hunt for Gillespie, she thought. A lot of manpower deployed to apprehend her attacker. But, Stevie told herself, even if he was the man who had so ferociously attacked her, had he killed those two red-headed boys? And that gentle old lady? What would Lorimer make of it? she wondered. Wouldn't he want to ask a different question?

If Gillespie was guilty of these crimes, then why was she still here at all instead of being flung into the bottom of the ocean?

'He must have realised who he was knocking over the head, surely?' Lorimer remarked as he and Solly drove back to Kilbeg from the incident room at Tobermory where they had met with the other members of Crozier's team.

'It would be dark,' Solly reminded him. 'And she was an intruder.'

'But to truss her up and dump her in that wee shed ...? Come on, what was he thinking?'

'Maybe he just wanted to frighten her?'

'Gillespie could just have given her an earful,' Lorimer retorted. 'No, there's more to this, Solly.'

'He's not been found then?'

'Not yet. But he must have been hiding something, surely?'

'Any words from DI Crozier at all?'

'Just what we know from big Calum. He did pass on one thing, though. DI Crozier wanted to let us know that there was a whole sheaf of Courlene on Gillespie's boat. That was the same stuff he used to tie her up.'

'Hm,' Solly said, staring at the road ahead as they passed the sign for the Mull Theatre and headed out of the Tobermory area.

'He gave her a fright, that's for sure,' Lorimer said grimly.

'Maybe that *was* all he intended,' Solly replied thoughtfully. 'If he'd wanted to strangle DI Crozier and dump her overboard then he had plenty of opportunity to do so.'

'What I was thinking myself,' Lorimer agreed. 'Is he or is he not the man we're looking to put in the frame for the murders?'

'What did the team tell you about this man, Gillespie, from the initial inquiry?' Solly wanted to know.

'He came to work at Kilbeg shortly after the Forsyths

bought the place,' Lorimer told him. 'They'd upped sticks and left their previous hotel at Mrs Forsyth's insistence.'

'She was still hoping that her boy would return.'

'Yes,' Lorimer agreed. 'What we need to know is the exact time when Gillespie applied for the job. Was it before or after Gary Forsyth's death?'

'Do you *really* think he might have been the one that murdered Gary?' There was a challenging note in the professor's voice that Lorimer recognised.

'Well, it did cross my mind.' Lorimer turned to look at the psychologist's raised eyebrows. 'I know, I know. I'm guessing that doesn't fit your profile.' He gave his friend a rueful grin. 'And that is something I have come to respect.'

'Thank you,' Solly replied gravely, giving a little bow of his head in acknowledgement.

'Right, let me see. You think that our man is someone other than the chef from Kilbeg. Someone who may have been around the fringes of the art world? Am I correct?'

'Hmm.' Solly nodded.

'Let's take it a bit at a time,' Lorimer said, pulling into a lay-by to allow the local bus to overtake them. They had reached the top of the Guline Dubh and Solly's glance out of the window became a head-turning stare as he looked at the view. The whole Sound of Mull stretched out from the peak of Ben Hiant in the west to the vague shapes of mountains in the other direction, the land below a pastoral landscape that hugged the coastline in a series of small coves. In the time he had been on this island, the psychologist must have been driven past this place many times but it had taken this short pause for him to look out and appreciate its full magnificence.

'Whoever killed those boys must have felt a great deal for them,' Solly said slowly, turning to face the road ahead once more. 'I think that each of these young men's deaths was an accident.'

'An accident?' Lorimer exclaimed. 'Do you really think so?'

'Hear me out.' Solly held up a hand. 'Whoever tied up the two boys waited with their bodies for a considerable time,' he reminded Lorimer. 'Until rigor had set in.'

Lorimer nodded silently.

'It was only then that he undid the bonds, taking them to a place where he could release them into water.' He looked back out at the expanse of the Sound below them. 'I wonder if it was a sort of farewell,' he mused. 'To have buried them would have been too great, emotionally speaking.'

The psychologist gave a sigh as though trying to put himself into the shoes of the man behind these tragedies.

'It was only when he had made some sort of peace with them that he could let them go. So he slipped Rory's body over the side of a boat. Probably tumbled Gary down the side of the river from somewhere upstream. Out of a car, possibly. We don't know such details yet, of course.'

'And what about Jean Erskine?' Lorimer insisted.

'By the time he knew about what Jean had witnessed that night, I think our killer had become desperate. I am sure that brief moment of strangling the old lady had nothing malevolent about it at all,' he continued sadly. 'One swift snap and she was gone. Like throttling a chicken.'

'You're saying that he had dehumanised her?'

Solly looked at him intently for a long moment. 'I think he had to,' he said at last. 'A man like that would never have been able to kill in cold blood otherwise.'

'Who are we looking for, then? A sentimental gay man with BDSM tendencies who happens to have access to a boat?' Lorimer tried not to sound overly sceptical.

'Perhaps.'

Lorimer threw his friend a quizzical look, then, signalling, he drove from the lay-by and down the twisting single-track road that would take them back to Kilbeg Country House Hotel and the deepening mystery of just who had taken these three people's lives.

CHAPTER FORTY-SIX

'Maryka's got something to tell you,' the police sergeant announced as he met the pair in the foyer of the hotel. The Dutch girl was hovering behind the big policeman, shifting her eyes to Lorimer then away again. He'd seen that sort of expression countless times before, especially in interview rooms when he knew that the person opposite was about to confess their guilt.

'It's about Archie,' the girl said, moving forward at Calum Mhor's prompting. 'I know why he went away in such a hurry. He was hiding stuff in that boat of his.' She glanced at Lorimer then down at her shoes.

'Cannabis,' Calum stated. 'Maryka, tell the detective superintendent exactly what you told me.'

The Dutch girl shifted her eyes back to Lorimer and Solly. 'He had stores of it in the boat,' she told them. 'Got more every time he sailed to Oban for supplies.' She shrugged. 'Suppose he was dealing for years around here.'

'And how did you come to know about this?'

Maryka looked to the side, making Lorimer wonder if she were about to fabricate the truth.

'I . . . we . . . had a few joints together in the kitchen,' she said, feigning a nonchalance that Lorimer was certain she did not feel.

'No, Maryka,' he insisted. 'How did you know about Archie Gillespie being a supplier?'

There was no reply from the girl as she continued to look beyond them at the open doorway. Then, as though something had come to mind, she looked up at the detective superintendent.

'He hated Rory,' she said. 'Told him he'd be eating with the fishes if Rory grassed on him.'

'So Rory knew too?'

She shrugged again. 'Think everyone knew Archie was a dealer,' she said vaguely. 'Not the Forsyths, of course. They'd have sacked him right away.'

'And Fiona Taig?'

'Oh, Fiona!' Maryka gave a superior sort of smile. 'She's such an innocent sort of girl. Only ever sees the best in people. Even in Rory,' she added thoughtfully. 'No, Fiona was never aware of Archie's habits. We kept that from her, all right.'

'Explains why he was so eager to get rid of DI Crozier and scarper,' Lorimer said grimly. 'And if we do find that boat you can bet there will be no trace of cannabis or anything else on board.'

428

'Just a lot of happy little fishes at the bottom of the sea,' Solly murmured, an enigmatic smile hovering above his beard.

Lorimer shot him a look. Had the psychologist dabbled in his younger days? Best not to ask, he thought, flicking through the files placed against the steering wheel.

They were sitting in the Lexus once again, Lorimer preferring to look at the case notes in private and out of earshot of anyone in the hotel.

'What does it say about the gardener?' Solly asked, his eyes resting on the file that Lorimer was examining.

'Not a lot,' Lorimer sighed. 'The officer who questioned him has very little on record. Does say here though that Lachlan Turner appeared to be dour. And monosyllabic. Can't see how that helps at all.'

'Oh, but it does,' Solly countered, sitting up and smiling.

'How so?'

'Don't you see?' Solly continued, smiling his enigmatic smile. 'This could be the suppression of emotion, could it not?'

Lorimer shook his head wearily. 'Or Lachlan Turner might just be a dour monosyllabic gardener,' he objected.

'Well,' Solly said brightly. 'Shall we go and see for ourselves?'

Bella Ingram's house seemed deserted when they arrived, with no sign of the gardener's van parked outside.

A knock on the door was rewarded by the sound of feet coming along a corridor, however, and the door opened, a woman's face lit up with expectation.

When she saw that two strangers stood there, Bella Ingram's expression changed at once, a wary shadow crossing her face.

'Yes?' The door was only half open, the woman's strong hands clutching the handle as though ready to slam it shut.

'Detective Superintendent Lorimer,' he told her, holding out his warrant card for her to inspect. 'And Professor Brightman who is part of the team who are looking into the recent deaths on the island.'

'Terrible,' Bella Ingram declared. 'Just terrible. Nothing like this has ever happened in all my life. No one's safe any more,' she said, accusingly, as though the tall policeman were personally responsible. 'We all keep our doors locked now. And not only at night. Never used to be like this,' she went on. 'Drugs and that. The world isn't what it once was.' She shook her head.

'We were hoping to speak to Mr Turner, your brother,' Lorimer said patiently.

'Lachie isn't here,' she said shortly.

'When do you expect him home?' Lorimer asked.

The woman shrugged. 'Who knows? When he's out fishing he could be away all day.' She looked past Lorimer at the bearded psychologist who had taken a step forward.

'Is there any chance we might come in and talk to you,

Mistress Ingram?' Solly asked, his quaint form of address at once disarming the woman who passed a hand over her hair and smiled coyly.

'Well, now, I'm not sure how much of a help I could be ...'

'Oh, I think you might give us quite a lot of background information about life in Tobermory nowadays,' Solly assured her. 'You've lived here all your life?'

Bella Ingram nodded. 'Well, why not come away in. I was just going to put the kettle on anyway,' she said, opening the door wide and beckoning the two men inside. 'Come through the house.' She ushered them into a room that was obviously the parlour, kept clean and tidy for special occasions. 'I'll just be a wee minute with the tea.'

Lorimer watched her go then glanced around the parlour. It was an old-fashioned sort of room with heavy dark furniture, probably passed down from one generation to the next. Solly stood looking out of the window but Lorimer's eyes had been caught by several fine watercolour paintings that had been fixed to the walls. They were all landscapes, mostly, he assumed, of Mull: one was unmistakably Tobermory, the curve of colourful houses around the bay with Calve Island in the background, now an iconic image found in calendars everywhere.

'They're good,' Lorimer remarked as Bella Ingram returned with a laden tea tray. 'Local artist?'

'Och no.' She gave a short laugh. 'Well, I suppose it is in a way. No, these were all done by our Lachie. Long time ago, now,' she added in a disapproving tone.

'He was a good artist,' Lorimer remarked. 'Self-taught?'

'Milk? Sugar?' Bella busied herself with the tea things as the men took the jug and sugar basin in turn.

'Well, now,' she began, sitting down on an upright chair that faced the visitors, 'our Lachie could have been an art teacher if he'd stuck at it. But he dropped out,' she said, lowering her voice as though admitting to something shameful.

'He was at art school?' Lorimer asked.

'Aye,' Bella agreed. 'In Glasgow. Terrible wicked place, that. Can't imagine why he'd want to go back there at all. Spent quite a few weeks there earlier in the year,' she mused. 'Of course he came home again after he stopped working for his art degree. That was when he was young,' she humphed. 'Never settled to anything much after that, though. Start with one thing then he'd drop out of that. Became a pattern over the years,' she added contemptuously. 'Never settled. Didn't even take up the fishing after my Dougie passed away. Well,' she sighed, 'our Lachie was always a little bit different from other men.'

The two men exchanged a look, their silent thoughts working in harmony.

'Nobody uses the boat at all now?' Lorimer enquired.

'The *Bonny Belle*? No,' she said, stiff-lipped. 'Lachie keeps her in decent shape, right enough. Takes folk out from time to time. For a wee trip around the bay. Not that it does more than pay for the diesel,' she added with another humph. 'What do you want to speak to our Lachlan about anyway?' she asked, turning to the professor as though she had just realised that he had not yet asked her one single thing about life in Tobermory.

'Oh.' Solly leaned forward, his hand hovering above a slab of what appeared to be home baking. 'May I try a piece of this excellent-looking fruit cake?' he asked, his gentle smile making Bella Ingram's eyelids flutter girlishly.

'Oh, please,' she answered.

'Mm, lovely,' Solly sighed, munching a corner. 'Lachlan is a lucky man to have a sister like you to look after him,' he declared roguishly.

'Well, now, that's as may be,' she replied, simpering a little under the psychologist's smile.

'Was Lachie at home the night of the ceilidh? When the boy, Rory, went missing?' Lorimer asked.

'What do you ask me that for?' Bella replied, a truculent frown shadowing her face.

'Oh, it's just a routine sort of question,' Lorimer told her, giving one of his own easy smiles.

'Hasn't he told you, then?' Bella looked from one man to the other.

'I've not spoken to your brother,' Lorimer said truthfully, though he suspected that the woman was asking a different sort of question: *hasn't Lachie spoken to the police?* was what she really meant.

433

'Was he here that night? With you?'

'Oh,' she said, a relieved expression softening her features. 'No, no, Lachie wasn't here,' she chuckled. 'You mustn't get them into trouble now, mind.' She leaned over and nudged Solly's elbow as if he had become her new best friend.

'Lachie wasn't in Tobermory at all,' she told them. 'He was with Ewan Angus and his boy at the splash.'

'That puts him out of the picture, then,' Solly said as they drove off.

'Only if the fishermen can confirm what Mrs Ingram just told us,' Lorimer declared.

'She seemed pretty sure,' Solly replied, raising his eyebrows in mild protest.

'Ach, one slice of cake and you're anybody's,' Lorimer rejoined with a shake of his head. 'Let's see what we can find out about Lachlan Turner's fishing activities.'

The water rippled as insects disturbed the tranquil surface of the loch. Somewhere, below, fish were lurking, waiting to nibble: brown trout, the tastiest of all fish to be found in this sea loch. Perhaps they were hiding deep within the shadow cast by the nearby boathouse where a motor cruiser bobbed gently, moored there until its owner returned with the next party of tourists. He'd be safe for another hour or more, the lone fisherman told himself. And until then the trout within the man's private loch were his for the taking.

Lachie stretched the muscles across his back, feeling the warm sun as he flicked the rod once more and saw his fly dip below the water, creating more ripples. It was a perfect day for the trout, the basket at his side already testament to his success. One more and he'd head on back home.

The sound of a car engine above him made Lachie turn his head and look up. There, on the road where he had left his van parked on a grassy spot past the lay-by, was the unmistakable sight of a Police Scotland squad car and two uniformed officers emerging.

He dipped his rod, watching as they walked around the van, peering inside the front, it seemed. He could hear their voices discussing something, though he could not make out the words they spoke.

Then, one of them turned and looked down to where Lachie crouched over his rod. 'Hey, you!' he shouted. 'Is this your vehicle? We want a word.'

Lachie Turner stood up and shaded his eyes, dropping the rod at his feet.

'Aye, you! Come on up here!'

For a moment the fisherman stood still. Then, as though galvanised by a sudden thought, he began to run towards the boathouse and disappeared inside.

'What the hell's he up to, cheeky bastard?' PC Roddy Buchanan asked the other officer. 'We just want to tell him his tax disc's out of date now that it's the first of August.'

'Looks like he doesn't want to know,' Finlay Simpson

435

remarked as they watched the man untie the boat and gun the outboard motor.

'Well, take his licence number and put it in the book,' Buchanan said, shoving his chequered cap above his hairline and scratching his forehead in bewilderment. 'Funny sort of behaviour, though, eh?'

'No.' Ewan Angus scratched his balding head as the tall policeman looked down at him. 'No, we haven't seen hint nor hair of Lachie for weeks, have we, son?'

Young Ewan shook his head. He was in big enough trouble after telling Calum Mhor about the night of the splash. Father had given him a right bawling out. But he had been brought up to tell the truth, he thought mulishly. And Da shouldn't have tried to cover up what they had found.

'That's right. Lachie Turner hasn't come out with us for quite a while, Mr Lorimer,' he said. 'Just me and Da on our own. Are they going to take the boat off us?' he asked, chewing his lower lip anxiously.

'I don't imagine so,' Lorimer replied. 'You've been assisting us with our inquiries so I expect that will count in your favour. Plus, Mrs Calum will still be hoping for the occasional pink fish, I dare say,' he grinned. He did not add that, because of her injury, being appointed SIO in Crozier's stead might give him some influence in this area.

But as soon as the two men were out of sight, that friendly expression changed to a frown of concern.

Lachie Turner had lied to his sister about his whereabouts the night that Rory Dalgleish had last been seen. How many more lies had the man told? And what had he really been doing that night?

CHAPTER FORTY-SEVEN

'Courlene?' Dr MacMillan remarked to her friend. 'Martin uses it all the time.'

'We think that was what made those marks on Rory's body,' Rosie explained quietly. She was aware of Abby at their feet, playing with a sheaf of printer paper and some coloured crayons. 'Little pigs have long ears,' she smiled, raising one eyebrow. It was an old saying Rosie had remembered from her own grandmother's day when she had been an inquisitive sort of child, always listening in on grown-ups' conversations. But Abby seemed content to play, absorbed in her childish drawings.

'Well it's a fairly common sort of thing,' Grace continued. 'I would expect most ships' chandlers to stock it.'

'What does Martin use it for?'

Grace shrugged. 'Oh, all sorts of things. It makes a good tight knot. Keeps boxes and things secured when he's out sailing. He has most things covered in bits of oilskin. You wouldn't want water to get into all that camera equipment,' she chuckled.

'He's still doing that project on the minke whales?'

'Oh, yes. Out most days, depending on the weather. Heads over towards Fishnish at some God-awful time in the middle of the night,' she laughed. 'That's where he's been having the best sightings.'

'Why does he go out so early?' Rosie asked.

Oh, he likes to be there at dawn or dusk,' Grace said. 'Best qualities of light, Martin tells me. Not that I know much about that sort of thing.'

'Does he know that chap they're looking for? Gillespie? He has a boat, too; lives in the darned thing, Solly told me.'

'Gillespie?' The doctor frowned. 'Not a name I'm familiar with. Not one of my patients,' she added. 'But people around here know one another *and* their boats,' she admitted. 'You need to. It's a sort of unwritten rule of the sea, I suppose, to help a fellow sailor if he needs your assistance.'

Rosie smiled and pretended to be engrossed in her daughter's drawings. If there had been a boat taking Rory Dalgleish's body into Fishnish Bay in the early hours of the morning following the ceilidh in Tobermory, would Martin Goodfellow have been out and about to see it?

Lorimer slammed the car door behind him and raced across Tobermory Main Street, his feet taking him up the stairs of the Aros Hall where several officers were seated at open laptops.

'Lachlan Turner,' he said loudly, making every head in the room turn his way.

'That's the man whose van we were looking at,' Roddy Buchanan said, turning to his fellow officer. 'Isn't that right?'

Finlay Simpson nodded. 'Strange sort of thing to do,' he agreed. 'Soon as he saw us standing beside his old van, he just got into that boat and headed off down the loch.'

'Oh.' Jamie Kennedy looked at the pair of them. 'That was George Ballantrae's boat! He's only just gone and reported it stolen!'

'I have reason to believe that Lachlan Turner may be the man we're looking for in connection with our three murders,' Lorimer told them, glaring intently at each officer in turn. 'And I need him found *now*.'

CHAPTER FORTY-EIGHT

He hadn't meant to do it, Lachie told himself over and over. 'It was a mistake, an accident,' he muttered, the words becoming like a mantra. The open sea surged below the boat, kicking salt spray into his eyes as he steered away from the dangerous rocks that littered this part of the coastline. He'd need to keep away from the cliffs if he were to avoid the Black Teeth, that series of sharp rocks that had taken many a good boat and its crew in times gone by.

A few more minutes and he would be clear of these waters, past the lighthouse then out into the Sound. And then ...? He had no plan and there was nothing in his mind but the desperate urge to escape.

They were coming for him, Lachie knew that now. Had known it from the moment that he had looked up from the bank of the loch and heard them shout out.

Twenty years, he thought. He had been running away from this moment for twenty years. And he had thought to be safe for so long, even after Rory ...

441

They must have found everything in the *Bonny Belle*, Lachie realised. Stupid to keep Rory's things; his clothes and his mobile phone. But they'd been so well hidden, secreted under the gunwales, wrapped in oilskin and tied with the very Courlene he'd used to secure the red-haired boy's bonds. The deep sigh that emanated from his chest turned to a sob as he fought the desire to relive those moments of passion.

Regret nothing, live life to the full, he thought, hearing half-remembered words that came to him now.

But who had spoken them? Had it been Gary, urging him on that night? Or had he himself whispered them in Rory's ear, pulling the bonds tighter?

The thought was lost as a rhythmic throbbing sounded behind him.

Lachie turned, looking astern. The unmistakable shape of a police launch was bearing down on him, a figure standing in its bows.

For a moment he hesitated, a sudden swell from the waves making him sway, threatening to push him off balance. He would not be taken, Lachie decided, seating himself firmly in the centre of the boat, face turned towards the wind, knowing now where his destination lay.

'Cut your engine!' Lorimer yelled through the loudhailer, his voice booming above the noise of the two outboard motors.

He stood, feet planted securely apart, his life jacket already wet with the spray that lashed against the bow. 'Turner, cut your engine! Now!' he repeated, steadying himself with one hand against the rail.

Above him dark clouds scudded past, a brisk north-westerly wind making foaming crests across these treacherous waters. He glanced back for a moment but the town was far behind them now, hidden from sight as they followed the path of the smaller boat around a curve in the coastline. Where was he heading? The lighthouse was fast approaching, a beacon of warning to sailors who might venture too close to these treacherous shores. Would he slow down there and let them board the stolen motorboat?

But there was no sign of the smaller craft easing up as they followed its creamy wake around the spit of land protruding into the seas.

Lachie thought he could hear them calling him back, *Turner! Turner!*

Or were they trying to make him change course? A different voice whispered temptation in his ear: *Turn her, turn her*, it said, in Gary's mocking boyish tones.

'No!' he screamed aloud, but the sound was carried away in the wind, leaving him to face the approaching rocks.

'Turner!' Lorimer called again but the man in the boat ahead gave no indication that he had heard his name.

Why did he not simply stop and give himself up? Surely

the man knew that the more powerful police launch would soon be overtaking the stolen boat?

Waves lashed furiously against a deep fall of black rock that sliced the hillside, several jagged shapes looming ahead.

'He's heading for the Black Teeth,' the pilot exclaimed. 'He'll never make it past them.'

'Dear heavens!' Lorimer exclaimed as he watched the passage of the motorboat.

A sudden memory of Solly's words came back to him then. *Perhaps he's not running away from anything. Maybe he's running to something?*

The knowledge hit Lorimer like the spray that stung his skin. The man they sought was not seeking to escape from his pursuers but running towards a fate of his own making. Lachlan Turner was deliberately heading to one of the most dangerous spots on this coastline.

He was close enough to see the clumps of sea pinks that survived on these harsh cliffs of his island, their tiny flowers blowing frantically against the whipping wind. And that gull, rising like a ghost from its perch, wings outstretched, lifting higher, higher. If he could fly like this gull, Lachie thought, become a bird and fly away . . .

'Turner!' Lorimer's voice was lost against the noise of crashing waves as he saw the boat ahead of them turn towards the sea cliffs.

444

There was a ripping sound as it hit the first rock, a shriek of wood against the harsh pinnacles of stone.

Lorimer watched in horror as the small boat was tossed high into the air and came crashing down, splintering like matchwood as it fell onto the Teeth.

For a moment he saw a pair of flailing arms as the man they sought rose into the air. Then the waters took him and his dark form disappeared, sinking beneath the foam.

The police launch slowed down at a safe distance from the rocks and Lorimer stared into the pounding waves where Lachlan Turner had ended his own life. There would be no answers now to the many questions he had hoped to ask but right now that had ceased to matter. He had witnessed the ending of another man's existence. He gave a shuddering sigh. Had it been a coward's way out or a moment of insane bravery turning toward these rocks? No earthly judge or jury would now decide Lachlan Turner's fate. And perhaps there was some relief that all those grief-stricken relatives whose loved ones had been taken might be spared that further anguish.

Lorimer shook hands with each of the officers in turn. It had been a difficult time for them all, he thought, their beloved island gripped by the fear that one man had generated over the past days. He stepped out of the Aros Hall, leaving the men to pack up the place as an incident room for the last time, and walked across the road. Standing at the railing, he looked across Tobermory Bay. There were still yachts in the harbour, gulls flying high above, their slanting wings grey against the white clouds. He breathed in deeply, smelling the sea. This had been a fishing port once, he knew, and still there were boats that plied that trade. His eyes fell on the brown varnished boat moored at Ledaig, across from the Old Pier. What would she do with it now? he wondered.

Bella Ingram had wept bitter tears when he and Solly had told her about the accident. And about the brother she had always thought to be *a little bit different from other men*. They had found Rory's clothing hidden on the widow's boat, enough evidence there to have sent Lachlan Turner to prison for a very long time.

How had Turner felt, Lorimer wondered, when Rory had come to work at Kilbeg? Had he begun to relive his time with Gary Forsyth all over again? And what had really taken place that night aboard the *Bonny Belle*? Had Rory struggled? Or had he, as Solly had suggested, been compliant? Had the older man been jealous seeing Rory with Richard Maloney? These were things that they would never know.

Freda Forsyth had shown him the watercolour drawing that Gary had sent her, unclipping the picture from its wooden frame; it had been the last birthday card she had ever received from her boy. Lorimer had taken it from her hands and looked at the landscape, the little jetty at Kilbeg and the Morvern hills beyond. It was so like the pictures adorning Bella Ingram's parlour walls that it did not even need the tiny *L T* in one corner that had been covered by the picture frame to identify it as Lachie Turner's work. It was, he thought, the final piece of the puzzle. Lachlan Turner must have wished for Gary to come to Mull. Yet his predilection for masochistic sexual gratification had taken the boy's life back in Glasgow, leaving Freda Forsyth bereft for all these years, never knowing and always wondering what had become of her son.

He took another deep breath, savouring the salt taste on his lips, then, turning away from the view, Lorimer headed along the street to where Maggie was waiting for him.

CHAPTER FORTY-NINE

Pamela Dalgleish slipped her hand into her husband's arm. It was over, she told herself. There would be no more nightmares, no unseen monster coming back to face a court of law here in Glasgow. And for that she was grateful. She looked at the flowers on her youngest son's grave, masses of white and yellow blooms given generously by so many of his friends. Pamela wiped away a tear. She had not known Rory had so many friends. And that was a grain of comfort after the horrors of what they had been told. Douglas would never come here again, she thought sadly. His son was lost to them for ever, the bitter knowledge of what he had been too much for her old-fashioned husband to bear.

Across the city another older couple stood, the summer wind blowing the petals of flowers from the surrounding graves of the Necropolis like so much wedding confetti. Hamish Forsyth bowed his head as his wife placed a posy of carnations on Gary's final resting place. The guilt of his actions rested heavily upon him, something he must endure for the rest of his days. That his only son's killer was dead and gone, smashed to bits on these notorious rocks, was little comfort. The man had been Gary's lover, too, the tall detective had reminded him, a fact that Hamish found both repugnant yet full of sadness. Lachlan Turner must have been living in a kind of hell all these years, the bearded psychologist had said.

The hotelier gave a sigh. Who would have thought that a man like Lachie could have done such things? He had wanted to recreate Gary in the person of Rory Dalgleish, Professor Brightman had insisted.

And Archie Gillespie? What would they do to his former chef? The man had been found halfway down the west coast and was now in remand in one of the Glasgow jails, having been refused bail for the several charges that had been brought against him.

Hamish tried to take his wife's arm but she shook him off as though the very touch of his hand had stung her. No amount of blaming the gardener from Tobermory would ever exonerate him in her eyes. Or, indeed in his own.

It was a windy day for a wedding, Rosie thought, as they left the car and headed towards the grey stone church, her hand clasping Solly's. Just ahead of them she could see the tall figure of Lorimer, Maggie beside him, clutching a little arrangement of pale pink feathers to her dark curls lest it blow away.

It was several months since they had last been here, she realised, looking up as the clouds scudded across a sky that threatened rain. The invitation to attend Jamie Kennedy's wedding had surprised them all, but the Lorimers had agreed to come up for the weekend and so she and Solly had made arrangements with Abby's nanny to stay over for a couple of days.

She gave a smile to Maggie as they settled into the back of the kirk, the pews almost full of townsfolk and well-wishers who were here to see the local policeman wed his childhood sweetheart. The ends of the pews were decorated with tartan bows and sprigs of white heather, a symbol for good luck. Rosie found herself silently wishing this young couple all the luck in the world. It was time for some good fortune to come back into this lovely town.

Outside the sound of bagpipes could be heard, heralding the arrival of the bride, she assumed.

Then, as the organ boomed into a rendition of Mendelssohn's 'Wedding March', all heads turned to see Fiona Taig make her entrance. A short lace-trimmed veil covered her face but there was no hiding the beaming smile behind it as she walked down, her hand tucked into Hugh McIver's arm. His daughter, Eilidh, resplendent in a scarlet frock with a Kennedy tartan sash, beamed at the assembled congregation as she followed her father and best friend down the aisle. The music faded into silence as the minister stepped forward and began to address his people.

'Dearly beloved . . .'

Rosie felt for her husband's fingers and was gratified by the squeeze that Solly returned. This town had suffered much, she knew, and it would be a long time before many of the scars healed. But life went on: there would be other weddings, children born and christened here in this place of worship, and in time these dark deaths would be forgotten, consigned to the history books. She listened as the minister's words continued, the two young people standing side by side, ready to commit themselves to a lifetime together.

She smiled as she caught her friend's eye. Maggie nodded; no words were needed to express how she was feeling today. They were staying in the cottage at Leiter for a few days as it was the school October break.

There were ghosts there too, Rosie suspected; images to lay to rest, she thought, glancing along at Lorimer's handsome profile. What was he thinking, she wondered? Did he look out at Fishnish Bay and remember the morning when he had discovered that poor boy's body? Or, like the birds he so loved, could his spirits rise above it all and take flight, seeing only the brightness of day to keep the midnight out?

AUTHOR'S NOTE

Those readers familiar with my beloved Mull will see that I have kept faithfully to its topography. However, there are a few places in *Keep The Midnight Out* created purely from my imagination. You may search in vain for Kilbeg Country House Hotel, the Black Teeth or any loch that spills its waters into the Sound of Mull near Tobermory Bay.

ACKNOWLEDGEMENTS

There are many people I wish to thank for their help in making this novel come to life. First, my cousin, Dr Andrew Noble, current owner of Leiter Cottage, for his kind permission to use it in my works of fiction. You know how much Leiter has meant to me since childhood, Drew. Also to my cousin, Elizabeth McIver, and to Ian Phillips for all the help in preparing background material and for being there whenever I needed a bed in Tobermory for the night.

Going back to 1995 has been an interesting experience and several police officers have made suggestions that helped to recreate that period when policing in Scotland was a bit different from now. As ever, my thanks go to DC Mairi Milne and to former DS Alastair Morris for their invaluable knowledge. Also thanks to Superintendent Martin Cloherty for his assistance in finding out technical details and to those officers in Oban and Lorn who gave me information. May they forgive my fictional imaginings of twenty-first-century policing on Mull!

To John Weir for his panama hat (the character who wears it is purely from my imagination!); to my sister, June, for help with researching Courlene; to the library staff at Glasgow Royal Infirmary for the invitation that gave me a chance to wander the hospital corridors; as ever to Dr Marjorie Turner for keeping me right about all post-mortem and other forensic details.

The crew at Little, Brown are perennially amazing, in particular my wonderful editor Jade Chandler and my dear David Shelley, not forgetting Stephanie, Rachel and Thalia. A special thanks to Moira who keeps me – and my diary – organised (and for looking after Puskas while I signed books all over the country and travelled around for research). Thanks, Jenny, the best agent a writer could wish for, and more than an agent, a dear and loyal friend.

Donnie, thanks for everything, especially for sharing the journeys (my, what trips across Ardnamurchan!) and for being a wonderful husband. And, yes, I couldn't do it all without you.